KING OF THE JEWS

KING OF THE JEWS

BY LESLIE EPSTEIN

Coward, McCann & Geoghegan, Inc.
New York

A chapter of this novel appeared in somewhat different form in *Esquire* magazine.

Library of Congress Cataloging in Publication Data

Epstein, Leslie.
King of the Jews.

1. Holocaust, Jewish (1939-1945)—Fiction.
I. Title.
PZ4.E6426Ki 1979 [PS3555.P655] 813'.5'4   78-14558
ISBN 0-698-10955-4

PRINTED IN THE UNITED STATES OF AMERICA

C.3

This work was completed with the generous support of The John Simon Guggenheim Memorial Foundation

Contents

KING OF THE JEWS

Chapter One

The Golden Age

I

In the winter of 1918–1919, on a day when the wind was blowing, I. C. Trumpelman arrived in our town. He was wearing a brown overcoat and a brown hat and had a large suitcase in either hand. The overcoat was a cheap one, woven from horsehair. "Mister," he said in Polish to the first person he saw on the platform, "find me a hotel." For such a large man his voice was high, with a trace of the lisp that Jews have in Vilna. Even at that time his hair was gray, almost white, and hung far over his collar. His eyes peered through the same pair of "American" spectacles—round lenses in black metal frames—that he was to wear twenty and twenty-five years later. The eyes themselves were also round, like a boy's, and were for a Litvak's remarkably blue.

Our main station, like many others built in the 1880's, was designed by the Italian, Donati. It is to this day still standing, with turrets of red brick, with stone buttresses, with slanted windows through which you can see clouds and birds and the lemon-colored lozenge of the Polish sun. The man on the platform, the one Trumpelman spoke to, led him through the station arches and out into the winter light. Although he was not a railway porter, and not even a member of the working class, this Pole carried both of the Jew's valises.

The newcomer, now standing on the steps of the Donati Station, put his hand on his hat and stared through the Central Square. There were carts there, and wagons, and several automobiles. Toward the east, over the rooftops, steam from the dyeworks steadily rose. Women passed with their bundles. Boys chased each other in the open air. Then the Pole pointed to where, on the far side of the Rumkowsky Monument, a flag was flying over the Hotel Europa. Trumpelman, with his teeth protruding a little, smiled. Then he picked up his bags and walked down the steps, into the square. The tails of his coat, as if angry at something, lashed round his legs.

The Hotel Europa, still intact also, though now the site of a state ministry, is even larger than the main station. It was generally thought to be the equal of the Britannia in Warsaw, and finer than the Zoppot Casino-Hotel in Gottentow-Lanz. The pastry shop on the ground floor had an international reputation. It made butter tarts, with crumb crusts that were toasted, and those traveling east–west, Paris–Moscow, or north–south, Danzig–Budapest, would buy them in between trains. In this hotel, in a corner room with a washstand, Isaiah C. Trumpelman stayed for three nights and three days.

It seems he spent this time walking, in wider and wider circles, so as to cover the entire town. Thus the first day he stayed near the Central Square, in the commercial district, and especially on Alexsandrowska Boulevard, with its travel posters and elegant shops. The next day he went to the residential sections, the Walburska quarter, the twin avenues, Leczyca and Pabianice, whose large houses were set into gardens and decorated with a pattern of banana leaves. Finally, he went past the New Market, to the working-class district known as the Baluty Suburb: here everything smelled from

12

the tanneries, the dyeworks and mills were always steaming, and there was mud in all of the roads. So much for Trumpelman's days. At night, at least for the first night and the second, no person saw him. Probably he was sleeping, or reading, or staring out the single round window high up on the wall of his room.

The third night was different. The Lithuanian walked out the front door of the hotel. Now he wore blue—the trousers, the jacket, the blue, white-dotted tie. A white shirt also. And a pair of long, narrow, shiny black shoes. Dressed in these clothes, which set off his eyes, and with his whitish hair brushed over his collar, he must have made a striking figure. He walked through the square and onto a side street, down which, blinking excitedly, were the lights from the Astoria Café.

That nitespot was not then as famous as it later became. Trumpelman took a table at the back. He ate a beefsteak and drank a clear liqueur. He bought four cigarettes. A thin comedian, losing his hair, told a number of jokes. About the Jew and the bathtub. About the landowner and the crow. Then a woman with black bangs and painted lips began to sing songs. She looked, with her straight, bare shoulders, like a statuette, like an Egyptian. The visitor at the far table ordered a hothouse flower and, when the songs were over, sent it to the stage. The singer pinned the rose to her waist, just above the split in her tight, gleaming gown. Then she blew that patron a kiss. It was in this manner that I. C. Trumpelman celebrated his forty-ninth birthday.

The following morning the guest checked out of the Hotel Europa and took a motor taxi to a wooden house in the Walburska quarter. To the front of this house, at Lepecky 6, there soon was affixed a bronze-colored plaque:

I. C. Trumpelman
Practicing Physician

13

That street, as it happened, was a lucky choice. Many of the houses on it were occupied by industrious and progressive Jews: the managers of the spinning mills, the owner of a furniture factory, lens makers, and such. Poles and ethnic Volksdeutschers, the sort who read newspapers, who wore wristwatches, lived in the rest. Moreover, from morning to sundown hundreds of men and women passed in front of Number 6 on their way to the nearby Rumkowsky Geyser—in fact not a geyser, but a branch of the municipal baths. Of course, such people, so hygiene-conscious, would notice the neat new sign on the wall—the only such sign, by the way, except for old Doctor Fosduk's, in the entire quarter. You will not be surprised to learn that the new doctor thrived.

Trumpelman rented three rooms in the old wooden house, one upstairs, in which he lived, and two on the ground floor: a surgery and a room for waiting. This last place always contained, for adults, the latest illustrated magazines from Berlin, from Warsaw; and for children there was a round bowl with two fish. The young Volksdeutschers especially would sit with their fists on their thighs, like little men, and stare at the creatures behind the glass. Some of them would knock on the sides of the bowl, or blow on the surface of the water, trying to make the minnows come from their porcelain castle.

The doctor treated most of his patients with pills, either long white ones, or green ones, which were round. How he knew which color to give which patient was a secret; sometimes he would insist that the very man he had previously given the green capsules should now take a white one, or vice versa. "Swallow!" he'd say, and you had to do it, on the spot. Trumpelman had another skill, which in our town was completely unheard of. Without warning, he would shoot out his left hand and take a sick man by the neck; then with his right hand he would twist the fellow's head like the knob of a door. If the person resisted, the doctor got angry. He would grasp his spectacle frames with one hand, so they wouldn't fall off; with his other hand he would strike the table.

14

"What's the matter with you? Are you the expert? Look, I am getting upset!" These different techniques—the pills, which did make people feel better, and the neck-twist, which worked wonders, too—were thought to be typical of medical science in Vilna, though there was no diploma from that northern city, or any other, upon the wall.

From the first days of his practice this physician cared for large numbers of children. There were not then in Central Europe—and perhaps there are few today—specialists in juvenile diseases; yet people brought to this stranger, a man with a foreign lisp, their little ones, even from distant parts of the city. "He treats my Meilech as if he were his own" was how one woman put it, and all the others in the waiting room nodded their round Polish or square Volksdeutscher or long Jewish heads. Trumpelman never gave pills to these children, or wrenched their necks. Instead, he had a box of hollow sweets, which, after you sucked them for a time, suddenly flooded your mouth with a syrup that turned your tongue, your lips, even the world before your eyes, the deepest raspberry red.

"Attention!" the doctor would say to the boys, and when they stood against the wall like soldiers, he would thrust a thermometer like a baton under their arms. The girls he rode on his knee, at a real jogging pace, until their pinched faces grew healthy and flushed. "Stop! Chaim!" they would call, using his middle name. In spite of his famous temper, he never struck, never screamed at, these patients. Once he stepped from the surgery into the waiting room and discovered a pale, pudgy boy with his arm in the fishbowl and the two little fish alive on the floor. "Ho! Ho! What big trout you have caught! Yes, my Franz! You're a brave hunter!" Then Trumpelman scooped up the minnows. As for the trembling Volksdeutscher, all the doctor did was pinch him a bit on the ear.

Trumpelman did not just treat these children; he tended their mothers as well. Best to say here that all through the

15

twenties and thirties his name was connected to one type of scandal or another. Much of that reputation—for being a roué, a ladies' man—began at Lepecky 6. People believed that with his blue eyes he knew how to hypnotize his female patients and make them do what he wished. It became a kind of fashion to develop a rash or a fever and then let it be known that the doctor from Vilna was attempting to bring on a cure. Rumors began to circulate about his past. You heard that he had already had three different wives, two of whom died in childbirth and one of whom was hit by a train. Or that, as a result of some liaison, he had killed a Lithuanian officer in a duel. Such stories explained why—crushed by tragedy, or a fugitive from justice—he had suddenly appeared among us. But whether they were true or not, or even whether his reputation was a deserved one, nobody could say for sure. Leib Korngold, who later grew up in our town, used to tell everyone how he once pushed open the door to Trumpelman's office and discovered Malka Korngold, his own mother, without any clothes. She was walking up and down, he said, on the back of the physician. The odd thing was, it seemed as if it were Trumpelman who had been hypnotized. He looked, with a dazed expression, right through the boy.

These are not pleasant stories. And there are worse things, terrible things, to come. Ladies and gentlemen, whatever you hear in the future, at least remember the true, genuine feeling of this man for all the little Leibs and Meilechs and Franzes, who were the first ones to call him Chaim. All too soon the whole town, or at least the Jews in it, tens of thousands of people, would call to him, would cry out to him, by that very name. We all became his children.

But first the years had to pass. In 1923 Trumpelman bought a new suit. This was camel-colored, and always had a neat white handkerchief in the breast pocket. The next year he got an overcoat to match. In 1926 the doctor hired a nurse, a Polish girl, Miss Wysocka. She had dark hair and a dimpled chin. All this meant that Trumpelman was prosperous, that he was respected. But it was only after the Walburska Pogrom in the spring of 1927 that he became a really well-known figure.

This disturbance differed from others in the quarter in that the hitting and beating, which went on through the night, reached as far as Lepecky. The waiting room at Number 6 became crowded with people suffering from wounds, from burns, from broken limbs.

By the time dawn broke Trumpelman was exhausted. The walls of his office, his new armchair, his wrists and thumbs, were smeared with blood. Plasters and bandages hung everywhere. A child with a crack in his head was lying on the movable table, and a middle-aged Jew, a complete stranger, was shaving in the surgical mirror. At this point the doctor happened to look out the window. In the first light two Poles were walking down the middle of Lepecky, carrying a rolled-up carpet on their shoulders. Without hesitating, Trumpelman picked up whatever came to hand—it turned out to be his little rubber hammer—and went into the street.

"Stop!" he cried. "What's that you have?"

The first Pole halted, but the second, a stocky man, kept going, so that the carpet looped in the middle. "It's a rug," said the lead man, with a smile.

"To walk on," said the rear fellow, who at last stood still.

"Where did you get it? Explain yourselves!"

"It belongs to my aunt!" said the first Pole, quick-witted. "On my mother's side."

From fatigue, not from fear, Trumpelman swayed. The crowd had come out on the steps of Lepecky 6. More Jews peered from the windows. The tall doctor stared down at the Poles.

"Describe the rug! Tell me what it looks like!"

17

The second man began grinning, too. "That's easy!" he said. "Blue! And green! Like when a peacock spreads its tail!"

"It's more of a yellow, a yellow-green. Not like peacocks, exactly." This was said by the more intelligent man.

"Roll it out!" Trumpelman demanded. With his left hand he grasped the frame of his glasses. With his right hand he waved his mallet, a foolish weapon. The Poles paused, shifting their feet.

"You see, sir, what's blue to one man is green to another—"

"At once! Unroll it!" Trumpelman's voice, always high, nearly screeched.

The two men obeyed him. A sigh, *ah*, came from the crowd. For the rug, a beauty, from Bessarabia, was bright red, except for a border of purple plums.

Wordlessly the doctor turned and strode to where two of the "mayor's police" were sitting on brown horses.

"Arrest them. They have stolen a valuable carpet. They have broken into a citizen's home."

The policemen looked at each other. One of their horses blew air through its nose. The sun was now high enough to give everybody a shadow.

"Why do you sit there? Didn't you hear? I, Trumpelman, order you to do your duty!"

The Lithuanian, bloodstained, white-maned, must have made an extraordinary impression. The two policemen advanced upon the thunderstruck looters and, between the flanks of their horses, led them away. Most people said that was the end of the pogrom. And it is true, within a few hours the whole Walburska quarter was quiet again. As for Trumpelman, he smoothed down his hair and returned to his work at Lepecky 6. Behind his back people threw their caps and their derbies into the air.

From that time onward, the doctor was a famous man. He

18

was invited to the best parties—the ones given by Madame Greenkraut, by Madame Zweideneck. He gave lectures on hygiene to the Zionist Association. You could see him at the local concerts and the light musical shows. In the late twenties he changed his membership from the Synagogue of the Fur Trimmers to the celebrated Italianate Synagogue, whose rabbi, Nomberg, he treated for pains in the lower back. In 1931 the Jewish Community Council was dissolved and new elections held. Trumpelman finished sixteenth in a list of forty and took up a position as Deputy Chairman of the Department of Public Health. For a stranger, a man from Lithuania, this was an astounding achievement.

Throughout those years, Trumpelman never stopped going to the Astoria Café. Only now he sat in the front instead of the back. There would always be a glass of clear liqueur hidden in his outsized hands. Kümmel perhaps. Important people dropped by his table, people like Fiebig, the financier, or Rievesaltes, who wore a pistol inside his armpit. Once Mosk himself, the owner of a hundred thousand spindles, sat down beside him and at once started to speak.

"Doctor, you don't know who I am, but if I told you that when I get up in the morning, when I sit up too fast, I see spots in front of my eyes, what would you say?"

Rievesaltes wanted to know if anything could be done about the fact that he had been born with one leg a little longer than the other. And why was it that Fiebig's gums had started to bleed? More than once Trumpelman would cut short such questions. "*Shhh!*" he would say. "Quiet!" Then he would turn toward the stage, where the singer, Miss Lubliver, was thrusting a leg through her slitted gown and staring from under her black helmet of bangs.

Then came the biggest scandal of all. Only eighteen months after he had taken up his position with the Community Council, Deputy Chairman I. C. Trumpelman was forced to resign. Not only that, but he disappeared from our town completely. The reason the doctor fell into disgrace was

19

his new insurance business, which he ran side by side his medical practice. He did not insure dry goods, or people's houses against damage from fire—no, he gambled with their very lives.

"Let me see if I understand this correctly," said H. Korngold, little Leib's father. "You take the position that I am going to live another twenty, thirty, or even forty years, and all that time I pay you seventy-five zlotys every month. I take the position that I might die suddenly, next year, or perhaps tomorrow, in which case you have to pay whoever I say twenty thousand in cash. Yes, that much is clear. But where I get lost is—isn't it like betting against yourself? Wouldn't you get the evil eye?"

The doctor—this was in the surgery—put his ear to the patient's pink chest. "You are too fat, Korngold. There is fat in the valves of your heart. I am a fool to write you a policy, even for five thousand, not to mention twenty."

"But we agreed to the higher figure!"

"Look at that! I slap your skin and immediately there is the impression of my hand. No, no, with circulation like that you are too great a risk. I could not afford it."

"Wait!" cried Korngold, the furniture factory owner. "You have to! I want to win!"

This life insurance became a craze in our town, like Mah-Jongg or buttoned shoes. Everybody had to have a certificate, even childless, even unmarried people. The most popular policy was for Zl. 25,000, which in those days was an immense sum of money. Rabbi Nomberg, however, by paying a premium of two hundred a month, had guaranteed for himself a lump payment of fifty thousand zlotys. Once Fiebig and Greenkraut and the mill-owning Jews heard about that, the race was on. Mosk was the first to go over one hundred thousand, but his record did not last long. It was as if people were climbing on top of each other. Someone who only yesterday was looked up to because of his enormous policy, with double indemnity, the next day wasn't worth notice—since

20

Blum, the importer, had secured a clause that paid a quarter of a million should he be struck by lightning or drowned in a flood.

No one could stand up to Trumpelman. What a salesman! He knew how to stalk you, to jump on you the way a lion jumps on a deer.

"What are you, Zweideneck, some kind of microbe? An insect? Or are you in fact a wealthy man who sells pneumatic tires? A maggot thinks about itself, but a man worries about his wife, his children, his dear little babes. Look what is happening! I am upsetting myself over you! What if I lose my self-control? When I think of your children—little Giza, with her violin, and young Mordechai—I become crazy. When you drop dead they will be orphans! Penniless orphans! A vision! I see them! Rags on their backs, sores on their feet. *Something to eat,* they are saying. *Something to eat!* It makes me tremble! How easily that hardship could be avoided. One hundred a month! One hundred and fifty! What about Madame Zweideneck? Has she not broken into a rash? That is a nervous reaction from worrying night and day about her little chicks, her darlings. In my opinion, it's almost murder. Not to save a life when you have a chance! It's filthy, swinish behavior!" And here the doctor did begin to tremble in fact. At the corners of his mouth, spittle appeared. Zweideneck, a man, after all, not an insect, took a policy for Zl. 200,000.

There were, however, a handful of people, Orthodox rabbis, Socialists, who refused to buy insurance at all. It cannot be proved, but many people believed that these holdouts were called on by Rievesaltes or by Rievesaltes' friends. Certainly many fires broke out and some things—a piano in one house, a broodmare in back of another—were burned. Also, at least one explosion occurred—in the office of Lipsky, the progressive lawyer. The long and short of it is that by the beginning of the new decade, the thirties, everyone who was anyone in our town was fully insured. That's why we felt so good about the future.

All this came to an end when Greenkraut, who had been insured for a quarter of a million zlotys, one day ate a sausage and died. Three weeks later the Widow Greenkraut received, inside of an envelope belonging to the Public Health Department, a bank check for the entire amount. But the next day, when she attempted to cash it, there were no funds left in the account. The poor woman looked once more at the envelope with the colorful stamps: postmarked Paris, Republic of France!

In minutes, it seemed, the news spread through the town. By evening a small crowd had gathered outside the house at Lepecky Number 6. Blum, the importer, was there, and H. Korngold, and the big furrier, Szapiro, in his wing-tip shoes. It got darker and darker, but these wealthy people refused to go. "Trumpelman! Trumpelman!" They shouted his name for hours.

Dawn came. The bells from the Protestant steeple started to ring. Finally Fiebig hurled his large shoulder against the doctor's door. It easily opened. Miss Wysocka, with her dark hair in a bun, was there.

"Gone!" she cried, shamelessly weeping. "He has disappeared!"

At that moment, from far down Lepecky, Mister Zweideneck appeared, shouting almost identical words. "Gone! Disappeared! Madame Zweideneck is missing!"

The Jews simply stood there, pulling on their lower lips. It was all clear to them now. The Lithuanian and his mistress had absconded, and not one among them—not Mosk, half-fainting from spots, or the bachelor Plumb, at the wheel of his Daimler Double Six, would realize from his investment of thousands and thousands the sum of a single grosz.

If only he had run off for good, if only that were the rise and fall of I. C. Trumpelman, practicing physician, then the fate of so many Jews would have been different. But he came back, he returned, like a burning bird from its ashes. Perhaps he had never left, that is what some people said. They

22

thought he and his paramour, the full-lipped Zweideneck woman, had hidden themselves in some part of the city, or else in a farmhouse nearby. There were reports that she would steal back to her old neighborhood, to visit her sleeping children, and that he sometimes went to the Astoria Café in disguise. Certainly such a thing is possible: ten years afterward a number of Jews, forty or fifty or sixty, managed to hide out that way in the Aryan part of the town. On the other hand, he might have gone to Paris, after all, or to Zagreb, or even to the moon. All we can say for sure is that he disappeared for two years and then, at the time of the epidemic, returned. And so our history changed. Or else—this is a thought that sometimes comes to us who are still living—it did not change, and everything that happened was destined to be. In that case the reappearance of Trumpelman did not affect the way our lives were twisted, like rags, one jot.

II

The attack of fever began in the Orphanage Number 2, the so-called Hatters' Asylum, early in the year 1933. This institution was located in a large house, with a garden, at the corner of Krzyzanowsky Street and Piotrkowska. Its funds came partly from the Community Council and partly from the Hatters Young Men's Benevolent Association, which was a group of Jews, with a Secretary-Treasurer and a Sergeant at Arms, who had emigrated from our town to New York City and who were not, or no longer, hatters at all.

What happened was that Julius Szypper, one of the foundlings, broke out in spots. No one at Krzyzanowsky Street had seen such a thing before. What's more, an hour later the six-year-old Rose Atlas developed the identical symptoms. By then poor Szypper was running a fever of forty-one degrees, and a bear and a zebra and also a camel, he insisted, were

23

circling around his bed. One of the older girls, pretty, plump Nellie Brilliantstein, had to cry, *Shoo! Shoo!*, and wave a broomstick, or Julius would tremble from fear. Then Nellie's own face grew hot, her eyes were running, and soon she too was in bed.

By supper thirteen orphans, eight boys and five girls, were covered with either round pink, or lopsided purple, dots. They all went to bed, warmly covered, but no one thought to call a doctor until Nisel Lipiczany, a boy with a chipped tooth and a squint, suddenly developed a terrific fever, swellings at most of his joints, and a way of rolling ceaselessly over the floor.

The physician who normally attended the Orphanage Number 2 was a young man from Warsaw, Zam by name, all of whose clothing was imported from abroad. At 3 A.M., when his telephone rang, he jumped from his bed, filled a hypodermic injector, and patted his face with cologne. But as soon as he opened the door his muffler blew out from his neck like a windsock and his knuckles turned white inside his gloves. Snowstorm. He called the orphanage back. "It's nothing!" he shouted into his end of the phone. "Hysterical rashes! We have seen this in Warsaw!" The ancient Fosduk, called upon next, promised to come, with his leeches, the following afternoon.

But it was not the old doctor and not Zam, who, that same storm-tossed night, knocked on the door of the Hatters' Asylum. Miss Bibelnieks, a large, damp-faced woman, threw back the latch and uttered a cry. For standing before her, in the camel-colored coat that everyone knew, was the former Deputy Chairman of the Department of Public Health. He was thinner than he had been, gaunt almost, and held his hat in his hand. A strong gust of wind sent his hair in every direction. "It's a mistake," Miss Bibelnieks said. "We were expecting Doctor Zam."

Just then, behind her, a small, swarthy child appeared on the stairway and wailed. "Help! Help! Spots!"

This little girl, so dark that many considered her a Gypsy and not a Jew, was rubbing and pinching her blotchy shoulders. Gutta Blit was her name. Above the wind more sounds came from the Asylum. Crashing noises. Shouts from children. Feet running up and down. Into this tumult, this plague, strode Trumpelman, pulling sweets from his pocket. He gave one to Gutta and another to Nellie Brilliantstein, upstairs in her bed; more to Szypper, to the Konotop brothers, to Myer Krystal, who was scratching the skin practically off his bones; and one to Usher Flicker, the single-toothed tot. Slowly, not right away, but as the drops released their magical centers, the children fell silent, rolled over, held still. By the time morning arrived, gray and snowy, the orphans were peacefully sleeping, as if under a single huge blanket, a raspberry-colored rug.

The days went slowly by. Trumpelman drew all the curtains, so that only chinks of light came into the Asylum. The children lay in their large, dim room, calm in the morning, calm through the early part of each afternoon. Then their temperatures started to climb. That's when they kicked off their bedclothes, scraped at their skin, and imagined bats swooping, and birds. By dinner, bedlam had come: Gutta clawing, Szypper howling, and Nachman Kipnis knocking his head rhythmically against the wall. Trumpelman came round with ice packs; he squeezed their calves; he straightened Nellie's wet, tangled hair. Finally, when the lines of light had faded from around the curtains, the children grew quiet. The sweet syrup inside the candies began to dissolve. It was at that hour that the doctor, seated on a wooden chair, himself not visible, told them a story. It became a regular custom.

It was not the stories that calmed the orphans, at least not at the start. No, it was the voice that told them, high-pitched, lisping on S's, rising and falling out of the gloom. Occasionally a sick child would cry out; often somebody sighed. But bit by bit they all lay back, staring with their brown or black

25

eyes, listening to Trumpelman describe his youth, his adventures, his journey to America when hardly more than a boy.

"My dear children, from my earliest days I have suffered from a wanderlust that has taken me to many places, in many lands. Only now, at the end of my life, have I struck roots—here, with you, in your town. One day, many years ago, I arrived at the port of Memel and for no reason, on an impulse, boarded the steamer *Morgenstern*, which was tied up at the piers. The decks of this ship were covered with great piles of coal, and seated upon these piles, and in the spaces between them, were hundreds and hundreds of Jews. In the center of the deck was a tall metal smokestack: black clouds, with live sparks in them, were even then pouring from it, covering the Jews, in their black clothing, with an even darker layer of ash. Children, as I stood there, watching this, I began to tremble. Something made me afraid. I knew that this little steamer—it was an old ship, of iron, with fittings for masts and sails—was meant to travel along the Baltic coasts. But then, the many passengers, the coal, the coal piles on the decks—that could only mean an open-sea journey, across the earth perhaps, perhaps to America!

"No sooner did this thought occur than there was the sound of a whistle, and a shower of sparks, all orange, shot into the air. The *Morgenstern* pulled away from the port. You can imagine my shock, my horror. I had no ticket. I possessed nothing but the clothes on my back. Yet strange as it must sound to you, as the houses of Memel grew smaller and smaller, as the shallow green sea turned steadily gray, my fear fell from me and I grew lighthearted. Many times since, in the course of countless dangers, I have experienced this feeling, this joy. It is the happiness of knowing one's fate has been taken out of one's hands. I know now that my life has been guarded for some particular purpose, some task, though what it may be I still cannot say.

"Our journey went smoothly for many days. The hot sun

26

hung always above us; the pale passengers turned more and more brown. Small fish leaped from the water, spread wings, and flew past our bow. At night, behind us, in the churning water, green lights and yellow lights were flashing and glowing, like a boulevard. Then, on the morning of the fourteenth day, when the piles of coal had shrunk almost to nothing, the ship began to move very much faster. The sky was blue still, but the wind flattened the tops of the waves. Some man pointed upward; the plume from the smokestack no longer billowed behind us; instead—and why did this sight fill us with sudden fear?—it stretched out ahead, as if we were chasing it, as if it were a black rope we had to follow. A small cloud on the horizon began to swell over the entire sky. The day turned as dark as night. The steamer raced onward, dropping for whole moments into the trough of a wave, then rising even more steeply until it burst through a cloud of its own soot and embers. This happened several times. Then the *Morgenstern*, with its coal, its Jews, and its white-shirted sailors, broke into two pieces and swiftly sank.

"My young friends, I do not wish to frighten you with my story. You know I am here among you. I did not after all drown. The reason for this is that in the violent swirl of the seas, as I was tossed this way and that, my arm became wedged in a floating fragment of wood. At that hour, in the darkness of the storm, and through the night which soon followed, I had no idea of what it was that had saved me. But in the dawn, under light clouds, I clearly saw the giant timber, still round like a tree, with the grain of the wood wet and glistening. Perhaps it had been part of a mast, or a rib of the ship; but of that ship there was no other sign—no person, no object, no stain on the water. It was as if Providence had sent this timber to me and fastened me there, as a reminder of earth and of the role I had yet to play upon it. I alone had been saved."

The room was silent and black. Most of the Hatters' Asy-

27

lum orphans were by then dozing. Those who had remained awake—Nellie, for instance, and Szypper, and one or two others—were staring at the place where the voice had been. There something was glowing, burning, then dimming, then getting red hot again. What was this? Trumpelman's cigarette.

"Now I must tell you that on this same day, when the thirst became more than I thought I could bear, I wished to end my own life. But my arm was broken, my legs numb in the water, and I could not twist from the grip of the jagged wood. I had no choice but to drift, cursing the God who had saved me. The thirst. I cannot adequately describe it to you. The sea salt was mixed into each breath that I took. And in the seams of my skin. Crystals of salt on my hair. And the sun hung above me, licking at me, like an animal's rough tongue.

"I cannot say how many days passed. For much of the time I was not fully conscious. I awoke at last to the sensation of movement—no longer drifting but cutting purposefully through the sea. Under a crust of salt, I opened my eyes. What I saw was this: the fin of a beast, protruding above the water, no more than an arm's length away; and a second fin, moving rapidly toward me, coming up to the timber on the other side. It is true that my spectacles had long since been swept away. And possibly my senses had become crazed. Was this a dream? An hallucination? I can only repeat I saw the double fins, and felt myself propelled swiftly—for the remainder of that day, the whole of that night—through the water. I remember the sounds the dolphins made: grunting sometimes, the snap of their air holes, at night a whistling song. Before the next dawn they suddenly dove away, and I continued forward a moment until I struck the shore. When the sun rose I saw a city, it was the city of Galveston, rising out of the sea."

Now everyone was sleeping. Even Nachman Kipnis, who

28

had struggled to stay awake. The minute his eyes closed, however, he saw a genuine city, with towers and traffic and windows of glass—and not the muddy little port, half on a sandbar, that Galveston must have been at the time.

Not long after, the orphans got better. In a week their fever was gone and their skin became smooth and clear, the skin of healthy young children. The drapes were pulled back from the windows. Bright daylight came in. Immediately Mann Lifshits, the toddler, rode young Krystal around like a jockey on a horse. And Gutta Blit walked upside down on her hands. Thus the Hatters' Asylum weathered the attack of what seemed to be spotted fever, but which turned out to be only measles of a new kind. Everyone knew the danger was over when Bettsack, the schoolmaster, and old Rabbi Lunt, with his hump, his sport jacket, returned to Krzyzanowsky for their regular lessons.

"Here. Here. Also here," Lunt would say, smearing honey with his finger onto their books. Then the boys had to read aloud: *Free will is granted to every man. If he wishes to direct himself toward the good way and become righteous, the will to do so is in his hand; and if he wishes to direct himself toward the bad way and become wicked, the will to do so is likewise in his hand.*

As for Bettsack, his question was, "How many legs has a spider? Six? Four? Twelve?" It was a thrill when he opened his shoebox and let the children count the eight woolly legs for themselves.

There was an exception to this rosy picture. Nisel Lipiczany did not get well. From the start his symptoms had not been like the others'. His fever went up to forty-one degrees Celsius, then held there all night long. His joints swelled, first in one part of his body, then in another. Worst of all, he could not hold still. Wherever you put him he rolled: off the bed, over the floor, in and out of your arms. Only during the stories did he seem to relax, throwing the balls of his wrists

29

over the side of the bed and turning his face, pinched like a monkey's, toward where the familiar voice was calmly rising, calmly falling, like the sea.

That's how things stood until one night in February, a really cold one—the children wore gabardine coats on top of their sleeping gowns—when as usual Trumpelman was talking around a lit Sport cigarette. Suddenly there was a noise in the corner, and on went the electric lights. Lipiczany was there, stark naked, squinting, doing a kind of dance. He lifted his knees, first one, then the other; then he did this more and more quickly, until it seemed the floor was on fire and neither foot could touch there for more than an instant without being burned. His black hair was flying. His head flopped around. Immediately the doctor ran over, trying to grab him. But remember he was then a man in his sixties. Nisel darted away. Nellie and Myer Krystal closed in behind him, while Miss Bibelnieks blocked his forward path. The crazy dancer, with his elbows, his heels, knocked Krystal and Brilliantstein down. With a whoop the other children came after, diving at his flashing legs, throwing their coats at him like a net over a bear. But Nisel leaped free. Then, with nobody near him, alone, he stiffly fell over, his arms at his sides. Everyone stopped, amazed at the force with which the back of his head struck the floor.

The boy was in a coma. They put him in a room of his own, overlooking the bare, snow-spotted garden. Lipiczany had been a lively, popular fellow, able to crack walnuts open with only the palms of his hands. Thus many friends crowded in to stare with real interest at the hollow spot in the center of his breastbone, over which a thin layer of skin was visibly shaking from the heartbeats underneath. To this spot Trumpelman hourly placed his ear. The rest of the time— for weeks, then months—he stood alone at the window, whose top pane was open in order to draw the smoke from his Sport like a thread through the crack.

It was by this same window, with its unwashed glass, that

Trumpelman was standing one day in late March. Behind him was Lipiczany. The boy lay on his back with his mouth open, his lips fallen away from his teeth. His wet dark hair stuck to his forehead. Another breath. Another thump from his heart. A breath again. There was a shout on the other side of the glass. All the children ran into the garden. Miss Bibelnieks began counting, while the wards of the Hatters' Asylum, like inverted bicycle riders, rotated their feet in the air. Springtime! Spring! For the first time since the epidemic, Trumpelman left the Asylum and took a walk in the town.

Where to? It's not important. Perhaps for a steambath under the Geyser's high dome. Perhaps for a walk by the boarded-up Lepecky Number 6. Or else he just rode here and there in the electrified trams. It is more interesting to note that no one recognized him until late that same evening, when he walked through the door of the Astoria Café. Then the whole crowd, which had been talking and eating and drumming their fingers, swung around. Baggelman, the orchestra leader, stood frozen, his baton in the air. "Please!" somebody shouted. "I have requested 'St. Louis Blues'!" Then all the men and women got up to dance. Trumpelman slid behind the same rear table where, years before, he had begun.

Soon the songstress appeared. The same black bangs. The white pancake makeup. The only thing different was the tiny twitch, like a tic, she gave to her head. Trumpelman once more sent a pale rose onto the stage. It came back to the sender, during the latest Yiddish hit song, stuck in F. Rievesaltes' sharkskin lapel.

"Well, Doctor," said the latter, "when was it you came to town?"

"That rosebud. It was meant to go to a different person."

Fried Rievesaltes frowned down at the tightly shut petals of the little flower. Then he gave them a flick with his finger. "Miss Lubliver has passed this gift on to me. Perhaps you do not know she is now my intimate friend?" With that he twisted that hat from his head and waved it in the direction of the entertainer. Her head jerked in response. She thrust her white leg through her gown.

Rievesaltes gripped the older man's arm. "What a neck!" he said.

It was the custom at the Astoria Café to bring the drinks on little metal plates with a watch face painted on one of the sides. By midnight Trumpelman had six of these "clocks" piled on his table; the seventh kümmel was just going down. The waiter, Popower, made the usual joke about the quick passage of time. The doctor put on his hat and walked out the door.

There was the moon, with a fat Ukrainian face. And there a horse, attached to a carriage. Otherwise, the city was deserted. When the former Deputy Chairman of the Public Health Department reached Krzyzanowsky, he took out his latch key and inserted it into the lock. All the lights in the Asylum were out. Trumpelman, using the banister, went up the stairs. In the sickroom, under the overhead bulb, he caught young Doctor Zam stabbing a needle into the child's wasted hip.

"I was sent for! They called me! It's the crisis!" Zam stammered, and quickly pulled his instrument out. The Warsaw physician was dressed in what looked like a riding costume, with leggings and spats. His colleague strode to him, at the same time clutching the arm of his glasses. Then he slapped the dandy's face.

"Out! I cannot restrain myself! I will snap your neck!"

Zam broke for the doorway. "That's alcohol, you know. I smelled it. I could have you reported."

But Trumpelman was already next to the bed. For a live person Lipiczany looked amazingly green. His breath came and went without enough force to shake a feather. And then, beneath the doctor's eyes, the nose of the poor boy started to bleed. Trumpelman dabbed at the stream with the handkerchief he wore in his breast pocket, then turned to the window and leaned against the black panes. He heard a door slam and an automobile engine ignite. Departure of Doctor Zam. From habit, from his gay nature, the young man gave two toots on his horn. The Lithuanian waited some time, until he thought he could see the outline of things—the top of a hedge, the frame of a bicycle against a tree. Then he returned to Nisel.

The bleeding had stopped. The thermometer inside his armpit read 39.4 degrees. The skin was once more a normal color. "Is it possible?" murmured the physician, and, as if in response, Lipiczany opened his eyes. They were black, wet, and held in miniature the overhead light and the figure bundled in a camel coat. Trumpelman leaned over the wizened little face, lined like a man's. He had sucked one of his sweetmeats to within a millimeter of its liquid center. He passed the fragile glazed ball from his mouth to that of his patient. It was a kind of kiss.

III

Approximately six months after these events, in the fall of 1933, the Widow Greenkraut received a brief message:

> *Madame:*
>
> *I know I have made you suffer. If I could cut off my right arm to avoid this, I would cut off my right arm. For years I poured on my head the ashes of shame, remorse, and regret. Now I am able to send you the sum of Zl. 1500, which is one-quarter of the total paid me by Greenkraut before he died. In this way I lighten my burden as I crawl through my last years to death.*
>
> I. C. TRUMPELMAN

In November, Szapiro, the furrier, received a similar letter

33

containing a slightly smaller amount. So did Fiebig. Rabbi Nomberg, the following January, got the same. In short, everyone who had purchased insurance from the Lithuanian was slowly, a little at a time, getting his premiums back. Even Zweideneck, who never again saw his wife, and who had lost his tire business because of the worldwide depression, was paid back half the zlotys he had invested.

Whether for good or for ill, the Jews are a softhearted people. They forgive and forget. As time went by, as the messages and the bank drafts for zlotys continued to arrive, people began to think of Trumpelman in a more brotherly way. Korngold, upon seeing the former Deputy in the Central Square, removed his hat. A more telling incident took place in the steam chamber of the Rumkowsky Geyser. A number of Jews were sitting on the wooden platforms, sighing now and then. Suddenly one of them stood up and walked to where Trumpelman was sitting, a little apart. "We are naked! This is how we came into the world, without any money, and how someday we shall depart. I am saying this for everybody to hear: we are all men here, just human beings, and nobody is different from anybody else." This was not just a rich man speaking, somebody like Szapiro or Plumb. It was Mosk, the magnate, himself.

The seasons passed, one after the other, and it became clear to all that Trumpelman had devoted his life to the Hatters' Asylum. He lived there in an attic room, with slanting rafters, in which he could barely stand. He was now the official physician of the Orphanage Number 2, for which the American Hatters gave him the same salary—every grosz of which went to pay off his debt—that had previously gone to Doctor Zam. As for young Zam himself, he never appeared on Krzyzanowsky Street again. His little blue roadster was often seen parked in front of the Hotel Europa, in an upper floor of which he maintained a suite of rooms. But what he did there, and why his patients were pale Polish girls, of good families, too, and indeed where his riches came from—

all that was simply a matter of speculation. This much may be said: the young physician, in his French cuffs and knitted vests, so intelligent, so expertly trained, a Warsaw product, seemed bound to disappoint those who had placed such high hopes in him and in his generation of Europe's Jews.

In 1936 a representative of the Hatters Young Men's Benevolent Association, the businessman James Faulhaber, came back to the town where he had been born. He was an American citizen now, a New Yorker, and wore instead of suspenders a belt. A camera was looped over his shoulder. The plan was to work out an arrangement whereby American cotton would be turned by our local mills into trousers with matching caps. Of course, while he was there, Faulhaber wished to inspect the various projects of the HYMBA. Thus Anton Schneour, the Chairman of the Public Health Department, and as such the Director of the orphanage, brought him one night to the Asylum door. Said Schneour: "This is our staff, both Jews and non-Jews."

Rabbi Lunt, Miss Bibelnieks, and the schoolmaster, Bettsack, stood against one wall of the downstairs hallway. The cook, the two maids, and the mute, microcephalic gardener boy curtsied and bowed on the other.

"Everybody together!" said Faulhaber in his rusty Polish. "And everybody smile!" With his photoflash camera, he took a picture of the crowd.

"And here," said Schneour a few minutes later, "here are our future scholars and rabbis and captains of finance." He meant the rows of male orphans, asleep in their beds. What a pretty sight! Each head on a pillow, a curled fist beneath every chin. The light from half a moon came through the window.

The American held his camera against his chest, peering down into the box. Something, alas, moved in the viewfinder. It was Usher Flicker, the four-year-old, blurring the picture. He threw his legs over the side of his bed; he stood straight up and down. Then, with his arms held before him, dragging his white sheets behind, he began to walk slowly across the floor.

"What's this? Halt at once! Return to bed!" Anton Schneour hissed at the orphan.

"*Shhh!* He is walking in his sleep." Bettsack, with Miss Bibelnieks, had come upstairs in the nick of time. The young schoolmaster held his derby, the way Faulhaber held his camera, against his chest. "It might be fatal to wake him."

Like a bride with a train, the boy moved down the row. Only his toes and his ankles showed beneath his long cotton nightgown. His eyes were closed, like those of any sleeper. When he reached the bed of Julius Szypper, a strange thing happened. The older boy—also with his arms out, with his sharp chin pointed ahead—slid from his bed and began to walk about, too. Nor was that all. Whether it was the power of suggestion, of unconscious imitation, or simply because of the moonlight, more of the orphans began to move silently, slowly, in various directions about the room.

The adults stood in the doorframe, dumbfounded. Perhaps it was they who were sleeping, who were having a dream? A feeling—it was like fear, like awe—went through them. The sleepwalkers, each with his sheet trailing after, seemed to be gliding through space, floating like phantoms, like ghosts.

Then little Flicker, turning slightly to his left and his right, came up to where these grown people were standing, and abruptly stopped. His arms, so long held stiffly before him, dropped slowly to his sides. He gripped his nightdress and lifted it upward. His little male member stood out from his body, and through it he released his water over the American's pants cuffs and the American's shoes.

Faulhaber jumped backward. His camera, with its flash reflector, crashed to the floor.

"This is a hoax! It's been planned!" cried the head of the Public Health Department, making a leap for Flicker. But the

36

boy had let down his nightgown and was already drifting away.

Miss Bibelnieks, with her strong, dimpled arms, yanked the sheet from one of the Konotop brothers. She did the same to Nachman Kipnis. But both boys—Konotop had thick eyebrows which, like an adult's, grew in a line over his eyes—continued to glide over the floor, as if in a trance.

"What about my shoes?" Faulhaber was asking.

"Stop!" Schneour commanded. "Stop them, Bettsack! It's an order!" But there was nothing the poor teacher could do. Indeed, just then Rose Atlas, Gutta Blit, and other girl orphans came from behind the folding partition that divided the room. Their hands were stretched before them. Sleepwalkers, too!

You would think the presence of young ladies, even with their eyes closed, would have made unthinkable the next thing that happened. But it did not. Mann Lifshits climbed onto a bedstead and, exposed there, like a statue in a fountain, sent a stream splashing against the lower part of the wall.

It was an awful moment. No one, not Schneour, not Bettsack, had any idea of what to do. Young Szypper was beginning to raise his nightgown. On a different mattress, Kipnis, with a look of rapture, was about to do the same. That was when Trumpelman, holding a burning candle, entered the room. Calmly, he addressed the orphans.

"This is Trumpelman. You are sleeping. Go to your beds."

The children did as they were told. The girls vanished behind the partition. The boys spread their sheets and put their pillows under their heads. The spell was broken.

Faulhaber turned to Anton Schneour. "Who is this person?" But Schneour only stared dumbly, refusing to identify his former subordinate on the Community Council. The physician blew out his candle flame. So Faulhaber's words came out of the dark:

"From now on this man is in charge."

37

It was in this way that Isaiah C. Trumpelman became the Director of what was called the Hatters' Asylum.

The old house at the corner of Krzyzanowsky and Piotr-kowska changed little over the next few years. Trumpelman had it repainted, in the style of a Baltic villa, white with green trim. In 1937, when the building next door became vacant, the Asylum moved in. The wall between the two gardens was razed, and in the common yard the children grew cabbages, beets, turnips; kept two goats and geese; planted trees for walnuts and plums. In the middle of the city, with its smoke, its trams, its thousands of people, it was like living on a farm.

The orphans of course grew older. The teeth of Usher Flicker came in. Mann Lifshits turned out to be left-handed. And a soft black mustache appeared on the lip of Myer Krystal. That was a sign that soon he would depart. But the odd thing was that neither he nor any of the other children left the Orphanage Number 2. Or if they did, with knapsacks, with valises, they quickly returned. Something there—the little bells around the necks of the goats, perhaps, or the yellow light burning late in the attic window—called them back from the task of seeking their fortunes.

This refusal of the older children to leave created two major problems. The first was that the gossip that had surrounded the doctor when he lived on Lepecky began to plague him at the Hatters' Asylum as well. Much of this talk—about the Polish cook, the Polish maids, or about Miss Bibelnieks for that matter—need not be repeated here. What if it were true that shortly after Trumpelman became Director, Miss Wysocka moved into a room next to his? Or that when Mathilda Megalif, the dramatic actress, taught the orphans pronunciation, she occasionally remained for the night? These things may have once shocked our Jews, in their corner of Europe; they would not faze many folk now—not in America, not in the modern world.

It was a more serious business when the talk tied Trumpelman to his charges—that is, to children, even if some of these same orphans now wore earrings and read novels half through the night. Then word got out that one of the girls was going to bear the Director's child. Imagine the scandal! For weeks no one talked of anything else. A Pole came around, a municipal official, and asked Miss Wysocka questions. Then a letter arrived from Mister Faulhaber—airmail, from New York. The news had spread over the ocean! In response to this, the Community Council announced that the Chairman of the Public Health Department would hold an investigation. For a time, it was an ugly situation. But Fried Rievesaltes, with his many connections, saved the day.

It was that gentleman who, early one morning, in the midst of a rainstorm, drove up to the Hatters' Asylum in a cab. Trumpelman, with his hat over his eyes, his collar up, climbed into the rear. A young Jewish girl, it was the dark-haired Nellie Brilliantstein, tightly held his arm. The taxi knew where to go. To the Hotel Europa. It stopped next to Zam's "Spider" two-seater. While the girl was above, in the medical suite, Trumpelman paced in the downpour. The pastry shop was already open. It was permissible to sit in the lobby chairs. But the Director would not leave the open square. There the rain drove at him from different angles. With an effort the pigeons flew by. At last Miss Brilliantstein came out the hotel door, openmouthed. Instantly the taxi, with Rievesaltes still inside it, drew up beside her, and she got in. Trumpelman shouted through the shut, streaming window. What he wanted to know was: *Had it been a male child, a son?*

At that time, however, other Jews were still having babies, and this was, for the Hatters' Asylum, the second big problem. No one was leaving, but new foundlings were coming in. Even with the house next door, there was no room to put them. Nor was there enough money for food or warm clothes. What Trumpelman did was go to the fine houses on

39

Lepecky, on Leczyca, and put his foot in the door. If no Jew was home, he waited. If he had to beg, he got to his knees.

Mosk, the man of a hundred thousand spindles, lived in an English-style mansion, made from red brick, with a row of white columns. One day Trumpelman forced the rich man to answer his door. There was no begging here. "My children are hungry!" the Lithuanian, in his high voice, started yelling. "Pay up! No chiseling! Trumpelman won't let you make a deal! A doctor has to do away with diseases! This wealth, this richness, is a sickness! You are a danger to us all!" It was as if the Asylum Director were having a fit. He put his arms around two of the pillars and began to strain. His face became red, his hat fell off, and it seemed to Mosk that the old man was full of strange power, like Samson, with Samson's wild, magical hair. In a moment the house would tumble down.

"Wait!" cried the mill owner. "I'll pay!"

So, like a salesman, Trumpelman moved through the city. And wherever he went, from doorstep to doorstep, at his table in the Astoria Café, or even riding in Plumb's twelve-cylinder Daimler, he was accompanied by a small, quick figure, like a pale shadow, never more than two or three meters away. This was Nisel Lipiczany, with the pinched face and the tooth that was chipped. He always held his head to one side, squinting, as if he were looking into the sun. Any light was too bright for his eyes.

"Poor little fellow," said Plumb, at the wheel of his two-ton limousine. "What's that noise he's making?" Both men turned to look at the boy, alone on the rear leather cushions. Nisel's heart sometimes swelled large inside him, making him suck in, and swallow, great gulps of air. He smiled at Chaim.

There is a certain kind of goose that thinks the first thing it sees must be its mother. If a member of this species should hatch on a day when its real mother is gone—let's say, for example, she has been eaten up by a wolf—and if a hen, or a

40

pig, or even a person, the farmer himself, is walking by, then the little gosling will peep with joy and follow the moving form wherever it goes, for the rest of its life. There have been cases of such geese running after clothes on a clothesline, or a cardboard box pulled on a string. When the actual mother comes back—there was no wolf, after all—the gosling will pay no attention. Don't be surprised to hear of this. Peasants, mimicking calls, have always led ducks to the water and sheep to the slaughterhouse. What is new, a contribution of our own times, is that the same can be done to a man. Lipiczany, his fever broken, waking from his coma, saw the light in the hair of the man above him, felt on his face the wash of his breath. At that instant the orphan—silly goose!—attached himself to his ersatz father.

Plumb parked his auto and turned the engine off. He was a bachelor, a diamond cutter, and wore three rings on one hand. He used that hand to write out a bank draft for a handsome sum. In that fashion the Hatters' Asylum solved its financial problems and went on happily, blissfully really, right through the end of the decade. Charity was the same as life insurance: once a few people had made a contribution, everyone else was eager to give.

On a bright afternoon in September, 1939, a small dot, a speck, appeared high in the sky. The children of the Orphanage Number 2 were in the garden, jumping over a little stream that Myer Krystal, with a pump, had forced from the well. A Polish girl was beating dust out of a rug. The gardener boy was clipping the lawn. A sunflower nodded. Walnuts, all on their own, dropped from the walnut tree. Then it became silent everywhere. The housemaid put down her broom. Workmen in Piotrkowska Street stopped their digging. Even the bells in the far-off Protestant steeple, which had been ringing, became completely still. No one, anywhere, spoke. It was as if the entire city were listening to the faint

41

sound of the airplane engine. The children looked up. The distant craft dropped steadily lower, in circles. Its wings, in the sunlight, were silver, then turned dark beneath a cloud. For minute after minute it lazily dropped; then two bombs tumbled from it and, whistling a little, fell all the way to the ground.

Chapter Two

The Elder

I

The sound of bells came down Krzyzanowsky Street first thing one morning. Not church bells, but a bright, cheery noise, like a sleigh. The sound grew louder, and the orphans put their heads out the windows to see. In a moment four white horses pulling a wagon—it was big as a boxcar, with a peaked roof like a house—appeared. They trotted briskly, jangling the bells on their reins and the straps tied around their middles. A brown dog barked at their hooves. The wagon was painted in fresh red, white, and black stripes, and leaned precariously when it went around the corner. The dust cloud behind it rose to the rooftop of the Hatters' Asylum.

After riding about the streets for nearly an hour, the horse-drawn wagon came to a stop in the Central Square. With its bright stripes it looked like a circus car. Immediately a crowd pushed up close. A man with a large, narrow nose and a handsome suit, gray, double-breasted, asked everyone to step back several paces. Suddenly the front side of the wagon, or the top two-thirds of it, swung down. The Poles, men and women, started to flee, as if the carriage had been full of lions. The tall man in the suit jumped onto the low-

43

ered wagon wall, which now formed a platform a little more than a meter off the ground. He held up his hands. "Stop!" he cried. "There is nothing to fear!"

Perhaps it was the tone of this man's voice; perhaps it was the sight of soldiers in uniforms who now joined the crowd—for whatever reason the Poles turned around. As a matter of fact, more people were coming up every moment, from the main station, the hotel, the various shops; they pressed against the backs of those in front of them, and even jumped a bit in the air. Everyone was trying to see into the interior of the wagon, all gloomy and black, except for low shrubs attached to the floor and dozens of stones that stuck up here and there. These were white or gray slabs, some square, some rounded at the top, and they were all crowded together, leaning against each other like bad teeth in a mouth. A shudder went through the hundreds of people. Tombstones! Markers for graves!

The thin-nosed man, he also had black, slicked-down hair, called out to the crowd. "Poles! Listen! Is it day or is it night?"

Many people swung their heads to look for the sun. There it was, round, bright, and hot enough to keep alive the late summer flies.

"It's daytime!"

"Yes! Daytime!"

The figure on the platform seemed to have swallowed his lips. There was just a slot where his mouth was. "No! It is night. Night. Look how many stars are out!" He threw his arms over the crowd where some Jews, wearing yellow patches on the front of their coats, and on the shoulders, shuffled their feet and laughed at the joke.

"Yes!" somebody cried. "Like Hollywood!"

A thick-armed Pole looked about him—at the Jews, at the soldiers, and at the Volksdeutschers, who stood at the back, with their leather straps under their chins. Then he crossed those arms on top of his chest. "We wanted a Poland without Jews. Now we've got Jews without Poland."

"Citizens! You are about to see something that really happened." The man in the gray suit motioned toward the dark box behind him and stepped to one side of what was, after all, a stage. "This is the Jewish Cemetery in Prague. Night. Darkness. Listen, the midnight bell—"

At those words there was a sound like a gong, hidden, deep, echoing. One of the white horses thrust his head downward and rolled his pink eye. On the stage a Jew was standing, wearing striped pants, a cutaway coat, a top hat. A gold chain glistened on his vest. There was a ring on every finger.

The black-haired, lipless man whispered, "Rothschild!"

The gong sounded again and a second Jew appeared from the opposite side of the wagon. This was an old man, his eyes red-rimmed, dressed in a long gabardine and a fur-trimmed hat.

"Aha!" the man in the gray suit exclaimed. "Another Elder of Zion!"

Then the gong rang once more, and a fourth and a fifth time, up to the midnight hour; with each stroke a new Jew appeared, until at last, in silence, with wolf lips and frizzled hair, the representatives of the twelve tribes stood shoulder to shoulder across the front of the stage.

The sun hung over the Central Square like a bare bulb on a cord. But the Jews on the wagon blocked out the light. Behind them everything was dark, lit only by a sliver of moon. Suddenly, at some secret sign, the Elders stepped into the shadows and gathered about a tombstone larger than all the others. One of their number spoke into the open grave.

"We greet you, son of the accursed."

"Soon, soon," the remainder chanted.

Then the first of the Jews, Rothschild, spoke alone. *"Already we have gold. More riches than the mines of California. We*

45

control the exchanges of Europe. Princes and governments are in our debt."

After him the others, Benjamin, Naphtali, Zebulun, bragged in a similar fashion—about their powerful leaders, their brilliant artists, the way the Jews in the parliaments and publishing houses controlled opinion throughout the world. *"Reason! Open debate! Free thinking! Now we have the same rights as Christians!"*

In the crowd of spectators men and women were crossing themselves. One or two Jews attempted to sneak away, but were stopped by Volksdeutschers. At the front two boys managed to work their way into the first row. One was Myer Krystal, with the silky mustache, and the other was the left-handed Mann Lifshits, seven years old. The latter wore short pants and a white shirt, the regular outfit of the Hatters' Asylum. But Krystal, in spite of the heat, the sunshine, was wearing a raincoat that came past his knees. The two orphans watched as the Elders of Zion continued to address the newly opened tomb.

DAN (an old man, stains on his jacket): *O Prince of Darkness! Physicians of our race have learned the intimate secrets of Christian families. The health and even the lives of our mortal foes are now in our hands.*

ASHER (leering): *Marriages between Christians and Jews are now common. Already the offspring of such unions, many with twisted bones and the thick lips of the mongrel, can be seen in the streets and alleys of Europe.*

THE AARONIC LEVITE: *Our ancient goal, world domination, as was promised to us by our father, Abraham, is at hand. Famine, pestilence, great economic dislocations—all have been propagated by our agents, from the celebrated international bankers down to the unknown governesses in rich houses. Even as I speak to you, highly trained Jews are descending into the metropolitan railways and underground trains. From these subterranean places we will explode all the cities of the conti-*

46

*nent. The whole of mankind is about to be plunged into anoth-
er world war! Arise, O Serpent! Wind the states of Europe
into your unbreakable coils!*

ALL TOGETHER: *Arise! Arise!*

The crowd watched silently, raptly, openmouthed. In spite
of their fear, they wanted to see what would come out of the
pit. But nothing did. Instead, from the front row, there was
a sound like this: *click*. Again the identical noise: *click*. A Polish policeman jerked his head around. A soldier, one of the
Others, turned his back to the wagon and began to search
the faces in the crowd. Mann Lifshits cleared his throat.
Click, yet again. Krystal, his companion, put his lips out, as if
to whistle, though no tune emerged. *Click. Click. Click.*

People began to murmur and shake their heads. Many
were looking in Krystal's direction, though Krystal himself
was looking at a cloud, or a bird, or perhaps just the sky.
"It's him!" somebody shouted, pointing out the boy, whose
raincoat button had come undone.

"Yes," responded some others, "that one there!"

At that moment the whole crowd heard a sweet voice singing a Polish song.

"Listen!" cried the man in the gray suit, still sitting on the
edge of the platform. "A sound like an angel!"

A boy picking flowers skipped over the stage. He had
blond hair, red cheeks, eyes that were blue. Instantly the
Jews on the wagon hid themselves behind the gravestones.
The child wandered toward them, still singing his song.

"Warn him! Help him! They must not catch him!" The
slick-haired man cried those words.

From the crowd: "No! no!"

"Stay back!"

"Run from there!"

It was too late. The play continued.

Boy dances into shadows. At once the Jews seize him. The

47

child utters a cry, but one of the Elders silences him, saying,
"Now the snake will arise!" Others remove his clothes and
lift him to the top of the largest tombstone. A Jew fetches in-
struments: a knife, a needle, pliers, and a golden basin. Two
hold the arms of the naked boy while confederates pierce him.
The blood, as from a bladder, spills out. A Jew collects the out-
pouring eagerly in the golden basin. Boy dies. The Hebrews
make passionate action, some dancing, some in vigorous
prayer.

"Alas!" cried the man. "Did you hear? Did you see? Who
will avenge him?"

For a moment the crowd stood stunned, motionless. Then
everyone shouted at once.

"We will!"

"We'll fix them for good!"

The spectators surged forward, so that Krystal and Lifshits
disappeared among them. The Poles were straining against
the edge of the stage, pounding upon it. Suddenly they staggered back. They fell against each other with a sigh.

On the stage the contents of the golden basin were poured
into the open grave. Immediately smoke and flames issued
from the pit. Then the Jews reached inside and pulled out,
by its head and its tail, a live green serpent.

The smoke from the wagon spread over the crowd. People
began to shout, to scream. All four horses reared upward.
One frantic stallion broke from its traces and galloped away.
The Elders lifted the reptile over their heads, above their top
hats and skullcaps, their black ringlets of hair. The snake extended its tongue from its narrow head.

"Satan! Satan!" everyone cried.

Watching the pageant were a score of Jews. You could see
where they stood by the little space, like magic circles, that
grew around them. But the Poles did not dare touch them.
They thought the Hebrews had some awful power.

The man in the gray suit, nearly lipless, called out, "Do not be frightened! Stay calm! Listen!"

Just then the bells from the church on the square began to peal. Out of the roof of the wagon, which was supposed to be Heaven, a cloud descended with soldiers on it, the Others, the Lords and Masters. They shot bullets from their guns and the Elders of Zion fell into the pit. Then the top part of the wall shut up and the bottom third of the wagon opened. You could see that the Jews had fallen into the mouth of hell. There were flames there, real flames, among which the Jews danced, calling out, *Woe! Woe!* They beat at their clothes; they beat at the air.

The folk in the Central Square started to cheer. Then they took hold of the Jews. What they did was shake them, not hard, not violently, but slowly, steadily, mechanically even. No one said anything. The three remaining horses stood peacefully switching their tails. The bottom wall of the wagon swung up and the fire went out. The only sound in the square, with its grand hotel, the station by Donati, and its monument to a hero, was the clacking of teeth and the ring of coins on the pavement. That's because some of the Jews were being shaken upside down.

Way off, from a side street, a man appeared and began to walk across the empty part of the square. People stopped what they were doing to watch. This big man, a bearlike man, was moving unsteadily, from one side of the square to the other. It was Fiebig, the financier. What caught people's eye was, he had his coat on, a fur coat, made out of mink, or foxes, as if it were not one of the hottest days of the year. Stranger still, he had it on backwards. The back of the coat was in the front, and up his spine some person had done all the buttons. As he went by, you could see the sweat on his face, the fat cheek, the long, wet black strands of hair stuck on his forehead. His arms just hung down.

It was comical, really—such a rich man, shuffling and

stumbling across the public square. Yet nobody laughed, perhaps because in front of Fiebig, waiting for him, were two Men of Valor, each with a skull, a death's-head, on his cap. The financier reached the first officer, stopped, took a half step forward, and then he hauled up his arm and with a fat wrist saluted.

"What's that? I'm not a friend of yours!" said the Death's-Header, and struck him smartly on one of his eyes.

Fiebig hung his head between his furry shoulders and trudged ahead, just three steps, when the other one hit him with a balled-up fist.

"Don't you salute? A Jew has to show some respect!"

This man Fiebig, a member of the Community Council, breathed in and out. Then he fumbled with his hand, like a drunken person, trying to get at his backward pocket. After groping a moment, he pulled out a matchbook. God knows why, he lit a match.

For a cigarette? For *them?* For a Sport brand of his own? To hurl, perhaps, into the face of his tormentor? Or was he going to touch it to the fur of his coat and go up—a terrible idea, a great gesture—like a torch, a ball of fire? These thoughts went at the speed of light through the mind of everyone there: Myer Krystal, in his raincoat; Mann Lifshits, standing nearby; the whole crowd of gentiles and Jews. But the fact is, he didn't do anything. He just stood there. In the sky the hot sun jumped a centimeter higher, like the hand of an automatic clock. It shone so brightly you could not even see the live flame of the match, which moved down the wooden stick until it burned Fiebig's fingers and then went out. That's when everybody went home, or else to a café for something cooling to drink. As for Fiebig, zlotys or no zlotys, he had simply gone mad.

50

In the early days of the war, there were still many wealthy Jews in our town. It is true that their money was impounded and that they had to register valuable items like jewels or furs. They weren't allowed to keep servants either. But in spite of these restrictions, there they were, out on Leczyca, on Pabianice, wearing high boots and walking their dogs. For a time it was the fad to own different kinds of animals, parrots or monkeys, which people carried about on their shoulders, or little lizards that turned the same color as the coat you wore. After that, cane furniture became the rage. Tables, chairs, lounges—everything was made out of wicker or bamboo. The clothes in that season: in addition to boots there were leather belts and brass-colored buttons. Madame Tort, the former Widow Greenkraut, actually wore padded shoulders and a pair of pants. Everyone wanted to look like a soldier. Do not ask how these pleasures were paid for. The money just seemed to come from the air. At a time when Polish officials had to walk to their jobs, when even the Others, for lack of petroleum, were forced to leave tanks and trucks in the depot, the "Spider" Gran Sport of Doctor Zam was parked in front of the Hotel Europa, and Plumb drove his Daimler Double Six wherever he wished in the town.

The problem for our upper-class Jews was not how to spend money but time. Professional people, doctors, lawyers, could not treat Polish patients, or serve papers, or appear in court. The fashionable shops had been taken over by Volksdeutscher trustees. What to do? Even the Rumkowsky Geyser, once a popular gathering spot, was—because of lice, of typhus—now closed to Jews. Which left the cafés, where you sat at tables and talked about the end of the war: *that month, that winter, sometime before the spring thaw.* Then the Occupying Power set a curfew at 9 P.M., and the cafés shut, too.

Not the Astoria, however. It was an exception. On the night following the pageant in the Central Square, for instance, you could find all sorts of well-known people—the importer Blum, Szapiro the furrier, bald Jacob Tort—eating broilings and meat balls behind the famous blinking sign.

"Boogie-woogie!" That was Plumb, the bachelor. "Boogie-woogie!" he cried, using the American term.

Baggelman raised his arms to conduct the orchestra of eleven pieces. His shoulders, from his years as a musician, had a slight hump. Rabbi Nomberg—his face was shining from a recent shave—stood up to dance with Malka Korngold. Schneour took the arm of the new Madame Tort. The linoleum dance floor filled up. The men and women took short little steps. Their cheeks were together and their eyes, with their painted shadows, stared.

The waiters, with towels over their arms, ran from table to table. Because of the cigarettes, smoke in a cloud hung in the air. Rievesaltes and Miss Lubliver were sitting to one side of the dance floor. He leaned toward her, with his lips near her ear. Not far away Isaiah Trumpelman drank off a clear glass of kümmel and strode to the window. It was already dark in the streets. A streetlamp, a second streetlamp, came on. At the front table Nisel Lipiczany, to keep the old man in sight, swung his head around.

On the stage the comedian, Schotter, began telling jokes. He was a thin man, and stood with his hands thrust into his armpits. His shoes turned up at the end. "Horowitz called on the telephone. That's not his real name. But his real name also begins with 'H.' Horowitz wants to talk to his Governor-General of Poland, to find out what he had done to the Jews. So the governor says, 'We took away their money, and we're going to make them work on the canals.' 'Not enough,' Horowitz tells him. Then the governor says, 'We banned ritual slaughter, and pretty soon they won't have a potato to eat.' Still Horowitz isn't satisfied. *What else?* he wants to know. Then the governor mentions his new ten-point plan: 'First, we have set up a Jewish self-help organization—' 'That's it! Stop!' Horowitz interrupts him. 'You don't have to go further than that!'"

People did laugh, but not loudly. It was a daring joke. It made one breathless to hear it.

"A Jew runs up to another Jew and says, 'Good news!' Naturally, the second Jew wants to hear what it is. 'I was walking down Alexsandrowska,' says the first Jew, 'and I saw where someone scribbled on a wall: *Beat the Jews! Down with ritual slaughter! Beat the Christ Killers!'* 'You call that good news?' says the other Jew. 'What's good about that?' The first Jew replies, 'Don't you understand? The old days have returned. The Poles are in charge again!'"

A real burst of laughter at this one. Schotter rocked back and forth on the rounded bottoms of his shoes. He tipped so the crowd could see the hairless spot on his head. He told one more.

"Horowitz has a wonderful idea to save on petroleum, so he calls the Prime Minister of England on the phone. 'Listen, Churchill,' Horowitz says. 'Why should we bomb each other? All that flying back and forth is a waste of gas. Let's make an agreement. You bomb London, and we'll bomb Berlin!'"

The whole crowd—waiters, orchestra members, everyone—was aghast. The reason for this was that even before the joke was over, four of the Others had come through the door. Two of these were in uniform, the black ones, Death's-Headers; the other two men wore civilian clothes. The gray-suited man, the one who put on the show in the square, spoke first. "Jew, who is the owner of this club?"

Popower, the waiter, was the person closest by. Fear gripped him. The dumplings, the calves' feet, slid off his tray.

The second civilian addressed the crowd. This was F. X. Wohltat, a native of the town—the same little Franz, in fact, who had once put his hand in Trumpelman's fishbowl. The Volksdeutscher had grown up. He was the head of a big

53

coffee business. But even though the Occupying Power had made him an important and powerful figure, the head of the whole Civilian Authority, he still took his hat off when he spoke to the Jews.

"My friends of the Mosaic fraternity. It's a pity we have to intrude on your evening. On your innocent pleasures. It just can't be helped. But at least I am not a stranger. No, no! I was brought up here, in the same streets as you. *I* am not ashamed to say that I played boyish games and swam in the blue Dolna with members of your community. Those were happy days! In later years my business has often drawn me away. Coffee! Coffee! But no matter where I travel, even in far-off Brazil, I always long to return to our beloved city. So it is your neighbor, Wohltat, speaking to you."

Upon those assembled in the Astoria Café, these words—spoken so softly, so mildly—made an agreeable impression. *Our beloved city! Your neighbor!* And above all, *My friends!* Those who knew Wohltat only by reputation began, a little, to relax. They had thought he would be tall, fierce, and—perhaps because he was a coffee roaster—somehow darker. But there he was—short, plump, white-skinned, like a popped kernel of corn. He turned his hat brim in his hands.

"With your permission we want to make a brief announcement, and then we shall be gone. The message is for the proprietor of this fine café. Would he step forward? Would someone perhaps point him out to me?"

No reply. Everyone in the crowd looked away from the owner—Putermilch, a huge, albinoish man, who went on drying glasses in back of the bar.

It was the lipless gray-suiter's turn to speak. "Three minutes! Three minutes only! If in that time the man we ask for is not before us, each Jew here must bear the consequences."

Immediately Wohltat's face broke into dripping perspiration. His brown eyes bulged a bit. The crowd was sweating, too. A whole minute went by. And then another. Putermilch, in his shirt sleeves, went round and round the rim of a glass. What awful tension!

"Heavens!" cried a woman. "Why won't he step forward?"

The next instant Schotter was speaking. "Horowitz, you know who he is, the Big Man, wanted a suit of clothes. So he orders three different tailors to make him one out of the material he furnished. Said the first tailor, 'There's only enough material here for a vest.' The second tailor said, 'From this I might be able to make a pair of pants.' But the Jewish tailor laughed, saying he could easily make three suits, with something left over: 'To them he's a giant, but to us he's only a pygmy!'"

You can imagine the horror that greeted this joke. Franz Xavier Wohltat put on his hat. Margolies, a waiter, choked on something. And both the Totenkopfers took out their guns.

Then Putermilch, round-shouldered, head hanging, came around the end of the bar. He stood in front of the gray-suited man.

"You are the owner of this club?"

Putermilch nodded. With his white, soft skin, and the way the electric lights caught the little hairs on his neck and his arms, he looked like a root that had been dug from the ground. A tuber. A yam.

"Name?"

"Putermilch, Herman."

The thin, black-haired Conqueror spoke right through the proprietor, as if he were not there. "Jews and Jewesses! The old Community Council is from this moment dissolved. It no longer exists. A new Judenrat must be formed. It will be known as the Council of Elders. Sixteen members, no more, no less. To be picked from those now in this room. This Council will be the instrument of our will among the Jews. It shall raise taxes and control its own police. It will run all religious organizations, all cultural affairs, all charitable institu-

55

tions. It appoints the judges, the teachers, the hospital heads. Putermilch! You are the new President of the Judenrat. The Chief Elder. Your first task will be to draw up a census with the name of each able-bodied Jew. All men between the ages of fifteen and sixty must work on the river dike. The only exceptions are those too sick even to lift a shovel, and of course the sixteen members of the Council itself. The rest will work, work!"

Once again Wohltat, the coffee roaster, removed his hat. The part in his hair was just over his ear; the long, damp strands of hair went over the dome of his head. His little red lips formed a smile. "My dear Jews. It is time for you to choose the members of your new Council. Please select whoever you want, in a completely democratic way. We won't interfere. We'll wait outside. If you will allow me, I have one small piece of advice. These are difficult and unhappy times. So in your deliberations, elect those who have the most to offer, the most intelligent, the most resourceful among you. We all have need of such leaders now."

The four Others went to the door. The man with the double-breasted suit had the last word. "No one may leave here until the selection of the Council has been completed. After the fifteen Elders have been selected, Putermilch, the President, will bring them to me in the road outside. Then the remaining Jews may return to their homes."

The door opened, it closed. A breath of the cool night air entered the room. Putermilch remained where he was. At last he looked up—he had light-colored eyes, he had invisible lashes—and said, "Does everybody have enough to eat?"

"This is no time, Putermilch," said Lipsky, the progressive attorney, "to be thinking of food."

A well-dressed man, with eyeglasses and a full black beard, stood up at a rear table. No one knew his name. "I am not from this city. I am from Budapest. I have a passport to prove I am not a Pole!" With that the stranger put on his top hat and his handsome coat. "What has been said does not apply to nonbelligerents. I shall leave here. I shall explain." To the astonishment of the entire café, the Hungarian went out the front door. No one moved. It was as if there had been an agreement to count to ten. Then Szapiro leaped to his feet as well.

"I have a residence at Carlsbad. At the baths. I go there each year for my health. I will show them my address at the spa."

"Jews will not have to go to Carlsbad anymore," Schotter announced. "Because Carlsbad has come to the Jews. We won't have any trouble losing weight." But the whole crowd was already abuzz.

"I'm going, too!"

"Let's all leave together!"

"Perhaps it's only a joke!"

There was a rush for the exit, a jam-up of people. For a moment everyone was pushing against everyone else. When at last the door swung open, the Hungarian was standing inside it—his beard chopped off, his glasses broken, and without his tall hat.

"The back door!"

Like a herd, like steers, the crowd ran through the café, to the rear of the kitchen. The cook, Gutfreind, wearing a white cook's hat, shook his head.

"Locked," he said. "They put a bar on it just this minute."

A line formed at the telephone. "Hello, hello, hello, hello," Mosk, the millowner, shouted into the receiver. "It's not working," he said.

Tort took it from him and dialed a number. "How do you explain it? There is nothing but a hum."

Blum, the importer, was next in line. "We are cut off from the world!"

There was a soft moan, a groan, and one by one the Jews—each with a star on the front and back of his jacket—went back to their tables. In a moment only the four waiters and their employer, Putermilch, were left standing. The latter softly said, "Who wants to be on the Jewish Council? Are there any volunteers?"

Silence. Blank faces. No one was willing.

Dorka Kleinweiss, one of the orchestra members, raised her hand. "Perhaps I should not speak. I am only a cellist. But I have an idea. Why don't we reelect all the old members of the Community Council? They already have experience in public affairs. Wouldn't that be the fair thing to do?"

Mordechai Kleen, a woodwind player, spoke up from the orchestra pit. "Miss Kleinweiss is right! What a wonderful idea! This will show the Lords and Masters that we can't be ordered about. That we have backbone!"

"Yes! Yes! Reelect the old Council!" many voices rang out.

"Ha! Ha! We are too smart for them!"

"Just a moment! A moment, please!" It was Rabbi Nomberg, himself a member of the dissolved organization. When he stood, the room grew still. "Let us look at the facts here. First, many members of the Community Council have fled to Warsaw or even more distant places. Of those remaining, some—Fiebig, for instance—are no longer able to serve. Then we must ask: How will the Occupying Power respond to Miss Kleinweiss' suggestion? Would it not seem to them a deliberate provocation? If they disband the old Community Council it can mean only one thing—they want a new one. Speaking for myself, I am going to refuse the honor of any such office. In my opinion not a single member of the former Council should be allowed on the new Judenrat. New blood! Fresh faces! That's what we need!"

Blum, also a member of the defunct government, Department of Commerce and Trade, supported his former colleague. "I refuse to serve! Anyone who goes on the new Judenrat has to be crazy. These Elders will be responsible the first thing that goes wrong. They could go to jail. They could be deported. No! Don't mention my name!"

But Mordechai Kleen held his ground. "Let's vote on the idea! How many want to reelect the old Council?"

But before a vote could be taken, Lipsky the lawyer climbed onto a chair. He was a slight man with a narrow face, whose hair stood up in the back. His ears were large, nearly transparent, and pointed. "I can hardly believe the things I have been hearing. From you, Rabbi. From you, Blum. I feel ashamed to be in this room because of what the musicians suggested. As for you Putermilch, you're a disgrace to us all. How dare you ask for volunteers? It's a scandal!"

Pale Putermilch turned completely pink. It was like dipping an egg into a dye. "But Lipsky," he said. "What else can we do?"

"Do? Don't do! Nothing! No elections! No Council! No police and no judges! Nothing at all! They are waiting for an answer? Here is our answer: *Do whatever you want to! We can't stop you, but we don't have to cooperate, either. You want to snatch? All right, snatch! You want to kill? So kill. But we will not do this work for you!* Putermilch, it's up to you! Go out there! Don't be so shy! Tell them: *Sorry, not willing.* If not, if we collaborate, if we hold this election, for sure sooner or later our own Elders will end up killing Jews."

For a moment no one even breathed. Little Lipsky stood poised on his chair, on tiptoe, with his chin up—it looked as if he meant to leap, to fly. Then Mordechai Kleen, the oboist, responded. "I withdraw my support from Miss Kleinweiss' idea."

"Bravo!" cried Plumb. "It's the resistance!"

Baggelman raised his baton. "We will play Chopin! Even if it's against the law! Yes, and Paderewski!"

The crowd cheered. "Bravo!" they yelled. The musicians— Salpeter and Murmelstein, violinists; Andrei Schpitalnik, the piano player; Kleen, Miss Kleinweiss, and all the rest—lifted their instruments, their gleaming trumpets, and prepared to play.

At which point a voice—high, forceful, lisping, a singsong voice—cut through the expectant hush.

"May a Jew speak?"

It was, of course, I. C. Trumpelman, the Director of the Hatters' Asylum. Like a man half his years, he jumped to the top of a table. The eleven-piece orchestra laid their instruments in their laps. Lipsky folded his arms.

"What patriotism! It's touching! What heroes! Maybe you'll let me talk for a minute and I'll tell you something these smart lawyers and businessmen don't even know." Trumpelman's head was practically level with the bulbs in the chandelier. His skin was tanned, healthy-looking, and his teeth and his hair were bright, white, gleaming.

"You heard the news that the Conquerors set up labor brigades. But they don't care about damming the rivers or blasting tunnels for mountain roads. No! The Jews dig the holes and then fill them in. They carry rocks from one side of the road to the other and then drag them back again. Jews working! That's what the Others want. They think it's a bigger achievement than making a farm from a swamp.

"Listen! Here's what happened this morning. In our Asylum were two boys, aged eight, aged ten. The Konotop brothers. These boys sold carrots from our garden in the market stalls. Today the Conquerors snatched them. They rounded them up. A whole truckload went to the Dolna. There the Jews were given pails to dredge with. They had to walk into the river, far into it, where it's fast. By the time I got there the water was up to the chest of the tallest man. But on my boys it rose higher, to their shoulders, their chins, and then—what else could happen? First one Konotop, then the other, floated away.

"And now you will allow this to happen, only to music! To patriotic tunes! Children! They can take children, as long as your hands stay clean! Lipsky wants to say, *No! No census! We won't do your work for you!* That's laziness! That's luxury! And worse! At least if there's a Judenrat to make a list, there will be exemptions. No one under fifteen or over sixty. And no one who's sick. To let children work in the river, to let sick people carry stones—it's the same thing as murder. Murder!

Listen! Either we have the courage to make this census or it will be made for us, according to whim, to passion, to chance! We have to do what we can! No one wants to be on the Council? Trumpelman will run! He'll be an Elder! He's not afraid to dirty his hands!"

Nisel Lipiczany lifted his head toward the blinding chandelier. A hero stood there, a giant. "Yes, yes," he shouted. "You have to run!"

Philosoff, the oldest waiter, scratched his chin. "Every argument sounds so good. My opinion keeps changing."

Indeed, for that instant the entire gathering seemed poised between the two points of view. Then Jacob Tort cried aloud: "But there is another exemption! Judenrat members won't have to drain swamps!"

That turned the tide. Szapiro made his voice heard. "I am a man with a wife and with children. I have to think of them! So I put my name up for my old position."

And then the importer, Blum: "I nominate my good friend, the rabbi of the Italianate Synagogue."

"I accept!" Nomberg shouted. "And I propose a man with great experience in Jewish self-government, the wise Nathan Blum!"

"Wait a minute! The old Council is nominating itself!"

"Put down my name. Popower. With two P's."

Plumb was banging a fork on his glass. "Popower! A waiter! You can't have such people on the Council! No workers allowed!"

"What about artists? I studied woodwinds with Lajpunger himself! In Crakow! I also play saxophone and flute! Write down Mordechai Kleen!"

"Yes! A waiter! A musician! The next thing we'll be hearing from actors and cooks!" Szapiro, whose name had already been put into nomination, went on in this vein. "What a spectacle! We might as well present the Others with a Council of women!"

Mathilda Megalif, the actress, replied. "Why not? It's a

61

good idea! I have performed in theaters all over the world. Madame Megalif accepts a place on the Council!"

"What's wrong with cooks?" the white-hatted Gutfreind wanted to know.

Mosk rose, blinking. "Nothing is wrong with cooks, except they should be in a kitchen. Just like actors should stay on the stage. We already heard who should be on the Council. Elect the smartest people, the best brains, the ones with the most to offer—that's what Wohltat said. We mill owners have a head for business. What's good for textiles is what's good for the Jews. I control a hundred thousand spindles! Every day in my pockets I carry thousands and thousands of zlotys. Look! Here are two thousand in cash. That's the kind of thing I have to offer!"

The room was in an uproar. Several young people shook their fists in Mosk's direction. "It's a bribe!" they were yelling. "He wants to buy his way onto the Judenrat!"

Putermilch, in his white shirt, was turning around and around. "Ladies and gentlemen. Friends! There are too many Jews for the Council. We have only fifteen places. How will we be able to choose?"

"Better to take the names from a hat!" Paradyz, the drum player, shouted.

"Why not have a rotating Council? First one group of sixteen serves for a month or two months, and then the next group has a turn. And so on. That way everybody will have a chance to be elected." That was Bettsack, the schoolmaster's, idea.

Philosoff: "But I thought it was a Council of Elders. Why not let the oldest on first?"

Pandemonium then. Everybody in the Astoria Café was on his feet, on chairs, on the tables. They all wanted Putermilch's attention. But they came to order when Rievesaltes shot a bullet into the ceiling with his gun.

"Jews," he said. "I don't want to hear a sound."

The storm ended. The patrons sat down in front of their plates. Rievesaltes, wearing a special shoe to make his legs even, stood on a tabletop.

"That's democracy, my friends. All for one and one for all, pretty soon everybody is at everybody's throat. I want to point out to you that while we have been throwing pitchai slices, and behaving like children, the moon has come up and the stars have risen. It's already bedtime, Jews! Let's put it this way: we have to settle our business."

Odd that Rievesaltes should mention the moon. That was what the other kids called him, *levune punim*, moonface, man-in-the-moon, when he himself was a boy. It was the roundness of the head, and the neckless way it sat on his shoulders, that did it. Strange to say, not one of Rievesaltes' associates—Mister Nodelman, Mister Pravenishkis, Mister Turski—had a neck either. Their heads lay on their shoulders like balls on a shelf. It is a type of body you often find on porters, on ritual butchers, on policemen. Rievesaltes, at age thirty-eight, was moonlike still. His hair had receded well up his bulging temples, and the habit of smoking had puffed the skin around his wide-set, narrow, browless eyes. His little ears seemed stuck flat to the side of his head. Where was his pistol? Disappeared. Vanished.

"The first position is the Vice-President of the Council. Mister Mosk, am I mistaken, or did you not mention two thousand zlotys?"

Mosk sat rigid, with a fork and a spoon in either hand. "No. It was my mistake. I meant four thousand five hundred."

"Mosk, of the Mosk Mills, is the Vice-President of the Judenrat. You can see my associate, Mister Turski, to settle details."

Rievesaltes did not pause. He waved the smoke cloud from in front of his eyes and continued speaking. "Next is the Department of Finance, a big position. More or less treasurer and tax collector for all the Jews. Fiebig's old job. Mister Plumb? Mister Schneour? Mister Szapiro?"

Each of those called held up a different number of fingers. Plumb, the bachelor, had to use three on his second hand.

"My good friend Plumb, the diamond dealer, is now Chairman of the Department of Finance. Eight thousand zlotys to Nodelman, my associate, please."

A murmur from the crowd. A pit-pat of applause.

"Now we turn to the third vacant position, the Department of Religious Affairs." Rievesaltes turned his circular face onto the restaurant patrons. Kornischoner, the rabbi of the Fur Trimmers' Synagogue, held up a single thin finger. Kelbasin, the dairyman, though a nonbeliever, put up four. But one man was frantically waving all ten.

"To Rabbi Nomberg it goes! An excellent choice!"

What an exciting half hour then! People were putting up fingers and waving their hands. There were shouts of encouragement, bursts of applause. Anyone looking in the window would have thought it was some kind of sale, an auction, not a matter of how the Jews were to govern their lives. No one thought of anything but the bidding, the suspense, the amazing sums. And as the vacant places were slowly filled, the higher their prices became. Szapiro took over the Housing Department, a fourteen-finger position, and Zweideneck, the balloon tire dealer, had to pay fifteen to become head of Charities and Welfare. Such prices left people dizzy. They were biting their tongues.

At last Rievesaltes, with his face wet and shining, declared, "Only one position left. The Department of Public Health. Do my ears hear ten thousand—?"

Immediately Anton Schneour, who had once held that office, put an end to all bidding. "Twenty-five thousand zlotys," he said.

There was a gasp, then a sigh.

"Mister Schneour once. Mister Schneour twice—"

"Wait!" Lipiczany was on his feet, squinting and wincing. "Chaim said he would run! It was his idea to save the children! It's because of him that we're choosing a Council. It's not fair that he won't be on it!"

The crowd at once responded. "That's true!" they cried. "Let's elect him Chairman of Public Health!"

Nisel was beaming, babbling almost. "Chaim is a wonderful doctor. He saved my life."

The whole room started to cheer—not so much for Trumpelman or for his skills as at the thought that they were the ones who were going to choose him.

"Twenty-eight thousand, in cash!"

Rievesaltes put out his hands. "What can I do, Mister Schneour? In this case we must bow to the will of the people."

The former Chairman of the Public Health Department pulled on his mustache, as if he meant to rip it off. "A wonderful doctor! Who has seen his diploma? Where are his credentials? Lithuania is not on the other side of the world!"

"Call the question!" That was the musician, Kleen.

"Vote, vote!" A regular chant.

The election was held on the spot by a show of hands. Rievesaltes announced the results. "Schneour, sorry. The new boss of the Public Health Department is I. C. Trumpelman. Eighty-seven to six."

A shout. A roll of applause. Rievesaltes climbed down from the table and made his way to the crestfallen Schneour. "A word," he said, "in your ear."

Dozens of hands pushed Trumpelman up where Rievesaltes had stood. "Speech!" cried the Jews.

And Trumpelman obliged them.

"Maybe a time will come when we can forgive our enemies. Maybe someday the war will end. Then we can all meet together. Even the six Jews who voted for the other person. Ha! Ha! Even that person himself. Then we can talk and

65

drink tea and read newspapers. Until then, too bad. We have to be the way *they* are. Like bandits. Like wolves."

Impossible to say whether it was those words, so strange and unexpected, that sent a chill down everyone's back, or whether it was the cold air that rushed through the open front door. Putermilch was standing in it, filling it, with only a small space for the black of the night.

One by one the new Judenrat members drew up nearby. They put on their hats, their expensive mufflers. But no one made a move to go. Putermilch, parsnip pale, continued to stare back at the café, at his four waiters—Popower, Margolies, Philosoff, Hasensprung—and at the bottles with their silver caps lined up at the bar.

Then someone in the crowd impatiently cried, "Leave! Go! The rest of us want to go home!"

"Wait! Wait!" Mosk, the new Vice-President, cupped his hands around his mouth. "There is just time for everyone to have a drink. An alcoholic drink. I am paying for everything!"

In seconds the atmosphere of the café was almost normal: the band playing, waiters running, and people ordering gin with aerated water.

Mister Turski came up to Trumpelman. "Somebody wants to see you," he said.

"Can't you see I am a member of the Council?"

But Rievesaltes' associate opened his hand under the older man's eyes. There was a hothouse flower inside. Trumpelman clutched it and followed the no-necker, who was already wending his way through the crowd.

Lipiczany followed, looking over his shoulder to where Schneour and Rievesaltes continued their conversation. He saw the zlotys the former handed the latter. To his dismay he also saw how the previous Public Health Director put on his hat and his coat and took Trumpelman's place in the line.

"Chaim! It's a plot!" The boy darted after the physician

66

and grasped his coattails. But Trumpelman had already arrived at one of the private booths that lined the far wall of the Astoria Café. Ignoring the warning, he parted the velvet curtain and stepped inside.

"Have you perhaps lost this, Miss Lubliver?" he said.

The singer was sitting by a little table, on an upholstered divan. Her cigarette was burning in a holder. Slowly, showing a trace of lipstick, she smiled. "Ah! My rose!"

Trumpelman was still twisting the stuff of the purple curtain. "Where should I pin it?" he asked.

The woman's gown was cut in the Chinese fashion—that is, with a long slit that ran well up one leg. This leg Miss Lubliver now lifted, placing the heel of her foot, with its sequined sandal, beneath her. "Here," she said, indicating the wisp of material between her waistband and her thigh.

But Trumpelman stood, half transfixed, staring at the whiteness, like fresh snow, like cream, on the underside of her leg. Above the strap of her garter there were two green-colored bruises. His hand, the one with the flower, shook. "Rievesaltes beats you!" he exclaimed.

She did not answer, though her head gave a short jerk, like a twitch, and her chest heaved, stretching her thin gown against the dark dots of her breasts.

"One day I shall kill him!"

"Cigarette?" She held out to him, across the tiny room, a rare pack of French Bleues.

"What? Cigarette? No, no, no, no." He felt that if he let go of the curtain he might actually fall.

"A drink then? A toast?"

"Miss Lubliver! I must not stay. The Council is leaving."

"But you have a moment, please. Sit by me on this sofa. Just here." She moved to the side of the divan, folding her second leg, like the first, beneath her. The Director of the Hatters' Asylum stumbled forward.

"Miss! The sound of your dress! It rustles!"

67

He dropped onto the cushion, sank right into it, and took the white cigarette. She put the hot end of her own to his cold one, put her hand over his, then drew in her breath. He saw the lines in her lips, like an accordion's, the down in her hollow cheek; and he felt, through the cloth of his trousers, her kneecap. His cigarette flared.

"Are you frightened?" she asked him. "Your hand is shaking."

"Of the Others? The Occupiers? Never! It's not fear, Miss Lubliver. It's anger! It's indignation! I know that only moments ago that man, like a goat, nibbled at your ear!"

Again her head jerked aside in a flinching movement.

"Miss, pardon me: now it is you who tremble."

She turned partly from him, stretching the tendons of her neck. He could just see her foot in her sandal. The toes were pinched together, as if squeezed by a hand. A tear hung on her lashes. With his thumb he smudged it on her cheek.

"Miss Lubliver! My old friend!"

But just then the velvet curtains parted and Nisel Lipiczany leaned through. His face looked anxious, his head tilted aside. "Chaim!" he exclaimed. "They're leaving!"

Beyond the boy's head you could see where the last of the Council of Elders—Jacob Tort, Chairman of the Water and Power Department, and Plumb, of Finance—were filing out the open door. The sixteenth member was Anton Schneour. Those left in the room, the regular Jews, were rushing to get on their coats. The band had stopped playing. The lights were already dimmed.

Trumpelman jumped from his place and ripped the curtains closed. "Miss," he said. "Time to go!"

But the singer did not seem to hear him. Beneath the black cap of her hair her eyes were fixed, not blinking. She spoke as if he were not in the little chamber. "This is not my home. I am from the seacoast, near the beach, the waves. In our village the boats left at night, with yellow lanterns on the bows. The little boats. The little lights."

68

Bai nakht verft der alter fisher, hoopla!
Zem netz ber de glanzende fish—

At night the old fisherman, hoopla!
Throws his net over the gleaming fish—

She broke off her song. There were real tears in her eyes and—because of the night, the rocking boat, the salty, moonlit waters—in his as well.

"Such a beautiful voice."

Her head twitched once more. "In the morning the boats threw the catch onto the sand, onto the shore. How they flipped and flopped! Curling! Covered with sand! How frightened the little girl was to see them struggling. Breathing! Breathing! She was frightened of the net!"

Trumpelman dropped to his knees before her. "No one will harm you! I swear this! It is I who will protect you, the Chairman of Public Health!"

She stretched her arm. She touched him, as if he were a knight, on the shoulder.

Automatically almost, his hand opened on the little flower. It was as fresh, as red, as young-looking as the one he had sent her two decades before.

"You remember?" he said to the lady above him.

She nodded.

He leaned forward, pushing the stem of the flower into the crack in the gown. The rosebud's perfume filled the room. He shut his eyes. For a dizzy moment, for many moments, he felt like the newcomer again, the Lithuanian just off the train. She had thrown him a kiss then, across the room. Yes! He would kiss her now!

There was a rustle, like wind blowing, and he opened his eyes. The singer was gone.

Trumpelman dashed from the booth. "Miss Lubliver!" he cried. "Where is she?"

69

Rievesaltes spoke up from his table. "Don't worry. Mister Turski is taking her home."

"The Council! What about the Council?" The physician was shouting. "I have a place on the Judenrat!"

Verble, just a ragpicker, a beggar, mumbled a reply. "The Judenrat left a long time ago."

Trumpelman looked around the Astoria Café. Chairs were on the tables. The windows were shuttered. Most lights were out. Yet the waiters remained there, with their dark suits, their white towels, and not one of the musicians had budged. Lipiczany turned from a crack in the shutter and, wide-eyed, gasping, stared at Trumpelman, through Trumpelman.

The Lithuanian struck his own forehead. "Yes! I see! It was a plot! Rievesaltes! You did this! You sold my office to Anton Schneour!" He descended upon the table where Fried Rievesaltes was calmly sitting. Pravenishkis, another no-necker, stepped between them.

"Don't blame me," said Rievesaltes. "I can explain."

But Trumpelman had already whirled around and was striding, with his long legs, toward the door.

"Wait! Stop! Don't go!" cried Gutfreind, his cook's hat collapsed on his head.

Trumpelman flung the door open and stepped boldly through. Then his strength left him. He tottered like an old man against the frame. It was what he saw, a little way down the lamplit street, that struck him this blow. There, between the gutters, in their underclothes, or wearing no clothes at all, were the Council of Elders, hopping like frogs over each other's backs. On either side, holding a pistol, stood a Totenkopfer. Laughing. Joking. Puffing a cigarette.

As soon as a Jew had jumped over a Jew he had to drop to the ground, so that the next one could leap over him. They were all doing it, the white shapes of their bodies shining strangely, the sexual parts of the naked men hanging down. Putermilch was on his hands and knees, his bent back milk-white in the light from the streetlamp. Mosk put his hands

70

on that back and pushed himself up, halfway up, and then, with his black mouth open, he climbed the rest of the way. Schneour bent his legs and jumped over Plumb. At the top of his leap, while in the air, he saw Trumpelman. The latter, under this gaze, backed into the café.

"See?" said Gutfreind. "I told you."

Rievesaltes came up to the taller man. He actually put his hand on his shoulder. "This I suspected. My connections said this would happen. That is why I asked her to see you."

Paradyz crossed the dance floor, dragging his set of drums. "We're free to go, you know. We don't have to sit here until something happens. Let's go home, brothers! Tomorrow is another day!" But no person stirred from his chair—not even the ruined Hungarian, so far from his home.

Some time went by. Mister Schpitalnik played a few notes on the piano. Not a whole melody. Naymark, a trombonist, took apart his trombone. After a while Schotter started to speak. "Did you hear how Horowitz and the statesman Weizmann were going to settle everything by fighting a duel? So on the day of the duel Weizmann doesn't show up. Instead he sends a messenger who gives Horowitz the following message: *Weizmann can't make it, please kill yourself.*"

No laughter. No comments. Klapholtz, the modernist painter, removed the cigarette from his lip. The Jews were waiting, calmly, quietly, to see what would happen to the Council: manufacturers and merchants, professional people, the cream of our crop. Then, slow enough to count them, there were sixteen shots.

Immediately Wohltat rushed in, followed by the man in gray. The Volksdeutscher turned his hat in his hands. "Listen, Jews! This is terrible. It's the worst day of my life. Who would believe what I have been through?" True enough, the man really suffered. His eyes were popping. There were circles of sweat under his arms.

"This can't go on, my dear people. One day it's a riot, like at the Central Square, the next day your coreligionists are actually shot. We'll have to set up a special quarter, just for the Jews. That way you'll be protected from anyone who wants to hurt you. The place is the Baluty Suburb. Take whatever you want with you. Don't worry! Poles living there will have to give up their apartments. We'll put guards there to keep them away. And you have up to seventy-two hours to make the move. That's three whole nights and days."

The waiters and musicians were too thunderstruck to say a word. The thin, lipless man spoke instead. "Everyone in this room is now a member of the new Judenrat. You must make arrangements for the transfer of population, for housing, for kitchens, for movement of goods. Your orders will come from the President of the Council. Every member of the Mosaic community, every Jew and Jewess, must obey the Elder's commands. Who, then, will be this first among you?"

It was Wohltat who pointed then at his childhood physician. Trumpelman, with his hair like a mane, with all his teeth showing, slowly rose. The black-haired man continued. "You are the Chairman of the Jewish Council. The Elder of the Jews. Your word in the Suburb is law. Anyone who shirks his duty toward you will be arrested and subject to further measures. Seed of Abraham! Run now to your homes! You will not see them again!"

The coffee roaster, the native son, was calmer now. He smiled. "You see? No more beatings. It's best for everyone." He put his hat on. Then he, with his companion, walked out the door.

In less than ten minutes the café was completely empty. Everyone was gone. And that, ladies and gentlemen, is how they killed the rich Jews in our town.

III

From the Astoria Café to the Orphanage Number 2 was not a long walk. For Trumpelman, however, there was a detour, since the old Council of Elders, arranged neatly head to toe, lay in what was the most direct path. When he saw this, the Lithuanian turned left instead of right. It is not difficult to imagine what his thoughts must have been, as he and Lipiczany walked through the windy street. Of course it was he, Trumpelman, who should have been lying there, with Blum's feet on his forehead and his own feet on Zweideneck's nose. It was as if God had put down His hand and, groping about on the darkened earth, specifically had forbidden this to happen. Perhaps that is why Trumpelman stopped and looked up at the nighttime sky. It was covered with stars, like a wizard's cloak.

At that instant, while they were standing there, an awful thing took place. Nisel was aware of it first. He pulled the Elder's arm and pointed to where a figure, half-naked and missing an ear, was running toward them out of an alley. This bleeding person threw his bare arms around Trumpelman's shoulders. It was Nomberg, the Italianate Synagogue rabbi.

"They missed! They shot at me but they missed! I fell down and when they weren't looking I ran away! I'm not a ghost! I'm alive!" The wounded man took Trumpelman's hand and kissed it. Tears dropped from his eyes. "I know why you were saved! You will be the new Moses! You will lead us out of the land of suffering. Happy am I! To have kissed the savior's hand!" Smiling, nodding, also weeping, Nomberg ran off, along a perpendicular side street.

The man and the boy—what choice had they?—continued. By the time they reached Krzyzanowsky, Nisel, from the danger, the excitement, was wheezing and gulping. He pushed the air like a pudding into his throat. Trumpelman grasped him under his arms, around his chest. He carried the boy into the Hatters' Asylum and up the dark stairs. What strength the Elder had! What power! For a man aged three score and ten!

Upstairs, at the center of the hallway, a light was on. At once Trumpelman put Nisel down. The light went out.

Then, a moment later, weakly, without many watts, it shone again. The Director moved carefully forward. The beams were coming through the half-open door of a closet for brooms. Inside were Mann Lifshits and Krystal, each in his long sleeping gown. Lifshits had a stopwatch in one hand and the light cord in the other. Myer Krystal was holding a pane of glass, with paper stuck to it, right up to the unshaded bulb.

"Time," whispered Lifshits, the left-hander, pulling the cord.

In the blackness the boys fumbled their way to the deep double sink, which was supposed to be used for wringing out mops. The water ran there. For a time you could hear it swishing around. Then the boys groped through the darkness again.

"Ready?" asked Krystal.

"Ready," said Lifshits, and the yellow light, with a wire in it, started to glow.

Trumpelman ripped the door fully open. "What is this?" he demanded. His voice rang through the whole Asylum. "Sabotage? Saboteurs?"

The boys stood petrified, wide-eyed, and silent. But Trumpelman did not give them a slap. And he no longer shouted. Instead he stared in amazement at the ceiling of the little room. There, with clothespins, on clotheslines, hung pieces of paper. These were snapshots, dozens and dozens of them, glossy, dripping, wet. The Director of the Asylum, with his neck craned, walked underneath. Here, a Jew in a top hat, wearing striped pants. There, the white horses. Photo after photo of the slick-haired, thin-faced, eagle-nosed man. Totenkopfers, with the skulls on their caps. Jews upside down. Jews, all blurry, running. Fiebig, in a fur coat, holding a match. A complete record, in short, of the events at the Central Square.

The orphans looked at Trumpelman. He stared back at the boys. At last he asked them, "Where did you get such a camera?"

74

Lifshits hopped to the corner and picked up an overturned pail. There was a black American Kodak, with a leather strap. Trumpelman took it, pushed at the bellows, and then pulled back his lips in a grin.

"Ha! Ha! It's Faulhaber's! From three years ago!"

It was indeed the American's camera, dropped by him on his visit to the Orphanage Number 2. Quick-witted Krystal had scooped it up and hidden it inside his bed.

"Ha! Ha! Ha!" It wasn't just Trumpelman, not just the boys, who laughed at this joke. Ten or twelve orphans were standing in the doorway, too.

"Hee, hee," they giggled. They put their hands over their mouths.

Trumpelman grew suddenly grim. "This is an illegal act! It could mean death and torture! You will be shot!"

Boldly, Krystal stepped forward. He took the camera from the Elder's hands. "No! We have to remember!"

Lifshits was holding the reflector for the photoflash. He cried out, "So people will know!"

Then, before the old man could touch it, the camera, with its metallic lamp, went off. The light in the room was blinding. It seemed to collect, to burn, in the strands of Trumpelman's hair. It was precisely this picture, with the face of the Elder part way to the side, his hair making a halo and with a star on his coat, that later appeared throughout the Baluty Suburb—in miniature on all of the Ghetto stamps, and blown up larger than life size on hundreds of buildings and hundreds of walls.

The flash lamp exploded again. The orphans who had gathered in the doorway—Gutta Blit, Rose Atlas, Szypper, Kipnis, young Flicker—took each other's hands or clutched their friends' nightgowns. Together they watched Trumpelman shining, melting, in the rainbows and spangles of light. Nisel Lipiczany shielded his eyes.

"Oh!" he cried. "He is the King of the Jews!"

Chapter Three·

Smuggling

I

As the winter wore on, and Poland tilted farther away from the sun, the weather made life hard for the Jews. How cold November was! How bitter December. If you hit the ground with a shovel, the shovel broke off. People who liked to keep a glass of water by their bed at night discovered in the morning a glass of ice. At any time in the Baluty Suburb you could see these two sights: first, on street corners, in doorways, with rag balls on their feet, children doing a jig to keep warm; next, crowds of women following the coal carts— they hoped that a single "black pearl" would fall.

Luckily, most of the Balut was made from wood: one house against another, a slum really, with dirt streets and no sewer pipes. So when the last tree had been cut down, the Jews began to burn buildings. Some of the houses had porches in front or in back. The occupants took up the planks and railings and sawed them to fit in the stove. Other people burned their wardrobes, their tables, their stools and chairs. By the start of the year 1940, whole walls were missing, as were floorboards, and the banisters on stairs. The entire Ghetto, with its chimneys smoking and smoking, was like a train rushing down an empty track, toward nowhere, while all the time the fireman chops up his boxcars for fuel.

There were quite a few fires. The Jews began to fear a conflagration, like the one in Crakow in 1850. But while houses sometimes burned, no one was killed or even injured until the Koscielny Place blaze. This occurred at Number 80, a large house, four stories, with many families living inside. In a single room at the front of the second story resided Professor Potash, his wife, and his wife's unmarried brother and sister. On February 16, which turned out to be the coldest day of that winter, Madame Potash picked up armfuls of her husband's books—the bookcase itself having long since been burned, along with the bedstead and the chest of drawers—and threw them into the stove. When the professor returned from his job at the Statistical Office and learned what had happened to his Schiller, to his Grillparzer first edition, he lost control of his senses. Off came his jacket and his shirt and his gold wedding band; with bare hands he groped in the hot iron stove. Then he began to throw the charred, red-rimmed pages over his shoulder onto the floor. Thus the tragic fire began. The rug caught first, then a mattress which lay on the rug, and then with a whoosh one of the curtains. Madame Dickstein, the sister-in-law, made the mistake of pushing open the window: freezing air rushed through like a bellows. Before you knew it the room was in flames.

The alarm went out to Smugowa Street, which was the headquarters of the Jewish Fire Brigade. The company owned two pieces of equipment: a bright red pumper, the duplicate of the one shown at the Grodno Exposition, 1922, and a ladder truck, which was steered in the back as well as the front. The members of the brigade were friends and relations of Rievesaltes, all of whom—Faybush, Bloygrund, Pfeffer, and the rest—received extra rations because of their dangerous work.

By the time the first vehicle arrived—it was the pumper, with Faybush at the wheel—the sun, already low on the horizon, suddenly dropped like a man into a manhole, and the only light on Koscielny Place came from the shooting flames. Awful vision! Jews, the tenants of Number 80, stood in the street, their faces black and scorched. More Jews were bunched on the neighboring rooftops, wringing out towels on top of sparks. From the second floor, where the fire was all about them, Madame Dickstein and Madame Potash were calling for help. One story higher, a family, the Bloomgardens, a mother and father, the four little children, were squeezed into the windowframe.

"Sisters! Sisters!" Dickstein, the brother, had just returned from his job in the millworks and was howling. "We shall be homeless!"

The pumper pulled up to the front of the burning building. Faybush jumped out, and with Bloygrund, a Rievesaltes first cousin, unwound the metal-tipped hose. Meanwhile, more firemen dropped off the back of the machine and, in their black and yellow slickers, ran without fear into Number 80's front door. A cheer went up from the freezing crowd. "What a good thing we live in the Ghetto," said one among them. And others nodded, saying, "Now we have our own policemen. And fire fighters who are Jews!"

The next moment the same rescuers bolted from the doorway and began to vomit their double ration of stew. But they had the two sisters with them, the one, Madame Potash, without any eyebrows; smoke was coming from the bun of Madame Dickstein's hair. Their brother ran to them, his tears frozen on his cheeks and nose. "But where is Potash?" he said.

As if in answer there was a tremendous crash, and ten thousand sparks flew into the air. The roof had caved in. The fourth floor was demolished. And now the flames were right over the Bloomgardens' heads!

None too soon the hook and ladder came roaring out of the darkness, into the flickering light. At the wheel was Pfeffer and steering the rear, the way a dinosaur's second brain steers its tail, was a Jew named Wax. Pfeffer turned his wheel left, onto Koscielny, but Wax, confused by the spectacle of the smoke and the flames, turned his to the right. The gigantic machine skidded in a huge semicircle, clearing the spectators off the sidewalk and running over the pumper's limp hose.

The crew went into action. Two men unhooked a ladder and, since it had little wheels on one end, rolled it to the front wall of the building. The others ran with a net to just below the third-floor window. They spread it out, like spreading a fan, until it made a circle. Nor had the pumper been idle. Bloygrund, by pulling and tugging, managed to free the flattened hose. Immediately Faybush spun the hydraulic valve to send the water streaming through. But nothing came out of the end of the tube. Not a drop. Worse, it turned out that the ladder reached only halfway between the first and second stories, well below the spot where it was feared that Potash, the professor, was trapped. Most awful, the Bloomgardens seemed to have gone into shock. They stared straight down, at the round net, at the firemen arranged around it, and then they pulled back their heads. Bloygrund kicked the side of the pumper. "Frozen!" he shouted. "A block of ice!"

It was at this point, with little hope left for those inside the blazing house, that Isaiah Trumpelman arrived at Koscielny Place. Hasensprung, the new chauffeur, drove the black car—it was the old Daimler Double Six, with a new yellow star on the door—directly down the center of the street. Then Trumpelman got out and Lipiczany hopped off the jump seat. It was amazing, the effect the Elder had on everyone there. A cry went up. Tenants waved their towels from the roofs. And the members of the Smugowa Street Company, sick, demoralized, breathless, snapped to attention. "Greetings to Chairman Trumpelman!" they cried, and saluted.

The Elder stood erect, hatless in spite of the bitter cold.

The flames, Nisel noticed, lit his face and were reflected in his spectacle lenses, so that for an instant it seemed that the fire itself was not occurring outside, in the building, but inside Trumpelman's brain. Then, above them all, Number 80 visibly trembled, as if it meant to fall to its knees.

"Laddermen!" Trumpelman shouted. "Lash the second ladder onto the first! Raise it to the second-floor window. Faybush! Build a fire under the pumper to get it thawed." Then he walked to where the fire fighters were still holding the net. Everyone looked up to the third story, where the Bloomgardens cowered. "This is Trumpelman! This is the Elder! Come to the window! It's an order from the Judenrat! Trumpelman commands you to jump!"

It worked! First the six heads appeared. Then one after the other, the youngest first, then the older ones, the family sailed down. After Ignacy, who was eleven, the rescuers began to stagger, the center of the canvas started to sag. The father came next to last, with his palms together, like a diver. Finally Zinta Bloomgarden—there were already flames burning along her shoulders—made the leap. In spite of the shortages, she was a heavy woman; when she landed the net split in two pieces, it flew from the firemen's hands, then wrapped itself around her, snuffing out all the flames.

Everyone burst into applause, not only because of the rescue of the Bloomgarden family, but because Wax, the tillerman, was now coming down the extended ladder, with Professor Potash on his back. The man of letters was living. He had books pressed in his badly burned arms.

"A miracle! It's a miracle!" the Jews were exclaiming.

Even the President of the Judenrat seemed stunned. "Can it be true? All my people saved? Every one?"

Everyone was crying with joy. Indeed it did seem a miracle, a supernatural event, that in that awful inferno not a single life, not one Jew, had been lost.

"Wait!" cried Madame Bloomgarden. "I don't see any Einhorns! Has anybody seen an Einhorn around?"

No, nobody had. Once again rescued and rescuers had to lift their heads toward the top of the building, to the fourth floor, into which the roof had already caved. There, in the back, the missing family had had their apartment.

Two things happened next, first one, then the other. In the fourth-floor window—only it wasn't a window any longer, just a gap in the roofless wall—the head and shoulders of a child appeared, undoubtedly one of the overlooked Einhorns. Then, just as it was sinking in that there was no way to save him, I. C. Trumpelman walked into the flaming house.

Minute after minute went by. Nisel attempted to follow the Elder, but Pfeffer, with his powerful arms, pinned him down. Parts of the building began to break and fall. There were loud crashes and thumps. Sparks like so many human souls flew into the blackened sky. On the ground the Jews prayed for the Judenrat Chairman's return. For the young Einhorn, no longer visible at the window ledge, there was no hope at all.

After a half an hour there was a sound like a moan, like a person sighing, but it was the building itself, its timbers, or the cold wind rushing through them, that made the noise. Then the whole structure, all four floors of it, began to settle, to tip, to sway. The Elder walked out. Not singed. Not smudged. Timbers in flames tumbled around him, but not one came close. His camel's hair coat had been removed and bundled around the Einhorn named Hersh, whose brothers, alas, along with his parents and grandparents, had all been burned to a crisp.

Even before the Koscielny Place fire, I. C. Trumpelman had been a popular leader. This was because of the soup kitchens, the ration cards, and all the boys and girls he had put into school. "Now we are learning, because of our President, Trumpelman!" the students all sang, first thing in the morning. And it had been the Elder who had thought up the idea of using the spinning mills to make the uniforms for the Conqueror's army. The Ghetto was on its way to becoming one great factory. Everyone in the Balut would have a good job.

But none of these accomplishments counted as much as the rescue of Einhorn. Not that they weren't important, critical even. But the opinion of the Jews was that another man, an equally skillful politician, might have done the same. To walk through flames, however! To go through burning walls! No ordinary man could do it, no person of flesh and blood. In short, this was a True Judge, a man who was no man: the savior of his people. The Jews began to say, in so many words: *Nothing can happen to our Elder. Bullets bounce off him. So nothing will happen to us, either.*

A last word about the fire. The heat from the crumbling building at Number 80 eventually thawed the water pumper, which stopped the flames from spreading to the wooden houses on either side. Professor Potash was taken to the hospital, in quite serious condition. The other tenants of the ruined building spent the night at the Housing Department, where, the next morning, they were all assigned to new rooms. As for the burnt boy, Hersh Einhorn: Trumpelman stretched him out on the back seat of his Daimler, got in the front seat himself, and drove off to the Hatters' Asylum, which had just been resettled within the Balut. On the trip there the Einhorn orphan opened his eyes. He whispered to Lipiczany, who was perched on the jump seat, "Hey! Look!"

Then, while Nisel—not squinting, but staring, amazed—leaned forward, the boy's scorched fingers fumbled at his yellow star and ripped it away. There was a red star underneath. "Soviet Army," Einhorn said. "The glorious Soviet Army." Then he closed his eyes, and they sped quickly on, their headlights dimmed, through the Jewish part of the town.

What came to be called the New Hatters' Asylum was located on the top floor of Trumpelman's country home, which
he named Tsarskoye Selo, after the famous summer palace
of the Tsar. It really was a country home, too—except that
the Elder slept in it the year around. To one side of the
mansion there was a barn, and at the right time of year
geese, goats, and sheep came out of it and wandered over
the lawns. On the other side were the gardens, with vegetables in them, with garlic growing, and different kinds of flowers. The front of the estate was decorated in the familiar ba-
nana-leaf design. Real grapevines climbed the walls.

Behind the mansion, the ground sloped away into untend-
ed fields and low, swampy sections. No one knew why the
Conquerors had included so much undeveloped land in the
Ghetto. One opinion was that young people were going to be
given agricultural training, to ready them for a life in Palestine. Once, the man in the gray suit was heard to say to
Franz Xavier Wohltat, "What's this? A park? A zoo? We
should put elks in it. They have the right kinds of noses."
But it was not long before people started dying; then everyone realized that the open area, the marshland you couldn't
walk through without sinking, was meant to be a graveyard
for the Jews.

It so happened that Hersh Einhorn was practically the last
child to be allowed into the New Hatters' Asylum. There was
no room for the hundreds of others who tramped out from
the heart of the Suburb to the estate walls. "I have no mother! I have no father!" they cried. "Let me in!" The fat orphans who lived inside the Asylum were not supposed to
have anything to do with the thin ones who lived outside. It
was a rule often broken. Szypper, Myer Krystal, and some
others made it a habit to throw bags full of sugar over the
walls, or, from the sheep's backs, miniature bales of nicotine-

colored wool. From these things the homeless children made a sort of living. The wool was sewn into patches, the six-pointed stars; the sugar spun—sometimes with sand added to it—into flower-shaped, iris-shaped, treats.

Patches! Pretty patches! Cheap! Cheap!
Irises! Good ones! An hour in the mouth!

The sound of these voices, the very sight of the children, must have been like a persecution, like torture, to Trumpelman. From the top floor of the mansion you could see them playing on the far side of the wall. Half would lie in a hollow dug from the ground, while the other half stood over them, with screwed-up faces, with sticks in their hands; then everyone would switch places, the Jews would become the High and the Mighty, and the High and the Mighty would lie in the ditch like the Jews.

One morning when the Elder was walking inside the estate, a boy went berserk and somehow or other climbed onto the wall. His mouth was foaming. "I am a dog, a dog!" he shouted. "Now the Others will pet me!" Then he jumped down and ran at Trumpelman, as if he meant to bite him. The old man scooped him up under an arm and brought him to the top floor of the Asylum. There he set the wild child, his name was Leibel Shifter, down. "Little birds!" he said to the orphans. "This is your nest. Let the whole world go crazy! Here—Trumpelman swears it—you will survive the war!"

But that same day the Elder went to the cellar and began to open the wine. He poured it out and then, with his boot heel, stamped on the bottles. He smashed them to pieces. That night a moon came up, almost a full one, over Tsarskoye Selo; the top of the wall sparkled from the layers of broken glass.

It was a relief—not only for the Lithuanian, but for the
84

Hatters' orphans—when night came, when the stories began. In the dim room, the windows were covered with droplets of steam. It was warm, it was dreamy; the voice with the lisp rose and fell. The cigarette glowed. The rest of the world, with all its unlucky children, no longer existed. It was like being hypnotized.

What happened to Trumpelman—it was enough to enchant any child—was that after his shipwreck, he was captured by Indians. Not a tribe with feathers, with painted cheeks. Not Indians who whooped or shot arrows from bows. These were not even "redskins" because some disease had turned them mostly yellow. They looked more like Chinamen than anything else.

Night after night, week after week, the Elder told the story of how the natives seized him, how they forced him, a boy not yet twenty, to march countless miles, and then held him in a trench with roots to eat. He knew it was winter, because he was shivering beneath a hide. But he had no idea of time, whether it was day or night, or whether the thoughts that he had were his own or pieces of an endless dream.

"At last, on a morning, three young men—they had baggy cotton pants and blankets over their shoulders—came under my roof, stooped down, and released me. They raised me to my feet and at once I fell again. So, half fainting, I was carried out, to what fate I did not know, into the dawn." The light in the Asylum was rushing out like a tide. The sun sank through the thousand crooked chimneys of the Balut. Only the tip of the Elder's cigarette, like a pulse, continued to glow.

"I was brought by the three yellow men to a fourth, lying upon the ground, surrounded by all manner of seashells. His skin was dry, his eyes shut, and his breath, when it came, made clicking sounds. My children, this was a sick man, and it was made clear to me that I, without knowledge, with no schooling, and truly half-dead myself, was expected to cure

85

him. Of course I protested, but to no avail: something had convinced them that this Jew, with his boy's Adam's apple, with his earlocks, was a man possessed of healing powers.

"Thus I dropped to my knees, and while in prayer it came to me to blow my breath onto the patient. This I did, and then I touched him with my hand. Whereupon the sick man sat up and declared that his pain had been driven away. When the others realized that he was well again, they all began to touch their breasts, and then rub their hands on my chest, and then touch their breasts again. A feast of oysters, a spitted hare, were set before me. It was from that day that I began my career as a medicine man."

Lipiczany was sitting on the floor, with his elbows on his bent knees and his palms helping to prop up his heavy head. He felt that his heart had run out of room, that it was about to spill over. If anyone had thought to place young Nisel's chest under a radium cannon, he would have found that the boy's heart was in fact so swollen that his lungs were squeezed nearly off the picture. Now the boy saw that Julius Szypper and Nachman Kipnis—not in their nightshirts, but in their padded winter clothing—were standing. Not just standing, but moving slowly, slyly toward the door. He opened his mouth, he tried to say something, but it was Trumpelman's voice he heard.

"From that time forth many Indians came who were very ill, some paralyzed, and by prayer, and with my breath, and by touching them, I restored each to health. This caused great amazement. Nothing was talked about in this country but the wonderful cures, and all who heard of it came to me that I might heal them and bless their children.

"Then I was brought a man whom I could not treat in that way. He was from a different tribe and earlier had been shot deep with an arrow, the head of which had lodged close to his heart. He said it gave him much pain, and that on this account he was ill. I touched the region and felt the arrowhead there, and so with a sharp shell I cut open the breast and found the point next to the tissue of the heart; with great difficulty I removed it. The man said he felt no pain, and with a deer bone I made simple stitches and sewed the wound. From this cure I gained such fame among various tribes among the country that there was much competition to have me. But my own village would not let me go, saying they had such confidence in my skill that they believed none of them would die as long as I remained among them."

"Come on," somebody whispered behind Lipiczany's ear, and his own heart, like that of the wounded warrior, practically stopped. He whirled, squinting, peering into the dark. Einhorn was there, with his flat nose, his eyes like a Tatar's, his perfect teeth. "Come," he repeated, stepping toward the doorway and beckoning Nisel to follow. "Hurry. A mission is about to begin." In the hall, at the top of the stairs, two or three shadowy figures, Kipnis probably, and Julius Szypper, were already waiting. Something in Lipiczany—the carefree boy, the cracker of nutshells—stirred. He got to his feet and, while Trumpelman went on with his tale, edged toward the open door.

The old man was describing his greatest challenge, the time that the Indians brought him to a patient who—from his upturned eyes, from the many mourners about him— Chaim knew had already died. "It was a trick! My enemies did this! The medicine men who had lost their power. I saw them laughing behind their hands. But I prayed, I breathed upon the cold body, I touched it—again and again, through the whole of the night. At dawn the dead man—whether charmed or, in fact, briefly expired—rose from his pallet, walked about, and asked for something to eat, because he was well. Then all the Indians there, even those who did hate me, raised their hands and said together that I was a Child of the Sun."

Yes! thought Nisel. *Yes! I too was raised from the dead,* and

87

the next thing he knew someone had grabbed him by the arm and was pulling him, half resisting, from the room.

"*Shhh,*" Hersh Einhorn warned, and placed his hand, still scarred from the fire, over Lipiczany's mouth. At the top of the stairway they were joined by Szypper and Kipnis; all four boys went down together, on tiptoe. They came to the front door of Tsarskoye Selo.

"Where are we going? Are we going out?" Nisel asked his companions.

"It's life and death," Hersh Einhorn replied.

They unbolted the door and walked without speaking over the hardened ground. They stopped at the barn, where the gardener boy, the deaf-mute, was waiting in his usual posture: one hand resting on top of his head. The other held a lantern.

Nodding and grinning, digging at Nisel with his elbow, the way a man does who has told a joke, he swung open the large whitewashed door. The orphan quartet stepped inside and squatted, the lantern beside them, on the cold, frosty straw. Einhorn spoke crisply:

"What about the gate? Did you pass the money?"

Julius Szypper, who had grown up to be a triangular-faced fellow, with a flat cap on his head and a narrow, dimpled chin, replied. "No use. They're not Jewish police. They're Chaim's Elite Guards." He showed the others his handful of banknotes.

"All right," said Einhorn, putting the zloty roll into his own padded pants. "We shall have to go by them anyhow. There is no other way. Not too fast, Comrades. And not too slowly. Steadily forward. Instruct Muszkat not to stop for anything. Not anything!"

Nisel had broken into a real sweat. "What guards? Who is Muszkat? Do you mean the guards at the mansion gate?" Szypper and Kipnis looked at each other, and then at the surviving Einhorn, who was clearly the person in charge. The latter leaned forward and put his hands upon Nisel's shoulders.

"Lipiczany! What a moment for you! What a decision! It's either forward, in step with historical forces! Or else be left behind, in the ash heap of the capitalist system. It's a choice that's up to you. You have no time to lose."

"I'm mixed up, Hersh Einhorn. I don't understand what you say. How is it you have so much money? What did you say about the Jewish police? Why are you squeezing like that on my shoulders?" At that, the other boy's grip relaxed a little. He even smiled.

"It's like this, friend. The fascist beast wants to exploit the Ghetto's labor. We've been turned into wage slaves; only our wages are the scraps they give us to eat. They have worked it out scientifically, to the last calorie even. Those who can't work will cease to exist. That means old people, sick people, anyone too young to run a hundred spindles. We have reports that the breasts of Jewish mothers are unable to produce milk. Already newborn citizens have started to die."

"That can't be true!" exclaimed Nisel. "The Elder gives everyone enough to eat. There are soup kitchens. There are ration coupons."

"Salvation through work. That's his motto. He is no different from *them*." The speaker was Julius Szypper, with the handsome chin.

Nachman Kipnis next: "The Elder of the Jews has been co-opted by the same forces from whom he wished to save his people. It is a common historical event."

Einhorn ran a hand through his wavy hair. "Lipiczany! I have faith in you. I don't even know why. But I am going to take a tremendous risk. I am going to tell you something top secret. Listen! The reports we have are true. There is an underground clinic, don't ask where, don't ask how I know; in this clinic the children are simply starving. It's a waste of

89

good, useful, productive lives! So what do you think? We are going to bring them milk in the form of a cow!"

"Ha! Ha!" Szypper laughed. "The Trumpelman Holstein! It's a stupendous operation!"

"Oh, hooray!" shouted Nisel, for an instant carried away. Then he felt his heart expanding, as if someone were pumping it up like a tire. "No! Wait! It's not possible. You can't succeed. Why don't you just send out some milk? Throw a liter container over the wall? A whole cow? Do you mean a live one? One that's still living?"

"This way," said Szypper, and led them all to the back of the barn. There a black and white cow was standing, chewing on something. "See that?" he continued. "We've already muffled her hooves." It was true. The beast was wearing, on all four feet, what appeared to be pairs of thick woolen socks. Nisel stared at her flanks, where the patches and markings looked like a map of the Mediterranean area, black for land, white for the sea.

"How is it to be done?" he found himself asking. "The gate is locked. It's guarded."

"Not tonight, Comrade. Tonight the funeral wagon has been delayed coming in and will be late coming out. Who knows why? A broken axle. A lame horse. Muszkat knows what to do."

"Muszkat," young Kipnis explained, "is the driver on top of the wagon."

"Inside! Don't you see? Inside the hearse! What a plan!" Szypper, in his enthusiasm, balled up his fist and struck the animal behind the ear. Her tail flew up, as if there were a mechanical connection between the two parts. To those present, this was hilarious, and before you knew it everyone was laughing and kicking the straw. Then the boys began leaping about the only cow that existed inside the Ghetto. Around they went, and around, in the opposite direction from the hands of a clock. And it may be said that Nisel Lipiczany, waving his arms like a monkey, danced about too.

Then the door at the end of the barn opened and the pin-headed gardener boy looked in, his finger against his lips. The smugglers then fell in a heap, gasping, holding their sides. Einhorn was the first one up. "Lipiczany, your task is to make sure the Elder does not suspect what is going on. He trusts you. If he asks any questions you have to answer. It's an indispensable job."

Nisel stood, squinting. "I am full of different emotions, Hersh Einhorn. The trouble is, the Elder saved your life and also my life, and he protects the lives of the orphans. How can we betray him by stealing his cow?"

Nachman Kipnis was busily changing into a suit of dress clothes. He put a forefinger into the air. "There is no room for sentiment in the struggle against reactionary forces. His cow! His cow! To each according to his needs! Are you with us?"

"Friends, friends—first I thought yes but now I think no. It's a crime. It's a capital offense. The Elder has ruled that all smuggling must cease."

"Comrade Lipiczany, it's too late. You, the same as us, have received your orders."

Lipiczany, his head off-balance, looked at the orphans. "Orders?" he said.

One after the other, first Einhorn, then Kipnis, Szypper last—the boys peeled back their yellow stars in order to show the red one below.

"Red partisans," Einhorn announced. "This is no game."

"But the Soviet Union is an ally of the Thousand-Year Reich! They have already occupied the eastern section of Poland."

"Ha!" laughed Szypper. "So you have also been fooled. Comrade Kipnis is able to explain everything."

Kipnis, a thin boy, who each year had to put thicker glass into his lenses, pointed once more to the top of the barn. He had a brown mole about the size of a five-grosz piece under his eye. "This is an error often made by the liberal press and bourgeois politicians, who do not understand the workings of dialectical materialism. All progress is the result of the clash of historical forces: the bigger the clash, the more gigantic the cataclysm, the greater the progress will be. Thus the Soviet Union waits silently and confidently; it bides its time, while the stooges of Western capitalism and the running dogs of fascism tear each other's throats. From this conflict of thesis and antithesis will emerge the synthesis of the dictatorship of the proletariat. Therefore, we see the present alliance of the Soviet Union is a correct strategical maneuver from the historical perspective. Our leader, the Man of Steel, has declared: *You have to deal with Satan to drive out the Devil!*"

Einhorn—he was the radical who had converted the others—began once again to squeeze Nisel's shoulders. "It's to make a better world, Comrade. A better world!"

At that moment the Holstein, as if she, too, wished to encourage the boy, took a padded step forward and scraped Nisel's cheek with her tongue. This animal had damp brown eyes that stared without blinking—like Kipnis', thought Nisel, blown up behind the spectacle glass. Then, as the cow took a second lick on the boy's salty cheek, Szypper threw a rope on her neck. All four boys pulled upon it, urging her, black and white herself, into the black and white night.

The smugglers came to a small hill and stopped to look around. The land lay like this: behind them the darkened, stubbly fields, the barn, the mansion with its lights already out; then the wall, with its gate, its guards, and beyond the rest of the Balut. Ahead and below were the ruts, the gullies, the impassable marshland. There, in a hollow, a group of people were energetically throwing up earth for a grave.

"Whose?" Kipnis inquired.

"Don't know," Einhorn replied.

Szypper: "Someone with connections."

"Zlotys you mean."

The Red partisans stared silently down at the distant

figures, some of whom were digging, some holding lit torches, a few just standing around.

It was the sort of funeral you hardly saw anymore. In the first days of the Baluty Suburb you could easily get a plot, a headstone, and a rabbi of your own. That was because people died more or less one by one. But only a little later, because of the hunger, because of the typhus, Jews seemed to expire at once, in bunches. It was already the custom to lay them out in the street, covered by pieces of paper, the paper weighted down by stones. After a while the Judenrat picked them up in handcarts and barrows, then threw them in unmarked and sometimes even common graves. There was only one real hearse in the Suburb, because there was only one team of horses. These belonged to Muszkat, the former liveryman, and it was he who had the monopoly of funerals in our town.

Comrade Kipnis, in his dress suit, went down the hill by himself. The suit was blue, and in a moment got lost in the gloom. His companions waited until they saw him show up again among the small knot of mourners; that was his job, to mix with the crowd. Then they, with their milk cow, started down too.

These three did not head for the grave but for the funeral wagon, which stood off to one side. There Muszkat was waiting. He had what were known as "boiled ears," like a prizefighter's, and his hair grew like a cap well down his brow. Stealthily, silently, the cow and the smugglers went around to the back of the wagon, where a ramp led to the ground. There she stopped, and would go no farther. Einhorn and Szypper pushed at the back half, Lipiczany tugged at the front. No movement.

"Let me," said Muszkat. "*Meow!* I know animals. *Meow! Meow!*"

At this the Holstein turned one hundred eighty degrees and stared, with her wet eyes, at the torches and the dark mound of earth; at the widow in black; and, under a blanket of flowers, at Fiebig, the financier, who was the dead man himself.

The rabbi held up his hand and cleared a frog from his throat. This was Kornischoner, of the Fur Trimmers' Synagogue, whose presence at the funeral of such an important and wealthy man was a surprise. Just this matter was taken up first.

"Nomberg," he said, "couldn't come."

There was a pause. The old man looked around. Hair was growing all over his face. You couldn't see a mouth in it except when he talked.

"Neither could Rabbi Lunt."

The Widow Fiebig, supported by three sullen sons, took out a red handkerchief, which she waved in front of her eyes. Kornischoner continued.

"I barely got here myself. A big order came in. For powder puffs. For shops in Berlin. They put in a quota. Four hundred puffs a person. Then you get your dinner. Kohlrabi in soup. Broad noodles. One ersatz egg. I started before it was light out. I stopped when the sun went down. Guess how many puffs I made. Eighty-three. And twelve got rejected. That makes seventy-one!" Here tears came out of his very small eyes, and were soaked up at once by his beard. "No soup. No egg. Nothing to eat! What will I do? Who can answer this question? Those little threads! Impossible to work with! I can't make four hundred puffs!"

Everyone, the torchbearers, the relations, stood perfectly still. Only the widow's handkerchief continued to dab at her eyes. Kornischoner slightly swayed. "Where was I? What was it I wanted to say? The hunger affects my mind! Once I saw a note for a hundred zlotys. That was in the town of Lvov. There! On the ground! I do not put my foot on it. I do not put it in my pocket. I tell my son, Lipa: *This might be the savings of some poor person.* That is the kind of man you see before you! A man who sets an example!

"Let's talk about Lunt. Let's talk about Nomberg. They

wear sport coats. That's because the Judenrat says, no more gabardines. Next thing the Elder will make us shave off our beards! Otherwise, you don't get kohlrabi! Kohlrabi! It's the stems you eat. The stems! Friends, remember this about Kornischoner. He would not wear a short coat. He would not trim his beard. Never mind if I'm crying. I'm weeping! Never mind. But when you speak of him, say that his coat came down to his shoes!"

Somebody said, "What about Fiebig?"

Kornischoner, with his sleeve, wiped the tears from his eyes. "Fiebig? The financier? Willy Fiebig?"

"Yes, yes. We want to hear about him."

"What is there to say?" asked the rabbi. "Fiebig was a rich man who went crazy."

No sooner had this eulogy ended than Fiebig's former wife opened her eyes quite wide. Then she uttered three little cries and pointed to where, with its head lowered and its horns pointed frontward, a tremendous black and white bull was charging straight for them all.

Of course this was the Tsarskoye Selo Holstein. Whether, like a bull, it had become enraged by the widow's red handkerchief; or whether like any cow it had been attracted by the smell of her ex-husband's flowers, there is no way of saying. For before it could reach either goal it fell headlong into the freshly dug grave.

"*Moooo!*" went the beast, in an international tongue.

Madame Fiebig swooned into the arms of Adolf, one of her sons. With the crack of a whip, the funeral wagon, still dragging its ramp, bounced over the frozen ruts, in the direction of the dim mansion. Hersh Einhorn ran at it from an angle, so as to cut it off.

"Stop! Muszkat!" he shouted.

The liveryman lashed his horses, a brown and a white one. "This was not our agreement!" he yelled. But before the wagon rolled by him, Einhorn had thrust his hand into his pocket and was waving a wad of bills in the air. The hearse quickly stopped. Clouds came out of each horse's nose. "What's that in your hand, young Einhorn? Zlotys?"

"Four hundred. Two hundred now. Two hundred when we get through the gate."

Muszkat leaned from the box of the wagon; a ribbon's worth of skin showed between his eyebrows and his hair. "Three hundred now. Later two."

The Red partisan considered a moment. "Agreed!"

Meanwhile, on the lip of the grave, Lipiczany was clutching his head of hair. "What are we going to do? We have to do something!"

Julius Szypper and Nachman Kipnis were pulling on the rope that still encircled the animal's head. The cow's tongue came out. "*Moooo!*" it repeated.

"In my opinion, this is not a difficult problem. It's a matter of physics. Of pulleys and levers." The speaker was Professor Zygmunt, a former scholar. "Over the load we erect a block and tackle. Underneath we establish a fulcrum. And then, all together! Alley oop!"

Bettsack, the Hatters' schoolmaster, ventured to make a suggestion. "Why not fill the grave with water? Then we could buoy the cow with corks."

A man wearing earmuffs looked at the cow shivering in the bottom of the tomb. "We don't have any corks," he said.

Kornischoner, the rabbi, spoke up. "Maybe we could cut her into pieces. Not so it hurt. Humanely. Then not only could we lift her out, but everybody would have something to eat."

Muszkat on his own hitched both horses to the Holstein. Then he backed up ten meters and called to his team. "Come! You darlings!" The mare surged in the direction of Tsarkoye Selo, but the white stallion veered toward the marsh. This created a situation in which the cow was about to be strangled. Muszkat cut one rope, the other snapped by itself. The two steeds disappeared.

The sons of the dead man were still trying to revive their

mother from her swoon. They kept patting her cheek and her hand. "What a fortune this funeral is costing," one of them said.

Kornischoner began to talk to himself like a madman. "Why don't we bury the cow?" he mumbled. "And cook Fiebig instead."

Professor Zygmunt, the university man, resumed his theme. "Let us return to the science of physics. We don't have a block and tackle. We don't have corks. But we possess picks, and many shovels. If we start to dig here, point X, and proceed gradually deeper, to there, point Y, the result will be an inclined plane. The animal can simply walk up from one spot to another."

"What a good idea!" the mourners declared, and at once set about digging into the hard-packed ground.

The plan worked to perfection. The Holstein, blue-lipped, her udder drawn upward, strolled up the ramp and into the back of the funeral wagon. Then Fiebig's friends lowered the corpse into its grave. They poured earth upon him, along with the petals of flowers.

The only way to get the hearse up the slope and out the gate of Tsarskoye Selo was for the Red partisans to push it by hand. More easily said than done. The boys were wet, cold, and weary; the hill slippery and steep. At one point they stopped, stuck. Muszkat cracked his whip, exactly as if there had been horses; Kipnis uttered the cry, "Forward, Comrades! Let us accomplish the task!" Painfully, the wagon moved upward again.

Nisel Lipiczany, his teeth chattering, sat high on the box, with a blanket over his shoulders. From his perch the boy was the first to see over the rise: there was the barn, the mansion, and the glass-covered wall.

At the gate stood two armed members of the Elder's Elite Guard. What a surprise to see that they had the brown mare between them, and were even feeding it sugar that had been pressed into lumps. These two men, the exporter Szpilfogel and Bass, a former tanner, came to attention and gave Muszkat a familiar wave. A good sign, surely. The boys pushed the wagon forward and Szpilfogel, a pure mesomorphic type, backed the runaway horse into her harness. Then Bass slid the large bolt from the gate and beckoned the funeral party through.

Suddenly there was a kind of muffled explosion and the whole hearse shook on its springs. The two guards looked at each other. "What's that?" Szpilfogel asked.

"Ha! Ha!" went Szypper, pretending to wipe his nose. "I must have caught a cold."

Then, from inside the wagon, the same loud report echoed again. Clearly, a sneeze.

Szpilfogel raised his hand, palm outward, which is what policemen do all over the world to indicate *stop*! "Open the back of the hearse," he ordered the driver.

Hersh Einhorn cried out. "Impossible! We have to go!"

"Muszkat!" cried Kipnis. "Shake the reins!"

But the liveryman sat there. What little there was to his brow fiercely contracted. With his knuckles he rubbed his boiled ear. Bass, the Guardsman, was pointing at him with the barrel of a gun.

Just then they all heard a voice with the accent of a Lithuanian Jew. "What's going on here? Who is making the disturbance?"

It was, of course, the Elder. No one had seen him arrive, perhaps because his new cloak, which was black, blended into the night.

Bass threw up an arm and saluted. "Chairman Trumpelman! It's smugglers! We caught them ourselves!"

"That is a lie! We have just come from a funeral! The funeral of Fiebig, the financier."

"This is a provocateur!" Kipnis shouted, pointing at Bass. "He wants to turn Jew against Jew!"

98

At last Muszkat, after his long silence, burst out. "My stallion! I lost him! Now what do I do?"

Isaiah Trumpelman sliced through the air with his hand. "Quiet!" he commanded. At once they all fell still.

"Don't think the Elder doesn't know what's going on in his Ghetto. He knows what goods are coming in. Your carrots, your beets, your butter. And fancy liqueurs! Cigars! Expensive meats! It comes over the wall, through the fences, up from holes in the ground. The pity is that innocent children are being corrupted in this dirty business. Turned into crooks! And why? To save the Ghetto? To keep people from starving? Don't make me laugh! Everybody in my Ghetto has enough to eat! Only they have to work! To work! The Elder won't allow Jewish loafers in the Balut! Someday an important official from Berlin—the Hunter, the Schoolmaster, maybe even the Big Man himself—will come to inspect our streets. He doesn't want to see merchants and middlemen: he knows that kind of Jew already. But when he sees workers! Real workers! Then he will be amazed. And in his amazement he will say, *Live! Live!*"

Trumpelman paused. His hat was on, and his white hair came from underneath in wisps, in billows. The orphans and guards stared at him, not saying a word.

"I'm smart! I know the smuggling is Rievesaltes' work. He takes fifteen percent of every load of potatoes, fifteen percent butterfat, fifteen percent coffee, sugar, and the rest! What a racket! But the Elder will root it out! He has a thousand eyes and a thousand hands. He will be standing at each gap in the wire, at each hidden hole in the earth. Nothing can escape him!"

"But we're innocent!" cried Szypper, trembling against his will.

Then the orphans were dumbstruck to see real tears in the Elder's eyes. "My dear ones," he said. "I am praying to God that is true. My own sons! My own life! You know how I love

99

you! But if you are guilty, even though you're my own children, you'll be punished like anyone else. To set an example! Lipiczany! You tell me! Tell Chaim! Is this a smuggling job or not?"

Everyone looked up at Nisel, who held quite still. Muszkat loomed over him, like an organ grinder over a monkey, and nudged him with his elbow. But the boy sat mute, screwing his eyes up, though there was no light. Then Julius Szypper, who was standing closest, reached up and patted Nisel's knee. He said softly, "Tell him, Comrade. It is your duty."

To see the face of the poor boy then! There was a deep crease in his brow, lengthwise, where he was being split in two. His head shook, as if he meant to say, *no, no smuggling here*. Then the tremor stopped. He blurted aloud, "But it's milk for babies!"

Immediately, as if to confirm this, the Holstein bellowed, "*Moooo!*"

The next thing that happened was that Kipnis jumped into the air and, though a small person himself, knocked Nisel Lipiczany head over heels off the wagon. "Fifth Columnist!" he cried.

At the same instant a shot rang out—impossible to tell whether the gun had been purposely fired or whether Nisel, in falling, had struck Bass' arm—and the bullet went past Szpilfogel's shoulder and spun harmlessly into the air. The terrified mare reared, then bolted toward the opening in the wall. The two Guardsmen jumped out of the way, and the wagon rolled safely through to the center of the Balut.

Trumpelman, meanwhile, had got hold of Einhorn by one arm and Kipnis by the other. Guardsman Bass tackled Szypper around the knees.

"My ears are ringing!" Szpilfogel said. "I could have been shot."

Bass lined the three guilty orphans against the wall. Each of them, defiantly, spat on the ground. Then Isaiah Trum-

100

pelman, with his huge hands, iron hands, struck them on the face.

"Einhorn! You! Einhorn! I wrapped you in my coat! I kept you alive like an ember! My darlings! My sons!" The terrific slaps went on and on. They made each boy's head slam back against the stone and left, on the skin, the whole hand's impression. Some distance off Lipiczany put his own hand to his own cheek, which was burning, as if on fire.

Chapter Four

The Wedding

I

If there were any doubts in the Balut about how smart the Elder was, what a wonderful politician, they all disappeared when he thought of a way to solve the smuggling problem. Only ten days after Fiebig's funeral, Trumpelman called a special meeting of the Jewish Council. There he announced his masterstroke. Why shouldn't the Ghetto, like any other state, have its own paper money? Polish zlotys, reichsmarks, American dollars could be turned in for a new Baluty pound at a fixed rate of exchange. The pound itself would become the only legal tender within the Suburb. If the citizens of the Balut wanted a roof over their heads, to give a single example, they would have to pay the rent to the Minister of Housing in the new currency alone. The cash would be distributed at a special purchasing office, in exchange for the jewels, the crystal, and the porcelain of the Jews. Blocked zloty accounts in the Aryan section would be converted. Holding gold and silver was henceforth against the law. It was astonishing how everything had been thought out.

"But what about the Others?" asked Popower, the former waiter. "Won't they object?"

There was a ready answer to this. "The Occupying Power

has already been contacted and has agreed to accept a fixed proportion of all goods exchanged. In addition, the foreign paper will go directly to them. The problem is not convincing the Others; it's convincing the Jews."

Rievesaltes, the Minister of Security, jumped to his feet. "It's the same as robbery! We cannot approve an act of theft!" It was no secret that Rievesaltes, as head of the Jewish police force, was the one who profited from the smuggling most. It was this irony, perhaps, that made Trumpelman smile.

"Too late," he said. "We can't call it off."

And he spread on the table, beneath the Ministers' eyes, banknotes in six different colors. The Elder's portrait was on each denomination, superimposed upon a Star of David. Cotton bobbins, symbol of the Ghetto's survival, were in the corners of the bills. At the bottom, in a bold hand, with an old-fashioned flourish, was the signature: *I. C. Trumpelman.*

The plan worked perfectly. First civil servants, then ordinary Jews lined up to get the new money. But these "Trumpkies," which is what everyone called the pretty bills, so valuable inside the Ghetto, were worth nothing anywhere else. The Poles only laughed when the children offered them the script in exchange for butter or potatoes. Immediately the smuggling dropped to half its former volume, and fell again to half of that. The Jewish police were losing tens of thousands of zlotys each week. They were becoming desperate men. And at just that crucial moment the Judenrat offered a bounty on all smugglers caught in the act. The result was, instead of assisting the children, the policemen were now putting them under arrest. It was as if the Ghetto had been hermetically sealed.

That spring the streets of the Baluty Suburb were full of the so-called wild children, who had nothing to smuggle, nothing to do. One of these was Nisel Lipiczany, who had exiled himself from the Asylum and sworn not to return. For the first time in his life the boy was thinking about his real father and mother: who they might have been, why they had left him, whether or not they were alive. Do not be surprised that he decided upon a mother who was blond. In those days everyone had become an expert on genetical law. Two tall sweet peas yield three tall and one short. A smooth-coated badger and a rough-coated badger produce a litter rough to smooth in a ratio of four to one. And it had been demonstrated time and again that Aryan couples, light-haired, gray-eyed, firm-chinned, could give birth to a dark, recessive Jew. Thus it was that, in the gloom of the night, sleeping within a doorway, Nisel dreamed of a woman who was faceless and bodiless, but who had, piled on her head, a mass of gold-colored hair. It was twisted in braids, like a *challah.*

His father's hair was black, brilliantined, shining like a count's. Not just a count's, a king—which meant of course that Nisel himself was really a prince, cast adrift the way Moses had been. Instantly the boy felt for Isaiah Trumpelman the deepest scorn. The old man was a stand-in, a substitute, a comical Jew. How surprised he would be when the truth was revealed, and the little orphan took his rightful place on the throne. Then the cold sky began to grow lighter, like color coming into a patient's cheeks; Nisel lifted his head from his knees. He heard a sound like the crack of a whip, and another sound too: gongs, or bells. *It's Muszkat!* he thought, half-asleep. *The funeral hearse!*

The boy got to his feet and trotted toward Brzeszinska, a prominent street in the Ghetto. From that direction he could hear the whip crack again and a voice cry out, "Faster!" That must have been Muszkat, calling to his mare. He heard the mourners, like in the Orient, ringing their gongs and bells. Then, from around Marysinska Corner, came the wagon itself. But this was not the black box of the funeral hearse. For an instant Lipiczany thought it was the Smugowa Street pumper, since it had the same low cylindrical tank, as well as a row of pails, like fire buckets, strung on either side. It was

104

these, striking against the side of the tank, that made the sound like bells.

The four Bloomgarden children, the ones who had jumped from the burning building, had more of these pails in their hands. They ran back and forth between the wagon and the front of each house they passed. There, at every doorstep, was a bucket of urine and feces, and it was this that the children had to transfer to their own pails and then pour into the big metal tank. It was work—there were no sewers in the Baluty Suburb—that had to be done. For doing it, you got a double ration.

"Faster! Hurry up!" Bloomgarden, the father, cracked his whip again. Nisel saw with horror that Einhorn, Kipnis, and Szypper were the horses; they had a kind of yoke over their shoulders, and a leather harness passed over their brows. The fecalists drew closer and closer. But Lipiczany, in the center of Brzeszinska, held his ground.

"Comrade Einhorn! Comrade Kipnis!" he began. Then he fell silent. He saw that around each orphan's neck there hung a square pasteboard sign. SMUGGLER! it said. Trumpelman had made them an example.

Nisel, directly in the path of the wagon, shut his eyes. The whip cracked. The pails clanked and clanged. The wheels ground around. Then the whole stinking contraption swept by him, without touching a hair.

For a moment the orphan remained alone between the four corners, squinting, swallowing air. Then more Jews came out—not to their work, however, but slowly, keeping together, to some other destination. Nisel followed the crowd.

Assisi Street Number 2 was a large two-story building, which used to belong to the furrier, Szapiro. That gentleman had used it as a storehouse and a factory for furs. The skins came into the big open hall on the ground floor; there they were sorted and sent for stitching to the smaller rooms above. As for the retail business of Szapiro & Son, that had been conducted solely in the Alexsandrowska Boulevard shop, the one with the plate-glass windows and the famous crystal chandelier.

By the time Lipiczany arrived at this address, hundreds of Jews were already standing on the opposite side of the street. Directly in front of the warehouse, wearing their green uniforms, stood the Men of Valor. Twenty or thirty in all. A pink ribbon had been stretched across the fur factory door, and Wohltat stood on a step beside it, shining the knobs of his shoes on his trousers. Nisel glanced up. The wall of the building had been freshly whitewashed; there were shutters by every window. And in each of those windows, along the whole second story, was the shadowy face of a Jewish girl. Wohltat, in his derby, began to speak.

"My dear Jews! The time has come to open the House of Pleasure. As the head of the Civilian Authority, it is my privilege to cut the ribbon in two."

One of the soldiers handed the Volksdeutscher a pair of shears. But before Wohltat could use them, a horn sounded and the fifty-horsepower Daimler raced pell-mell down Assisi Street at tremendous speed. Everybody—Jews on one side, the Brave Ones on the other—leaped out of the way. But two lads remained in the street, not flinching even when the jet-black fender came to a stop not more than half of a meter away. It was the team of Krystal and Lifshits, with their camera and flash clearly displayed.

The back door of the Double Six opened and the President of the Judenrat stepped into the lightning strokes of the photoflash. There was thunder also: *Trumpelman! Trumpelman!* The word echoed and rolled. Then the coffee merchant called out from the warehouse.

"Come! My friend! Take half of the scissors. As co-workers we shall cut the ribbon together!"

In Yiddish they say, the same as you do in English, "to die from shame." That was how Nisel felt then, though he had

106

no real idea of what a House of Pleasure might be. Somehow it was connected with the Warriors in their helmets, with the lavender-colored ribbon, and most of all with the six windows, with the actual window glass, against which were pressed, so that their features were flattened, the faces of the Ghetto girls. It was that, the spreading mouths and splayed noses, the distortion of people, that made the boy's own face feel hot and burning, as if the Elder—*my friend, co-worker*—had slapped it again.

In giant strides, his cape alternately swelling behind him and sucking the back of his legs, Trumpelman crossed the roadway. When he reached the steps of Number 2 Assisi he climbed them, then swung around.

"A Jew speaks to Jews! Citizens of the Balut! The Judenrat has not issued a permit for the operation of this building. We have not given approval. Therefore, no one may pass!" With those words, the Elder threw both arms high against the doorjambs. The top of his hat brushed the lintel. Then the flash lamps went off again. Everyone in the crowd was excitedly talking. Lipiczany had heard and seen what had happened, but it took him an extra moment—gulping and gulping, like a fish—to realize that the Judenrat Chairman was actually blocking the door.

"A permit is an unnecessary formality. The arrangements have already been made." Wohltat was speaking loudly, so that the whole crowd could hear. "Let me be frank. These are not normal times. Our men are fighting a war. Think of the things they have seen, the things they have had to do. This house will allow them to forget, to relax. Here there is a bar, music, games of chance. Upstairs—yes, upstairs. That is the problem. But these are young men, far from home, from their sweethearts and wives. You must see it is better this way for the Hebraic population. A more humanitarian solution. Now your daughters, your Rachels and Sarahs, will be protected from random attacks. Come, join with me. Cut the ribbon in two!"

Eagerly the Warriors pressed closer about the doorway. But Trumpelman did not cut the pink cloth: he merely strode through it, into the depths of the former warehouse. A moment later a large gaming table flew out the open door and landed with a crash in the midst of the uniformed men. Before anyone could react, a wheel for roulette came after and shattered to pieces. Then Trumpelman appeared in the doorway, with a gleaming slot machine in his arms. With what must have been superhuman effort, he raised it over his head and stood there—like a prophet, thought Nisel, a righteous man—bathed in the exploding flash lamps. Then, while the Warriors broke ranks, while they fled in every direction, he dashed it to the ground. Coins burst from it like shrapnel; springs shot out and gears whirled around.

Once more the Elder turned on his heel and plunged into the dark building. This time nothing came from the doorway, but Nisel noticed that one by one the heads of the girls were vanishing from the upper windows. A moment later the whole crowd saw the same six maidens walk onto the steps of Assisi 2. There was rouge on their cheeks and their eyelids were painted. Their hair had been curled with an iron. Then Trumpelman appeared behind them. "My people!" he shouted. "Your daughters are safe! The Judenrat has put a stop to this immoral business!"

The Jews let out a terrific cheer, then cheered even more loudly when the Elder spread his arms and encircled the girls, in their pretty new dresses, within his cloak. They hugged him; they kissed him. Once more the President of the Jewish Council addressed the Jews.

"My people! Return with your daughters to your homes. Remember what you have seen this day. The day we stood up to the Others! Don't tremble! Don't fear! The House of Pleasure will never open again. In its place your Judenrat will build a House of Culture, a Temple of Art. Here you shall see great dramas and listen to symphonies. Poets will speak! We shall show wonderful paintings! This place of shame will become a home for the spirit!"

He opened the cloak. The girls ran toward the street, toward their homes, while Trumpelman backed in the other direction, into what had been the factory for furs.

Lipiczany stood alone before the black, blank doorway of Assisi Street 2. Then he stepped inside. Overturned tables. Upended chairs. A smell from hides. Stray light was reflected from bits of glass and fragments of mirror. Overhead the crystal rods of the Szapiro & Son chandelier struck each other, tinkling constantly. Directly beneath it, in a plain wooden chair, with his white hair shining and his glasses turning themselves on and off, sat the leader of our Jews.

Nisel walked toward him. Trumpelman did not stir. His hat, like a beggar's hat, was upside down on the floor. The pink ribbon lay loose on his chest like a sash. "I would have been a wonderful actor! Ha! Ha! I could perform in the Temple of Art!" He did not look at the boy, who drew near him. "Wait! Tomorrow the whole Ghetto will be covered with pictures! Trumpelman will be a hero!"

The orphan squatted by the chair. He reached for the old man's hand. "I haven't a sweet," said the native of Vilna. "I used to carry them in my pockets."

Nisel did not reply. He sat there, squeezing the Elder's fingers. The chandelier tinkled above them, and, like a reflector in a ballroom, filled every corner with mothlike light.

After a moment or two, from high up, far off, a person sang a snatch from a song.

Bai nakht verft der alter fisher, hoopla. . .

Instantly the Elder was on his feet and moving up the flight of stairs. As fast as he could, Nisel followed. He saw

109

Trumpelman standing at the end of the hallway, with his ear by a shut door. Just as the boy reached him, the Elder threw his shoulder against the wooden panel. The two Jews—when you think of it, there was more than a half century between them—went inside.

There was hardly anything in that windowless room. A bed, with two tulip-shaped lamps screwed to the wall above the headboard. A single table. Only two chairs. Under the bedcovers, with black hair, a white neck, and smooth, broad shoulders, was a naked woman. One of *them*—it was the thin-faced, lipless man—was sitting nearby.

"Miss Lubliver!" Trumpelman exclaimed.

Instinctively the woman sat up and turned away. You could see all the way down her spine, to where two little dents broke the skin, like on a statue of Venus.

With one motion the Elder removed his cape, spun it in the air, and brought it down over the singer's shoulders. The old man was red-faced. His bucked teeth showed. He stammered.

"I don't know what to say. There has been an error. An awful mistake. How thin you are, Miss Lubliver! Your face. Your little bones. I can't help trembling. What if I had not been here to save you? What then?"

"Save her? But she is here of her own free will."

It was the man in the gray suit, speaking in Polish. Only he was not wearing that clothing now. He was dressed in a uniform—silver, with black piping and black trim. There was a death's-head on the cap. By then the Ghettoites had learned who this was: Grundtripp, the boss of the Totenkopfers, not just for the city, but for hundreds of kilometers around. An Obergruppenführer.

His voice brought Trumpelman to his senses. "Do you know who this is? How can you think she would come to the House of Pleasure? Miss Lubliver is a valuable artist in the Jewish community and is under the Judenrat's protection."

110

"I repeat that she came because she wanted to come and may go when she wishes to go. No one has said he would shoot her brains out."

Perhaps it is true that the life one leads shows up in one's appearance. For Grundtripp, after just six months among us, looked somehow different, altered, as if he had sat for one of Klapholtz's futurist paintings. One eye, for instance, was slightly but definitely higher than the other, and the left nostril seemed larger than the right. Now, when he leaned toward the singer, only half his mouth smiled. It was as if he, too, like the Jewish maidens, were pressed to a pane of glass. "Will you stay with me? Here with me? Or will you go?"

The woman was clutching the top of the cape to her chin. She stared at the Obergruppenführer. She turned to Trumpelman. "Is it you? The Elder? How can you remember me? What can you want with me? A great man with a worthless Jew?"

"No, no, no! It is I who am the worthless one! I throw myself before you! You could walk on me with your feet, the way a queen walks on a cloak!" Trumpelman gripped her arms. He helped her rise from the bed. Without resisting, willingly, she walked with him toward the door. But when they reached it, she stopped. Then she jerked her head.

"Listen!" she said.

There was a noise in the hallway outside. It was like a clock's pendulum, making a tick, a tick, but missing on each beat the tock. The Jewish Elder gripped his eyeglass frame. "I know that sound," he murmured.

The door opened and—with the sole of his special shoe striking the floor—Fried Rievesaltes walked into the room.

Instantly Miss Lubliver wrenched herself from the grip of the older man. Her face was pale and, as Trumpelman said, bony. Her head twitched sharply again.

The round face of Rievesaltes was glowing in the light from the twin tulip lamps. Between his nose and his lip he had started a mustache, just a thin one, as if a child had penciled it in. "This is a private room," he said to the Elder. Then, to Lipiczany, who stood pressed to the wall: "This is no place for a child."

Enraged, Trumpelman advanced on the Chief of Police. "Now I understand! You arranged this! You brought her here! As a favor for the High and Mighty!"

"Who then," answered Rievesaltes, "give favors to the Jews. For example, there is this lovely gown."

The garment in question was clutched against Rievesaltes' pearl-button vest. In color it was orange-red, with lace along the neckline and with swollen satin sleeves. Miss Lubliver's arm darted from the cape, which slipped aside. But she already held the soft silk dress before her. "Lace!" she exclaimed. "Silk! The only one in the Ghetto!"

Trumpelman still towered over the Security Minister. "It is forbidden for anyone except the President of the Judenrat to contact the Occupying Power. To do so is treason against the Balut. As the Elder of the Jews, Trumpelman informs you that you are relieved of your official duties. You are no longer head of the Jewish police."

"That is not possible, no, it cannot be," Grundtripp intervened. "Only last night I returned from Berlin. There I received two new orders, vital orders, for the Jews of the Suburb. Both will require tremendous efforts from everyone—but especially from the Jewish police. The leadership of that organization cannot be changed."

Rievesaltes, with a handkerchief, wiped his bulging temples. Trumpelman turned to the Obergruppenführer.

"What orders?" he asked.

"There is to be an increase in production. The millworks will have to make winter uniforms for the army. There must be woolen linings. Jackets are to be filled with feathers and down."

"Impossible," Trumpelman snorted. "Where will these linings come from? And where the feathers, the down?"

112

"We will supply the raw materials, you the labor force."

"But our workers are already exhausted. They will rebel! It can't be done. The Elder refuses to do it."

"This command," said the Obergruppenführer, "came from the highest circles."

There was a sudden silence. Trumpelman seemed to rise a bit on his toes. "When you say *Berlin,* when you say *highest circles,* do you mean, have you talked to—?"

Grundtripp nodded.

"Ah!" The Elder sighed.

Here Rievesaltes quietly put in a word. "May I ask, how many of these uniforms, of these wool linings, do you have in mind?"

"We demand ninety thousand complete outfits for each two-month period."

At this even the Police Chief objected. "But that is a doubling of production! One hundred percent! It would take a miracle to do it!"

"Quiet, Rievesaltes!" Trumpelman commanded. "You will round up the wild children. Bring them into the mills! The Elder will give our clock watchers a good kick, a good slap or two! We'll triple our output!"

Grundtripp stretched out his legs, with one shiny boot on top of another. "In Berlin everyone says the same thing. That our Jew is a magician, a Houdini. For every zloty brought into the Balut—for cotton, for cabbages, for materials of any kind—fifty zlotys come back again in the form of finished products. We expect the same miracle with the winter clothes."

"I shall call the Big Man on the telephone. As one head of state to another. I shall invite him to our Ghetto. He will see our spotless streets. He will see how everybody works, nobody complains! When he sees what my Jews can do, we can discuss the role Trumpelman will play after the war."

For an instant Grundtripp seemed honestly puzzled. "After the war? What do you mean, *after the war?* In springtime we prepare for the winter campaign, and in the winter you have to spin linen so we can fight in the spring."

"Look! Miss Lubliver!" It was Lipiczany who cried out that way. He was pointing at the singer, who still—so tightly—held her gown. In all this talk she had not said a word. Now, with the bangs lying girlishly on her forehead, and in a girl's voice, she was talking just to herself.

"This is the kind of dress I wore for my first solo performance. It came to my ankles. It had lace at the neck. That was not in my village, but in the city. A full orchestra. A mixed chorus. My sisters in the audience. My two sisters! *Israel in Egypt,* by the composer Handel. It was about Moses and Pharaoh and the terrible plagues. The locusts, the lice, the flies. The chorus sang first. Their voices boomed. Hailstones! The cattle dying! The withering wheat! Then the whole sky came down in a storm of dust. It was time. Time for me. My spotlight! Oh, my pretty dress! The piano alone. Then the double bass. Thirteen years old. *Thou didst blow with the wind. Thou didst blow! Thou didst blow, blow, bl-ow, bl-ow, bl-ow-ow-ow! Ow! Ow! Ow! Ow!"*

It was not a song. The woman stood stiffly, beating her fists against her thighs. Her head lashed. Trumpelman ran to her and gripped her arms.

"Miss Lubliver! Don't cry! I swore to protect you. Like a soldier! I will take you to my summer palace. My Queen. You can have whatever you wish."

Phelia Lubliver swayed against him. Like a child, she repeated, "Whatever I wish?"

"You will be the mother of my sons! Your wish in the Ghetto is law!"

Everyone turned to the woman to see if she would accept the proposal. Her head twitched just once. "No more singing! Print that on the posters! No music allowed!"

"A problem. One problem. I wanted to tell you before." Grundtripp had pulled his oversized cap onto his head. His uneven eyes were hidden beneath the visor. "Oh, there are no objections to this marriage. I congratulate you. I myself

114

will attend the wedding. The difficulty is in the second order I received in Berlin. Jewesses in the Suburb are forbidden to give birth to more babies. The reason for this is the same need to increase production in the mills. No more useless mouths to eat up our food. No interruption in the worktime of women. This order takes place at once. Those who are already pregnant will be allowed to receive abortions. The Jewish police are to enforce the measure. And it is to be announced to the population by the Elder of the Jews."

Those in the room then saw something that no one else in our town had seen before. The Elder on his knees. He held his hands together like a Christian praying. "Please. I'm just an old man. Just an old Jew. I'm not even from here. I'm from Vilna. A little town near Vilna. I didn't want this job. I'm too weak to do it. Look at my white hair, look how my old hands are shaking. Look, I'm even crying. I resign! I'm not the Elder anymore. If you want, you can shoot me. Yes! I'll drink poison. I'll jump from the Zgierska Boulevard Bridge. Don't make me announce such a thing to the Jews!"

"Stop this weeping!" Grundtripp commanded.

"Weeping! Yes, I'm weeping! Because a man like me has to beg from a man like you."

Before the officer could respond, there was a clatter in the hallway and F. X. Wohltat burst through the door. He pointed a finger at the Elder, who was still on his knees. "Chairman Trumpelman, you broke our agreement. You overacted your part. Valuable property—the roulette, the card tables, it's all been destroyed. You were only supposed to send the girls home. Now you will have to pay! We have confiscated the Judenrat limousine!"

Was it because the Jews had become so much thinner that the Volksdeutscher looked actually fat? Lipiczany noticed how the man's arms took up the room in his sleeves, how his neck pushed down his collar.

The tears dried up in the Elder's eyes. "What?" he said. "The limousine?"

Grundtripp walked over. He seemed to have swallowed his

115

lips altogether. Without speaking he struck Trumpelman on the side of his head, near his eye. The "American" spectacles flew off, shattered. Blood came from a gash in his cheek. The Obergruppenführer swung across his own body, like a back-hand in tennis, and the Elder's head snapped back.

"'A man like me!'" the Other repeated. "'A man like you!'"

Wohltat was excitedly walking up and down, wincing, making faces. "Never mind me," he said. "I'm just a little sausage." Then he darted in and gave the Judenrat Chairman a kick with his shoe.

Suddenly the two Others pulled back. Miss Lubliver, with the gown only half covering her body, spoke once again. "Day and night. They must work day and night. Smoke will come from the chimneys, flame from the mills. Two shifts! Two shifts until the men drop!"

Nisel, pale, squinting, wrung his white hands. He could not understand why Chaim, such a big man, such a strong man, did not fight back against his attackers. Was he a coward? Afraid of the Others! The thought made the boy choke. He wanted to shout, *Get up! Fight them! Kill them!* But when the two men closed in again, when they again started to beat him, the great hands of the Elder hung limply down.

II

Late that same afternoon Trumpelman arrived back at Tsarskoye Selo. The Obergruppenführer dropped him off in his new Double Six. The Elder could hardly walk. His clothes were ripped, his cloak gone. There was only one lens left in his frame. He did not go into the mansion, but around it, to the gardens in back. Though early in springtime, the fresh green stems of garlic were pushing out of the ground. Trumpelman sank down among them; wearily, he shut his eyes.

No telling how long he might have stayed there if Bettsack, the schoolmaster, had not walked by carrying what looked like a gigantic squash. *Smuggling!* said the Elder to himself, and keeping low, keeping hidden, he followed the young teacher to the edge of the plowed-up field. There the orphans—both the old-timers and the ones who had joined the Asylum in the last years before the move to the Balut—were waiting. They all had caps on, and coats, and were holding such things as nuts, the head of a cabbage, and a pink India-rubber ball. The sun had dropped well down in the sky, and the air was chilly now. Bettsack was a thin fellow, poorly whiskered, with threads that stuck up from his collar. He made his way to the center of the field, set down the gourd—it was as big as a washbasin, really—and began to call through his hands.

"Stations, children! Positions, if you please! You! Shifter! Leibel Shifter! Further back. Further back! Tushnet! You go back, too!"

The children began to scatter over the field. Shifter, the mad boy, the dog, kept going backward. Every minute or so he would stop, but Bettsack waved him farther on, until he was practically out of sight. "Stop!" the schoolmaster shouted. But Shifter still backpedaled, and the message to him had to be passed from orphan to orphan, from Krystal to Atlas to Tushnet, across the length of the field.

Finally they all held still. Bettsack bent down and picked up the dried squash; he just had the strength to lift it over his head. The next thing you knew the schoolmaster, a grown-up, responsible person, was rapidly spinning around. "Flicker!" he gasped to the boy who was nearest. "Citron!" he called, to the lad next farthest out. "Begin rotation!"

Trumpelman could hardly believe what he saw: both boys, and then Gutta Blit, and then all the others began to spin on the spot. It was like madness. Round and round they went, stepping all over their shadows. "West to east, Miss Atlas! Not like a clock!" Rose Atlas stopped; she reversed direction.

117

The rest kept going, holding their little spheres. Bettsack had begun to stagger a little. The breath came visibly from his mouth.

"Now! Revolutions!"

Little Usher Flicker—between his fingers he had a pea from a pod—began to trip around the teacher, in a circle more or less. A bit farther out Citron was doing the same. The amazing thing was that as both boys went in this circular orbit, they did not stop whirling about. Gutta Blit, with the pink rubber ball, was spinning like a dervish too, and also Krystal, and so was everyone soon. Even Leibel Shifter, way out on the edge of the field, a half kilometer off, had started to run. However, because of the distance between him and Bettsack, he hardly seemed to be moving. Flicker, for instance, had run three times about the center, before Shifter, his legs thrashing, covered any noticeable ground. It would take him forever to complete a revolution.

"Attention! Moons!" Bettsack, with red patches that showed through his beard, with his necktie coming undone, practically shrieked this.

From behind the hill that led to the cemetery grounds fifteen, twenty, more than twenty children came pouring. What they did, with a whoop, with a shout, was to pick out some of the whirling orphans—Gutta, Rose Atlas, the puffing Mann Lifshits—and then begin to race as fast as they could around them. For a time the whole field was covered with these whizzing children, making circles inside of circles, curves within curves.

Then Trumpelman stood up in the dimming light; he walked into their midst. Through his split, puffy lips, he demanded of the reeling Bettsack, "What is the meaning of this? Speak!"

The schoolmaster dropped his squash. He started screaming. "It's the whole solar system! Including the new planet of Pluto! In correct proportions! According to the system of Sir

118

J. Frederick Herschel!" Then he threw his arms around the Asylum Director, clinging to him the way a drunkard does to a post. Just then Nathan Hobnover, an eight-year-old boy, came roaring over the hilltop, making a sizzling sound: zzzzzzz!

"Comet," said Bettsack, and sank down about Trumpelman's ankles.

The exhausted children saw the old man in tatters; they wobbled to a halt. Mann Lifshits, whose heavy cabbage represented Jupiter, simply dropped, as did his eleven moons. One by one the others collapsed. They lay on their backs, with their coats spread, their breath coming up in a mist. Only the man from Vilna, for all his scratches and bruises, remained on his feet. Then he sat down, too. Tushnet caught his breath before anyone else and addressed the schoolmaster.

"Sir, what will happen when the sun goes out?" He was some way off, but it was so still you could easily hear him.

Bettsack said, "What do you mean, Tushnet? It goes *down*. It does not go *out*."

"I mean, when it burns up. Will we burn up, too?"

A high voice broke in. "It can't just go on forever. Sometime it has to run out of fuel."

"That is only a theory, Flicker. It has not been proved."

"But what if it's true? What then? Everything will be dark. It makes me nervous." That was Rose Atlas.

"I don't think it will burn up," said Mann Lifshits, from his spot on the ground. "It'll just get colder and colder. Everything on earth will get colder, too. It will be like the ice age. Nothing but ice."

"But it scares me," Rose replied.

"Listen," said Bettsack. "This is speculation. In any case, it won't happen for thousands of years."

"See? You said it was going to happen! It's going to happen!"

119

"We'll all be frozen to death!"

"Please!" their instructor said. "Why do you worry? In a thousand years none of us will be alive."

"I don't care! I don't want it to go out! I hate the idea of the cold!"

"I do, too!"

"No one alive! No one! There won't even be animals on the earth. It's terrible!"

"Don't talk about it! Don't think about it!"

The children began to whimper and moan. So Bettsack spoke in a loud, firm voice. "Pay attention, if you please. The sun is not going to stop burning. It is made in a certain way. And even if it should go out after all, by then men will have invented spaceships, and they will fly off to live somewhere else. To other planets, to other worlds. There is nothing that science cannot achieve. Perhaps in the universe we shall meet other forms of life. Perhaps even people just like ourselves. Think of that! What a wonderful day that will be! How much we shall learn!"

The moaning had completely stopped. Everything was quiet. Then, so that everyone's heart leaped and pounded, there was an awful wail from Leibel Shifter. "Help! I'm so far away! Help! I'm afraid!"

Trumpelman, sitting upright, answered. "Come. All of you. Come closer."

Silently, on all fours, the boys and girls began to crawl toward the center. They drew near to Trumpelman, who, through his swollen eyes, his single lens, was staring off to the west. They looked, too.

There, on the horizon, the real sun was leaking something. Red stuff, like jam, came out of it and spread over the nearby sky. "Like a raspberry drop," said Usher Flicker. He took the Elder's hand. Citron, a new boy, had curly blond hair coming from under his cap. He laid his head across the Elder's knees. Dark Gutta Blit leaned on his shoulder.

"It's beautiful," she whispered, gazing off to where the sun, cut by the earth's edge, still pumped the sweet-looking syrup from its center. All the children—the planets, the satellites, Hobnover the comet, and at last even Shifter—pressed close to Trumpelman, and to each other. They were like his missing cape.

III

There was no synagogue in the Baluty Suburb. Not allowed. And *over there,* in the Aryan section, the Italianate Synagogue, the Central Synagogue, the synagogues of the Devout Butchers and the Fur Trimmers—all these had been burned down. But there was, on Lutomierska Street, the Church of the Virgin Mary. This was a big, solid building, made from brick and stone. Here, every Sunday, gathered our Christian souls. Some were converts and some the sons and daughters, or even grandsons and granddaughters, of baptized Jews. There were even cases of worshipers who had not known, until they found themselves in the Ghetto, from whom they had descended.

No matter, the Judenrat treated all of them well. They received double rations and worked in this or that department of the Council itself. Inside the church there was a big picture of Jesus, coming down from the cross. A man in a red robe was kissing one of his feet. A man in a green robe kissed his hand. The ex-Jews prayed to this. They knelt before it. Around the head of everyone in the picture there was a circle, a halo, painted from melted gold.

Shortly after the closing of the House of Pleasure, the Occupying Power began to store inside this fireproof building hundreds and hundreds of bolsters and mattresses and sofa cushions. This bedding was the property of people in the hospital, people in the Tsarnecka Street jail. No one dared ask what the sick people would sleep on once they got well. It

121

was the feathers the Conquerors wanted, to put in their winter uniforms. All day long women sat on church benches, slitting pillows, pulling the stuffing out. They had to wear face masks because of the lint. The down always hung there, drifting and blowing on currents of air.

Three months later, at the end of June, Klapholtz, the artist, walked into Mary's church. He had a soft hat on his head and a cigarette stuck to his lower lip—habits he had picked up during his studies in Paris. With the help of Brauwatt, the carpenter, he built a tall scaffold, so that he could paint directly onto the ceiling. Then he stretched canvas panels to hide his work from view. Day after day he painted, week after week. Finally one of the feather cleaners called up to where he was lying on his back.

"What are you painting?" she asked.

"A mural," he answered. "A surprise for the Elder's wedding."

The wedding! The wedding! Now that the secret was out, no one talked about anything else. It was said, for instance, that the Bulgarian king had been invited and that Weizmann, the statesman, was pulling all sorts of strings to reserve a seat in the church. There was even a rumor that the Big Man would appear. That summer, in honor of the occasion, the Judenrat provided little gifts—a pot of ersatz honey, a double ration of bread—to each couple getting married. Thus, weddings became a fad. Jews who hardly knew each other got engaged. It wasn't unheard of for the same bride and groom to show up in front of two different rabbis. Such marriages— this was a joke that went around—lasted only as long as the extra loaf of bread.

But the truth was that the wedding fever was caused not so much by hunger as by hope and joy. It was as if the citizens of the Balut had been waiting for a reason to be gay. In the great wave of optimism that swept the Ghetto even the most disturbing news was seen in a favorable light. When the pa-

122

tients were suddenly removed from the hospital, when the prisoners disappeared from the Tsarnecka Street jail, everyone accepted the explanation that the former were being transported to rest homes, the latter to work on the unfinished dikes. Then all the clothes came back, but not the people inside them. Suits and shoes and dresses piled up inside the Virgin Mary Church. Here was a difficult moment, a time for unthinkable thoughts. But before the Baluters could give way to despair, a big patch of postcards came through the Jewish mail. Each one—including that of Professor Potash, who had been seized in the hospital, not yet recovered from his awful burns—said much the same thing. *Life goes on. We grow stronger. Here there is marmalade.*

It was the same with the prohibition on births. The majority argued there was no room for babies in a full-employment ghetto. These infants, nonworkers themselves, forced pregnant women and new mothers to leave the factories, to abandon their sewing machines. What did it matter that the increased production made huge profits for the Lords and Masters? Or that they were putting uniforms on their own oppressors' backs? What counted was that because of these very things the Jews had become indispensable at last. Thus, to the Baluters, the marriage of Trumpelman was not to any particular person—no one even thought of Phelia Lubliver, who had not been seen or heard of for months—but to his people as a whole. The union was like a pact between them that they would survive.

If the bride had vanished, there was no shortage of the groom. From somewhere the Elder had found a pure white horse, a stallion, and he rode it throughout the Balut. It must have been Muszkat's runaway nag, except this horse seemed larger, more splendid. It was like one of the pink-lipped team that had pulled the Conqueror's movable stage. Wherever Trumpelman rode there was a crowd. Sometimes it would press closely around his stallion, so that the Elite Guard had to link hands to hold everyone back. At the

Chancellory, at Dworska Number 20, it was impossible to get near the Elder's door. But here, in the streets, you could come close; if you wanted to ask, "What about horsemeat? Can a Jew eat it? The rabbis won't tell," you got an answer: "Never mind the rabbis! It's an emergency! Horsemeat is kosher!"

Some in these crowds managed to hand up personal petitions. Trumpelman, on his horse, higher than anyone, would read the scraps of paper, and then announce: "The Jew, Windman, is excused from the house tax for the month of August!" or "The room of the glassblower, Pincus Lining, is not to be fumigated. Notify the fumigation squads!" Most people, however, had no petition to give him or favor to ask. They simply wanted to see him, to hear him, to touch his hanging cloak. There was a special relationship between the Elder and his Jews. It was democratic, like Roosevelt in America, and at the same time it was royal. Just to be near him was considered good fortune, good luck.

Sometimes the President of the Judenrat would get off his horse and plunge right into the masses of people. Then the Jews saw that he now had a limp and walked with a cane. "I know what you're thinking!" Trumpelman cried. "Look at the Elder! How old he's getting! He has to walk with a cane! Listen, Jews! Your Elder works every night until dawn! He doesn't need sleep. His eyes are always open. Every minute he's thinking of your welfare! That's what gives me energy! What keeps me young!" Then he picked out a girl in the crowd, a pretty young woman, and to the delight of them all he whirled her around, as if there had been music and they had been at a ball.

At night, curfew or not, there were always a few people gathered at the edge of the Balut. They liked to point to the light that burned in the top-floor window of Tsarskoye Selo. It never went out. It proved to the Jews that Trumpelman was still awake, thinking, working, finding new ways to save their lives.

124

In short, the summer of 1940 was the height of the Elder's popularity in the Ghetto. Wherever you looked you saw his picture—on money, on postage stamps, on the sides of buildings. There were parades in his honor, with the chimney sweepers, tall, thin Jews, in black, with brooms, always at the front. One day, as Trumpelman was riding past the Vocational School, the door flew open and the children rushed down the steps and surrounded his horse. They gave him a gift, an album, with the names of all the schoolchildren in the Suburb. There were also prayers in it, and pictures, and poems. The Elder did not read it at once. He sat, with his white hair and black boots, completely unmoving. He was like the Rumkowsky Monument, an iron figure on an iron horse. Then he swung his cane over the heads of the students.

"My darling boys and girls! Dearest children! The woman I am going to marry has been ill, but now she has recovered. The wedding will be in the middle of October, on the first anniversary of the founding of the Balut! Welcome her! Open your hearts to her! She will be a mother to you!"

The students cheered, then ran off to spread the news. The wedding album they gave the Elder still exists. It's in a museum. On the cover it says: *Adonenu Ha-Nasi*. "Our lord, the Prince."

Ladies and gentlemen, the wedding at last. It took place on a Tuesday, a lucky date, because twice on that day of creation God said, *It is well*. Another good sign: The sun was out, round and bright. The Church of the Virgin Mary shone in its rays. At noon the children were let out of the schools; they lined both sides of Lutomierska and waved cardboard copies of the new Baluty state flag. It was a half day in the factories, too. The dyers and tanners and cutters, the thousands of sewers and spinners, stood in back of the boys and girls. There were special marshals—the porters, the sweepers—to keep order in the crowd. Everyone was in a happy

125

mood, laughing and chatting. A cheer went up whenever a special guest or even a Judenrat member drove by in a rickshaw. "Long live Chaim! Greetings to Chaim!" cried the Jews, straining to see if the Elder, or the Elder's white horse, had come into view. A wonderful holiday!

Inside the church, with its thick walls, you could barely hear the shouting. But the sunshine came through. It struck the colored glass in the windows and made red spots, and blue spots, and blue and green ones, like lily pads, on the floor. Everything had been scrubbed and polished. Though the feathers and clothes had been carted away, the fluff floated through the rays of light and stuck to people's hat brims, or to those few Jews who still dared to wear beards.

The wooden benches had been turned lengthwise and placed one tier above another, so that a kind of grandstand ran down either side of the aisle. The Judenrat, along with the top workers on the Jewish Council, were on one side, the distinguished guests on the other. At the end of the passage, on a platform, there was a canopy raised on four poles. Eight Jews, our biggest rabbis, held it up: Trunk, of the Devout Butchers; Kornischoner, from the Fur Trimmers; also Rabbis Martini, Lunt, Chill, and Wolf-Kitzes; Lakmaker, a proven cousin of the Zlotchov maggid; and lastly Kanal, who some said was a descendant of the zaddik of Pshiskhe himself.

Down the long aisle the last of the guests paraded. The church organ sounded a fanfare and Schotter, the announcer, made a megaphone out of his hands.

"Jews! Honored guests! The Security Minister!"

Krystal, with Lifshits helping, set off the flash lamp, and Fried Rievesaltes, in his pearl-button vest and built-up shoe, strolled between the two rows of benches. There was a woman by his side. She had a little bulge above her nipped-in waist, and the bare skin of her upper arm, where Rievesaltes gripped it, was plump and reddish. The dark-haired Nellie Brilliantstein. The couple stopped at a large table, already

126

covered, overflowing, with gifts. They added theirs to the pile, then took their seats on the right-hand side.

Another fanfare. Another announcement. "Presenting the Mayor of the Poles!" This gentleman had not thought to wear a hat. The skin of his scalp, completely hairless, still had a deep summer tan. *Poof! Poof!* The boys took his picture. He placed a large box on the gift table and turned to his left, toward the distinguished visitors' section.

The Big Man, after all, was not seated there, though he had sent, it was rumored, a diamond or an auto or some other fabulous gift. The King of Bulgaria was also missing, as was Weizmann, the Zionist leader. But there were at least two other heads of state: Lender, the Chairman of the Lukow Jewish Council, and, from Sosnowiec, Chairman Moses Merin. They sat stiffly, in top hats, separated by an empty chair.

Andrei Schpitalnik, the pianist from the Astoria Café, made the organ thunder again.

"Jews! Guests! What an honor! Look who is coming now!" Schotter, in his excitement, kept thrusting his hands into his armpits. "Here is the boss of the biggest ghetto of all! Ladies and gentlemen, the head of the Quarantine Area of Warsaw—Czerniakow, Certified Engineer!"

The President of the Warsaw Judenrat stood at the far end of the aisle. Then he slowly marched down it. Everyone leaned forward to get a glimpse of such an important man. He turned to his left and to his right, tipping his hat. He was bald underneath it, with just a fringe of hair around the back. He had a bow tie and little fluttering eyelids. There was an obvious hook in his nose. Hard to believe this was the king of hundreds of thousands of Jews.

At the gift table Czerniakow stopped, pulled a plain white envelope from an inside pocket, and set it down. Then he took his seat, between the two other Council Chairmen, in the distinguished visitors' section.

A delay, a pause. People began to grow restless. Delicious

127

smells, maddening smells—from real soups, from yellow butter—drifted up from the banquet tables at the back of the church. While they were waiting, the Jews tried to think of something else. Some reached for the colored sunbeams, which turned their hands green and blue. Others, for a distraction, began to whisper about what Klapholtz had painted on the ceiling. Billowing strips of canvas hid the actual mural from view. The artist himself was still there, as he had been each day since June, putting on final touches. What could this work be? An abstract design, in the modernist manner? Some people thought so. But others argued that the wedding gift would be a portrait of the Elder, with his cloak stretched over the Ghetto, like a gigantic enlargement of a six-grosz stamp.

Schotter, to fill this time, started to speak again. "Ladies and gentlemen, what a great and happy day! A day for celebration. And that reminds me, not long ago I met a wise man, a real sage, and he told me that there wasn't a doubt that Horowitz was going to die on a Jewish holiday." What was this? Impossible! A joke! The Jews in either grandstand stared across at each other, with widening eyes. "Naturally, I wanted to know how he could make such a prediction. Where did he get his information? 'Any day that Horowitz dies,' the wise man told me, 'will be a Jewish holiday.'"

This story undoubtedly went back to the days of the Pharaoh. Perhaps that is why no one laughed. Or else it was because just at that time the guests saw the bride.

Completely in white, with white shoes and long white gloves, Phelia Lubliver stood at the far end of the aisle. Franz Xavier Wohltat, in a cutaway coat, had his arm linked in hers. The bride took a step, and then another. Because of the shawl over her head she could not see where she was going. The Volksdeutscher, who was shorter than she was, had to guide her along the way. There was a chair on the platform, with many silk cushions. Miss Lubliver was placed on

128

this throne. She sat with her knees together, her arms on the rests. Her whole head was hooded in the chalk-white veil.

Outside the church the crowd was cheering so loudly you could hear it through the stone and brick. The sound swelled and swelled. The rabbis holding the huppah stood straighter. The organ played the wedding march of Mendelssohn-Bartholdy, and Schotter, through his cupped hands, announced the groom.

Trumpelman appeared, in black. But his cloak was white silk, embroidered in purple, and swept down to the heels of his shoes. He did not look to the side, but strode firmly, without a cane, toward the front of the church. How fine he looked! Tall and splendid! His white locks curled from beneath his hat to his shoulders. An audible sigh filled the room. Compared to our Elder, Czerniakow of Warsaw was nothing, nobody.

A ninth rabbi, Nomberg, stepped off the platform to meet him. He had long since trained his hair to cover his missing ear. The melody stopped. There was a hush. The Minister of Religious Affairs asked Trumpelman if he was prepared to fulfill his obligations as a Jewish husband. The groom signified assent by grasping the handkerchief that Nomberg held out. Then both men stepped onto the platform.

At this point two gentlemen left the Judenrat section. One was Margolies, the former waiter, and the other was the Hungarian, whose name was Urinstein. They crossed the aisle together and stood at the base of the platform. Margolies reached into his jacket pocket and began throwing grain, for fertility, for many children, into the lap of the hooded bride. Urinstein's beard had grown back completely. He was now the Minister of Vital Statistics. "May you have a sweet life," he said, and hurled a handful of raisins at Trumpelman's chest. Then the two Judenrat members, bowing slightly, returned to their seats.

The groom turned and faced the woman in white. How

129

quiet it was. Not a rustle. Not a word. Slowly Chaim bent at the waist and took hold of the bottom of the veil.

"Oh, sister!" Nomberg chanted. "Be thou the mother of thousands of millions!"

I. C. Trumpelman lifted the veil.

"Ah!" everyone said, but from custom only, since the blinding flash lamps and the broad cloak of the groom blocked off any view. But Trumpelman nodded, satisfied. It was a Rachel, not a Leah. He dropped the cloth back over the face of the woman he had chosen.

Rabbi Lunt, in his usual sport coat, declared, "Now it is time for the huppah."

The bride rose unsteadily and felt her way beneath the blue and white canopy. Trumpelman joined her, ducking a little. Then the maiden began to circle her husband-to-be. She walked around him once, and then once more, and then a third time—which meant, symbolically speaking, that months and months were going by. Still she continued, slowly circling, solemnly circling, and she did not stop until she had completed four more rounds: and thus she entered all seven spheres of her beloved's soul.

Then Nomberg produced a pretty little goblet of wine, over which he spoke the benedictions concerning the blessedness of the Lord and the holiness of His people.

> *He who is strong above all else*
> *He who is blessed above all else*
> *He who is great above all else.*
> *May he bless the bridegroom and bride.*

The Elder of the Jews took the goblet and, since it is written, "There is no joy without wine," he sipped the contents, red as rubies are red, and gave the cup to the bride. But before she could pass it beneath the veil, to her lips, the organ burst out once more into its trumpetlike notes.

"Obergruppenführer Grundtripp!" Schotter declared, and Grundtripp, tall and bony, in silver and black, walked down the aisle. Beneath his cap his eyes were deepset, in shadows. His mouth was like a cut in his skin. The loose cuffs of his trousers flapped over his boots. He halted at the gift table, though it was clear to all that he was empty-handed.

"Seed of Abraham! My apologies! Allow me to explain to you the reason I have arrived late. A message has just arrived from Berlin: our Leader, while not able to be here in person, has decided to send a magnificent gift in his stead. Listen! All Jews of Poland, and later all Jews everywhere, are to be resettled on the island of Madagascar. There you will live in peace and security, without enemies of any kind. Think of it, Jews! The ingathering of your entire nation! A kingdom of your own at last!"

Rabbi Wolf-Kitzes, straining to keep up his huppah pole, wondered out loud, "But what is Madagascar?"

"It is," replied Grundtripp, "the fourth largest island in the world."

Now Trumpelman broke his silence. He was smiling, not angry. It was apparent to all that he had expected this interruption. "Not just an island! No, no! A garden! An Eden! There the sun always shines! Even at night! The streams flow with milk, not water. If you strike the earth, from that spot nectar flows! Peaches are the size of melons; if you pluck one, a new one grows overnight. No hunger, Jews! Fish, the salmon, throw themselves onto the riverbanks. This is our paradise!"

Another rabbi, the zaddik's Descendant, said faintly, "Melons? To eat?"

"Salmon?" That was Rabbi Trunk.

Trumpelman, like a bird, a peacock, opened his cape. "We shall live there together. In time we shall build a magnificent city. A new Jerusalem. With sapphires at the foundations and emeralds on the roofs. At the center we shall raise the Tem-

131

ple again. How its white walls will gleam in the sunlight! Like alabaster! Like hills of diamonds and pearls! Across the ocean the gentiles will see it and say, *If only we could be Jews!*"

Trunk was in a daze. "I never thought I would eat a salmon. I told myself, all right, it's something you have to do without."

"On behalf of his people, the Elder accepts the gift of the Jewish preserve. We shall build a kingdom there to last a thousand years!"

Rabbi Kornischoner, thin, almost, as the pole he was holding, and with hair growing from every spot on his face, then asked a question: "Who will be the king of this place?"

All eyes turned of course to Trumpelman, who bowed, who beamed. But Obergruppenführer Grundtripp was looking at Czerniakow. Czerniakow, of all people!

"That," said the Other, "remains to be seen. The Elder who rules best here will rule overseas."

And at those words, Czerniakow, as if accepting a challenge, lifted his hat with both hands.

Grundtripp continued. "Jews! I also have a wedding gift! A gift of my own! President of the Judenrat Trumpelman and his bride are to be exempt from the prohibition on Jewish births. They and they alone are free to have children."

On the platform, Trumpelman swayed, then straightened. "Rabbis!" he said. "Pray that the Elder fathers a son. A broad-chested boy! That is a Judenrat order!"

The holders of the huppah all talked at once.

"Mister Chairman," said Rabbi Martini, "you have to put the head of the bed toward the north and the foot part to the south. It is a proven method."

"Eating cucumber is good. Both green ones and the squirting kind."

"But there are no cucumbers in this part of Poland."

With a wave of his hand Trumpelman silenced the rabbis. "Nomberg, read the contract. Read it quickly. The Elder and the Elder's wife will give birth to a line of kings."

The Minister of Religious Affairs rushed through the marriage contract. First came the date, the third day of the week, the sixth day of Tishrei, 5701 years since the Creation; then the place, the Jewish State of the Balut, on the western shore of the river Dolna, within the General Government of the Reich; then the bride's name and the groom's name and how the latter sought out the former and was accepted, and so forth and so on in the regular way.

When the reading was finished, Trumpelman turned his back on the crowd. Solemnly he grasped the bride by her shoulders and turned her toward himself. It was the moment of final unveiling. Once more he took the lower fringe of the cloth and centimeter by centimeter lifted it upward. A neck showed. A chin. A wide, thin-lipped mouth. At that instant two different people stood at two different spots in the right-hand benches. One was a man and the other—also dressed in white, which was an insult to the bride—a woman. They both began to make their way to the platform. When the man arrived he stopped and thrust his hand into his pocket. Everybody thought he was going to throw raisins or nuts. From another angle the woman rushed to the platform, too.

The next events occurred so quickly it is difficult to sort them out. First the man shouted loudly, "Trumpelman! You're no Elder! You're a traitor to the Jews!" From his pocket he drew a gun. Then the bride's veil came off, like a cover from the cage of a bird. Miss Lubliver twitched her head.

"It should have been me!" the woman screamed and, just as the gun went off, hurled herself at the groom. The bullet meant for I. C. Trumpelman went into Madame Zweideneck, who had not been seen in our town for years.

"Lipsky the lawyer!" somebody cried.

Then the whole church erupted in shouts and screams. There was a wild rush to escape from the rows of raised benches. People stepped over each other. Women fell down. The bulk of the crowd made a charge down the center aisle.

133

The gift table turned over. The soup spilled across the stones of the floor. Then the back doors flew open; the first one through was little Lipsky.

"After him!" was the cry.

There was a tremendous surge to the outside. Grown men butted each other. In the awful crush, the crowd shoved against the painter's scaffold. "Watch out! Don't push!" But the next moment the wood and the tubing started to buckle. Then with a rip the canvas parted and, with Klapholtz still wrapped in the billows, plunged all the way down.

In spite of everything people paused and raised their heads. Then all together they moaned. There, along the entire vault of the ceiling, in brilliant colors, was the *Tricouleur* itself. Across it the enormous legend:

VIVE LA FRANCE!

"Sabotage!" Trumpelman roared.

The last of the Jews fled through the doors.

On the platform Miss Lubliver pointed to where Klapholtz, although an arm and a leg had been broken, was trying to crawl away. "There he is! There! Get him! Catch him! Don't let him escape!"

Grundtripp himself sprang forward and collared the painter. He shook him the way you shake a broken machine. Then he dragged him to the street outside.

The church was now deserted. No rabbis. No Wohltat. Even the Zweideneck woman had been taken away. There remained only shambles: benches thrown over, the huppah tangled in its sticks. Trumpelman stooped for the canopy. He stretched it over his own head and that of his bride. Her teeth were clamped on the white cloth of the veil, as if she wished to tear it in pieces.

The Judenrat Chairman took the fist of her hand from her glove and placed a round gold ring on her finger. "Behold you are consecrated unto me," he said, "according to the Law of Moses and Israel." Then he faced north, the direction of demons, and smashed the little goblet under his heel.

134

It is said that God Himself is a bridegroom and that all Israel once, on the mountain of Sinai, became His bride. What that means is that every Jewish wedding is in some way a reflection of that distant and shining event. Even I. C. Trumpelman's.

IV

A last glimpse, that's all it will be, of that day. Quite late, when they should have been sleeping, Nisel and the other orphans moved in file down the stairway of Tsarskoye Selo. They gathered at the newlyweds' door. One of the boys, Shifter perhaps, nudged it open. Then they cried out together, "Sing for us! Sing for us! In your shiny dress!"

Madame Trumpelman was sitting in bed, with her black hair twisted behind her. Her husband, in a robe, was standing nearby. They both turned toward the shaft of light that poured through the crack in the door. "They're here!" she said.

"Only the children," the Hatters' Director replied.

"No! Up there! I mean over there!" She was whispering, hissing. She pointed over the heads of the orphans to where a tiny white-winged moth, the last of the season, had flown into the room.

Trumpelman laughed. "Ho, ho! A moth, Miss Lubliver!"

"Kill it! Drive it away!"

The children shrank back, into the hallway, onto the stairs. The Elder leaned over his wife, touching her shoulder. "But why, my dear?"

"It's an act of darkness! Forbidden to see!" She clutched him, then pushed him off.

Groaning, Trumpelman left the side of the bed. He moved into what looked like a film projectionist's beam. "Go!" he commanded. "Leave!" He waved his arms. The moth flew

135

upward. He stretched on his toes. The little creature went higher. He leaped at it, and the moth disappeared.

"There!" said the woman. "On the wall!"

It is the custom among some Orthodox Jews to sweep clean a room before each act of love. They rid it of mice. They catch all the flies. They put insects in paper bags. Like one of these zealots, Isaiah Trumpelman now flung himself at the dusty mark on the wall. He chased it from one side of the room to the other. At last, using his robe, he maneuvered it out of the door.

"There is another!" cried the bride. She was pointing at empty space. Trumpelman did not move. He stood there, unclothed. "I have it," he said.

"One more! See? A fly! A fly!"

He closed the door. Quietly he said, "I have it, too."

Then everything was still. Lipiczany did not retreat with the other children. He lay down, like a dog, before the shut door. Behind it, he knew, the Elder was making the long line of his sons.

Chapter Five

The Five Day Strike

I

A new year, this one 1941, came around. At six in the morning thousands of workers poured from the mill gates, and thousands more tramped in. The sky was dark and the moon still out, cracked like a dish at the edges. The two shifts did not exchange a word. Each man had his own thoughts, which did not much differ from those of another: *So what if horsemeat is kosher, if there isn't a horse?* No one dared think back even as far as Trumpelman's wedding. Those times, the good times, were gone. As for the lives the Jews had lived outside the Suburb only a short while ago, they were already fading into a fabulous, forgotten past.

It was a normal day in the Mosk Works buttonhole section. The men bent in rows as far as the eye could see. They wore their caps, or didn't wear them, just as they pleased. They snapped the thread with their teeth. At eleven o'clock, after hours of work, the buttonhole makers lined up for their ration of soup. The finishers were already there. Like finishers everywhere, they were loudly complaining.

"My friend Mister Pipe has broken his needle. But they won't give him a new one. He's too shy to say anything."

Pipe hung his head and merely murmured, "Without a needle I can't sew."

But Sheftelowitz, the friend of Pipe's, spoke, even louder. "They want him to pay for it. They say it's a needle tax."

Then Kleiderman, a finisher with a toothpick completely inside his mouth, shouted out, "That's not all. I know for a fact there will be all sorts of work taxes. I learned this from Luftgas himself. For instance, they are going to take away our chairs. If you want to stand, you can stand. Otherwise the chair tax will be fifteen zlotys a week."

"Fifteen zlotys!"

"Each week?"

Pipe, white-haired, said smiling, "But my knees are too weak to stand."

"That's because of the food allotment. The soup is practically water. There is no meat in it. No potatoes. Only peels from potatoes."

"And where is it, the soup? Mister Marx is here. Mister Kemp is here. I see Mister Trilling. We are here, but the soup isn't."

Sheftelowitz stood on a chair. "Jews! Finishers! Luftgas says there is plenty of work and plenty to eat. Don't laugh! It's true! There's plenty of food—"

"For him!" the workers replied.

"And there's plenty of work—"

"For us!"

From this demonstration the buttonholers, with their tin cups, stood apart. "*Shhh, shhh,*" some of them said. "You'll get us in trouble."

But the fiery finishers—Bundists, many of them, Socialist thinkers—continued to shout. "No chair taxes! Luftgas! We're human beings!"

"Thank goodness," said an elderly buttonhole maker. "Here at last is the soup."

The doors opened and a huge steaming kettle, placed as usual on a platform with wheels, came rolling in. What wasn't

138

usual, what made the finishers fall silent and the buttonhole experts drop back a step or two, was the fact that the two ladlers were missing and in their place stood a Warrior, along with Trumpelman, the Elder of the Jews.

The latter was bareheaded, with lines that ran from his nose to his mouth. He leaned with both hands on his cane. By the time the tureen arrived at the front of the room, the workers saw that the other man wasn't a soldier at all. It was Luftgas, the supervisor, wearing one of the new uniforms. More of these uniforms were piled at the edge of the platform. Luftgas threw up his arms, as if the crowd were still demonstrating.

"Finishers and buttonhole makers of the Mosk Works," he began. He pulled the brim of the Hauptsturmführer's cap over his eyes. He struck the top of his boot with a little whip. "A serious situation has arisen. Jews, you're involved, so pay attention." What Luftgas did was button his green-colored jacket. He got halfway to the top when one of the buttons burst. "You see?" he said. "What did I tell you?"

"That's nothing," an anonymous finisher cried. "The fit is too tight."

"Wait!" Luftgas commanded. He removed the jacket and took another from the pile. He put it on and did it up. This time nothing happened. Luftgas turned this way and that, as if he were examining himself in a mirror. How proud he was of his little belly, in which pieces of lamb meat, with waxed beans, were at that moment floating. He stamped his boot, he straightened his back, and with a stiff arm he saluted. A second button noiselessly bounded away.

A gasp rose from the crowd.

Said Luftgas, "Once is a coincidence. Twice is not."

A different finisher, Marx this time, said a word. "It's carelessness, Supervisor Luftgas. Or maybe it's the quality of the thread."

The supervisor took off his officer's cap. His hair was matted down. The knees of his trousers looked, all of a sudden, swollen. From the uniform heap he pulled out another tunic. "Look, fellow Jews," he said, plucking a button. "It just comes off in my hand. This is a catastrophe. When I first found this out I thought I must be having a dream."

"We need more soup," said a finisher, fearless. "With more soup we could pull the thread tighter."

I. C. Trumpelman made his hand into a fist. "More soup! More soup! Who is that genius? Write down his name! Don't talk about carelessness! About rotted thread! Look at this!" The Chairman dashed to the clothing and threw the things about. "The button is here. It's firmly secured. But the buttonhole is missing! And it's missing from this one! And this one, too! This is deliberate! It's sabotage! Buttonhole makers of the Baluty Suburb! For such actions you could be shot!"

There was an indescribable commotion among the old craftsmen. They looked at each other with shock. You can imagine, then, their amazement when from their very number a high-pitched voice came piping: "Comrades! Workers of the world! Stand fast! Do not let the fruits of our labor clothe the backs of the oppressor!"

Who was that? Everyone looked around. But the speaker was so short that, in the milling buttonholers, you could not see him at all.

"Comrades, let's be shot! Let's be hanged together! Better death than to assist the Race of Masters in their crimes!"

"An outside agitator!" Trumpelman cried. "Seize him, Jews! It's one of Lipsky's men!"

But the hundred buttonhole makers, instead of converging on where the provocateur's voice had been, drew swiftly apart, leaving Nachman Kipnis, with his mole, his thick glasses, and his fecalist's cap, all alone on the floor. "Greetings from the proletariat to Chaim, the exploiter," the youngster said.

"Ah! Assassin! He'll shoot me!" Trumpelman cried.

But the boy pulled pamphlets, not a pistol, from his pock-

140

et. He pressed a manifesto on everyone. "No twelve-hour shifts! No work taxes! We will not stitch for the Blond Ones!"

The Judenrat President pulled his lips back from his teeth. "Needle trade workers! There's only one way to survive. Our Ghetto must become the number one clothing center in Europe. We have to produce every uniform the Conqueror wears. There's no shirking in such a project. If you don't work, you don't eat. You die!" So saying, Chaim reached for the gigantic cauldron.

"But that's the soup," said Kleiderman, horror-stricken.

With a superhuman effort the Elder gripped the kettle, which was nearly as big as he was, and alone tipped its orangish contents onto the workroom floor. It took a few moments to pour out. The Jews stood there dazed, with hot, steaming shoes. Then Pipe, the finisher, fainted. Sheftelowitz stepped forward.

"Listen, Chaim. This is Pipe. He took part in the Russian Revolution of 1905. They want him to pay for a new needle. Of course now we won't have anything to eat?"

Trumpelman slapped him on his face. In many speeches he said, *Slackers and clock watchers will feel the weight of my hand.*

"This way, Comrades! Toward a new day!" Little Kipnis, walking backward, beckoned the Mosk mill workers to follow.

Sheftelowitz started forward, then stopped. "But what about Pipe?"

"Mister Pipe is on strike," said Edmund Trilling, a known Bundist, and he hoisted the unconscious man on his back.

"So am I!"

"I'm on strike, too!"

"Everyone out!" shouted Kleiderman, reversing the points of the toothpick in his mouth. "No chair tax!"

Five finishers, then ten, then the entire guild marched behind Kipnis, out the Mosk Mills door. A minute later the first buttonhole maker, Mister Marbled, walked out as well. One by one, then in groups, his fellows came after. Before the soup had dried, the last worker was gone. Trumpelman turned to Supervisor Luftgas. He said, "Lock all the doors."

From our town there are not many Jews still living. Maybe two hundred in all. Some of them say that the catastrophe of the Baluty Suburb began then, on the day that Luftgas burst a button. Others trace our misfortune further back, to the disruption of Trumpelman's wedding, or to the day when Trumpelman himself, with his two suitcases, stepped off the train at the Donati Station. Yet, once again, it is possible that everything would have happened just as it did, even if there hadn't been a terrible strike, and even if the Elder had never arrived. Ladies and gentlemen, you decide.

At first it seemed that the strike of the finishers and buttonhole makers would end as soon as it began. The Judenrat did not stand back and watch. At midnight the Elite Guard, with a detachment of chimney sweepers, broke into the rooms of the left-wing Bundists and searched everywhere. They were looking for—but they couldn't find—Lipsky. They arrested Edmund Trilling instead. Before dawn Trumpelman put out a new wall poster decree: every political party was banned. No more than five people could gather on the street, no more than ten unrelated Jews to be allowed in a single room. It was a brilliant stroke. Not only was the organized opposition suddenly shattered, but—more important— the soup kitchens these parties ran had to be closed. That meant you had to report to work in order to eat. That same morning, however, when the hungry pants workers and tailors—in other words the nonstrikers—arrived at the Mosk Works, they found that the gates were closed. Lockout.

It was an ugly scene. The cutters, the pressers, the cloakmakers shook the black bars. "Luftgas!" they cried. "Open up! We want to work!"

The supervisor, hardly visible in the darkness, walked back and forth behind the gates, eating sunflower seeds.

142

"Nothing doing! No more work until the ringleaders surrender. That includes Sheftelowitz and old man Pipe!"

The pressers, giant-armed people, turned on the intellectual finishers and on the small band of buttonhole makers. "Hand them over! They are taking bread from our mouths!"

"Just a minute! There's more!" In the dim light you could just see the white hulls on Luftgas' shoulders. "From now on all trimming-class workers must pay a ten-zloty deposit on silk spools. Too many valuable spools have been cracked or lost. That's ten zlotys for every spool. The next rule applies to everyone, even the knee pants experts and pressers. You will be charged for electrical power. Why should the Judenrat pay to make things easier for you? It's possible to use a hand press, if you want to, or a foot-pedal machine. Otherwise the tax is one zloty every two hours, six zlotys per day."

A wail went up from thousands of workers. "You want to kill us!" they cried. It was not clear whether they meant Luftgas or the finishers, those malcontents, who had brought this down on their heads. In any case it was toward the latter that the mob advanced. Nachman Kipnis attempted to head them off.

"Comrades! The events of last night have many positive aspects. First, Lipsky, our leader, was not captured. Second, the Jewish police did not take part in the search. A significant point!"

But the angry crowd, the cutters with shears in their hands, kept coming forward. Here was a classic case in which, instead of uniting to face a common enemy, Jew was fighting Jew. It was a short struggle. The finishers and buttonholers drew together about Mister Pipe, who had overnight become a popular figure. The big pressers simply knocked them out of the way. They seized Kipnis by the collar and pinned Kleiderman's arms. In less than a minute they had taken both Sheftelowitz and Pipe. No strike can be won in such conditions. It's the bosses you have to fight, not each other. The captured leaders were dragged to the locked met-

143

al gates. Luftgas stood behind them, his arms crossed on his chest. Surely the strikers had been defeated.

Then, from far off, came a faint droning sound.

"What's that?" asked some of the workers.

"*Shhhh,*" some others, listening, replied. It was the sound of a motorcar. Swiftly coming closer.

The sky was by then a little brighter. The sun was partly up and the moon, like a soap chip, was melting away. Thus everyone saw, while it was still a full block in the distance, the black Daimler Double Six. It roared toward the crowd of workers. There were strips of black paper across its yellow lights. Then, with its brakes screeching, it came to a halt.

From one rear door stepped Obergruppenführer Grundtripp. He was wearing a revolver on his belt. He went around the trembling auto and opened the other back door. The wife of the Jewish Elder slid off the seat. She was wearing a dark gown with dark gloves that came to her elbows. The Mosk mill workers nudged each other. They were trying to determine, through plumpness, or paleness, whether or not the Chairman of the Jewish Council had conceived an heir. But Madame Trumpelman stood straight and thin, her eyes narrow, her cheeks sucked in.

"She's not," sighed a presser, "in the family way."

Sheftelowitz plucked Pipe by the edge of his jacket. "Tell her," he said, "about the needle."

But other Jews had cried out to her first. "They want to charge a tax for cracked spools. But the spools are cracked before we get them!"

"Not fair!"

Chaffer, a buttonhole maker, actually dropped on his knees. "Mercy, lady! Your dear husband poured out the soup!"

At that instant, without any warning, a band of Jewish policemen came around Jakuba Corner. They wore their special blue hats, with the orange hatbands, and three-quarter-length coats. Each man carried a leather stick. They formed

144

a line between the workers and the luxury car. Then they forced the Jews back, against the factory wall. One worker, Marbled, cried over their heads, "We demand politeness and consideration!" But the rest stared at the Double Six, whose front doors now sprang open, too.

Out of the car came four Warriors in black. They marched back to the luggage compartment and opened its waxed, shining door. There was a sack of some sort wedged inside. Two of the Death's-Headers pulled it out. Then all four, with their rifles on their shoulders, dragged this load along the frozen ruts of the street—not in the direction of the Mosk Works, however, but toward the blank brick wall of the telephone exchange on the far side of Jakuba. When they got there they stood the sack up and untied the rope at the top. There was a living person inside.

"Klapholtz!" The Mosk mill workers strained to see over the heads of the Jewish policemen, who kept their own eyes pointing down.

It was the modernist painter. No doubt about it, though his face was swollen and blue. He stood for only a moment, and then he fell down. His knees pointed out in a way that was not possible for a person whose legs were not broken. A Death's-Header picked him up and pushed him against the bricks. But Klapholtz, like a rubber man, dropped down into another odd position. No matter what the Warriors did they could not get him to stand. His head dangled from his neck and his arms hung down without helping at all. It was frustrating work. At last Grundtripp, accompanied by the former Phelia Lubliver, strolled to the wall. His face had grown thinner, like a Ghettoite's. It was beginning to resemble the skull on his cap.

"Hold his legs," he ordered one of the men in black clothes. The officer did so. Propped up that way, Klapholtz stood swaying. The three Others unstrapped their weapons. Grundtripp and Madame Trumpelman moved off to one side. The Men of Valor pointed their rifles at Klapholtz, at

145

his heart it looked like, and his head. It was shocking how close they stood—only a meter away from their victim. If his arms had not been broken, the artist could have reached out and touched, practically, the barrels of the guns.

"Jew! Be still!" one of the squinting officers demanded.

But Klapholtz continued to sway, and his lips, though swollen, moved.

"Is he talking?" Grundtripp, the Obergruppenführer, wanted to know.

Sheftelowitz, from twenty meters away and in a trembling voice, responded. "He wants a cigarette. It's his right!"

The head of the Totenkopfers stared at the finisher as if he could not believe his ears. It was as if a dog, or a tree stump, had started speaking. Even Trumpelman's wife, so silent, so still, jerked her head.

Grundtripp dug in his pocket and took out his "Virginia" cigarettes. He put one into Klapholtz's mouth. The officer who had been holding his legs jumped up to light it. Yet, without support, and in spite of his shattered bones, the painter did not fall down. Instead, his back somehow grew straighter. His head lifted up. He even cocked it a bit, and took a puff. Then the whole street became very quiet. Not a person moved. Everybody had to wait until Klapholtz finished his cigarette. It hung on his lip, barely burning, in the French manner.

High above this scene, halfway up the Mosk Works chimney, Krystal and his assistant, Mann Lifshits, looked dizzily down. "Higher!" said Krystal, hauling himself upward by the rust-covered rungs. Near the top the boys stopped again. Young Lifshits—he was that year not even ten—hung by his strong left hand and passed the camera to Krystal with his right. The amazing thing was how far they could see. Kilometers and kilometers. Fields with hoarfrost shining. The silver strand of the river Dolna. Below were the rooftops of the city and streets in which Poles moved around. Throughout

146

the Balut the chimneys were steaming and smoking. How peaceful the Jews looked! How small!

The photographer, leaning perilously out from the smoke-stack, looked into his camera. Klapholtz came into focus. Either the smoke from his cigarette was, at that distance, not visible, or the stub on his lip had gone out. Two of the Death's-Headers crouched on a knee. The other two leaned over their shoulders. The four rifles fired at once. Krystal snapped his shutter, capturing this. The dead Jew fell down. Then Grundtripp, with his revolver, shot Klapholtz in the back part of his head. This also the two daring boys put on film, so it would last forever.

"Jews! Jewesses! On the morning of January 28, 1941, the saboteur Klapholtz was publicly executed at the telephone exchange wall. Beware, Chosen People! All those who violate the laws of the Occupying Power will be crushed the way lice are crushed. Do not make trouble but return now to your work. It is warm inside. There is soup. If you refuse, you will end up the same as this garbage. For him the shit wagon is coming. Spinners! Seamstresses! Watch out it does not come for you!" That was the speech that Grundtripp made. Then he, with the Ghetto Queen and the shooting squad members, got into the limousine, which at once drove away. The line of Jewish policemen likewise disappeared.

Instantly Luftgas swung open the mill gates. "Now we will forget what happened," he shouted. "Everybody who comes to work is forgiven!" But there was no surge toward the factory grounds. The pressers and cutters, along with the finishing and buttonhole sections, stood in place. They were watching the fecalist wagon which, with pails clanging, had turned that moment onto Jakuba Street.

The Bloomgarden children pushed the wagon to the spot where the shooting had taken place. Pipe took Klapholtz's heels and Sheftelowitz lifted his head up. They handed him to Zinta, Bloomgarden's wife, who pulled him atop the barrel. Then the driver removed his cap. It was not Bloomgarden, it was Hersh Einhorn. A leader of the underground forces! "Comrades! Look what they have done to him! They have murdered him!"

Meanwhile a second fecalist wagon drove up behind the first. The driver was young Julius Szypper. He stood on his seat. He was openly wearing his red star. "The members of the Fecalists' Guild wish to show solidarity with the plight of the spinning-mill workers. There will be no more movement of sewage!"

A bit of a cheer went up. The finishers were taking heart. But Luftgas made himself heard. "You're making a big mistake! Come back to work! Today there is kohlrabi leaf in the soup! And pea bread! It's illegal not to be at your spindles!"

No one paid any attention. Now a third wagon, with Jews pushing its metal-rimmed wheels, rolled up next to the others. The driver had a cap on, and his coat collar was pulled over his face. "Citizens of the Balut! Look at Klapholtz, shot full of bullets! How skillful he was! How expressive! He could have been a gold medal winner! But they broke his legs and his arms!" The fecalist removed his cap. A shock of hair stood up in back like a cardinal bird's. You could see the tips of his pointed ears. Lipsky the lawyer! The outlaw!

"Who did this thing? Mosk workers, have you got eyes? Wasn't the tyrant's wife right on the spot? What kind of government is this that shoots its own people? Jews are now killing Jews! They're collaborating with the Others! We repudiate the authority of the Judenrat! We are the tens and tens of thousands! We shall get weapons! We'll throw the dictator down!"

There was, for a hair's breadth, a split second, a pause. Then Marbled, all his life a buttonholer, ran forward, seized Bloomgarden's harness, and slipped the leather strap over his head. It was just what was needed. Pipe and Sheftelowitz and Kleiderman threw their shoulders against the spokes of the wheels. A roar went up. Hundreds of workers broke ranks and raced across the street. Even the shirtwaist girls were coming. They surrounded the excrement wagons and turned them around. Then they began to march behind them out of Jakuba Street. Their voices rang out: "Food! Fuel! A better life!" Their fists were in the air.

On Wesola Street passersby stopped and stared. The rickshaw drivers made their customers get out of the rickshaws, and they too fell in line. The caravan swept by the shed of the crystal sorters, and those workers, mostly old women, came outside and joined the throng. They tramped straight up the thoroughfare. There was not a soldier or policeman in sight. The ground shook. The buildings seemed to tremble. At Brzeszinska the comb-and-cork shop emptied out. Brush makers lined the sidewalk, waving strips of paper like flags. The demonstration grew and grew. What a spectacle it was. A procession of resolute Jews! They seemed to themselves to consist of an irresistible force. The world, which had been snatched from them, would be seized once again. What could they not do?

The broken body of Klapholtz, draped over the wooden staves of the leading wagon, rocked back and forth. His arms and legs and the head on his neck seemed full of energy. Someone ran up and attached a flower to his trousers. He was their martyr, their hero. Ladies and gentlemen, what other artist—not even Victor Hugo, not Michelangelo—has moved men so greatly, or filled them with the conviction that they could change the course of their lives?

So began the first day of the Five Day General Strike.

II

Strike Day One

Everything remained quite peaceful the rest of that morning. No raids by the Guardsmen. No Warriors called in. The

149

spinning-mill workers set out their pickets, and here and there in the Suburb you could hear clanking pails, rather like cow bells, as the fecalists drove to this shop and that one, urging the workers to strike. Then large wall posters were stuck right over the Judenrat's official announcements—FREE EDMUND TRILLING! REMEMBER KLAPHOLTZ! MARCH OF THE JEWISH WAR VETERANS!—and no one came to tear them down. Next the tanners voted to join the protest, the carpet workers did likewise, and the weak-current technicians, a crucial group, threatened to leave their stations if new Judenrat elections were not quickly held. It seemed likely the printers would follow. How rapidly the movement was spreading! A fight broke out between the Balut market porters and pickets from the Strike Committee. But the Jewish police only stood there, pretending not to notice. What did this lack of response mean? Had Trumpelman given up? The Ghetto waited to see.

The suspense ended late that same afternoon, when the hook and ladder and the red pumper drove out of the Smugowa Street station. For a moment—since there had been no report of a fire—people thought that the Jewish Fire Brigade had joined the General Strike. But the face of Faybush on one truck, of Wax and Pfeffer steering the other, did not respond to the cheers of the crowd along the road. The two machines went the whole length of Wrzesnienska and then turned down the Piwna Boundary Road. Finally they took up stations on Stefanska Street, in front of the food depot for the Ghetto. A detachment of sweepers was already there, stringing wire along the length of the warehouse. On the roof, with a rifle, was the Guardsman Szpilfogel. There were more Guardsmen at the windows and these men had rifles, too. Henceforth the policy of the Race of Masters—to wit, starvation—would be carried out by the Jews.

Strike Day Two

Obviously, whoever controlled the food supply in the Suburb would win the strike. It was a victory, then, when the

150

kosher butchers, and at least half the bakers, agreed to supply the pickets with fish sausage and bread. The Judenrat, however, had stored only enough food in the factories to feed those who still showed up to work. No fish, no flour, came into the other shops. At noon on the second day the brush makers, so full of enthusiasm during the funeral procession, cheering and waving streamers, showed up at their factory benches. Why? Because on their half-kilo loaves there was a choice of two jams. An hour later a fistfight occurred between the striking and nonstriking carpenters, some of whom broke into their own locked shops. The picketers hardly had strength to hold up their own banners and signs.

The only thing to do, and it had to be done quickly, was break the Judenrat blockade of the Stefanska Street warehouse. Now in the winter of 1940–41 there was in that building, besides the usual flour and tinned goods, one item of special importance. Long before Luftgas burst a button—that is, before the spinning-mill movement began—a deal had been made by which the Judenrat, in exchange for a hundred thousand uniforms, would receive from the Blond Ones the entire butterfish catch of the distant river Bug. This had arrived in December, turning the entire depot into a gigantic icehouse. It was possible to see the little fish, twisted and openmouthed, inside the hundreds of milky-white blocks.

It was these fish that the strikers were determined to snatch from the depot. The first confrontation occurred at three o'clock on the afternoon of Strike Day Two. The hungry workers marched down Stefanska, until they came to the wire strung across the road. From that spot the finishers, Kleiderman and others, hurled bricks and stones toward the warehouse. All fell laughably short. Then somebody found a hole in the wire and the strikers, some with clubs, some with heavy spindles, came pouring through.

To the amazement of the advancing workers, the warehouse doors, which had been firmly bolted, swung open wide. What a cheer went up from the spinners then! The Poles must have heard it on their side of the walls. But the next moment the bright red pumper roared from the depot, Bloygrund the hoseman, Faybush at the wheel. It bore down on the column of strikers, some of whom turned and ran back toward the wire. Bloygrund swung the water cannon toward those who stood their ground. It was this device, capable of sending geysers to the tops of buildings, that had made such a stir at the Grodno fair. A spray of water came from it now, scattering the Jews, tumbling them, breaking their ranks. A band of protesters sat down. They linked their wet arms. Then Bloygrund twisted the nozzle, making a hard flat blast, with no arc at all. Kleiderman's hair, normally curly, streamed straight from his head. A shoe of Chaffer's came off. Then they, with their comrades, went rolling and skidding away.

But the progressive forces were not defeated. Two fecalist wagons, their buckets clanging, turned the corner of the Piwna Boundary Road onto Stefanska. With the strikers regrouped behind them, they rolled right over the sharpened wire. The water from the water cannon splattered harmlessly against their cylindrical flanks. "Onward!" cried the advancing spinners as, crouching, trotting, they drew near their prize.

Just then the Elite Guardsmen appeared on the rooftop, and in the windowframes, too. The fecalist wagons ground to a halt. The Jews trembled behind them. The guards pointed their rifles upward, like hunters aiming at geese. At the sound of the shots the strikers dashed backward, running with their hands before them. Little puffs of smoke rose from the rifles, which from the safety of the coils of wire looked as harmless as sticks.

The sun hung on the edge of the sky, like a shiny spot on a pair of trousers. Then it fell below the horizon and the night grew black. The workers shivered, from habit, expecting the air to get colder. But, a blessing, a little southern breeze sprang up, and the temperature held steady, and even rose. Wet, hungry, discouraged, the men built fires, boiled

152

kettles of ersatz coffee, kettles of caraway-flavored soup. No one sang. No one told jokes. Everyone knew that the battle was lost. Meanwhile the temperature, instead of dipping, continued to climb.

Strike Day Two: Night.

Everyone in the headquarters of the Strike Committee was in a fever of excitement. It seemed to them that the eyes of the world were fixed on the struggle in Stefanska Street. What was the outcome of the battle? Had the blockade been broken or not? Old Pipe, in a pullover, had actually broken into a sweat.

"Have I a fever?" he asked.

"No, no," Sheftelowitz responded. "I'm sweating, too."

Only then did the members of the Committee realize how warm their little room, an airless cellar, had become. Everyone removed his winter coat, his woolen sweater. But the tension was as great as ever.

"Hello? Hello? Is this Bialystok? Comrades, come in!" Nachman Kipnis had earphones on and was turning the handle of a transmitter. It flashed and sparked.

Said Szypper, "Try Baranovichi! Try Siemiatycze!"

But neither Baranovichi nor Siemiatycze, nor any other town in which the Red Army was quartered, answered the call. There was, however, a loud knock at the door.

The finishers went pale. They trembled. One of the watchmen, a big, broken-nosed presser, put his head in the doorway. "Someone to see you," he said.

Then Kleiderman entered, and stood in a puddle.

"Woe!" Sheftelowitz sighed, seeing his drenched co-worker. For Kleiderman, with his hair undone, with dripping sleeves, with little spouts coming out of his shoes, was the image of defeat.

"They shot their guns," he said.

The wife of Edmund Trilling, Madame Trilling, did not succeed in stifling a sob. "We're going to starve."

153

"It's true," Mister Marx added. "Our picketers are dropping from line. They can't hold out one day longer."

Mister Pipe said, "But what about our smugglers? Can't they bring in more food?"

"No, no, my dear friend," Sheftelowitz answered. "The High and Mighty are all around the Ghetto. As soon as a child goes out, they grab him."

"Can this be?" asked a number of people.

The presser, who had been listening in, burst out like this: "Do you know what I ate yesterday? The top half of a shoe! Ha! Ha!"

It was the same as with the change in the weather: in all the excitement the band of Jews had not noticed how hungry they actually were. Now they groaned from the pangs.

Kleiderman wrung out his hat. He produced a toothpick that all this time had been in his mouth. "Brothers, this is what I saw after the battle. On my way to this cellar. It's why I'm so late. On Jelsky Street a group of Jewish policemen had placed a rope around a woman's neck and were pulling her down the steps of Number 29. They would not touch her. They used the rope instead. What was the matter? Did she have some kind of catching disease? I came close to see. The woman's hair was not combed. Her face was dirty. Above her people were leaning out of the windows. *She's a cannibal!* That's what they shouted. Oh, Jews! She had eaten the buttocks from her own dead son!"

"Poor woman," said Mister Kemp.

"A pity," Marx responded.

Hersh Einhorn snatched the earphones from his fellow orphan. Frantically he spun the transmitter dial. "Hello? Is this Pinsk? Reply, please, Comrades! Is this Grodno speaking? Help us!"

Without warning a stranger came in, walked right pass the watchman, and took off his hat and his glasses and, to everyone's amazement, his mustache and nose. It was Lipsky, their leader, in a disguise. The Strike Committee crowded around

154

him, teary-eyed, and at their wits' end. The little fellow took out the pistol he owned. "They're shooting? That's easy! We shoot back. We attack the warehouse with guns!"

"That means revolution! It's the revolution!" Nachman Kipnis, his thick lenses full of the lamplight, raised a finger to the ceiling. "Friends, this is what Rosa Luxemburg said: *From the whirlwind and the storm, out of the fire and glow of the mass strike and the street fighting, rise again, like Venus from the foam, fresh, young, powerful, buoyant trade unions.*"

Julius Szypper stood on a chair. "This is a great moment for the Balut. *The mass strike is inseparable from the revolution.* Comrade Luxemburg said those words, too!"

It was Hersh Einhorn's turn. "Remember this, Comrades. We are not fighting simply for the Jews of the Ghetto, but for the proletariat in every land. First we must contact the Polish workers. The left-labor parties. They will carry our strike to the Aryan section. Thus it will spread—from the Balut, to the city, throughout the General Government, from nation to nation. The hour of the working class is at hand!"

"What we do is of world historical importance!"

"Our struggle is the Götterdämmerung of capitalism! We are doing it! We simple Jews!"

Lipsky called for silence again. One of his eyebrows was thick and bushy; the other one, the narrow one, was his own. "First things first," he said. "We need guns. We have to seize them from the Tsarnecka Street jail. At the same time we'll free the prisoners there. It's a dangerous job, brothers. Is anyone willing?"

Madame Trilling stepped forward first. "I'm coming! They are holding my husband there."

The three orphans were next. "We too!" they cried.

"We are the forward scouts of the glorious Red Army!" Hersh Einhorn declared.

Marx, Kemp, Kleiderman linked arms with each other. "We're ready!" they shouted.

In no time, everyone volunteered. All together they rushed

out of the cellar and opened the narrow trapdoor to the street. They were met by a hot, bitter wind. Not only that: three no-neckers—Turski, Nodelman, Officer Pravenishkis—were stationed there, flanking the Chief of Police. Each had a gun.

"Rievesaltes!" cried Hersh Einhorn.

A spinner shouted, "Betrayed!"

But Lipsky kept his head. He pushed his way forward to where the two groups confronted each other. "Minister Rievesaltes! On behalf of the workers' movement, I inform you that the Tsarnecka Street jail no longer exists. From now on Jews will not arrest Jews! No exceptions! Anyone who violates this order will be dealt with by our armed units. There is only one enemy: the Occupying Power, along with its collaborators on the Judenrat. We'll take care of them, too. I order you to hand over your weapons to the officers of the Strike Committee!"

Behind the lawyer's back somebody shouted, "Free the prisoners!"

Nachman Kipnis cried loudest of all. "Attack the depot! Distribute the wealth of the Ghetto according to need!"

Then the workers demanded, "Free food! Free food for all!"

It was, of course, a wild, daring maneuver—as if the strikers, not the policemen, were the ones with the guns. Yet Rievesaltes was smiling. His voice was soft when he spoke.

"Yes, yes, we know what your plans are. That's why we came here. To bring you what you need." With that he waved his arm and the policemen stepped away from the entrance to the cellar. A whole crowd—smugglers, wood burners, thieves—was standing by the roadway. There was even the famous "broadcasting station"—that is, two Jews, one of whom tuned in the foreign newscasts, after which the other stood on a corner and for three zlotys a person read the bulletins out. And there, with the others, was Edmund Trilling, the Bundist. In short, it was the whole jail population.

156

As if that were not astounding enough, the Security Minister next handed his gun to the hatless Lipsky, and ordered his men to do the same.

The strikers instinctively shrank back. "It's a trick!" somebody shouted.

But the Police Chief was completely unruffled. "We don't have to fight each other," he announced. "You want to get the food out of the warehouse and so, as a matter of fact, do I. It follows we can make an agreement."

"The revolution doesn't bargain with class enemies," Kipnis shot back.

"Or with Judenrat members," Szypper added.

But Lipsky put up his hand. "What do you mean, an agreement?"

"Advocate Lipsky, you want to get into the warehouse but can't because of Bloygrund, my close relation, and the rest of the Smugowa Street Brigade. Also, there is the Elite Guard with its guns. I, too, want to get into the warehouse, but the strikers, your comrades, are camped all around it. What could be simpler? I'll talk to the firefighters and you talk to the spinners. That way we can all get the food together and not a drop of Jewish blood hits the ground. That's my proposal. We can clean the whole depot out!"

"What's in it for you?" Edmund Trilling, still standing with the group of freed prisoners, wanted to know.

Rievesaltes grinned. "One thousand ice blocks, one hundred fish in each ice block, at ten zlotys a butterfish is, to answer your question, one million zlotys."

Nachman Kipnis was horrified. "It's economic speculation!"

"True. But what do you want? To feed the Ghetto or not? If we agree, no one is hurt, everyone gets a meal. Your way people will be shot. How much is the life of a Jew worth? Ten zlotys for a butterfish is these days an excellent price. If a Jew can't afford it, he'll get a loan from Rievesaltes Associates! At good interest! Ha! Ha! The Ghetto will bless the Police Chief's name!"

The raiders were thrown into confusion by this clever plan. For no reason Szypper turned his cap backward. "It's wrong," he said. "But I can't say exactly why."

Pipe kept throwing his hands up. "What can we do? But what can we do?"

Even Lipsky hesitated. "And if the Elite Guard starts shooting?" he asked.

Rievesaltes: "Here are the guns to shoot back. The old man controls the Guardsmen, but I am boss of the Jewish Police."

At that moment, when the whole venture seemed to hang in the balance, one of the prisoners stepped into the light that came from the open cellar door. The sight of her made the boys pale. They shook. They moaned. This was the cannibal woman, the one who had been accused of eating parts of her son. Her hair flew like a person touching an electrical wire. In her open mouth you could see her tongue. She walked up to Rievesaltes. "The prisoners of the Balut agree to your plan," she told him. "We shall march to Stefanska together!"

"We agree! Yes, we agree!" the other prisoners shouted.

Above the din, Edmund Trilling made himself heard. "The Bund also accepts the Rievesaltes proposal!"

Then the prisoners and their former jailers started off down the deserted road. The Strike Committee, for all their doubts, their misgivings, followed along, into the dawn of that steaming day.

Strike Day Three

The hot wind was blowing, stronger than ever. The sky in the morning was half yellow, half blue, like a gigantic armband. Overnight, in places like the Marysin district, little blades of grass had sprung from the ground. On the other side of the walls and fences, where Jews weren't allowed, it was like summer. In front of the Hotel Europa gay umbrellas, green ones and red ones, had been stretched on their

158

frames. Poles sat beneath them with ices. It was as if all nature had been turned upside down. No one in the Baluty Suburb could remember anything like it.

"It's because of sunspots," said Zygmunt, the professor. But others said they heard of a new, terrible weapon, so powerful it could blow up a mountain, and that each time it exploded it caused such a wind. The opinion of the Pshiskher's Descendant was that the Master of the Universe had created the phenomenon on behalf of the workers, so that throughout the strike they would be warm. "No, no," argued Wolf-Kitzes. "He who judges will smite the Blond Beast with the plague of fire. *And the Lord brought an east wind upon the land all that day, and all that night.*" But Trunk, of the Devout Butchers, merely smiled. "Isn't it nice?" he asked. "Isn't it balmy? This is what our life will be in Madagascar."

In the heat of this day marched the newly armed Jews. Up the whole of Wrzesnienska they went, sloshing through the fresh mud. When they reached the bottom of the Piwna Boundary Road, where there weren't so many houses, the sewage smell from the melting excrement buckets stopped— rather, it was covered over by a different odor, a real stench, from no one knew what. The farther they went, the worse this stink became. Then the orphans, out in front, noticed fresh water running down both sides of the road.

"The pumper!" Kleiderman shouted. "The battle has already begun!"

The whole crowd ran forward. But now Jews, with rags to their faces, were going the opposite way. The boys rounded the corner. "There's the warehouse!" one of them cried. The front ranks slowed. The rest crowded behind them. They all stopped and stared.

All of Stefanska had been turned into a lake. The strikers were knee-deep in water. Some of them were lying in it, rolling around. The fire brigade had retreated to the top of the hook and ladder. As for the Guardsmen, they were all on the roof, on the edge of it, with their legs hanging down. Beneath them, from every window of the Stefanska Street depot, water was gushing and streaming. It came in a flood through the open front doors. It even trickled between the seams of the bricks. And where the waterfalls landed, at the spot where the geysers struck, a great silver mound was building higher and higher. In the sunshine it gleamed, dazzlingly, blindingly, like a hill of coins. It was tens of thousands of thawed butterfish.

One man sloshed forward to the band of raiders. He had a handkerchief over his nose. "Rotten! All rotten!" he cried. His mask fell aside. It was Marbled, of the Buttonhole Makers' Guild. He swept his arm back toward the glittering pile. "The Jews who ate it are poisoned!"

Rievesaltes sighed. "A million zlotys."

"This," said Lipsky, "was one of Trumpelman's bargains."

A moan came up from the stricken men, upon whom the sun unrelentingly glared.

The Mosk Works presser folded his giant arms. "It's the winter staple, you know. The whole February allotment. Ha! Ha! We're going to starve!"

Ladies and gentlemen, for the government of the Ghetto, and for its plain citizens, too, this was a crisis. First of all, what to do with the fish? The smell had already reached the neighboring villages, and in the Aryan section people complained that the fumes were making them ill. The bald Polish mayor drove to the Chancellory at Dworska 20. He took off his shoe to pound on the Chairman's door. Madame Trumpelman, not the Elder, came out. She was wearing a black hat over her black bangs, and there were little dark dots on her veil. This is what she said—and to an elected Polish official:

"Put your shoe on! Don't be a fool!"

And it was this same Phelia Trumpelman who, beginning with the morning of Strike Day Three, did the most to restore some kind of order. Her first step was to send the fumigation squads to Stefanska, to spray the thousands of fish.

160

The mound was by then surrounded by visible vapors. It seemed to float off the ground. The fumigation experts raced forward, squirted a little, and then staggered back. Not effective. Then the Ghetto Queen, watching from behind her spotted veil, ordered every member of the Gravediggers' Guild to be placed under special arrest. The Elite Guard rounded them up and set them to digging an enormous trench down the length of the street. The men worked in shifts through the rest of the day and into the night. When they looked over the lip of this grave they saw that, in the darkness, in the midst of the blackout, the fish, like phosphorus, had started to glow.

Strike Day Four

And what a day it was! If you were not there, if you did not see the suffering, the chaos, how can you understand? Actually, thanks to Madame Trumpelman's efforts, it didn't begin so badly. That woman seemed to be everywhere at the same time. First she sent a group of chimney sweepers, with their long-handled brooms, to commandeer the excrement wagons. These sweepers rode on top of the tanks and, as in normal times, poured the buckets in. Later that morning, when the weak-current workers voted to join the action, it was Madame Trumpelman, with a detachment of porters, who forced them to stand by their switches. Her most dangerous foe was the panic everyone felt about food. Bread riots broke out. Bands of desperate people smashed the windows of shops and raided the homes of the wealthier Jews. They stood up to the Jewish policemen and snatched the leather rods from their hands. But at the sight of the Ghetto Queen, tall, thin, with hollowed cheeks—even those crowds melted away. By noon, for an hour or so, a feeling of calm had been established. Could it be, the Ghettoites thought, that the worst has already been done?

The worst is never done. In spite of Madame Trumpelman's efforts, the situation became chaotic again. First, it was discovered that the fecalists had sabotaged their own wagons by drilling dozens of holes. So there were trails of raw sewage in half the streets. The hunger-looters did not reappear, but they soon joined forces with the Bolsheviks, under the influence of Lipsky. You could tell by the posters that were plastered everywhere on the walls. DAWN TOMORROW! MARCH OF THE JEWISH WAR VETERANS! MARCH TO TSARSKOYE SELO! Madame Trumpelman had them torn down; but new ones, worse ones, always appeared. DOWN WITH THE DICTATORSHIP! FOOD FOR ALL! One such poster proclaimed, in plain Yiddish, not Polish: *A Toit Zu Trumpelman,* DEATH TO TRUMPELMAN! It was, as Luxemburg had predicted, a revolution.

Still worse. Much worse. The final straw: there was another new smell in the Ghetto. The gravediggers were at work on a hole for the fish; so no one dug a grave for the Jews. They didn't stop dying, either. On the contrary, they piled up in the streets, swelling with gases to over life size. Beer yeast is what they smelled like. Muszkat, with his hearse, could hardly make a dent in such numbers of corpses. Besides, he had only one horse now, instead of two. It was difficult to believe this was the same dark steed that had carried Fiebig to his grave. Its skin hung on its bones like clothes on a hanger, and all of its muscles were twitching, as if to shake off invisible flies.

"Come! Onward! You darling!" Muszkat cried. He cracked his whip. He wrinkled his narrow brow. But the bigger the load became, the more the horse labored, until, with the rear door of the wagon jammed full of bare ankles, it simply halted. Muszkat jumped from the box. With his fist he hit the top part of the animal's head. "Forward, my beauty! My sweet one! *Bow-wow! Bow-wow!*" In response to this the animal gathered all four of its legs together, as if it were perched on the top of a barrel, and fell on its side. The liveryman stared. It was his own death he was seeing. "Help, Jews! You have to save her!" he called; then he ran off waving his arms.

How long was the hearse driver gone? Five minutes? Ten?

At the Marysinska Corner he stopped and turned around. "What if she's only fainted?" he said. But by the time he returned there was no horse in the harness, only a horse's bones. Even the head and the tail were missing. Even the hooves. It is not so important to know who, precisely, stripped the creature clean. Boys perhaps. Hungry people. With the tail of a horse you can make useful things. What mattered was that now there was no one to move the dead Jews. They just lay there. And all day long, the whole fourth day of the strike, an awful day really, the sun kept getting hotter. It sat over our heads like the blade of a sawmill, shining, gleaming, spinning around.

Strike Day Four, Evening

Where, in this confusion, this misery, was I. C. Trumpelman? For the whole of the strike he had not been seen. Rumors flew about, saying he was no longer in the Balut. Where, then? That depended on which Jew you asked. *On a battleship with Roosevelt,* said one man. Said another, *Everyone knows he is telling the Pope about the sufferings of the Jews.* And a third: *Not the Pope. Our President goes right to the top. To Horowitz himself!*

But the truth was, Trumpelman had not left the Ghetto. He was, on the evening of Strike Day Four, just where he should be: in the dining room of Tsarskoye Selo, having his meal. First Lipiczany would take a bite of chop and then, when he did not die, the old man was supposed to eat the rest. It was the same with the wine, with the potatoes. The boy tasted and tasted, but the Elder did not swallow a morsel or sip a drop.

The following were also present: Nomberg, Minister of Religious Affairs; F. X. Wohltat, representing the Civilian Authority; and Hasensprung, the President's bodyguard. Not present: Madame Trumpelman, whose chair was empty. The guests were discussing the March of the Jewish War Veterans, which was less than twelve hours away.

Nomberg: "Don't make a mistake. These are revolutionaries. Trained Bolsheviks. They don't recognize the legal order. The decrees of the Judenrat don't interest them. What are we going to do?"

Wohltat was sitting with his coat unbuttoned and his pants cuffs hiked well up from his shoes. "If the march is not crushed, if the strike is not quickly ended, everything will be lost. Our investments. Our profits. A fortune in reichsmarks."

Hasensprung, a little tipsily, waved his hand. "We have reinforced the estate walls. We are digging trenches. Nothing to worry about."

"These are starving people!" Nomberg was becoming excited. "Thousands of people. They know we have food here! A trench won't stop them! Sandbags won't stop them! We must request Grundtripp to bring in the army!"

"Yesterday I was shown a letter. It was from Warsaw, from Czerniakow, the Elder of the Warsaw Jews." Wohltat's skin was pale and glistening, like a sliced pear. "In this letter he says his Jews will make uniforms cheaper than ours. With no strikes and no buttons missing. That is why we must crush this demonstration!"

"I am a religious man, a rabbi. Everybody knows the reputation of the Italianate Synagogue. But we are facing atheists now! Therefore we need automatic guns, a half dozen of them, all along the wall! What is the point of killing one or two out of such a mob? It gives them martyrs! Another excuse to hold a parade. No! We have to have continuous shooting, a regular crossfire. That will cut them down!"

Hasensprung pulled the cork from a bottle. "It's an idea," he said.

"I am the best friend of the Hebrews," said Wohltat, "and I admit freely the Hebrews are like friends to me. It's a symbiosis. I am a Chinaman, yes, a Chinaman, and the Jews are the silkworms I keep in a box. As long as they spin silk, I supply them with mulberry leaves. But if the spinning should stop, when there's no more thread—then off you go to the east."

164

Lipiczany, who had not spoken, now jumped to his feet. "Chaim! Chaim! They want to use guns on the Jewish people! They want to call the Death's-Headers in! Stop them! Don't let them! You have to meet the marchers! Tomorrow you'll make a beautiful speech!"

The Judenrat President did not respond to the boy, any more than he had to the others. He sat hunched up, his cape around him, staring out the window. "It's getting bigger, bigger," he murmured. "It will burn through the night." He was watching the sun.

Lipiczany swooped some air into his lungs. He wrapped a fictional cloak around his body. He gave the speech he thought the Elder would give. "Jews! This is Trumpelman speaking. Go home! Go home! The strike is over! No cut in wages! No new taxes! The Elder promises meat for your soup! He loves you! He protects you! The way a father protects his children! Go home! Trumpelman has heard the voice of an angel! The angel said, *Chaim, you will lead your people from bondage!* The angel said, *Together you shall arrive in a new, promised land!*" The boy's pinched face, the squinting eyes, were shining. His heart must have been terrifically beating, because his whole body shook.

Just then, outside the window, like a glowing horseshoe that is plunged into a bucket of water, the hot red sun went out. Immediately a coolish breeze—the first in days—swept over the table, lifting the corners of napkins. Trumpelman seemed to wake from a trance. He turned his head.

"This Czerniakow. The engineer. Has he got any sons?"

Nobody answered. In the silence you could hear the chop-chop-chop of the Guardsmen cutting wood. They were preparing to defend the Tsarskoye Selo wall.

The Elder put on his hat. He wrapped a muffler around his throat. Then he questioned his guests again. "Who can tell me? Where in the town is Miss Lubliver? Where should I go to find her?" But he did not wait for a reply. Wrapped in his scarf, Trumpelman went out the door.

* * *

165

It was already cooler than in the daytime, and the Baluters lay on their doorsteps to catch the stray puffs of air. Against the smell they wore handkerchiefs, like in the influenza year of 1918. Trumpelman, passing them, saw only the top halves of their faces, their foreheads, their eyes. Whether because the curfew was coming, or because they recognized the Elder, the people drew away. In a short while the live Jews had all disappeared and only the dead ones remained. These corpses, pale, puffed up, looked like sea mammals that together had run aground.

Then Trumpelman heard somebody scream. The sound came from a narrow alley, off Nowozgierska Street. Of course there was nothing unusual about a scream in the Ghetto. They were as common as, in the old days, motorcar horns. What made Chaim freeze, then? It was a woman's voice. It rang out once more, urgent, piercing, full of pain. This time another noise followed, a deep sound that the Elder had heard somewhere before. He took a few steps down the alley; by putting his arms out he could touch either wall. After a moment, from nearby, the woman cried out, an awful shriek; again the moan came after, a low sound, like a blast to warn ships of fog. Why was it familiar? Where had he heard it in the past?

Trumpelman came to a door. Locked. He put his shoulder easily through. Inside there was a large abandoned stable, with stalls and carts and cartwheels everywhere. Off to one side there was a stairway, blocked by barrels of different sorts. What a lot of valuable firewood! Then the cry, *eeeee*, and the response, *ooooo*, sounded again, directly over the Elder's head. He sprang forward, knocking the barrels aside. He strode up the steps two and three at a time. At the top there was only a landing with no exitway. Then he saw, on the floor, a trail of dim yellow light. A disguised doorway, then! It swung open to his touch on hidden hinges.

The bright light in the room blinded him for a moment. Then he saw, on a table, on her back, a naked woman. Her

166

legs were held up by straps attached to the ceiling, and her arms were tied down by her side. Two people, with masks on, wearing robes, bent near her, where her sexual parts were plainly exposed.

"A torture chamber!" the enraged Elder exclaimed.

The two persons whirled around. "Chaim!" one of them cried, and removed her linen mask.

Trumpelman was stupefied. "Is that you? Miss Bibelnieks?" So it turned out to be. Her companion likewise lowered his disguise.

"Doctor Zam!"

But before the ex-Warsaw dandy could say a word the woman on the table emitted the worst scream of all, and a small, dark, greasy head appeared out of nowhere between her thighs. Then the whole room shook from the deep answering call.

Trumpelman half turned and strode to where a curtain was strung. With a single movement of his arm he swept it aside. There, with dried grass in her mouth, and the map of the Mediterranean on her side, was the cow from the summer palace.

The Judenrat Chairman did not know what to think. "My Holstein," he finally stammered.

"Moo!" the animal responded, as if she actually remembered who he was.

"The mothers don't have enough milk," Miss Bibelnieks explained. "It's because of their deficient diet."

But the Elder was beginning to recover. "Mothers? What mothers? Everybody has enough to eat!"

Just then young Zam interrupted. "Madame Gumbiner! Look here! It's a boy!" He held the fresh Jew upside down by the ankles and gave him a slap. This caused him to open his mouth, and then to cry.

Trumpelman was beside himself. "Quiet! Quiet! This is strictly illegal! It can't be allowed!"

The infant, perhaps because he was still upside down, continued wailing; then, from behind a false wall, a second baby joined in. Immediately a third, and then a fourth one, took up the cry. There was nothing for Miss Bibelnieks to do but slide back the movable wall. Thus was revealed for the first time the Ghetto's secret maternity ward.

A corridor ran down the length of the building, and on both sides there were cots and cribs, full of new children. Some had their mothers with them. Most were alone. But every last one of them, because of the light, because of the excitement, was kicking, waving, and howling with all his might.

"It's a factory!" cried Trumpelman.

"The sound of life! Of life!" Zam shouted. "When the history of the Baluty Suburb is written, our ward will be its brightest chapter!" The doctor was ecstatic. His eyebrows were lifted. Heaven knows what had happened to his sporty car. "Think of it! Someday these infants will grow into strong men and women. They will be scholars and lawyers and financiers. Perhaps they will never know they were born in a stable, in a building without plumbing of any kind. And I, I too, have been reborn! I am a new man! A different kind of person!"

But the leader of the Jews was yelling louder than Zam was. "Make them be quiet! I can have you put in jail! *Shhh! Shhh!* They will hear in the street! Hopeless! It's hopeless! There must be two dozen at least!" The Elder had apparently lost his self-control. He began to run up the aisle between the screaming children. "You are under arrest!" he shouted at one of them. To another, whose body was scarlet, who had shining gums, he said, "Twenty-four hours to get out! The Judenrat is closing the building!" Then in a mad way he began to rattle the crib slats.

"Mister Chairman! Our President! Help me, Messiah!" It was the naked mother, whose frantic eyes were fixed on her newborn child.

Somehow Trumpelman heard her. He came back up the aisle. Before anyone could do or say anything, he plucked the infant from Zam's hands and turned him right way

168

round. At once the dimpled fellow stopped crying. His whole head was covered with wet, wavy hair. There was even a little fur on his back. Then, amazingly, he gripped Trumpelman's hat brim and fiercely, reflexively, hung on. It was a terrible moment. The Elder was scowling. Even the pink and creamy infants fell silent, waiting to see what the man would do.

"Gumbiner, listen," said Trumpelman to the husky boy. "I have a horse. A stallion. You will ride him! Above the crowd."

Miss Bibelnieks sighed. "Have I lost my mind? I can't help hearing music."

"It is music," the obstetrician replied.

So it was. From far away, over oceans it seemed, an Italian tenor was singing his heart out. A whole orchestra—violins, woodwinds, a trumpet, everything—struck up, and then a woman came in, singing mostly vowels.

Trumpelman, holding the boy in his arms, cocked his head to listen.

Zam, with his Warsaw background, whispered, "*Aida*."

The Elder found his wife on the way back to the mansion. He had only to follow the sounds of the opera, which never ceased, which kept repeating themselves: the Italian man, the orchestra, the Italian woman—then all three elements playing at once. There was Phelia, standing with the sole of one foot against a wall. An elbow was cupped in one hand; the other held a cigarette. Her veil was up and in the starlight, and light from the sliver of moon, she looked silver-plated. Trumpelman swayed; he caught his breath to see her. His heart beat like a boy's. A faint curling smoke stream came from her lips and her nose.

> *Vieni meco—insiem fuggiamo*
> *Questa terra di dolor—*
> *Vieni meco—io t'amo, io t'amo!*
> *A noi duce fia l'amor.*

* * *

169

The song, with its senseless words, gibberish really, came to an end.

"Again," said the Ghetto Queen.

The Elder shifted his gaze. A few meters off there was a two-wheeled cart and on it an old gramophone player, the kind where the music comes from a horn. Smolenskin, a well-known figure, with a two-pointed beard, picked up the mechanical arm and put it down at the start of the recording. "It's wearing out, lady. I have to do this for a living."

"I'll pay. I'll give you a monopoly for the Ghetto. All other instruments must be turned in."

So Smolenskin turned the handle in a clockwise direction. *Let us together flee this painful earth,* sang the Italian tenor. Miss Lubliver, like a statuette, in silver, silently listened.

Trumpelman, barely breathing, remained in the shadows. What was the famous opera about? He hardly knew. Ethiopians. Elephants. Something about the river Nile. Was Madagascar, he wondered, such a land? Would Jews sing songs there to each other? About *l'amor?* Then he shivered. The temperature had dropped all the way down to what was normal for that time of year. Smolenskin, turning and turning the handle, audibly panted. Above them, with its chin practically touching its forehead, was the profile of the old Polish moon.

Strike Day Five, Dawn

The March of the Jewish War Veterans was beginning. The earth temperature, because of so much recent sunshine, was high, but the air was only five on the Celsius scale. The result was one layer of mist on top of another. The defenders of Tsarskoye Selo could hear the crowds coming—the tramp of their feet, the crackle of ice on the road—but they could not see a soul. The King and Queen of the Ghetto, the one in his cape, the other in furs, peered from the top of the reinforced wall. Mist only, white and gray. Szpilfogel squinted, and so did Elite Guardsman Bass. Nothing, just the fog,

170

sprawled like some great bear over the ground. Nomberg's teeth were clicking together. Hasensprung felt particles of ice form in his nose. Behind the defenders, on the top floor of the mansion, Flicker, Hobnover, Atlas, the curly-blond Citron—all the New Hatters' Asylum orphans pressed their flushed faces to the window glass.

Nisel Lipiczany sat on the edge of the wall, cupping his hands to hold his head. His legs dangled over the side. The whiteness of the mist hurt his eyes. He raised them to the clear air and saw, moving above the lumpy clouds, a red flag on a pole. He touched Trumpelman's boot.

"Yes," said Chaim, calmly. "The Elder has seen it."

Nomberg saw the flag, too. "It's a Bolshevik banner!" he shouted, and began to hop from log to log, moving toward the gate in the middle of the wall. "Fire!" he screamed. "Fire!"

Grundtripp, in his silver and black uniform, stood over a Death's-Header quartet. There were two of his men for each of the Gatling guns, a shooter and a holder for the belt full of shells. It was one of the marksmen who spoke. "Herr Obergruppenführer! The flag is ours!"

Everyone stared as hard as he could. The icy wind whipped the banner out. There was a black iron cross on a field of red: the flag of the Kaiser in the Great War past. Another flagstaff came into view, this one with a banner consisting of geometrical figures and stripes. "The battalion of Montenegro!" Hasensprung, himself a veteran, declared. A third flag, and a fourth, and then a whole series of pennants appeared above the mist. They stretched all the way back to the Suburb center. In what armies had the Baluters not fought? There, higher than all the others, came the black Austro-Hungarian eagle, spread on a field of white and red. The Rumkowsky Regiment! Poland's own! The bird had its talons out. With its double head it looked in two directions. Even Nomberg was moved.

Wohltat, excited, flapped his arms. "Look! Ha! Ha! The

171

bugs are spilling out of the mattress!" What he meant was that, about two hundred meters off, the Jews were coming from the bank of fog. Some had their Imperial uniforms on, and here and there was a helmet with a spike. More Jews materialized. They kept marching forward. A thousand, two thousand. Not speaking. Not singing. But silently moving toward the sandbagged wall.

"Those are not veterans!" Rabbi Nomberg had noticed the strikers, the militant finishers, the comb-and-cork workers, who were mixed into the line of march. Pipe was there, and Kleiderman, and the Bloomgarden family, arm in arm. Kemp, Chaffer, Trilling, and Marx became visible, too. It seemed that the whole Ghetto was hidden there in the fog.

Bass and Szpilfogel picked up their long-distance rifles. They held their fire, though. The only thing you could hear was the swish of the sleeves of the marchers' coats. Then both Guardsmen shot a bullet well over the heads of the crowd. They fired a second time, also into the air. The front of the column, the Rickshaw Guild members, halted, just thirty meters away. The Baluters bumped into each other. Confusion. Some people started backward. Then the cannibal woman stepped out of the fogbank, the wisps of fog mixed up in her hair. Kipnis and Einhorn came after, motioning with their arms. The whole procession started forward again.

On top of the wall Trumpelman's wife dropped her veil over her head. Like a hangman. Trumpelman raised his cane; then, as a signal, let it down.

"*Feuer!*" said Grundtripp, in his native tongue.

Both Gatling guns started to fire. The first one was aimed incorrectly, too low, so that the bullets merely struck the ground. But the shells from the other one, on the right-hand side of the gate, went into a group of carpet workers. Some women fell. The rest ran in all directions. But in spite of the shouts, the screaming, the bodies underfoot, the march was not over. The veterans had been under fire before. With

172

their banners aloft, they continued to parade out of the fog.

On the wall, the leftward gunner raised his weapon higher, and a whole series of bullets came out of it, one of which struck poor Marbled right in the head. That was not all: Sheftelowitz was shot, fatally it developed, and so was Mister Kemp. A bullet struck Edmund Trilling in the knee, and while he was sitting a second shell pierced his neck, snapping it. Wherever you looked people were tumbling down. Blood came from the veterans' wounds. What could they do? They retreated. They ran into the arms of the misty cloud. Then the automatic guns stopped shooting. Eighty or so of the hunger marchers lay behind on the ground.

One or two Jews dared to race forward again. One was Zam, who had a red cross sewn on his sleeve. He found Sheftelowitz propped up on an elbow. Lipsky also ran out, with his false nose dangling from his false eyeglass frames. He bent over the body of Marbled. The buttonhole maker was already cold. *We demand politeness and consideration:* those had been his wonderful words. The living lawyer, the leader of the underground forces, looked up past the still, stony figures on the distant wall, to the top-floor windows of the mansion. The window glass was filled with children, screaming through the holes of their mouths, pulling the strings of their hair.

III

That was the end of the March of the Jewish War Veterans; but it was not the finish, quite, of the Five Day General Strike. The reason there wasn't a sixth day had little to do with the massacre of Tsarskoye Selo. What's a few dozen Jews in a Ghetto of tens of thousands? Hundreds die anyhow every day. What stopped the strike was the weather. It got colder and colder all morning, all noon, and then, at dusk, within a matter of moments, the temperature dropped another thirteen degrees.

Suddenly there was a pinging sound in the air, like a huge string being plucked. It sounded as if the sky itself, blue, brittle, were cracking, as if the hot metal ball at the world's center were changing to ice. It turned out that the sound was that of the river Dolna, freezing from bank to bank in two seconds flat. Here is a true story: The Blond Ones, the Masters, were at that moment fording the Dolna with a herd of twenty-two horses, each one of which became trapped in the grip of the ice. What an attraction! For the rest of the winter the Poles came out of the city to see the thrown-back heads, the glazed, glittering hooves, the manes which had crystallized. They were like the horses that had lived in Pompeii.

Chapter Six

A Decision for the Judenrat

I

That summer there were more flies than usual in the Suburb of the Balut. They dropped, fingernail-sized, into the tin bowls of soup. They banged like hailstones against the sides of the excrement wagons. How awful it was when they whirled over the Ghetto in clouds, touching down now and then like tornadoes, making a roaring sound. "And there came a grievous swarm of flies," said Rabbi Wolf-Kitzes, quoting his text by heart. He thought the Jews were suffering the seven plagues. But the other rabbis answered him calmly. "The war is going to end in a few months," said Trunk, of the Devout Butchers. "In November." This is how such true believers reckoned: the new Hebrew year, which fell in November, would be 5702; and was not 5702 the numerical value of the Hebrew phrase *The Sabbath Brings with It Peace?* Meanwhile, in 1941, the flies hung in the air, like spots in front of a sick man's eyes, like ashes, like dust.

Because of these buzzing insects the windows of the Chancellory, Dworska Number 20, had to be shut, in spite of the heat of the day. Inside, the Judenrat members also were certain the war would soon end. Not on account of the New Year, but because Russia was at last in the war. It was to cele-

175

brate that event that the Council, before the start of its regular meeting, was having a party of sorts. Schotter, of course, had been invited. There was creamed herring and, in wineglasses, purple wine. Popower, once a waiter, was speaking.

"Listen! Horowitz has gone crazy! He thinks he's Napoleon now! That's why he invaded Russia on June 22. The same date as the *Grande Armée*!"

Margolies, another ex-waiter, Minister of Justice now: "But Kiev has not fallen! No, they won't take Kiev!"

Schotter, thinner than at the wedding, with fewer teeth, less hair: "They say that at the start of the Russian campaign Napoleon wore a red shirt, to hide his blood in case of a wound. Horowitz just put on a pair of brown drawers!"

There was a peal of laughter. Schpitalnik, the piano player, inhaled some snuff into his nose. "It makes me feel happy," he said.

Next to speak was the Minister of Water and Power, the percussionist, Paradyz. "I have also thought of a joke. What is the difference between Horowitz and the sun? The sun goes down in the west and Horowitz goes down in the east!"

"Ha! Ha! In the east! In Russia, you mean! It's clever!" The person laughing had just that moment come through the door. It was F. X. Wohltat. He had on a white linen suit with wet stains under both arms. As soon as the Jewish Government saw him, they jumped up from their places. Off went their hats. Even Schpitalnik stood up, dizzily swaying.

"Sit down, ladies. Gentlemen, please, replace your hats. All men are the same to me." Then Wohltat did something unique, something new: he held his right arm outward, toward the shocked Jews, as if he wanted to shake their hands. "Friends! Let us greet each other as colleagues. As equals. If you won't put your hats on, look, I'll remove my own." In one hand he gripped his derby; with the other he squeezed the fingers of Gutfreind, Minister of Education.

"This is because of the resistance of Kiev! There are pos-

176

itive reports from the eastern front! That's why you're shaking hands!" said Margolies.

"No wonder he wants to be our friend. The shoe is on the other foot now!"

"Yes!" cried two or three others. "The other foot!"

Then Nomberg, still the Minister of Religious Affairs, held up his palms. "Jews of the Judenrat! What kind of talk is this? We should welcome the head of the Civilian Authority as an honored guest."

"Please, that's all right," the Volksdeutscher said. His damp skin shone in the window light. He stared at the Council, member by member: waiters and musicians and actors and cooks. Yet, in their black jackets, their stiffened shirtfronts, they were dressed better than he. They laughed, they swaggered, they would not shake his hand. How could this be?

The fact was, it had been ages, a lifetime, since Philosoff had carried dishes, or an oboe had been played by Mordechai Kleen. It was in another world that Verble had begged for a living. Now the Minister of Housing decided who was to live in what house and what room. He had under him hundreds of inspectors and almost one thousand clerks, not to mention two private armies—the fumigation squads and the chimney sweeps. And every other member of the Judenrat had his own private office, his own desk and telephone. All day long Jews stood outside the House of Lords, that's what they called the building at Dworska 20, waiting to get a food coupon from Miss Kleinweiss, or a tax receipt from Popower, the Minister of Finance now. No wonder then, that in Wohltat's presence, they dared to light up cigars.

Kleen, presently Minister of Public Works, had not only put his hat on, but hitched his pants up by the belt. "What do you want, anyway?" he demanded. "This is an official meeting."

"Maybe some herring," remarked Paradyz, of Water and Power.

"Or snuff!" said Schpitalnik, holding out to the Volksdeutscher his little tin. "It makes you feel you are floating in a bath."

"Ha! Ha!" The whole Judenrat brazenly laughed.

Schotter rocked forward on his turned-up shoes. "I just heard the following news. Horowitz has requisitioned every chair in the Ghetto."

"I know why!" said Margolies, waving his arm like a schoolchild. "Because he's tired of standing outside of Kiev!"

Wohltat turned to Dorka Kleinweiss, the Minister of Provisions and Supply. "I will tell you why I have interrupted your meeting. I need one hundred Jews. It's for a farming project. Light work. In the open air. There will be meat to eat, and vegetables and dairy products. All the Jewish Council must do is draw up a list of names. Old people, Madame Minister. Or young people. Or healthy or sick. It is completely up to you to decide. Each Jew is allowed to make up a bundle of twenty kilos. They must be at the Radogodsh Station tomorrow at noon."

The former cellist changed color. It was as if someone had drawn a green shade over her face. "They want a hundred Jews!" she screamed.

"Only a hundred. You choose which ones."

The Security Minister, Fried Rievesaltes, who up to then had been silent, now uttered a single word: "Deportations!" He dropped with a thud into his chair.

"Deportations, deportations," murmured the Council, also sitting down.

"*Ga-a-a!*" It was old Philosoff, older even than Trumpelman. Ninety. Perhaps ninety-five. His face had gone red. "*Ga-a-a!*" he said again.

But no one paid any heed. Everyone was thinking that in the Church of the Virgin Mary there would soon be new piles of feathers, fresh mounds of hats and shoes.

"This," said Mathilda Megalif, of Posts and Telegraph, "is a punishment for the Five Day Strike."

178

"A punishment from the Almighty!" a different Minister cried. "He sees us sipping wine and eating creamed fish!"

"True! It's true!"

They all were sighing and groaning. Philosoff, the Minister of Charities and Welfare, continued to make a rattling sound in his throat. Wohltat wiped his cheeks and his brow.

"Ministers! Council members! Listen to what I am saying. I am saying more than is allowed. You are right. It is because of the troubles on the eastern front. Because of Kiev. But if reinforcements are called up from the homeland, who will plow the fields and milk the goats on the farms? The answer is, the lucky one hundred Jews! They just have to pluck fresh eggs out of the nests. It will be like a vacation. In any case, you have my word that the Judenrat will be exempted. My dear friends, you don't have to worry at all!"

Here old Philosoff came to his senses. He dried the tears from his eyes. "A soft bone," he said, apologizing. "From the herring."

Then Dorka Kleinweiss, the only Minister still standing, said the following words: "What if we refuse to do it?"

"What? What did she say?" She had spoken so softly that no one had heard her.

"What if we say to the Blond Ones, *No, we won't do it. You do it*. What then?"

There was a gasp from the Judenrat.

"Then," said Wohltat, "we'll do it."

Mordechai Kleen pounded his fist on the Council table. "The Minister of Provisions and Supply, Miss Kleinweiss, has the right idea. It's a scandal for Jews to put down the names of Jews!"

"Hear! Hear!" cried Margolies, whose eyes were set only millimeters apart, on either side of his nose. "How do we know they're going to a farm? Maybe they'll have to dig dikes, or ditches. We are in office to protect our people, not to send them away."

It was amazing how brave the Jews became. One minute it

179

was as if someone had hit them on the head with an ax; the next thing they were shaking their fists in the air. Baggelman, with his rounded conductor's shoulders, arose. "To send citizens out of their own country in time of war is a violation of international law!"

The Volksdeutscher looked genuinely perplexed. "But we are the winners," he said. "We make the law."

"I have written your words down on paper. Exactly as you have said them. I shall thus record each of your statements. Now continue. You were saying you wrote the law." It was the Hungarian, Urinstein. He had a green fountain pen.

Wohltat swung around. "Who is this person?"

Urinstein tipped his black silk hat. "Ministry of Vital Statistics."

Baggelman had more to say. "In the last Great War no one was deported. The invaders behaved with honor toward the Jews."

There was a drop of sweat on Wohltat's nose. Another formed on his chin. "The Great War was a long time ago."

Gutfreind, of Education: "Wait a minute! He said sick people. What good are sick people on a farm? Or old people either? What kind of farm is that?"

"No list! No list!" cried the Judenrat members. It was a moment of courage and heroism. "Why should we give you a list when you can't enter Kiev?"

The Volksdeutscher replaced his hat. "Because it's either you or the Death's-Head troops, that's why! Do you want them to make up the quota? Do you know what that will be like? They grab the first person they see. No matter who. The more important, the better. It could even be a Judenrat official—or a member's wife, or a member's child. They do the job with rifles and fists. And no one's counting, either! Take everyone you can! By the neck! By the throat! Get a good grip on their hair! Take two hundred, or three hundred! Watch them squirm!" Wohltat was like a different per-

180

son. He was panting. His eyes were rapidly blinking. A button had come loose at his collar.

Paradyz, the percussionist, said, "Maybe we could ask for volunteers."

"In my opinion," said Nomberg, "we have acted hastily, spontaneously, without enough thought."

Verble, the Housing Minister, twisted his waxed mustache. "What about the Jews in the Tsarnecka Street jail? They went before. Why shouldn't they go again? The Judenrat has to feed these antisocial elements, the same as productive workers. That is something I never could understand."

Urinstein—in his top hat and silk tie, his beard and his glasses, he looked like a statesman, not a commercial traveler—Urinstein stood up from his chair and leaned with his hands on the table. "It seems we are not able to come to a decision," he told the head of the Civilian Authority. "We shall need time to continue our debate."

Wohltat replied, "I am willing to turn my back for three minutes. You have three minutes to make up your minds."

Schpitalnik's neck was so relaxed from the snuff he had taken that his head kept nodding loosely, as if to a tune. "Three minutes is a short time. What about four minutes? Or even fifteen or twenty? Everybody wants to give his opinion."

Schotter: "Not I! I have no opinion! I am not a Judenrat member!"

"Ten minutes then! After ten minutes Grundtripp will be informed that the Jewish Council requires his assistance."

"You see?" said the pianist. "He's a reasonable man."

Wohltat turned on his heel and went to the window. He clasped his chubby hands behind his back. The flies, he noticed, were bumbling against the glass. He looked into the dusty, deserted streets. He imagined himself pulling a person through them. A Jewess perhaps. By the hair. He dwelled on this, on the little pulls and jerks he would give her, and his throat swelled, like an amphibian's, under his shirt. Mean-

181

while, behind his back, like more flies, the Jews were buzz-buzzing. Then that sound came to a stop.

"Ahem-ahem—" Some person coughed. Wohltat swung around.

A Jew was standing there, swinging a timepiece from his outstretched hand. This was Popower, Ministry of Finance, an erstwhile waiter. He held his top hat against his chest, so that his skull, with its bony, fuzzy ridge, was apparent. He laughed to break the silence. "Everybody wants to live."

"Show him how it strikes the hour," hissed one of the Council members.

"Like this!" said the Minister, pulling at the crown of the watch. "Let us say it is eleven o'clock. There!"

A number of little bells inside the clock started to chime. They played a tune. "An American watch," Popower said. "From the St. Louis Exposition."

Then there was silence. No one could guess, at that difficult moment, what Wohltat would do. "Pretty watch," he said at last.

"Take it, take it," all cried out.

The timepiece went into the Volksdeutscher's pocket.

Mathilda Megalif stepped forward. She had the face of an artist, with dark semicircles under her eyes, and lids that came halfway down. There were many tight curls in her hair. "A bundle of twenty kilos is a pathetic and paltry load. A Jew, instead of necessities, like food, bedding, and saucepans, ought to be able to carry books and albums and certain mementos. The Judenrat therefore requests that the twenty-kilo limit be doubled. Forty kilos is all that a strong man can carry. Let a Jew take whatever he is able to lift!"

Wohltat pondered. "The limit is raised to thirty-five kilos," he announced.

It was an important concession. Some of those assembled broke into applause. Verble, of Housing, was especially excited. "People say the Judenrat is a worthless institution. That it should be abolished. But look what we've done!"

182

Now Paradyz stepped from the group. He was holding a number of rings in his palm. "Noon tomorrow is too soon. People need time. Twenty-four hours more! Just twenty-four! To wind up one's affairs. To say farewell."

"The time limit is extended from noon to 4 P.M.!"

The Council let out a collective sigh. The Minister of Water and Power slipped the gold bands into the Volksdeutscher's hand.

"This is real diplomacy!" exclaimed Gutfreind, like so many cooks a baby-faced man.

Now the Ministers urged Urinstein forward, so that he faced the head of the Civilian Authority alone. His red lips showed through his distinguished beard. "Let us speak frankly," he said. "I have been authorized by the Judenrat to offer you a certain sum—not jewelry, not watches, but so many thousand of zlotys, in exchange for a reduction in the number of listed Jews. It has already been mentioned: what good are old people and criminals upon a farm? We shall raise a special tax, and with the proceeds you can buy tractors and fertilizers, which will take the place of the Jews."

"One tractor," said Wohltat, "costs forty thousand zlotys."

"Agreed!"

"The Jewish quota is reduced to eighty five!"

Urinstein was far from finished. "Then we shall raise eighty thousand zlotys. Am I correct when I say that makes a total of not more than seventy Jews?"

The membership became agitated. "*Shhhh!* For God's sake!" some of them said.

Nomberg whispered, "Urinstein, Urinstein. We've done enough. We've saved fifteen lives!"

But to the amazement of everyone Wohltat crooked a finger in his damp collar and said, "All right. Very well. It's a hard bargain. Seventy Jews."

The relentless Urinstein pushed on. "By that token, a further forty thousand zlotys would bring the total to—" But before he could finish his colleagues ran to him and grabbed his arms. The bald Popower stepped on his toes. They feared he would undo the good that had been accomplished.

"To fifty-five Jews." The coffee merchant completed Urinstein's phrase. "If the sum you mention, the full one hundred and twenty thousand, is brought in cash, I shall make the final total exactly fifty. I cannot reduce that number by a single Jew. Do you accept, or don't you?"

Margolies, among those there the most Jewish-looking, was the first to respond. "We definitely accept!" he cried. "The number has been cut in half!"

"We've saved them!"

"Yes! And at what risk to ourselves!"

"I told you," said Rabbi Nomberg, "that this was our friend. He is practically a Jew himself."

Minister Verble: "We thank our good friend Wohltat!"

"Yes, yes, many thanks!"

They all turned toward the Volksdeutscher. He remained where he had been, the sweat rolling off him, like rain from an awning. "But where," he asked, "is the list?"

"The list?"

"The fifty names. Write them down. You—" He pointed to the Minister of Vital Statistics. "You with the pen. Draw up the names."

"I am a stranger here," Urinstein hastily said. "A Hungarian citizen. I hardly know a soul in the Ghetto. In my opinion, to choose a name, one name and not another, that is an ethical question. It has a spiritual dimension. Perhaps the Minister of Religious Affairs—?"

"But I represent only a single congregation," Nomberg responded. "And the Italianate Synagogue has been burned down. I would need the advice of the wisest rabbis. The Pshiskher Descendant and other scholars. However, these matters also come under the jurisdiction of the Security Minister. After all, his men will have to deliver the quota. Ask Mister Rievesaltes about it."

Rievesaltes did not have to be asked. "The Jewish police

know their duty. Whoever we have to, we'll bring to the train. But since the Jews are being sent to another country, it's mostly the job of the Minister of Foreign Affairs, who, as the whole world knows, is Trumpelman himself. Alas, the Eldest of the Jews is not present. These days he rarely leaves his summer estate."

"Let's call him in!" the Judenrat ministers shouted. "We can't act without his permission!"

"Enough! No more talking! I know this is an attempt to stall for time! I have been here already an hour! Do you know I have the right to shoot anybody I wish? That is the strain that I live with. It's anguish!" The pudgy man was beside himself. His eyelids fluttered wildly. He blew air from his cheeks. "Watch out, Jews! Watch out! I'm changing!"

It was at that dangerous moment that old Philosoff chose to come forward. He walked right up to Wohltat, who had a bubble in the corner of his mouth. "I made a list. Since it had to be done." In truth he did have a list, a long sheet of paper, with names on it, written in ink from Urinstein's pen. Nobody made a comment. Nor did anyone attempt to hold him back. Freely, he handed the document to the Volksdeutscher. The latter read the first name out loud.

"One Ferdinand Philosoff."

"Present," answered the waiter. His beard hung down in long separate strands, as if he were having a meal of noodles.

"Ferdinand Philosoff," Wohltat repeated.

"Also present."

And then, before anyone had grasped what had happened, the head of the Civilian Authority began to giggle, then to guffaw. He pointed at the list of names. "*Philosoff!*" he roared. "It says *Philosoff!*"

It turned out that the waiter, after starting with his own name, had printed it again, forty-nine times. "What's so funny?" he asked—not only of Wohltat, but of his colleagues, who were tittering, too. "Who else could I write down?"

Wohltat was taking little steps, wiping the tears from his

185

eyes. "Ha! Ha! My good spirits have returned. I will do everything that you ask. You—" He pointed at Schotter. "Fetch the rabbis. All the ethical scholars. I, myself, will inform Isaiah Trumpelman that his presence is requested here. Ha! Ha! Ha! He put his own name down! He wants to be a farmer! Ha! Ha! Sit down, Jews! Talk it over! Seek advice! You now have until sundown, precisely sundown, to write the names."

The Jews did sit down—less Schotter, who, a step ahead of the roaster-importer, darted through the Judenrat door.

Two flies had come in when the two men went out. They hopped from one dish of herring to another. They walked skillfully around the rims of the glasses of wine. One flew up and performed the letter *Z* several times before Popower's nose. The other clung to Fried Rievesaltes' cuff. Neither man noticed. The whole membership sat silently, like nappers, with their chins on their chests. At last Mordechai Kleen, who had turned recently forty, spoke a sentence or two aloud.

"At first I thought I would play the flute. With that instrument the breath passes over and not into the mouthpiece, so the sound it makes is that of breathing, of life. Nevertheless, I took up the oboe."

Baggelman, the orchestra conductor, spoke after another short pause. "In 1885, when I was a boy aged eleven, my family moved from our village to the great city of Vienna. Here there was much to see: the fountains, the gardens, the men and women at tables, sipping red and green drinks. Once on the street I saw a man wearing a turban. That same year I went for the first time to the Vienna Opera. What did I see there? A stone statue singing! A pink cloud above him when he sank to Hell!"

A third pause. Then Margolies: "My first post as an apprentice waiter took place at the three-star Scotch Hotel, in Bialystok. This was March, 1900. I was just seventeen. One day, not long after this job began, there was a stir in the grand dining room. All the waiters and headwaiters were gathered around an oval table. I will tell you who was sitting there. With a cigarette in a holder and a dark blue gown: Sarah Bernhardt. Then on a world tour. Imagine my feelings when I, remember a mere apprentice, then leaning against a distant wall, realized that the famous actress was making a signal to me! *'Un café crème!'* she demanded.

"In those days my hair was black and curly, and I wore the curls mostly on one side. Also, I had a mustache. That is how I looked when I came up with a cup and a saucer and a pot of hot coffee and a pot of hot milk. I combined these elements without a flaw. Sarah Bernhardt, dear friends! With earrings! With eyebrows! What a terrible blow when I read in the newspaper that they had to cut off her leg."

Verble: "I suggest we look at things this way. Not who should go but who should stay. The biologically sound material. The socially valuable elements. From this perspective, it's obvious we should put down the names of the fifty oldest people in the Suburb. They've lived their lives. We haven't!"

The assembly of Ministers groaned, as if they had been awakened. Fried Rievesaltes slapped at the fly on his wrist.

"Dry leaves," said Nomberg, "must fall."

Dorka Kleinweiss: "I disagree completely. I have not changed my mind. How can you bring yourselves to do the Masters' work for them? How do you *know* it's not because you've been promised an exemption? What if one of us writes down a name because of some private quarrel, to settle some personal debt? We are not, fellow members, the Lords of life and death."

Paradyz turned to the Minister of Provisions and Supply. "Come, come, Miss Kleinweiss. What an exaggeration. It is not a question of life and death. We are simply deciding who is to continue to live in the Suburb and who shall live on a farm. It's not as if we were condemning people to prison."

Gutfreind, of Education: "Minister Paradyz, how can you

187

be so certain? The letters from the earlier deportees, the ones from the hospitals, stopped coming a long time ago."

Baggelman: "I have a question for the Minister of Provisions and Supply. Suppose you were driving a van down a narrow mountain road. The mountain is on one side, and on the other is a cliff measuring hundreds of meters. Unexpectedly you see before you a child on the right-of-way. No time to stop, Miss Kleinweiss. My question is, what do you do?"

Without hesitating, Dorka Kleinweiss responded, "Swerve over the side."

Baggelman: "Aha! I thought you would say that! Now, what if the van were to be loaded with people? Then what do you say?"

Minister Mordechai Kleen: "It's a completely hypothetical question."

Paradyz: "Not hypothetical. The driver is the Judenrat. The loaded van is the Ghetto. The child is the few who must go."

Gutfreind: "But we can still put on the brakes. By saying *no*."

The snuff was wearing off Andrei Schpitalnik, the Minister of Culture and Entertainment. "We are not getting anywhere, my friends. We have to take turns, so everyone can speak. First, here is my opinion. We should not worry, because no one will be deported. A miracle will definitely happen first. Now it's the turn of F. Philosoff, who sits on my right. And so on around the circle. Mister Minister, what do you think?"

"I pass," said Philosoff.

Miss Megalif, Posts and Telegraph: "I am the next speaker. I propose an appeal to world opinion. We could circulate a petition with thousands of names."

"I have a plan that will meet every objection." It was Verble, of Housing, once again. "Miss Kleinweiss said that the Judenrat might act from self-interest. To pay off old scores,

188

and so forth. Very well, then. Why don't we pick the names completely by chance? Then fate will be the guilty party."

Paradyz: "It's a wonderful idea. We could put the names into a hat!"

Schpitalnik: "Yes, yes. We could even put our names in. Out of a population of over a hundred thousand, the chance of one of us being picked is practically nil."

Popower: "That won't be necessary. We have already been picked by chance—for our positions on the Judenrat. Isn't that burden enough? Now let others run the same risk."

Many voices spoke together. "Yes. Do it by lot! What could be fairer!"

But the membership of the Jewish Council had yet to hear from the Minister of Vital Statistics. The Hungarian removed his spectacles, which had little black ribbons attached to the lenses, and rubbed his eyes. He licked the whiskers nearest his mouth. "No," he said, "it will not do. If we are going to leave the decision to blind chance, we might as well allow the Death's-Headers to do it. They'll seize whomever destiny puts in their way. I have been thinking and thinking. Why does the Conqueror wish us to become his accomplices in this matter? Why doesn't he simply take the farmers himself? It can only be because he is going to commit a crime so big that even he dares not do it alone. What could such a crime be? I have not thought so far. I only know if I were one of the Others the thing I would want most is for the Jews to do it for me. And the thing I would want least is for the Jews to resist. Judenrat members, here's my advice. Let's set a fire, a big one, and order everyone to break through the walls, to swim over the river. *Run!* That is what we should tell our people. *Run! Run! Run!*"

"Be quiet, sir!"

"What is he saying?"

"He's non-Polish born!"

"What about women? What happens to them during this

189

fire? What about the children who don't know how to swim?"

"The official policy of the Judenrat is *Cooperation and Production*. Urinstein is taking an illegal line!"

"He talks just like a Lipsky agent. It's defeatism!"

The Minister of Security waved his hand for silence, which he received. "Nobody here heard a word on the subject of swimming in rivers. No one said a thing about fires. Am I right, Minister Urinstein? It is your duty to report it if you come across such a punishable offense."

Urinstein, instead of responding, hung his head.

Mordechai Kleen, one of the cigar smokers, now ground out his stub. "What," he demanded, "are we going to do?"

"Maybe," said Schpitalnik, "we could write down a list of fictional names."

Margolies: "Listen! We only have to hold out a little longer! Kiev is a fortress! America will enter the war!"

Philosoff was standing at the side of the table. The mop strings of his beard shook and shook. "I can't stand it! It's too much of a strain! Why didn't I choke on the bone?" And he started to beat his own head through his hat. Everyone wanted to stop him, and yet everyone, whether in or out of his chair, suddenly froze.

For this reason: the door had opened and inside it was the zaddik of Pshiskhe's Descendant, accompanied by Rabbis Wolf-Kitzes, Kornischoner, and Lunt. It was not their sudden arrival that astounded the Council of Elders; they had been, after all, expected. It was what they looked like. One sleeve of Lunt's sport coat was missing and both his eyes were swollen shut. Kanal, the Descendant, had only half of a beard, not to mention the cut on the bridge of his nose. Something had happened to Kornischoner's neck that caused him to keep his chin down, the way a violin player holds his violin. As for poor little Wolf-Kitzes, he had no coat, he had no trousers, and someone had taken his shoes.

"They beat me," said Kornischoner.

The Pshiskher Descendant said, "They pulled my beard."

Popower, the Minister of Finance, thumped the table. "It's an outrage! What intolerable behavior! They have gone too far at last!"

Baggelman: "Members of the Judenrat, I give you my resignation. I am no longer the Minister of Industry and Labor."

Schpitalnik: "Then I resign, too."

"That's it! It's the solution!" Paradyz shouted. "We'll resign from the Council!"

All members, together: "Yes, yes! Why didn't we think of it before?" They put on their hats and headed for the door.

But the four rabbis were still standing there. "Where am I?" said Lunt. "It smells like herring."

Verble told him. "It used to be the Chancellory. But not any more. Ha, ha! We've resigned!"

Rabbi Wolf-Kitzes refused to get out of the way. "You cannot resign. You can't leave, either."

"Why not?" Nomberg, his colleague, wanted to know.

"Look out the window."

The Ministers ran to the shut windowpanes. They leaned over each other to get a look out the glass. Then they recoiled, they staggered backward, wringing their hands. There was not a single Jew on the street below. No wonder: a Totenkopfer battalion stood at intervals of two meters the whole length of Dworska, on both sides of the street. Between those lines, in command of everything, was the Mighty One, Grundtripp himself.

Surrounded.

"It's the leapfroggers!" cried Mordechai Kleen.

"Remember Putermilch! Remember Anton Schneour! They'll do the same to us as the first Judenrat!"

Thus the memory, long suppressed, of Mosk jumping over Plumb's back, and Blum over Szapiro's, came back to each of the hostages trapped in the hot, airless room.

Gutfreind, still by the window, cried out in alarm, "Look! It's falling!"

191

The Ministers knew immediately what those words portended. The sun, which had been at the peak of its orbit, was now like an egg yolk slipping down the glossy side of the sky.

Urinstein looked at his wristwatch. "Not much time!" he groaned.

"Not much time for what?" asked Rabbi Lunt. "What's going on? Everything is completely dark."

The one-eared Nomberg stepped forward. "Fellow rabbis, we need your guidance. You must make a decision for the Judenrat."

"Why bother with us? No one asked us whether horsemeat was kosher." That from Wolf-Kitzes.

The Descendant of Yaakov-Yitzhak, the Pshiskher, stroked from habit the missing half of his beard. "On what subject do you wish a ruling?"

"The Others have given us until sundown to give them a list," Nomberg explained. "On this list there must be fifty Jewish names. These citizens will be transported to the fatherland of the Race of Masters."

"Reduced from one hundred!" cried Verble. "Don't leave that out!"

"Oh!" There was a tiny, high-pitched shriek, and Lunt, originally from Yambol, fell flat on the floor.

"He's fainted!"

The members rushed over and began to slap at the rabbi's bruised face. "Wake up! Wake up!" shouted the Minister of Water and Power. "It's not what you think! They are only going to work on a farm!"

Lunt nonetheless could not be roused. The Ministers cleared room for him among the plates and glasses on the table. They laid him carefully down. Then Nomberg turned to the three remaining sages.

"What is your conclusion? Give us your advice."

"Advice? Nothing could be more simple." Wolf-Kitzes was keeping his hands crossed in front of his gray underdrawers. "It is written, *The Law is the Law*. Draw up the list of names."

The oboist, Kleen: "And does the Prince of the Pious agree?"

Everyone turned to the Pshiskher, whose opinion was worth more than that of any single Jew. "If the whole may be saved by the loss of the part, then the lesser evil must be done."

"My position exactly," Nomberg replied. "After all, if the few refused to go, wouldn't they be guilty of an injury to the many?"

Rabbi Wolf-Kitzes: "The fifty are the lucky ones! Chosen to sanctify God's Holy Name!"

Verble's mustache, a long one, was distinguished by the hairs at the ends, which had been waxed to a fine line. "At last! All authorities are in agreement. Urinstein, we'll just use your fountain pen—"

"Not quite all authorities. Not every one." The rabbi of the Fur Trimmers, even with his wrenched neck, started to speak. "My fellow scholars have overlooked the words of the mighty Rambam: *If heathens say to the Israelites, 'Surrender one of your number to us, that we may put him to death, otherwise we will put all of you to death,' they should all suffer death rather than surrender a single Israelite to them.* Thus wrote Maimonides."

There was a murmur in the crowd. "There were not," remarked Paradyz, "Gatling guns then."

The hair, the beard, stood out wildly from every spot on Kornischoner's face. But his small round eyes were wet and shiny. "Furthermore, the Jerusalem Talmud says that if a company of Jews is walking down the road, and the heathens approach them with the same demand, then, *though they be all killed, they shall not surrender a single soul from Israel.* Not a single soul, Baluters!"

"But why do we keep talking about killing, about death? It's just a trip they are taking."

"What about a soul that *isn't* from Israel? We have many Christians in the Ghetto."

Margolies, narrow-eyed, worried-looking, approached Kornischoner. "Rabbi! Say something else! Make a different suggestion! Tell us what to do!"

But the rabbi, thin as sticks, turned aside. "I can't talk! My neck is twisted! I can't make puffs this way!"

Rabbi Wolf-Kitzes, solemnly: "Everyone in the Baluty Suburb should start to pray. We will blow the shofar the entire night. Something will happen to make these hard hearts softer."

"Pray? Is that what you have to tell us? Pray?" There was, in the House of Lords, general consternation.

Then an idea came to the Descendant. "One moment, please. There are certain exceptions to the rulings that the rabbi of the Fur Trimmers has quoted. If the demand of the heathens is not for just anyone, but for a named individual, Jew X, Y, or Z, then in order to avoid greater bloodshed he should be given up. Examples of such cases abound. Was not Johoiakim surrendered to Nebuchadnezzar, in order to save the Temple? When King David's forces declared they would destroy the city of Abel unless Sheba, the traitor, was given to them, was not the head of Sheba forthwith thrown over the wall? Give them, I say, their fifty heads, rather than let the whole city suffer."

Suddenly the Chancellory was in an uproar. Everyone talked at once. Gutfreind's voice boomed the loudest. "But these victims were named by the heathens. In our case, we, *we alone,* must pick and choose."

The Minister of Housing: "But we could ask the Others to give us hints. They could name the ones they wanted, and we would just write them down."

Wolf-Kitzes: "No, no. The Judenrat may not set its hand to any such list. However, it may cause the list to be drawn up by its clerks."

The Judenrat members saw through this argument at once. There was no way for them to reach their clerks. No phone. No telegraph. And the sun was steadily sinking.

"We will have to hop like toads!"

"Aha! Aha! I've thought of something!" It was the Fur Trimmers' rabbi again. "It is true, the case of the person specifically named is an exception to the rule *Not a single soul from Israel.* But there is an exception to the exception. Resh Laquish has ruled, and Rambam has accepted this teaching: not even such a named person may be surrendered, *unless he is deserving of death!*"

Popower: "Wonderful! Grand! It's the criminals! I said that all along!"

"The question is," said Rabbi Kanal, the Descendant, "is the exception to the exception truly an exception? What is meant, beyond the obvious instance of capital cases, by *deserving of death*? Do we not say that a student of Torah is 'deserving of death' if he happens to have a stain on his garment? Is not the man who holds his own organ when passing water called 'death-deserving' too? To whom, then, does this phrase not apply?"

Wolf-Kitzes: "A married man may support his organ from below."

Rabbi Kornischoner said thoughtfully, "What our Master now teaches is valid. All men are guilty. There is no person who can say that his death is not just."

"True! True! Us most of all! We are bad, guilty people! Let's put our names down and be the first ones to go!" Old Philosoff was rocking from one foot to the other. The rosy light in the room lit his swaying beard, like the strands of a beaded curtain.

Then Mathilda Megalif began weeping, from both her eyes.

The next to join in was Schpitalnik, and after him Margolies. "Why are we weeping?" Verble asked, sobbing too. In no time, the whole room, including the rabbis, was quietly shedding tears. The answer to Verble's question was that each man and each woman was thinking of the reason why he or she deserved to die. Their faces were red, partly from this intense emotion and partly because the sun—round, im-

195

mense, purple, like a gigantic beet root—was setting opposite the House of Lords. They all turned toward it, with bright pink tears on their cheeks.

Then Kornischoner sighed and wiped his wet beard with his sleeve. "Let's keep trying," he said. "We might find a way."

"There is the case of the one hundred blessed loaves," said Wolf-Kitzes. They all turned toward the half-dressed rabbi. "The heathen demands one such loaf on pain of defiling the remaining ninety-nine. Many authorities write that all the loaves must suffer defilement; but Rabbi Joshua ben Hananiah has ruled that while the single loaf may not be delivered directly into the heathen's hand, it may be put on a stone within his reach. Thus, by analogy—"

"I know!" Kleen interrupted. "We can write the list and leave it on the table!"

"A perfect solution!"

The Pshisker Descendant: "Not so perfect. A loaf is a loaf and not a person. Why is this distinction important? First, because the former is not capable of feeling pain, but the latter is. Second, because one loaf is exactly like another, while no two people are the same. With the bread there is no true process of selection."

Another disappointment. The tears, which had nearly stopped, started again. The sun, meanwhile, was flattening out at the bottom, and looked like a Bulgarian hat.

Rabbi Wolf-Kitzes brightened once more. "Do not despair. The one hundred loaves reminded me of the one hundred women! The heathen demands that of this number he be given one to use for his pleasure; otherwise the whole community shall be defiled. The ruling is that no woman may be surrendered—except that one who is already unclean, since that would do her little harm."

Baggelman: "I do not understand. Are we to write down the names of fifty harlots?"

Nomberg: "No, no. The principle is, one may allow the

196

defiled to be defiled. Thus we may hand over farmers to farm, or even those already dying—the aged, the critically ill—to die. I wholeheartedly support the interpretation of Rabbi Wolf-Kitzes!"

The light in the room was draining away like puddles. The last of the sun dropped beneath the line of rooftops. Everyone knew this was their last chance.

"And what is the opinion of the Most Pious?"

"A negative opinion," announced the Descendant. "I am shamed even to think of women of that kind."

"What says the rabbi of the Fur Trimmers?"

Kornischoner, with much difficulty, shook his head. "No." His final word.

"Ah," said Dorka Kleinweiss. "The vote is two to two."

The dusk was now so thick that the Jews had to grope for the backs of their chairs. They sat in them, not noticing that the rabbi from Yambol was no longer unconscious but, on the contrary, sitting upright, rubbing his swollen eyes.

"What am I?" Lunt asked. "Living or dead?"

"Rabbi!" the Council members exclaimed. "Can we make the list or can't we? Tell us! Break the tie!"

"Alas, living," said the rabbi, whose back was humped.

"Speak! Tell us what to do!"

Lunt looked at the Judenrat. Impossible to tell whether or not he could really see them. He smiled. "Jews, you don't know?"

"No! We can't make a list and we can't not make a list! Where is the logic in that?"

On that rabbi's face there was a dreamy expression. "Look what they did to my sport coat. They ripped off the sleeve."

Urinstein leaned forward. "Tell!"

Lunt did. "We have to kill each other and the last person alive has to kill himself. I saw that at once. That's why I fainted."

There was absolute silence. Not even the sound of breathing. The white plates on the table were the brightest objects

197

in the darkened room. After some time Schpitalnik remarked, "It's a good idea."

"Hee, hee," Popower tittered. "We could resign after all."

Paradyz was actually laughing. "Ha! Ha! Like at Masada! We would be written up in history!"

The other ministers began laughing too. "I would like to see their faces! When *they* come into the room."

"Yes! This will teach them a lesson!"

Suddenly, from five meters off, Gutfreind ran as hard as he could against the wall. "Look!" he cried. "I ran into it!"

Then everyone rushed this way and that, trying to put Lunt's plan into effect. Wolf-Kitzes squeezed his throat with his own hands. More Jews did the same. Philosoff looked up from where he was beating his head against the plaster wall. "I am doing it!" he wailed. "But nothing happens!"

Margolies stood on the table. "What if I unscrewed the bulb from the lamp? And then put my finger into the socket? We could do that, one after the other!" The Scotch Hotel waiter stretched upward and removed one of the unlit bulbs. Then he groaned, "It only tickles!"

Said Kornischoner, "I don't have to kill myself! I'm not even alive! Yesterday I produced sixteen puffs, five rejected. For this I was given only as much soup as could be soaked into one slice of bread. The fewer puffs I make, the less food they give me, the smaller my strength to make puffs the following day. It's a vicious circle!"

"This is awful! It's so hard to kill a person!"

"I have it! Let's throw ourselves out! Onto the cobblestones!"

"Yes! That's the way!"

There was a rush for the window, a big jam-up. Two or three members tried to pull up the sash. Then the ones in front noticed, in the lamplight, the men in black uniforms below. "Watch out!" they warned. "They'll see us!" Then they all whirled around and ran back to the table, where they dropped in despair into their chairs.

198

Somebody said, "It was too low anyway. Only two stories." Then it was quiet again.

In not much more than a whisper, Fried Rievesaltes finally spoke. "Ladies, gentlemen, rabbis. I am sure you have noticed my buttons, those on my vest and the matching ones on my cuffs. These are real pearls. Is there anyone here who knows what a pearl is? I shall tell you. Long ago each one of these buttons was inside an oyster, the kind that people eat in France. Indian boys dive for these oysters at the bottom of the Indian Ocean. This button here, which cost at Palfinger's one thousand zlotys, I am not speaking of the mounting and trim, was at one time nothing but a grain of sand. It's a fact, Jews! This sand annoys the oyster, which makes a ball around it, the same as a gallstone, or a stone that is passed through the kidney. See? How smooth? How shiny? This takes the oyster years and years. Many times I thought how delightful to be an Indian pearl-diver boy. The Indian Ocean is blue. Here, feel it, Minister Verble. Minister Baggelman, you feel it, too. You have to open a thousand shells before you get this good a pearl. Those brown boys have just a scarf wrapped around them, and they dive down carrying a heavy stone. Past all the different varieties and kinds of fish. I read they can stay under at one time five or six minutes. I also read it's like a garden there, with the pink rocks and the sea flowers. It was not my fate to be one of those people. My fate led me elsewhere."

The moonfaced Minister, while he was speaking, tore the pearls from his clothing. Then to the amazement of the Jews, he tossed the matchless collection onto the Chancellory floor. "Years and years and years," he repeated. It was not clear whether he was referring to the time it took the oysters to manufacture the gems or to the decades of suffering that Rievesaltes had undergone—yes, and inflicted—in order to pay Palfinger for them.

"A fortune," Schpitalnik said.

"No," said the head of the Jewish police. "Only sand. *This*
199

is the fortune." So saying, Rievesaltes took from his jacket pocket a small vial filled with oblong white pills. He took the cap off and distributed them about the table. "Priceless! Priceless! Who would not give for just one of these pearls all that he owns?"

"What's inside?" Verble asked.

"Darkness. In just one minute. Painless darkness. Can you think of a more valuable gift?"

And without more ado, using the dregs in his wineglass, Rievesaltes gulped his tablet down. There was a gasp. No one stirred.

Rabbi Lunt: "They say that in paradise the sky is gold and the roadways are lapis lazuli. In other words, not darkness, Jews: light." Lunt swallowed the capsule. So did Baggelman, and, a half moment later, Miss Megalif did, too.

Popower stood up at his place. "Everybody wants to live! That's obvious!" Then he put a pill on his tongue and drank it down with a sip of wine.

"A toast of thanks to the Minister of Security!" exclaimed Philosoff, raising his glass. The Ministers of Culture and Entertainment, of Public Health, of Water and Power, likewise lifted their goblets and swallowed their pills.

Thus, in turn, all those in the room followed suit. The Minister of Justice was last. "If only there had been a breakthrough at the Kiev front," he said, rolling the pill in his cheek until, by accident almost, it went down.

"I don't feel any different. I feel just the same," said Rabbi Wolf-Kitzes.

"So do I! No! Wait! Now I am lightheaded!"

"Minister Verble," said Gutfreind, "I am definitely lightheaded, too."

"Yes! Yes! It's as if I drank a bottle of wine!"

Then there was a calm. Everybody was sitting around the long table, with his or her head propped on an elbow, like a person who is feeling bored. The silence continued. Philosoff closed his eyes. So did Popower. Baggelman, of Industry and

Labor, let his head fall onto his folded arms. About two minutes had gone by altogether. Finally Verble, the former ragpicker, weakly said, "Would the Minister of Justice tell us again about Sarah Bernhardt? About the *café crème*?"

Margolies' chin was on his fists. He could not speak above a whisper. "Gladly. It was at the Scotch Hotel. Bialystok. 1900. The curls of my hair, all on one side. She motioned for me. Forward I glided. A pot of hot milk, a pot of hot coffee, the saucer and cup. Now the cup is before her. Now with both hands I grip the silver handles: skillfully I pour out an equal measure of coffee and milk. A three-star hotel. A cigarette in a holder."

The voice of the waiter trailed away. Everyone's head had fallen down, either onto his arms or the back of his hands, or directly onto the table. Another moment went by. Kleen lifted his head up. "It's not working," he said; but then, seeing how dark it was, he changed his mind.

Not long afterward the Chairman arrived at Dworska Number 20 and, by the light of a match that he struck, saw what had happened to his Judenrat. Lifeless, the members were draped over the table, while a fly or two zoomed by their bodies. The match went out. Trumpelman stood on the table and screwed the loose bulb into the socket. He turned the fixture on. In the electrical glare he saw the vial. He picked it up, shook it, sniffed. Then, though it was hopeless, he began to smack the dead men on their backs.

"Up! Get up! Loafers! Bums!" Of course no one responded. So the physician put his arm around the neck of the Minister of Religious Affairs, precisely as he had done years before, in the first days of his practice, and cracked the bones.

"Ouch!" Nomberg declared.

Then the President moved quickly among the Council, snapping the necks of the members; with a gasp, a groan, each one returned to the land of the living. "*Psst*, Minister Verble," said Minister Paradyz. "What's going on?" Verble

201

looked around. At the far end of the table he saw the white hair, the flashing eyeglasses, of the Elder of the Jews.

"Messiah!" he called.

Baggelman saw him too. "Giver of life!"

"I exist!" exclaimed Urinstein. "I am!"

The four rabbis held up their hands, to chant, to pray. Schpitalnik shouted over the din. "I knew it! I said so! A miracle has happened!"

But Rievesaltes, round-headed, was not celebrating. Shakily, he rose. He pointed at the Elder. "You gave those capsules. You dispensed them. Cyanide, you said. Dear cyanide! To kill us in one minute flat!"

The physician wrapped his cloak about his body. He raised his chin. "So you could run out? Escape? There is no escape! It is I, Trumpelman, only Trumpelman, who decides who lives and who dies."

"But I'm the Police Chief! The Security Minister! I have a right to that power, too!"

"You? You? I made you sleep like a baby—with little pills!"

There was a loud wail from Philosoff. "Sleeping? Only sleeping? Does that mean we still have to make the list? We don't know what to do!"

Nomberg: "We do whatever our President orders! The Almighty has sent him to guide us!"

In a low voice Trumpelman said, "The list has to be made."

Immediately two of the rabbis—Kornischoner and Lunt—broke into heart-rending sobs. Their colleague, Wolf-Kitzes, touched each man on the shoulder. "Don't cry. Don't. We will pass a resolution: *The Jew, Kornischoner; the Jew, Lunt; also the Jews Kleen, Paradyz, Popower and others hereby forbid the King of Heaven from punishing His people any longer. It's enough! We demand that the suffering stop!*"

This was the answer the rabbi got: "You cry! You weep! You have fine feelings! You think I don't want to weep, too?

202

Like a woman! A baby! But the Elder has to think of the entire community, not Jews one by one! He has to keep it alive until the war comes to an end! Maybe the Red Army will win and Horowitz will be defeated. But remember, the Bolsheviks know we've been working day and night for the Race of Masters. They are not going to embrace us, to kiss our cheeks. Or else the Conqueror will march straight to Moscow and even England will have to surrender. Then we go to Madagascar. Then we make the new Kingdom of Zion. That won't be the end of the world."

An anonymous voice: "Maybe you'd prefer it that way?"

"A hero! A roomful of heroes! You think you're big shots because you tried to kill yourselves. Martyrs like in the Bible! Listen! If you don't make the list, then the Others will take one hundred or two hundred instead of fifty; they'll take children instead of adults. It's not just yourselves you're killing! You're murdering the ones who want to live!"

"Mister Chairman! Help us! We can't choose the names! Tell us which ones!"

The President of the Judenrat's veins stood out in his throat, and on his forehead. "Which ones! It doesn't matter which ones! I am a physician. I know that sometimes you have to cut off a gangrened arm to save the rest of the body. Look at me. My whole life has been devoted to the welfare of children. But even I have to let the newborn baby die in order to save the mother's life. Now we have to give them fifty people, so that our dear Jewish children, our hope, our future, can live. Be brave! When a great boat is sinking, like the *Titanic*, not everybody can get into the lifeboats. Some have to stay behind."

"But the captain of the *Titanic* went down with the ship."

"Who said that? Who dared?"

Not one soul responded. That made Trumpelman smile. "You think I want to save myself? That I'm a coward? I invite you to put me on trial when the war is over. Get a jury.

203

A judge. I'll explain before the Jewish people, before history, what I had to do. And what if they find me guilty? Let them put me inside a cage, like an animal! Yes, I'm guilty! Because I did not sit wringing my hands! I dipped them in ink, the same as blood!"

With those words the Lithuanian sat at the table and—on white paper, with a black-capped pen—began to write name after name. Silently the ministers took their places. Verble stopped the Elder: to the three names already listed, he added a like number of his own. Rievesaltes was next. He leaned over the sheet. He scrawled and scrawled. Five hands reached for the pen. Around the whole table it went. There was no sound, except for the scratching the gold tip made.

When the task was completed the Judenrat stood from their chairs. Paradyz was the first to speak. "I won't think of the few who are going. I'll think of the many we've saved."

"I put down rich people," Rievesaltes said. "But my men won't touch them. We'll bargain. We'll talk. After we come to an agreement I'll write out the names of any three Jews."

Popower was grinning. He beamed. "A moment ago life seemed terrible to me. I didn't want to go on. Now it seems sweet and good."

Baggelman lifted his arms, as if conducting. "Yes! Thanks to our redeemer! Our Moses!"

Trumpelman held up his hand, in which the filled sheet of paper was lodged. "Do you mean the Elder? Don't thank the Elder. He has done his duty, no more."

"No! No!" Schpitalnik shouted. "It was you who brought us back from the brink!"

The rest of the Council members crowded around their leader, tears of relief, of gladness, in their eyes. They cried, "Bless you! Bless you!"

And that, ladies and gentlemen, is the way people thought in our town. It did not matter what the facts were. Never mind that the poison was just sleeping pills. There would always be Jews to believe, even in the last days of the Ghetto, that the Elder possessed the power to call the dead back to life.

II

That night a wind blew and dark clouds whistled across the sky. A kind of humming could be heard throughout the Suburb. The sound rose, fell, then died out completely—only to strike up again. Was this the moan, the sigh, of those fifty Jews who even then were being taken away? For some time it was too dark to tell where the strange sounds were coming from. Then, out of the bottom of a hen-shaped cloud, dropped the shining white egg of the moon. At Tsarskoye Selo the ripe fruit on the fruit trees began to glow, and the glass on the wall lit up also, like a gunpowder trail. It was the mansion itself that was growling, droning, like a hive of bees.

On the ground floor the Trumpelmans, man and wife, were sleeping. Far above them, inside the attic, hundreds and hundreds of musical instruments were heaped into piles. Gleaming brass—the trumpets, the bugles—leaned against the walls. Woodwinds of every type were stacked in the corners. There were pianos, clavichords, harps, guitars. The violins and violoncellos formed wooden mountains. Standing apart, biggest of all, were three double basses. They throbbed, they groaned, although no one was bowing their strings.

These were the instruments that had been confiscated from the Ghettoites. Only Smolenskin, with his gramophone, could make music now. Yet each time the blast of the gale blew through the old house, the taut strings, the piano wire, began to vibrate and trill. Chimes tinkled against each other. A quiver ran through the stretched skins of the drums. It was as if the missing musicians of the Balut had picked up their instruments and started to play.

205

In his sleep Trumpelman smiled. It was daylight in the dream he was having, not night. The sunshine poured through the picture windows. Stalin, the People's Friend, and Churchill, the Bulldog, had to wear smoked glasses against the glare. Roosevelt shielded his eyes. Only the thin little Pope looked quickly around without blinking. Then Wohltat came in with coffee cups.

"The plantation is doing well," he said. He motioned for everyone to look out the window, where the coffee trees were growing on the side of a hill. An antelope stepped out of the forest, and so did deer, and gazelles.

"Have you a peach?" Churchill asked, and at once a real peach showed up in his hand.

This was the Jewish preserve, the sleeper knew. But where were his people, his Jews?

"There they are!" exclaimed Pius XII. He pointed to a number of gentlemen strolling past the window. They were speaking softly together and glancing into various books. "This is how Jews live now."

Just then a red ball bounced into the room, followed by a broad-chested boy. It was young Gumbiner, who was somehow already grown. Trumpelman smiled at his guests. "Have you met my son?"

The Englishman leaned forward, his forearms on his knees. "Fine boy!" he said.

The boy said, "Father, is he here yet?"

Everyone understood the person they were waiting for was the Big Man. Like the peach, he suddenly appeared. The guests rose to meet him. He looked like his photos, with his hair combed over his forehead. They did not call him Horowitz. They used his right name.

"The whole world thought we were going to kill the Jews," he began. "But what a fine farm we gave them! The Kingdom of Madagascar will last a thousand years!"

"The Jewish question has at last been solved," Roosevelt stated.

Stalin said, "Now the war can be ended."

"No more suffering for the peoples of the world!"

The Pope put his fingers together. "All men—brothers!"

Then the man with the black shock of hair said, "Let us hear from the peacemaker!"

"Speech! Speech!"

Trumpelman stood. His heart was swollen with happiness. The tears stood in his eyes. "Friends!" he began. He knew full well that he was only dreaming. But he felt the dream was a prophecy, a vision of the way things would be. That meant his Jews, with their courage, their discipline, and their patience, would survive. "Friends!" he said again, but the wind howled in the mansion and woke him up.

For a moment he struggled to remember the events of his dream—the end of the war, the homeland for the Jews, the husky child—but forgot them. Then Madame Trumpelman woke by his side. "Stop trembling," she said.

Her husband groaned. "Gumbiner," he said. "The boy!"

"We will have our own son."

But Trumpelman stared ahead. "His mother is on the list."

Madame Trumpelman put her arms around him; they wound their legs together. Above their bodies the instruments whooped and jangled and pounded. In the Ghetto, and even in the rest of the town, people heard how the whole house was moaning, like a great Aeolian harp.

Chapter Seven

The Yellow Bus

I

Where were you, ladies and gentlemen, when the Japanese struck the port of Pearl Harbor? There are hardly any Americans who do not seem to know. Down to the clothes they were wearing, and what they were thinking, and even the food on their forks. It is one of those magical moments capable of undoing thirty or forty years. Of all the stories that might be told of that unforgettable day, none is more marvelous than that of James Faulhaber—who, like many others, is no longer alive to tell it himself.

First, it was dusk, not dawn. The bald pate of the sun, peeping above the edge of the blue Pacific, had, over Poland, already gone down. In other words, the day of infamy, which on one side of the world was just getting started, on our side was practically done. The American citizen was standing at the gate to the Baluty Suburb, through which so many thousands had entered, without a single return. The streets were quite dark. No movement anywhere. Then an unusual event: two members of the Occupying Power, both in uniform, stepped forward and correctly saluted. Not only that, they actually picked up both of the Jew's leather bags.

"That's all right! Don't bother! I know my way!" Faulhaber managed a smile.

The guards spoke in English. "Is better please for your protection," one of them said.

The other added, "Safety from Jewish police."

The two of them strode through the gate into the Ghetto. Faulhaber, favoring one foot, followed. He wondered: was the Suburb always so still? It was too early, he knew, for the curfew. But where were the rickshaws? The peddlers? The half-frozen excrement buckets were, in fact, the only sign of life. And what did they mean, thought the officer from the Hatters Young Men's Benevolent Association, *protection from Jewish police?* He did not dare, however, to ask any actual question. The Men of Valor led him down Reiter Street, which was narrow and twisting, and where only a single lamp was lit.

Suddenly, into this light, a coatless and hatless figure came running. He cupped his hands around his mouth.

"Jews! A bulletin! Wait a moment!"

Then he dashed back into the doorway from which, it seemed, he had come. The pair of Blond Ones stopped and looked at each other. A window, several windows, opened over their heads. Inside some rooms the lights went on.

The man returned to his spot under the streetlamp. "Zlotys!" he shouted. He was trying to catch his breath. "Zlotys!" From five or six windows the coins came ringing down. "Bulletin! Bulletin! They just bombed an American seaport! In the paradise of Hawaii!"

Many more windows simultaneously opened. Jews hung from every one. "Who?" the Baluters demanded. "Who did it? When? What kind of bombs?"

"One moment!" The man—he was half of the same broadcasting station that had been held in the Tsarnecka Street jail—ran off into the adjacent building.

"It's nothing," said the neutral citizen to his uniformed escort. "Just a joke. On to Tsarskoye Selo." Neither guard moved. One of them, ominously, put down the suitcase he had been holding under his arm.

"Japan! Japan did it! It's a sneak attack!" The transmitter had come racing back. He clung to the lamppost. Grozys and zlotys struck the ground all around him.

Then a second man appeared in the doorway. He had earphones over his ears. His hands held a wire antenna. "They sank a battleship! Roosevelt will make a speech! That means war!"

The other soldier also put down his suitcase. He took hold of Faulhaber instead. "War?" he said, in English. "America in war?"

Faulhaber's head of course was spinning. When he had sailed from New York everything had been quiet and calm. He did his best to collect his wits. "Don't believe them! America is a peaceful, friendly country. The holiday of Christmas is only a few weeks away!"

The armed guards simply stood there, confused. Before they could decide on a course of action, the crowd, the people hanging from all the windows, began to shout things at their heads. Remember—these were Jews speaking. Saying things they had not dared even to think before.

"Hangmen! Murderers! The tide has turned. You can't beat the American army!"

"The Americans will build hundreds of tanks and bombers. On the assembly lines of Henry Ford!"

"Hail the liberators! Roosevelt! Morgenthau!"

James Faulhaber closed his eyes. Were prisoners of war, he wondered, permitted a phone call? But whom to telephone? He tottered a little, because the enemy suddenly released his arm. Alas, he felt something hard poking his rib cage. A gun muzzle? Bayonet? Then the crowd fell silent and all he could hear was the sound of windows slamming to.

"Faulhaber, James?"

The American opened his eyes. A gun, he had known it,

210

was pressed against his body. But it was held by a short-statured stranger, with a stocking over his head. The members of the Occupying Power, both of them, were standing against a wall with empty hands in the air. A second figure, also wearing a stocking, was keeping them covered with a pistol of his own. There was a third stranger, too. Also shortish. With eyeglasses over his cloth disguise. "Hurry up! This way!" he cried. It was an odd, high-pitched voice. More important, the words were in Polish. The speaker trotted down an unnamed, unlit alley.

"Wait! Where are we going? I am an officer of the HYM-BA! I am here on regular business. The Judenrat expects me. I must see Chairman Trumpelman."

But the man with the gun only jabbed it painfully into the area of his kidney. "Go now!" he ordered, in the same boyish voice as his partner. "Or else I'll shoot!"

Faulhaber found himself stumbling down the dark alley. A moment later the last hooded man came running toward them. He had the Conquerors' rifles in his arms. Then the foursome, Faulhaber limping a little, moved swiftly away. They made many turns. The prisoner had no idea of where they were going—except that it was not in the direction of Tsarskoye Selo. His heart was beating wildly, from exhaustion and fear. His only thought was that he had fallen into the hands of Ghetto bandits.

Suddenly one of the kidnappers held up his hand. "Stop!" he said. "Listen!"

Poor Faulhaber could hear nothing at all. But his captors grabbed him and threw him into the nearest doorway. One of them put the palm of his hand over his mouth. "Not a word," he warned. "Don't you hear?"

There was something, a few streets off. Feet tramping. Shoes shuffling. A noise like pots and pans. All this came steadily nearer. The American heard weeping, too. And dull, soft thuds. Unmistakably blows.

Then, turning a corner, a whole procession emerged from

211

the gloom. The man in the lead—though Faulhaber could not know him—was Officer Turski. Behind him, on either side of the street, were more Jewish policemen. They carried rubber clubs in their hands. In the center, between the two lines, was a mass of some two hundred Jews. They were the ones who were weeping. They had boxes on their backs, or they dragged tied-up bundles, like laundry, over the ground. The line of march passed in front of the doorway where the four men were hidden. Faulhaber was surprised to feel one of his captors tremble.

"The shame! The shame!" this man kept repeating.

Another bandit groaned and bit on the cloth of his stocking. He trembled, too.

There was still a gun barrel in Faulhaber's wool suit. The person who held it leaned closer and fiercely whispered. "Pay attention. Look carefully. Those are Jews dragging off Jews! It happens every second night. The quota is now eight hundred to one thousand weekly. They are taken to the Radogodsh Station and loaded onto a train. This train takes them to an unknown place. Remember this, Faulhaber. Remember the faces of the policemen. You have to tell the rest of the world."

"Can such things be?" the visitor groaned, watching the end of the procession move out of sight. The next thing Faulhaber knew someone had pulled a black stocking—this one without any eyeholes—over his head. They led him blinded through the narrow streets.

After ten minutes they went inside. But the journey was not over. They climbed stairs. Faulhaber bumped his head on a doorframe. He had to crawl on his knees through a tunnel. He even, it seemed, stepped out a window. At last, after going into and out of a series of connected low-ceilinged rooms, he was allowed to stand still. He could hear everyone huffing and puffing. A chair was pushed against the back of his legs. Without being pushed he sat down. They took his hood off. Then they removed their own.

"Hee, hee, hee!" They began to giggle wildly, like children. Which is what they were, Faulhaber saw. Three boys.

"Who are you?" the grown man demanded.

The oldest boy recovered first. His face grew stern. "Faulhaber, James," he declared. "You are the prisoner of the Edmund Trilling Brigade."

The American glanced around. He was in a small room with a slanted roof—an attic, he thought. There was paper over the windows. In one corner, a wireless machine. In another a hand printing press. Bags of sand were lined up along the floor. There were no pictures on the wall, except for a large poster, with the familiar mustache and pipe of J. Stalin, the Workers' Best Friend.

Faulhaber turned to the boy who was closest, the one with the thick milky glasses. He had a mole, a birthmark, under his eye. "I know you! You are from the Hatters' Asylum!"

"We know you, too, Mister Faulhaber. A monopolist exploiter. A Yankee boss!"

That speaker, with his wide forehead, the narrow, indented chin, was also familiar. "Is your name Szypper?" Faulhaber asked.

The third lad spoke for his companion. "Yes, it's Comrade Szypper. And I am Comrade Einhorn. Although there remain ideological differences between us, the time has come to forge a popular front. *Together the democracies shall crush the fascist forces.* Those are the words of the Man of Steel!"

The other two boys simultaneously shouted, "Death to the jackal!"

Then silence. Faulhaber became aware that a fourth boy was also sitting in the room. He still had his stocking on, and his featureless head kept falling onto his chest or his shoulder. Then Faulhaber saw the rope that bound his feet together and the rope that tied him to his chair.

Julius Szypper started speaking. "I have subjected my earlier remark, about the Yankee exploiter, to self-criticism. Of course America will now enter the war. We shall be allies.

213

You must insist to your government that they open a second front. To relieve the pressure on Moscow."

"Meanwhile," Einhorn put in, "you will contribute your American dollars to the Edmund Trilling Brigade."

Faulhaber felt as if a school of fish were swimming in his inner parts. "What American dollars?"

Nachman Kipnis: "Our agents have discovered the nature of your mission to the Balut. We know you have brought secret funds from American Jewish organizations. But neither you nor they know where that money goes. Into the tyrant's pocket! It pays the salaries of the policemen you saw tonight!"

"We are not obliged to make explanations!" said Szypper. "At this moment Leningrad is under siege. I know where he's hidden the money." The boy dropped to his knee and with great cunning pulled off Faulhaber's right shoe. It was full of green dollars.

"Aha!" shouted Einhorn. "I thought I saw him limp!"

"Bandits!" cried Faulhaber, his argyle sock showing. "Thieves!"

"How much?" Kipnis asked.

"Ten thousand! All cash!"

Szypper and Kipnis childishly cackled. "Quack! Quack!" said the former. "What a fat duck!"

But Einhorn's face was grave. "Do not call us bandits," he said to the courier. "Every penny shall be accounted for. The Edmund Trilling Brigade is a commando force, an advance unit of the Red Army. Five thousand dollars will be used to buy weapons from the Poles. The other five thousand will go into the ransom fund. In case our comrades are caught."

"But the money was specifically for medicine! For food! Why do you need guns? Do you think you can attack the Occupying Power?"

"That time will come," Einhorn replied. "For now, we have different targets. Nodelman, Turski, the rest of the police

214

command. Including Rievesaltes himself. Warnings have been sent to profiteers in the Ghetto. They'll be eliminated, too. Next come the traitors on the Judenrat. We shall execute them one by one."

Faulhaber jumped up, then sank down. "It's madness! Kill the leaders of the Ghetto? That's anarchy! You have to have a government here!"

"False!" Szypper shook his triangular head. "Such incorrect logic proves you are ignorant of world historical forces."

Kipnis: "I quote from V. I. Lenin. *While the state exists there can be no freedom. When there is freedom there will be no state.*"

Einhorn: "Everyone knows that in the higher phase of Communism the state, in the words of Engels, shall inevitably wither away."

"Yes! *Wither* away!" Faulhaber could not help himself from debating. "But you are talking about violence! About shooting people!"

"*Force is the midwife to the birth of every new social system.* Karl Marx."

"But, but, the Ghetto is a special case. Who will care for the sick? Who will teach the children? And feed the Jews who are hungry?"

Heish Einhorn addressed this point. "Faulhaber, that was the Jewish state marching those people away. The more government, the more of us disappear. First they wanted fifty. Then one hundred a week. Then two hundred. Now it's nearly a thousand. Starving isn't fast enough. Typhus is too slow. So the Judenrat itself will speed up the slaughter. Without a government, it's true, there will be chaos. People will suffer and people will die. But it won't be like it is now. The way it is now there won't be a Jew left in Poland!"

Kipnis came up. His eyes, and the tears in them, were magnified. "You saw? Faulhaber! You saw?"

Szypper also came closer. "The cursing? The clubs?"

Faulhaber: "Yes. With my own eyes."

215

Einhorn gripped the American's shoulder. "Comrade," he said.

At that moment footsteps were heard on the nearby stairs. The boys sprang for their weapons—the pistol, the two captured guns. A warning light flashed. A large man put his head in the door. It was the presser with the broken nose.

"It's our men," he announced.

Then a group of ex-Mosk Mill workers, led by Lipsky, squeezed into the room: Kleiderman, Kemp, old Mister Pipe. Also the woman who they said ate her son. Thus one of the most important results of the Five Day General Strike: those who had taken part in it had become progressives. There was a stranger, too, who stood a little off to one side. He was wearing an English raincoat and had the kind of bald head that bulged in the back, as if from brains.

"Comrades!" Szypper exclaimed. "Faulhaber's with us! He understands!"

Lipsky's hair was still standing up in the back. He spoke as fast as an automatic gun shoots. "That doesn't matter. The situation has changed. We've got to do more than shoot one or two people. Listen, the attack on America has been confirmed. Tomorrow or the next day one side or the other will make a declaration of war. Not only that, Stalin himself has issued a secret order for the counteroffensive. The slogan will be: *Victory in 1942!* Quiet! Quiet! No time for chitchat. We can't wait for the Americans to open a second front. The Jews of Europe will become the second front! Kipnis! Try to contact the partisan groups. Call Bialystok! The time has come for the Suburb to arise!"

Comrade Kipnis sat down at once at the wireless set. He cranked the handle around.

Hersh Einhorn struck his fist into his hand. He shouted, "Tell us what to do!"

"The Ghetto shall throw off its tyrants!" Lipsky responded. "We'll destroy them in their very nest! Yes! We're going to blow up Tsarskoye Selo!"

216

"The Elder! The Queen! But how—"

"How is up to Professor Zygmunt."

Yes, that is who the stranger was. How greatly changed he appeared! How much older! In the Jewish graveyard, just two years before, he had not been bald at all. Now what hair he had grew out of a fringe and hung, snow white in color, to his shoulders. The Professor held up two shaking hands.

"Stand back! Do not come closer. You see before you a human bomb!" So saying, he clutched, and parted, the front of his waterproof slicker.

Everyone gasped, including Lipsky. For inside that garment, strapped to his body, were dynamite sticks and gasoline bottles, all of it wired to a large spring-wound clock. "I have solved completely the technical problems. The results of a bomb blast of this type will be a forceful explosion followed by fire. The summer palace will dissolve in flames and smoke."

Kleiderman, with his tongue, pushed a toothpick from his mouth. "But how will it work?"

"By elementary chemical and mechanical principles. The explosives involve the former, the detonator the latter. The most difficult problem was the fuse and the timing device."

"No, no, that's not what I meant by my question. The Elite Guard is everywhere. How will you plant the device without being detected? And how will you know when to set if off? What if the dictators aren't actually there?"

"Easy, easy, I walk into the mansion and request an audience with *him*. As everyone knows, *she* has not left the mansion for months, not since she became pregnant. Once I receive an appointment there is nothing to do but wind up the clock and set the alarm. Perhaps I shall have time for a small cigar. I have some dandelions, which I like to smoke in a cabbage leaf."

The cannibal woman—they still called her that, even though everyone knew she had not eaten her son, only kept his death secret in order to use his ration card—asked the question in all of their minds: "But where will you be when the alarm goes off?"

Zygmunt gave a little wave of his hand. "Oh, where will I be? Where was I when Madame Zygmunt went off to the distant farmlands? *On the other side of the fence,* my dear. So frightened that I could not prevent myself from releasing the contents of my bladder. The urine went completely down my leg. You know, do you not, that I was once a professor at Crakow? I taught young men and women about the conversion of heat into light and how all energy in the universe is saved. My damp trousers, I believe, were seen by my wife. Do you remember the financier, Fiebig? The first of us to die? Do you remember the way, in the Central Square, he lit a match? This Fiebig is our example. Similarly, I light my match."

James Faulhaber stood up so quickly his chair flew to the rear. "But the Hatters' Asylum is located inside the mansion! All our orphans are there!"

"I have already thought of that problem," said Lipsky. "That's why we have brought him here." He meant, it was clear, the prisoner still bound to the chair. "Take off the hood. Untie him."

Hersh Einhorn jumped to obey. Nisel Lipiczany was the person inside the stocking. There was a tape across his mouth. Einhorn removed it as well.

"Lipiczany, you have heard everything. No need to repeat it. Your role is to get the children out of the building. One way or another. Out of the estate completely, if you can. It's a big job. You are responsible for many lives."

Nisel was doing his best to breathe calmly. The light, after the hours of darkness, stung his eyes. He said something. No one could hear it. He said it again.

"If I refuse?"

"You won't refuse."

"But if I do?"

218

"The tyrants," said Lipsky, "must die."

"It's not possible!" Faulhaber shouted. "I won't allow it. The property belongs to the Hatters' Association! Even if the orphans are not harmed, where will they go?"

Nachman Kipnis was sitting by the wireless machine. The tall tubes flashed and glowed on the glass in his spectacle frames. "To make an omelet, said Lenin, you have to break eggs!"

Faulhaber: "I can't believe I am here. It's like a dream. It's appalling!"

"Don't forget, Comrade, what you saw on the street tonight."

Lipiczany, between breaths, managed to speak. "What did he see? What? He saw Jews leaving the Ghetto, but not where they were going. The Elder has assured us they are not in danger. That they are being sent to the farms."

"Then why don't we receive any letters? Like we did from the people before?" Mister Kemp then lowered his voice to a whisper. "I believe they are being deported to forced-labor camps."

"The most suspicious thing," said young Einhorn, "is the way the same train always returns. Every two days. The same engine. The identical third class cars. Obviously the Jews aren't going far. It's an ominous sign."

Lipiczany, quickly: "But that's all been explained. They're probably switched to a second train. Along with the Jews from other ghettos. There must be an express to the west."

"Is this true?" asked Faulhaber. "No one knows where our citizens go?"

Lipsky: "This is what we know. The Baluters leave, they don't come back. Not a single letter arrives. We have a report that the engine was seen thirty kilometers east, not west. That's all. It is madness to assume anything but the worst."

Nisel's body jerked, as if from hiccups. His face was twisted. "I'll find out where the train is going. It won't take more than two or three days. If I can't get the information, I'll take the orphans out of the summer palace. I promise! I give my word! It's not fair to kill people because of rumors! What will happen to us without the Elder? Did you hear what happened to the Lublin Ghetto already? All the Jews have disappeared. Every one! Here we work! Here we have productive jobs! Thanks to Chaim alone!"

"Hello! Hello! Bialystok? I've got Bialystok! Comrades! Our fraternal greetings!" Kipnis turned toward Lipsky for his instructions. Everyone else turned toward him, too. He hesitated. He rubbed the top of his pointed ear.

"How will you get out of the Suburb?" he asked the boy.

"From the Zgierska Boulevard Bridge," Nisel answered.

"No good. They'll pick you up in a moment. Let me go. I don't look like a Jew." Einhorn, with his flat nose, said that.

Now Szypper interrupted. "There is only one way to find out where the train is going, and that is to put an agent aboard. He can let himself be caught in a roundup. Of course, he'll hide his gun."

"At the very least," added Kipnis, "he can leave a message inside the carriage."

Said Szypper, "I'm the one for the job!"

Lipsky had made up his mind. He gave the following order to Kipnis: "Inform Bialystok that we shall postpone the operation." Then he turned to Nisel. "You have only four days."

"Oh!" A cry came from Professor Zygmunt. He was shaking all over, like a palsied man. "I was definitely prepared to do it!" He began to stagger first this way, then that. You could hear the gasoline sloshing inside the bottles. "I had worked myself up!" With that he stiffened, like something frozen, and fainted onto the floor.

"Help!" cried the cannibal woman. "He's ticking!"

The members of the Edmund Trilling Brigade rushed forward. They opened the coat of the human bomb and disengaged the wires to the clock.

In the sudden silence, everyone turned toward Lipiczany. But Lipiczany, quick as a monkey, had already darted away.

II

Zgierska was an Aryan thoroughfare even though it cut through the middle of the Ghetto. The only way to go from the one half of the Balut to the other was to climb over the bridge. This was a tall wooden construction that passed over the boulevard at a height of three stories. It had a steep stairway on either side. There were always Jews on it, passing in both directions. For some reason, this structure had become a popular spot for the Baluters to kill themselves. Three people had been known to jump off in a single day. The Conquerors posted two regulations on the uppermost railing:

It is strictly forbidden to interfere with any Jew who is attempting suicide.

And:

Jews wishing to commit suicide are requested to make certain they have proper identification cards in their pockets.

After a time, though, these signs were removed. Perhaps because, by the winter of 1941, not so many people were using the bridge for that purpose. It wasn't really high enough. There were cases of men and women who had to lie on the pavement, while the crowds of Poles passed around them, as if they, with their broken limbs, did not exist.

At five in the morning the bridge was empty. The sky was as black as tar. Lipiczany moved slowly up the stairs. He had on a cap and gloves and an overcoat that hung to his ankles. The sleeves were held back with pins. Halfway up the stair-

221

way he stopped. He swooped the hard air noisily into his lungs. It felt as if the huge, thick coat were completely filled with his abnormal heart. Without removing his mittens, clumsily, he tore the six-pointed patch from his breast. Then he pulled himself higher.

At the top of the bridge he took a coil of rope from his pocket. It was thin as a clothesline. His intention was to drop from the end of the rope into the avenue. From there he would make his way to the train tracks and follow them to wherever—it couldn't be far—the engine turned around. The road below was deserted. Not a Pole. Not one of *them*. He tied the end of the rope to the base of the railing and threw the length down. He squeezed between the wooden supports. In the brown horsehair coat, he must have been nearly invisible. And even if someone did see him, he'd think it was only another despairing Jew. Nisel sat on the edge for a moment, clutching the rope, letting his feet, like a boy fishing, dangle down.

Then, from the south, from beyond Brzeszinska, the light of dawn appeared. It moved toward him quickly, blue-colored, and yellow and orange. Nisel pulled the visor of his cap over his tender eyes. But the light kept drawing closer, making a snapping noise. It wasn't dawn; it was the first run of the Zgierska Boulevard No. 4 trolley. He knew that, with one part of his mind. He could see the tramcar itself, swaying and jerking past the Baluter Ring. But in the other part of his mind, the part that made him lean forward, slack-jawed, gaping, the light that raced at him along the taut cable was like a star's. It sizzled. It shot out sparks. He thought he felt the hot blue bits of flame burn on the cloth of his coat and touch his face. Then the tip of the trolley passed under the bridge.

"There! It's a Jew!" An Aryan somewhere was shouting.

Nisel opened his mouth, as if to let his heart fly out, and fell toward the humming wire. Something ripped his glove off and scorched the palm of his hand. At the same instant a hot tongue of flame licked across his cheek. Then the rope, which had slashed him, ran out; he dropped hard onto the roof of the tram. He lay there, with his head twisted about, looking upward. The lights parted above him, like the phosphorescent wake of a ship. It was like staring into the gleaming crystals of the Szapiro & Son chandelier. Then, while he was watching, the lights grew dim and soon faded completely. That meant he was falling unconscious, or else, behind the clouds, from a distance of billions of kilometers, the spark of the sun had lit a new day.

The No. 4 trolley, stopping and starting, rolled over its route. Poles climbed onto it. They stood in the narrow aisle and clung together at the platform in the back. By the time they reached Piotrkowska Street, there wasn't room for another passenger. With its bell ringing, the old car ran right by the crowds who were waiting. No one, either inside the trolley or in the streets or looking down from their windows, saw the boy stretched out on the roof. At last the tram swung off Alexsandrowska into the Central Square. It made a complete circuit, right around the Rumkowsky Monument, and came to a stop. End of the line.

Nisel lay there, half fainting. His bones were not broken, but there was a rope burn on his hand and his cheek. One glove was missing. The cap remained on his head. He knew he had to jump down, to run off, or else he would surely be seen. But he did not move.

The reason for this was that the No. 4 line terminated directly in front of the Hotel Europa. Every few seconds a bell would ring, the pastry shop door would open, and the smell of the buttertarts, the ones with the toasted crusts, would expand through the street, through the air, to Nisel's nose. The boy could taste them. He could see them, piled up on their white paper doilies, the bottom of one resting on the crust of another, as if there had never been a war. Pyramids! Out of gold! Once Chaim had led all the orphans into the shop: "Tarts for everyone!" Nisel remembered the way they dis-

223

solved, without any help from the eater, onto the tongue. How warm they made you feel! How contented! Why should he move? Why fight? Why run? He would stay here forever, the muscles of his body, the whole of his waking mind, both tensed for just one thing: the cheerful tinkle of the pastry shop bell.

Instead he heard the whistle, a kind of shriek really, from the resettlement train. He sat up. The black engine and black tender, the blue third-class carriages, were just disappearing behind the Donati Station, only to appear in a few seconds again. Smoke, like link sausage, shot above the locomotive. The shades were pulled down inside every car. It was going from Nisel's left to his right. Eastward! Not west! He buttoned his greatcoat and leaped to the ground. The Poles, bicycling by, paid no attention.

Lipiczany followed the tracks for more than half an hour. For much of that time he kept the transport, which moved no more quickly than a man can walk, in view. The light gray sky still had a few birds in it. Here and there the sun nearly came out, the way a picture appears in a rubbing. After a few kilometers all the east–west tracks drew together, in order to pass over the Dolna. It turned out that, since the formation of the Russian front, the bridges over the river were guarded. Nisel had not thought of that. He saw how the Men of Valor stopped all the traffic, whether on foot or not—how they went through people's papers and searched their carts. There was even a gun there, a big one, which pointed upward in case of planes.

There was nothing to do but veer down toward the river. At the embankment there was a rope-driven ferry, but Nisel did not dare risk getting on. Instead, as soon as he was out of sight of the sentries, he went to the water's edge. He took off his cap and his shoes and thrust them deep within his pockets. Then, without hesitating, he stepped into the icy Dolna.

The trouble was, he could not swim. Worse, the water

came up to his chin. One more step forward and he found himself revolving downstream. It was amazing, the speed of the current. It stripped off his socks. By holding his breath and moving his hands, Nisel could keep himself on the surface. But the coat he wore grew heavier every moment. It was weighing him down. Soon he could barely lift his arms to tread water. So he tried, half submerged, like a Houdini, to free himself of the garment. However, the buttons stuck. The wet hide clung to his body. He went under. As he sank, rolling over, he thought he was being embraced by I. C. Trumpelman, whose greatcoat this was. *Chaim!* he called, swallowing mouthfuls, and the horsehair coat slipped from his shoulders. He shot up, near the eastern bank. On his hands and knees he climbed onto land. The Lithuanian coat washed up fifty meters down the shore.

Have you ever seen a big, furry dog coming out of the water? How puny it seems! Only a third of its former size. That is how Nisel looked, half drowned, gasping, in just his shirt and his pants. But he could not lie there, exposed. Boats were passing. People could see him from the opposite shore. He crawled to the heap of his greatcoat. It was too heavy to lift. He dragged it to the top of the embankment and fell with it, exhausted, into a clump of reeds. He had not slept in the night; no wonder he dozed much of that day. He woke in the afternoon, his overcoat dried out beside him. His bones ached. He sneezed. Also, he was hungry. He put on his shoes, his wrinkled cap, and arose.

From hunger, and from a fever perhaps, he felt slightly dizzy. He walked with a little weave. He found the four sets of rails and started along them. Soon he had to make a decision. The tracks divided, two branching south, the others moving side by side straight ahead. It was something else he had not considered. How could he ask a Pole which way the blue passenger cars had gone? While he stood there, uncertain, a train came toward him speedily from the east. He scampered down the roadbed and hid behind a shack. It was a large, long, olive-green train, with as many cars as the old Warsaw–Berlin express. The people in it, staring out the windows, leaned on their hands. The train roared by, rotating its gold-colored bell. Nisel discovered the shed behind which he was standing was open. There were tools inside, and sacks filled with root vegetables and potatoes. The land here was divided into small plots, tended by inhabitants of the city. The boy stuffed his pockets with turnips, with beets, and resumed his journey. He chose the rails that bent away to the south.

That proved a mistake, though Lipiczany could not guess as much for quite some time. He plodded forward, kilometer after kilometer. With his head at an angle, he gnawed at a beet. After dark, he walked on the tracks themselves, adjusting his gait to the space between the ties. He stopped once, to improvise a pair of socks from his shirttails. Then he grew too cold and tired to go on. He saw the silhouette of a barn in the fuzzy moonlight, and made for it. When a dog barked there, he simply dropped where he was and wrapped himself in the horsehair coat. He fell asleep, instantly dreaming of his unknown mother and father: the woman with the gold hair and the man, in profile, pomaded. Three trains went by, waking him—all the wrong ones.

By afternoon of the next day Lipiczany, dawdling, his head reeling, understood that he had gone the wrong way. For by then the resettlement shuttle would have had to pass him on its journey back. There was nothing to do but turn around. This he did, reaching the place where he had made his error at midnight. He slept in the same shed from which he had taken the beets. Many trains passed; he slept through them. His skin was now hot to his own touch. At daybreak he started tramping again, on the east–west track. Two hours later the train with the blue carriages caught him by surprise, blowing its whistle close behind him. It rumbled by. The windows were closed off as usual, but Nisel, lying flat by the roadbed, saw a single hand clutching a single shade.

When he came to the next spot where the tracks diverged—the two rails suddenly becoming four, crossing and crisscrossing each other—the boy sat down, clutching his knees with his arms. The next day the black locomotive with the three blue cars returned. Nisel saw that he must bear to the left. It was the afternoon of December 11.

There is no need to retell each of Nisel's adventures. Many did not remain clear in his own mind. One day passed into another. A light snow fell, the sun shone, once it rained. A boar, or so he thought it must be, chased him with its tusks. He slept in barns, in ditches, in open fields. He drank from wells, from potholes filled with rain. One time, grinding his teeth, he stole a chicken. Unflinchingly he wrung its neck. His black hair grew over his eyes.

The reason this trip, not a long one in terms of distance, took so much time was that at every new switch Nisel had to wait for the shuttle, full or empty, to go by. He came to know each detail of the train. He memorized the serial numbers on every carriage. He knew where a certain window was cracked. Sometimes he could see the men in the cab of the engine throwing things into a purple fire.

Only once did this familiar sight change. Between the first two and the last two passenger cars there was suddenly a flat-bedded wagon. Warriors stood there, holding guns. Nisel saw this late in the day. He was in a plowed field, covered by stubble and frost. No place to hide. The black locomotive, its yellow light burning, was practically upon him. Lipiczany hurled himself down and buried his head under his collar. From the moving machine he must have looked like a dead horse. No one fired a gun. Huddled there, beneath his sorrel skin, Nisel kept counting the cars: four now! Four! More Baluters than ever! He remained there; he fell asleep. During the night he woke himself with the sound of his weeping. You have to remember that this wild Jew was just a boy of fourteen.

Two nights later, when it was cold and clear, Lipiczany ar-

227

rived. The train tracks curved off side by side into a forest. The rails, of new metal, were gleaming, like the path left by a pair of giant snails. The forest itself seemed enchanted. The frosty trees had no leaves. High up in the crossed branches, in the switches and twigs, the moon was sitting, like a bright owl. There are many folk tales in which a child, with a kindly, befuddled father, and a mother who wishes to kill him, is left in just such an unnamed wood. Nisel, his head spinning, plunged in.

In reality, of course, there was nothing mysterious about this spot. You can look it up today on a good map of Poland. Indeed, one hundred years ago there was a town nearby, and a small industry based on pulp from the trees. But Nisel did not know where he was. To him, half delirious, the solid ground gave way like a mattress on springs. A sign of high fever. Suddenly the trees stopped, although the twin rails continued. In the center of the cleared space there was a guardhouse, from which a zebra-striped barrier protruded over the tracks. There were also four wide-awake guards. Totenkopfers! With moonlight, in patches, stuck to their helmets.

Nisel detoured. But the break in the trees went on and on. He would have to run through fifty meters of stumps. He tried it, tripping and stumbling, and got halfway across. Then he came to a wire fence. It was twice as tall as he was, taut and barbed. He squinted. There was a second, identical, fence just beyond this one. At that moment, between the two barriers, three men and a dog sauntered along. Nisel ran back as far as he dared, then hurled himself down. The patrol passed him by. Then he doubled back, stooping, to the rim of the standing trees.

He sat for some time without being able to think of a thing to do. At last, when his breath quieted down, he heard a gushing, gurgling noise. Keeping parallel to the swath of felled trees, he made his way to what turned out to be a swift, dark, downrushing stream. White boulders stuck up in the current like huge mushroom caps. The boy hopped from one to another until he came to the place where the wire was stretched over the water. What luck! Lots of room to get through. Nisel ducked under the lowest strand and made his way uphill to the inner forest. He climbed and climbed. When his strength gave out he curled around the bony white base of a birch tree. All night he heard it groaning and creaking, as if it were a mast of a ship in the wind.

Dawn. Nisel woke up. The sky grew only so bright, no brighter, as if there had been a reduction in current. He saw the pale, straight trunks of the trees. Then the familiar train whistle hooted. Nisel jumped to his feet and scrambled quickly to the top of the hill. He peeked over. There, just below him, making smoke, was the black locomotive, its tender, its passenger cars. It was already backing up, already moving away. The shades were up, the carriages empty. With a second blast of its whistle, it rolled out of sight.

The track ended where the train had been standing, against an embankment of logs. On the far side of the rails, on the edge of the bubbling stream, there was a large three-tiered building. It must have been a mill, because a water wheel was turning and turning. Lipiczany could see the top third of it, the black, wet buckets rising out of and dipping below the shingled roof. This was the noise, the creak and the rumble, he had heard during the night. It had not been the slim trees.

It was dangerous to look any longer. The Blond Beast was everywhere. One group was standing between the train tracks and the building. Two sentries remained at attention on either side of the millhouse door. A Warrior walked down an exterior staircase, pulling on a pair of gloves. Nisel lay flat on his belly. The whole sky was full of dark, low clouds, like sacks about to burst. Why were the windows of the mill boarded up? What was it grinding?

Then, as if in response to these questions, the heavy doors

opened inward and thirty Jews emerged, carrying bundles. There were men and women. They still had the stars on their chests. Though this was not even a half-carriage load of people, the doors were already shutting behind them. No others came out. The little crowd stepped over the tracks, toward where Nisel was hiding, then turned to their right, his left, and began to walk around the foot of the wooded bluff. Nisel ran diagonally across the top of the ridge, to where he thought he could head them off. At the sharp edge of the slope he looked down again. The Jews were just coming around, in their black coats and hats. Awaiting them were a small number of Death's-Headers and an old, yellow, hand-starting bus.

The front of this vehicle was pointed toward Nisel's cliff, or rather toward a kind of flat gully, a dry riverbed, a bit farther to his left. He could see its old-fashioned round headlights, one cracked, the other without a lens. The double-winged hood was lifted and a Warrior in uniform was lying across the bulging fender, at work on the engine inside. The yellow rooftop was battered, dented, as if it had been stoned. A layer of dust covered the windshields. At this distance, through the hundreds of trees, Nisel barely heard the mill's grindstone, the mill wheel's creak.

The Jews came to a halt near the rear of the bus. They were Baluters. Lipiczany recognized four or five of the crowd: Palfinger, a jeweler; one of the Fiebig sons; the Widow Tort who had also been the Widow Greenkraut; and, with her black hair in a bun, holding a small, white, neatly tied bundle, Madame Dickstein, a survivor of the Koscielny Place blaze. They all stood quietly, looking down. Then one of the Lords and Masters walked over to the Jews and said something to them. Right away the deportees put down their sacks and valises and began to take off their clothes. They took all their things off, in spite of the winter's cold. The men and the women tied their shoes together by the laces. Then they stood up, approximately in a line.

How white they were! Whiter than birches! How thin! Nisel had never seen a naked adult. Some of the Jewesses, some of the Jews, kept their hands in front of their bodies. But the rest were exposed. It was a shock to the boy to see the black sexual hair, especially the women's, growing so far up their bellies. He looked at their faces, at the half-open mouths, the half-open eyes. Then the back door of the bus swung open and the thirty-odd Jews from the Suburb climbed inside.

Nothing happened, except that the door was shut. The Blond Ones stood in various places, with their arms crossed or with their fingers in their belts. Finally, the mechanic slid off the fender, clapped his hands together, evidently to warm them, and turned the crank. The motor started. The bus body shook. It rattled. One half the engine cover slammed down, and the raised part clattered against itself. Nisel thought the bus would drive up the ravine, to transport the Jews to a different spur of the railway. But it did not move from the spot.

Then the boy noticed two things: first, that the front wheels were missing; and then, through the grime on the windshield, that there was no driver inside. This was not like a fairy tale—the tracks like snails' trails; the white, mushroomy boulders; the moon like an owl in a tree. It was like dreaming. A coach without wheels, with no one to drive it: yet the engine roared, the body shook and swayed, for all the world as if it were speeding along on a journey. Minutes went by, one like another. A black bird, as large as a crow, flew from Nisel's hilltop and floated downward. It perched, like a black knot, on top of Madame Dickstein's white bundle. The motor ran for another quarter hour. The bird filled Nisel with dread because of its tameness. It was like a person's pet.

When the Jews came out of the bus, all of them—Palfinger, Adolf Fiebig, the others—were dead. But to Lipiczany they were simply sleeping. Who would wake first? he wondered. He, himself? Or they? A team of matched horses came from

231

the direction of the mill, hitched to a rubber-wheeled cart. It was they who pulled the Ghettoites to the ravine. The clothing, the luggage, the shoes—that remained behind.

And the pile grew larger as each new batch of Jews—always in groups of thirty—added its share. Nisel almost always saw a person he knew: Pincus Lining, the maker of glass lambs and glass storks; Naymark, the trombonist, who had run away rather than serve on the Judenrat; the well-known Rabbi, Martini.

In one such group, in his flat cap, was young Julius Szypper. Nisel could hardly believe it. A member of the Edmund Trilling Brigade! It had to be a dream! But Szypper took off his cap, his coat, his shirt and his pants. He tied together his shoes. The boy on the hill felt a surge of anger, of envy. Why didn't the resistance fighters wait for him? Why did Szypper have to smuggle himself aboard the train? Because they didn't trust him, Nisel, to return! He knew, too, that somewhere nearby the partisan had hidden his gun. He thought that at any moment his comrade would lead a revolt. What actually happened was that Szypper climbed into the bus; the bus shuddered and shook; and then Szypper, with all the others, was brought out again. Even then Lipiczany was certain the boy would escape. Where was his gun? His gasoline bombs? His secret plan? He waited for the Red hero to wake from his slumber.

The day passed that way. The gray sky hung thicker, lower, like a drooping eyelid. Four different times the bus was washed out with barrels of water. Once, with Jews aboard, something went wrong with the engine. It ran for a bit, then sputtered and stopped. How quiet and peaceful the spot became! A Man of Valor, the same one who had put on his gloves on the staircase, walked to the side of the coach. He placed his ear against it.

"Just like in a synagogue," he said.

Then they cranked the engine and the old omnibus—did those inside think they were on a highway, going past fields and forests and towns—came back to life, vibrating. It was dark by the time the work ended. The rubber-wheeled cart took on the empty water barrels. The Warriors walked beside it, toward the mill.

The night fell without a moon, without stars. Lipiczany walked over the hill like a blind man, hands out. It took him more than an hour to reach the ravine, though it was only a few hundred meters away. The bottom was covered with hard, smooth, flattened stones that clattered as he walked upon them. He could almost see them, they were so intensely white. After a time he came to where the Jews were lying on the ground. He did not stop. He moved forward, among them. His fingers had long since come through the cloth of his remaining glove. He touched the cold, damp skin of the bodies. They were as white as the stones.

"Wake up! Wake up, Jews!" he cried.

It must now be clear that at some point in the day—perhaps at the instant the dark crow settled upon Madame Dickstein's bundle—Lipiczany had lost his mind. It never occurred to him that the Jews might be dead. He hurried, crouching, from one person to another. He touched their foreheads, their noses, their tightened lips. "Wake up!" he told them. "I'll lead you to the Suburb. I know the way."

Something touched his own face. Snow! The flakes were as dark, as weightless, as burned paper. They filled him with urgency. "Widows! Baluters! It is dangerous to sleep in the snow! We have to stay awake! Let's tell each other stories! About the way it used to be! Do you remember? We lived on Krzyzanowsky Street. The Director gave us raspberry drops. You sucked them until you came to the center. What a center, Jews! Sweet and delicious! Szypper! You know! You remember! In back of the Asylum there was a garden. We grew flowers! Bees came there! It was like heaven! We beat our rugs with a broom!"

Nisel sat cross-legged, chattering happily. Then, while he rested, the others took turns. Madame Dickstein described how the Elder—what strength, what courage he had!—walked into the fire to save her. How all by himself he had rescued everyone. After her, Rabbi Martini. He said he had been in the crowd outside Assisi Street 2. He told everyone how the Elder had saved Jewish daughters from defilement at the House of Pleasure. Next came Pincus Lining. The Elder had personally accepted his petition and saved his room from the fumigation squads. Then, to entertain the Baluters, to pass the time in the night, he blew some glass animals, the kind he used to sell in the street. The biggest one was a bird. It grew and grew. Its glass wings spread over the Jews to protect them. It kept off the black snow.

In the morning Nisel woke, perfectly lucid. He knew he was surrounded by corpses. There was excrement on their legs; some of the women were bloodstained. He also knew he had to get away. Farther along the ravine people were working. They stood halfway up the canyon wall, tumbling dirt into the ditch below. The entire riverbed was being turned into a grave. Ahead of this falling earth, a platoon was walking slowly downward. They stopped over this body or that. One of these had already worked his way quite near. He was dressed like a Jew, shabby, middle-aged. But he was no bigger, or older, than Nisel. There was a pouch strapped over his shoulder and a blade of some kind in his hand. He turned slightly. Then Nisel realized that this was Konotop, one of the Konotop brothers, supposed to be drowned. His eyebrows still grew in a line, thickly, over his eyes. The two boys stared at each other. Nisel, on his journey, had nearly forgotten how to speak.

"I have to tell the Elder," he finally said. "He doesn't know the Others are killing the Jews."

But Konotop, having no idea who this person was, did not answer. He bent over an anonymous woman and cut off the long, dark locks of her hair.

Lipiczany ran for his life, straight up the canyon wall. He

234

thought each instant there would be a shot, an outcry, the yelp of a loosened hound. He reached the top, where the birches grew, and rolled onto his back. There he breathed, and swallowed, the air. He knew that he would die before he could follow the railway back to the Ghetto. Even if he had had the strength, the trip would take too long. At that moment a fresh load of Jews was leaving the transfer station. There would be trainloads more. So he simply lay there, listening to the roar of the grindstone. One miracle was that his cap, with its little button, was still on his head.

All that day the cart went back and forth, bringing the clothes, the bundles, back to the mill. The buckets rose wet over the rooftop, like mouths that bit and chewed at the sky. Nisel could not help sleeping. In his dream, his imagination, there was a spinning wheel inside the mill, like at the Mosk Works; and on this loom all the clothing and rags, the gray dresses and dark coats and dark trousers, were being woven into one gigantic cloak.

At dusk the train woke him up. The whistle blew and the steam came from many places, as if the engine had been punctured with holes. Out came the farmers-to-be, the mowers and threshers, the milkmaids. They went directly into the mill. In the course of that night Nisel crept down the hillside to the last of the third-class wagons and secretly climbed inside.

And that is how, the following morning, Nisel Lipiczany set off for the Ghetto. The trip, as we know, took the entire day. Most of that time he spent hiding beneath one of the wooden benches. But now and then he sat up and looked calmly out the window, like a passenger with a ticket. They arrived on schedule, well after dusk. It was a roundup night, and so the streets were deserted. The Radogodsh Station was empty, too. Nisel trotted into the Baluty Suburb. He did not look like a boy any longer. Scratched, crooked, filthy, he looked like a beast.

235

The organ in the Church of the Virgin Mary could no longer play: not because of the ban on music within the Ghetto—from this it had been specifically exempted—but because the little holes in the pipes were clogged by feathers. Yes, feathers and feather dust! In short, the church was once again filled with the bolsters and pillows, the soft downy cushions, that belonged to the deportees. Thus when the Jewish Christians wanted to sing, there was no instrument to accompany their voices.

It was past midnight, and all the converts were singing. In the still Ghetto you could hear them far and near. Actually, although the church was crowded with worshipers, not every person sang along. Some mumbled the words and others went *tum-tum-tum*. These were the people who didn't know when to stand or when to kneel, and who crossed themselves in the wrong direction. The question was, were they Catholics at all? In the Office of Vital Statistics there were documents pointing out that the Christians were the only group inside the Suburb that had not—because of sickness, deportation, acts of despair—shrunk in size. Indeed, they had constantly grown. And on this night, when there was sure to be a roundup, people who had never been there before flocked to the church. They looked around to see what the next fellow was doing; all too often that Baluter was mumbling, too. The newcomers did not know whether it was proper to remove their hats. None knew the words of the song: *What means the turmoil among the nations? Why do the people cherish vain dreams?*

The priest of the congregation motioned with his hand, and everyone moved toward the altar. The priest himself looked like a merchant, a Jew. He was stocky, with short, pudgy fingers. His nose was flattened onto his mustache, and when he breathed he made a sniffing sound. On the other hand, the boy who helped him had blond hair that fell in waves almost to his shoulders. There were two candles on the altar, sputtering steadily from the bits of suspended fluff. They lit the child's head, so that it looked as if it had been painted in gold.

The line passed the altar and moved to a place where the Catholics were kneeling. There were animals there, made from wood and paper. Lots of powdery sheep. Brown donkeys. A cow with a real bell. The people who took care of these beasts, the shepherds, the cowherds, were also there. They had red dots on their cheeks and cardboard crooks and stiff paper staffs. They were kneeling. In front were three dark-faced kings, with jeweled fingers and jeweled crowns. Their eyes were made of white shells. Everyone, the kings, the shepherds, even the dumb beasts, was looking into the mouth of a cave. Inside was a light, and you could see a man with a beard and a woman in a blue gown and a child in the woman's arms. The little doll of the infant, with red lips, with pearly teeth, was gaily laughing. Even those Jews who had never seen such a thing fell to their knees.

The priest with the flattened nose began to speak in Polish. "Dear children, we are fortunate tonight to have with us a man who has proved to be our true friend. We are honored that he has agreed to speak to us during our mass. Is it not God's work that he has been sent to protect us? Let us hear his words."

The celebrant, with his acolyte, both in white robes, went behind the altar. The worshipers at the crib rose and returned to their former places. Then Isaiah C. Trumpelman appeared. There was a gasp, a murmur, and a few of the Jews started applauding. The Elder, hatless, taller than anyone, held up his hands. He spoke in Polish, too.

"Here I am, the same as I have always been, a poor Lithuanian Jew. I never tried to hide that from anyone. Some of you here were surprised to find out you shared that fate with me. The question is, what is a Jew? A lot of philosophers and big scholars have tried to answer that but they didn't know anything about it. A Jew is whoever Horowitz says is a Jew. That's why we're all here together.

"But we're also here because of the birth of this child. Soon heaven will bless me with a son of my own. That is why I cannot help feeling moved when I see this little baby in his mother's arms. It's an outrage that it has to be in a stable, with horses and cows. Even great kings have to kneel in the straw! I'm no expert on the life of this person. It's possible I'll say something that's wrong. But wasn't it because of the Conqueror's tax? Yes, the family of Jesus made the journey so they could pay their debt to Caesar, and when they got there no one would give them a room at the inn. The child had to be born the way it's shown here, in a cave. Then right afterward they had to flee again, because Herod, the king, wanted to seize him. When he couldn't find Jesus he was like a madman, like a savage, and killed all the children who were less than two years old. All the little ones! Don't worry! You don't have to worry! That can't happen here! No matter what Herod demands! In our orphanage the children are our number one concern!

"Next, the boy returned to Nazareth, and when he grew older he started to preach, telling all whom he met that the Kingdom of God was at hand. At that time the devil took him to the highest mountain and showed him the shining cities of the world and offered them to him as a gift. But Jesus rebuked him, and chose four fishermen, and other disciples, and traveled with them. Wherever he went he was followed by enormous crowds. He had the power of making sick people well. Just by touching them. There was a man with a withered hand, and he made it like the whole one. After Lazarus died and was in his tomb four days, Jesus called him out as a living person. He cured the deaf and the dumb. One time his disciples saw him walking on top of the water, to calm the waves. Another time he turned water into wine and five loaves of bread into five thousand.

"This was his message to men: that you should not love your neighbor and hate your enemy, but love your enemy too, blessing him when he curses you, doing good when he hates you, because God, the father of men, made the sun rise on the evil the same as the good, and sent rain on the unjust and just. He blessed the poor, the meek, and the children. He said the last would be first.

"But the rabbis, in spite of these miracles, did not accept this message. Not even when he went onto a mountain and his face began to shine like the sun and his cloak turned as white as light. They were cowards! Fearful men! When Jesus denounced these hypocrites, they plotted together how they might kill him. Alas! Alas! Even worse, it was a Jew, one of his disciples, that betrayed him. For money, and because of an envious heart. This disciple came to where he was walking in the garden and threw his arms up and kissed him. It was a sign for the followers of the rabbis to make the arrest. Then they took Jesus to the chief priests, who asked him whether he was, as he had said, the Son of God. The high priest stood, tearing his clothing, when Jesus answered, *I am*. And the rest spit at him and struck him for his blasphemy.

"I tremble! Tremble! How hard it is for me to say these things! Listen! The council turned Jesus over to Pilate. That man questioned him and, unable to find any fault in him, offered to let him go. But the Jews would not hear of it. They insisted: *His blood be on us, and on our children!* So the Roman let Barabbas go and, because of the clamor, had Jesus crucified on a cross. The crowds passed by, mocking him, asking where were his miracles and his wonders now. When he was thirsty a soldier gave him vinegar, poured on a sponge. Then the sky grew dark and he cried out and, as it is written, gave up the ghost. That is the story of the birth, the life, and the death of Jesus, who some say, even after he was buried, rose again."

"Yes! We do!"

"He sits on the right hand of God!"

"Praise Him!"

The congregation of the Church of the Virgin Mary was standing, crying out. The priest, behind the altar, wrung his fat hands. Trumpelman leaned on his cane. The converts at the Christmas mass shouted more loudly still.

"That's why the Jews suffer now! Because they wouldn't believe!"

"It's because they killed him!"

"Even the Elder admits the blood is on their heads!"

"And on the heads of their children!"

Trumpelman nodded. He smacked his lips. Then he started to laugh. "Ha! Ha! Ha! You've got it backward! Backward! You didn't understand a word!"

The whole of the congregation stared at him in amazement. "It's not because the Jews killed Christ that they have to suffer, but because they gave Christ to the world! Look! There! At the cave! That's where our troubles began! Turn the other cheek, ha-ha-ha! A Jew said that! Turn the other cheek and let them hit you again! If someone takes your coat, let him have your cloak also! Think about that! It's fantastic! It's like a joke! Love your neighbor! Love your enemy! Ha! Ha! Ha! That's a burden no one can bear! Horowitz knows it! That's his secret! He knows how hard it is to be good!"

The door at the back of the church opened and closed. In a moment a small black figure, its hair matted, its head held at an angle, came from behind a pile of cushions. Trumpelman saw him, and stared.

"Julius! Julius!" cried the apparition. Its voice was croaking.

Trumpelman steadied himself on the point of his cane. "Lipiczany!"

The boy howled: "Julius Szypper is dead!"

"Szypper?" The Elder staggered. "One of my little ones?"

Lipiczany gripped his own body, as if to force out the words. "Chaim! You have to stop the roundup! Stop all the

240

roundups! Warn the people! The Others have betrayed you! The Jews are not going to farmlands! They are being killed in a forest! Every one!"

The crowd in the church heard what Lipiczany was saying. Immediately the Jews began to cry out to each other, to wail. There was a tremendous, earsplitting commotion. Then, in her dark dress, in her dark-dotted veil, Phelia Trumpelman rose from the chair on which she had been sitting. Her belly was far too swollen to hide.

"Don't listen to him! This is an agitator. He wants to spread panic. He's a known Lipskyite!"

"No! No! They take off their clothes! There's a mill wheel! The Baluters are in a ravine!"

Now the converts joined in the wailing. They beat their breasts like the Jews.

"Don't stand there!" cried the Ghetto Queen. "Seize him! It's a Bolshevik plot!"

Two or three men lunged forward, but Nisel darted away. He ran to the Elder and gripped his hand. He was still wearing the old man's horsehair coat. "Chaim! Listen! A yellow bus!"

Trumpelman drew his lips back from his teeth. It was a tic he had developed. "What nonsense! It's nonsense! There is no forest!"

The boy was shaking. He squeezed the Elder's fingers. "I saw this with my eyes!"

"What if it's true? What do you want the Elder to do? To announce it? What suffering then! What a massacre! It's better if they think they're going to a farm."

Nisel stepped slowly backward. He turned his face, black like a chimney sweep's, away.

"Oh!" he cried. "You knew!" Then the sooty tears rushed from his eyes.

Just to the rear of Madame Trumpelman a man stepped forward. This was one of those Jews who did not know enough to remove his hat. Now he did so, revealing a head

241

that bulged in the back. Professor Zygmunt! Next he threw open the front of his raincoat and took out a ticking clock. "I-I-I-I am not afraid!" he shouted, and at once set off the alarm. For a bit nothing happened. Then there was a flash of light, all around the professor, followed by quite a loud bang. An immense cloud of feathers—feathers from chickens, from geese, from swans even—rose into the air, swirling everywhere. It was during that storm, like a snowstorm, that Madame Trumpelman lost her unborn male child.

Chapter Eight

Makbet

I

On Assisi Street, inside the House of Culture, a number of boys and girls were ice skating. At least, from the orchestra seats, from the balcony and boxes, it looked as if the stage must have been covered with a sheet of ice. That's how smoothly the children moved across it. They kept their hands behind their backs, the way skaters do, and glided about on bent knees. These were the students from the Vocational School. The girls wore red mufflers and plaid, pleated skirts. The boys were in black—black trousers, black cutaway coats, but with white shirts and, at the neck, white ruffles. From one side of the stage to the other they went, hand in hand, or alone. Sometimes a girl would throw up her arms and start rapidly to spin, or a boy would loop or leap; but mostly the whole group just skated along, swaying a little, with serious, thoughtful faces. Alone in the orchestra pit, on his gramophone machine, Smolenskin played marches from *Aida*.

When the children were done, they ran off the stage to tremendous applause. People were stamping their feet on the floor. They whistled and shouted. It's difficult to say why the skaters appealed so much to the Ghettoites. Naturally everyone knew the performance was an illusion. There wasn't—in

July, in Poland—any ice. You could see that the young men and young women were wearing regular shoes. Still, the applause got louder and louder. It would not stop. So the vocational students appeared once again. They slid forward on one foot and held the other one up behind. They leaned into the wind. This time Smolenskin was not playing a tune. The feet of the skaters went *shhh-shhh* over the wooden boards. In the audience no one spoke a word. The Baluters looked dazed. Perhaps it was because they were reminded of other places? Of prewar times? Perhaps it was because the pantomime was so carefree and—the bright skirts, the ruffles—so gay? The girls from the Vocational School had their hair done in braids, which swung across their faces. How red their cheeks were! It was exactly as if they were crossing the surface of a frosty pond.

Down from the rafters descended the Szapiro & Son chandelier. There was a light bulb inside it and this, with the houselights, came on. The Jews sat for a moment, staring quietly at the empty stage. Then more Jews pushed in. They came through the back doors and milled in the aisles. The men and women were wearing elegant clothes: jackets and trousers that matched and, in spite of the heat, shawls and long dresses. No one could remember seeing so many jewels, such brooches and rings. It was a stunning gala. "We want the skaters, too!" the latecomers shouted. The rest of the crowd took up the cry. "Encore! Encore!" But the skillful students did not reappear; the two halves of the big purple curtain swung shut, from either side of the stage.

It was amazing how the old warehouse for furs, briefly the House of Pleasure, had been transformed. The whole upstairs, where the skins had been stored, did not even exist. In the huge open space a balcony, and some boxes, had been constructed on poles. Underneath these, covering the entire floor, was the orchestra section. The back part was just wooden benches, but farther on there were regular seats, with cushions and armrests and, the same as in a cinema theater, bottoms that folded up. At the front were two rows of separate, upholstered chairs. That's where the Judenrat, the bigwigs, sat. Right now, however, these places were empty. The last stragglers found their seats and twisted about, hoping to catch a glimpse of the ministers when they came in. It was becoming a long delay.

Just then a disturbance broke out overhead. From the edge of the balcony, sheets of white paper came slipping and sliding down. There were dozens and dozens of these. The first-nighters stood on their seats to catch them. Something was written on each. ONE DOESN'T PUT ON SHOWS IN A CEMETERY! That was the message on one. Another one went like this: NO DANCING ON THE GRAVES OF THE DEAD! In short, it was the Lipskyites. They wanted the Jews to boycott the House of Culture! There was a sudden silence. People were staring upward, to see where the agitators might be. Then a plumpish man with black hair parted in the middle—it was Mister Luftgas—folded one of the broadsides in half and in half again. He threw it scornfully over his shoulder.

"We've heard all that before," he said.

True, true. Everything that Lipiczany announced at the midnight mass—the forest, the bus trip, the naked Baluters on the dried-up riverbed—all this had been printed on paper and dropped from building tops. The same documents showed up beneath people's doorways and on the benches of the spinning mills. The big presser, a member of the Edmund Trilling Brigade, walked all over the Suburb, carrying a leather suitcase. It was so heavy he had to keep setting it down. When he picked it up again a slogan was cleverly stenciled on the ground: DEPORTATION=DEATH, for instance, or DON'T GO LIKE SHEEP TO THE SLAUGHTER! The Ghettoites could not say they hadn't been warned.

Still and all, they didn't believe it. Everyone maintained that the only eyewitness was little more than a child. It was possible he had dreamed up, or misunderstood, the entire scene. And even if he had reported everything accurately, that didn't mean that all the deportees were subject to the same measures as those on that particular train. Besides, what if—just for the sake of argument, to take the devil's part—what if it were true that all the Jews were being killed, what were they, the Baluters, supposed to do? Fight back against tanks and airplanes and machines for flames? One might as well put the warnings out of one's mind. There were cafés to go to. Casinos sprang up. And above all, this great event: the grand premiere of the House of Culture. Eat, drink, and be merry, that's what people wanted. Ladies and gentlemen, wouldn't you?

Meanwhile, on Assisi Street, someone was standing at the lip of the stage. It wasn't a Bolshevik, not a pamphleteer. It was—in a tux, in a top hat—the master of ceremonies. The crowd clapped rhythmically, impatiently. They wanted to see the show.

"Look," Schotter cried. "It's Baggelman! And Urinstein! Also Verble and Mordechai Kleen!"

The audience turned around. In a bunch, in the doorway, were the members of the Jewish Council. They were dressed in special frock coats and polished shoes. All the big rabbis—Nomberg, naturally, and the Descendant, Wolf-Kitzes, Trunk of the Devout Butchers—were standing there, too. With Margolies in front, the officials walked toward the front of the room. Nobody cheered. But there weren't any catcalls, either. The procession went slowly, only as fast as Philosoff, using two canes, could shuffle. While they took their seats, the plush ones, Schotter spoke.

"Distinguished Ministers! Fellow Baluters! Did you hear what happened in the town of Stok? That's far from here, over the mountains, and the whole place has only eight or ten thousand Jews. It's not like our town at all." The master of ceremonies was rocking on his turned up shoes. Many of his teeth had fallen out of his gums.

"In Stok, like everywhere, they had a Jewish Council. It had a Minister of Housing and a Minister of Public Health, and all the rest. Yes, even a Minister of Water and Power, like our friend, Paradyz. One day—in this respect, it's true, their town resembles our own—the Others ordered the Judenrat to make a list of one hundred Jews. If the Council refused to do it, the Lords and Masters would snatch up a thousand on their own. Of course there was a big discussion. Some members would not put down even a single name. But a different faction won out. They said, *We are rescuing nine hundred Jews.* The problem was, the Others were not satisfied. They kept asking for more. Every time was supposed to be the last time, but it never was. Pretty soon only half the town of Stok was left, and then only a quarter. And so on."

Spittle came from Schotter's mouth. It flew to the nearest rows. "To make a long story short, before you knew it, in the entire town there were only two people left, both members of the Judenrat. Then the train pulled in once more. The one Minister says to the other, 'You go. Otherwise it will be harder on the rest of us!'"

"Ha! Ha! Ha!" Only three people were laughing—Schotter himself and, with their arms linked, Fried Rievesaltes and Miss Brilliantstein, who were just starting down the aisle. Then the rest of the crowd joined the Police Chief in the joke. Wave after wave of laughter rolled up past the gleaming, quivering lozenges of the chandelier. People were holding their chests, they were wiping their eyes. One minute—with the skaters—tears; the next moment laughter. How to account for such glee? Something about the story—the deserted village, the train, the gall and scorn of the Judenrat member—must have struck them as funny. Unless it was because they were sitting in the House of Culture, in the Baluty Suburb, with jewels on, and not in the town of Stok.

Suddenly there was a gasp, then a whisper, then a general murmur. The Chairman and Madame Trumpelman were in the building! A flash lamp went off. *Bing, bing*—it exploded twice more. Young Krystal, as usual, was taking pictures. The couple walked into the glare. This was the first time Madame

247

Trumpelman had appeared in public since the catastrophe of the Christmas mass. The citizens of the Balut had started to think they would not see her again. In the new cafés they had begun to play music. Yet here she was, clutching her husband's arm with both her hands. Her veil was down, at the line of her lower lip, which was unpainted. She was as thin, in her tight, shiny gown, as a silver fork or a spoon.

The Elder wore a black cape with gold trim, and a hat just as black on his head. He was stooped and his spectacle frames had slipped down the bend of his nose. There were lines on his cheeks that made him look like a man aged one hundred. The two of them—with no Guardsmen to help, no sweepers standing by—reached the end of the aisle. Alone, they sat in the two biggest chairs.

Then the chandelier speedily rose up and up, and Schotter, with his hands in his armpits, made an announcement.

"Our show is ready to start! It's by a world-famous author. It takes place hundreds of years ago, before there were clocks or gas lamps or engines for steam. Here we are, in a faraway land. This is a country without any Jews. A place where it's always misty. What a fog! If you put your hand up, you can't see your fingers! Look! It's like smoke from a fire! Seed of Abraham, close your eyes! You have to imagine these things, the way children do!" And, taking the edge of the curtain in his hand, the master of ceremonies walked across the stage: like magic the great purple sheet parted behind him.

At first the stage was dark, like a pitch-black box. But an owl, or something like an owl, was hooting. Then a yellow light came on and you could see the fog. It was yellow, too, and looked like clouds of sulphur. In the middle of the stage was a large, leafless tree. Its limbs were black and twisted. Suddenly, from either side of the stage, a really frightening figure trotted out. The members of the audience asked themselves, *Are these men or women?* For both creatures wore

248

ragged gowns and sandals with heels—that suggested the female sex, as did the locks of hair that spilled from their conical caps. But the beards on their chins were just like a man's. These marvels met at the center of the stage and, from under the palms of their hands, peered anxiously about. What nails they had on their fingers! How the fog bank swirled about their tattered clothes! Yet neither was any taller than a half-grown child.

Then, from behind the trunk of the gnarled tree, a third crone came leaping. Smolenskin cranked the gramophone handle and the three witches—what else could such fiends be?—linked their arms together and danced in a circle. They went, as they hopped, *hee-hee-hee!* The latecomer jumped so wildly that his hat dropped off. Some people, by his close-cropped hair, by the shape of his skull, recognized him. It was the pinhead! The gardener boy! Grinning, his head lolling, he loomed over his partners. These two began to speak, piping away:

1st WITCH: *Fair is foul, and foul is fair:*
Hover through the fog and filthy
air.
2nd WITCH: *The weird sisters, hand in hand*
Posters of the sea and land.

The voices belonged to Tushnet, with his face blackened, in a wig, and to Leibel Shifter, in a similar disguise. The children of the Hatters' Asylum were putting on a show! What a sensation! No one could remember when the orphans, the Elder's favorites, had last left the estate grounds. And why had they kept everything—the long preparations, the months of effort—such a secret? Was it to give Trumpelman and Madame Trumpelman a grand surprise?

From some spot overhead a thunderclap sounded. A bright light, the forks of lightning, lit up the stage. An orphan, standing where no one could see him, was shaking a

249

piece of tin. The Jews in the crowd knew that, but they shivered anyway. The rumble and roar echoed like cannonballs. Once more the arc of white light spilled over the spectators' upturned, fearful faces. The slave dance from *Aida* stopped. The three demons, in the wind and the rain, cupped their hands to their ears.

1st WITCH: *A drum, a drum!*
2nd WITCH: *Macbeth does come!*

Two warriors, holding swords, moved from the back of the platform to the front. The furious storm broke about them. The lightning glanced off their breastplates and shields. It was as if young Krystal were setting off all his flash lamps at once. One soldier took a step forward. He wore something like an airman's helmet, with leather flaps for the ears. Fixed to his face was a curly black beard. "So foul and fair a day," he shouted, into the boom-booming blasts, "I have not seen."

The other soldier was gaping at the withered sisters. His mouth opened and closed. From fear his knees knocked together. Despite his slight beard you could tell it was really Usher Flicker, who ten years before was just being born. He hugged his comrade-in-arms. "Hail! Hail!" cried the hags, capering this way and that before them. At last the dark-bearded swordsman, holding his weapon skyward, addressed the apparitions: "Speak, if you can. What are you?"

The gardener boy—people thought he was a deaf-mute, without any tongue at all—put his hand on top of his head. Then he said, in the same poetical Polish that everyone else was speaking, "All hail, Macbeth, that shalt be King hereafter!"

No sooner had he spoken than a whoosh of fog rose up about him and, to thunder, to sizzling lightning, he and his companions vanished inside it. Banquo ran here and there, slashing at the mist with his sword. But when the clouds lifted, the weird sisters were gone. The storm was over. Everything was clear and calm. The green eyes of the owl—there it was, on a limb of the tree—began to glow. Banquo approached his friend. He leaned by his ear.

You shall be king.

Do you want to know who it was kneeling down? It was only the left-handed Mann Lifshits. The clue was that the sheath for his sword was on his right side. He was like a rock, not moving, not speaking. Banquo, baffled, turned his back and stood by the trunk of the tree. All the lights on the stage were fading, fading. The eyes of the owl stood out, bright and green.

Just before the whole theater was swallowed up in fresh darkness, Lifshits, still kneeling, raised both his hands. His fists were balled up at the sky. Then—it was almost as if we were hearing his thoughts—he spoke these words:

Stars, hide your fires.
Let not light see my black and deep desires.

And then the curtains closed.

The Manchester of Poland, that's what people called our town, with all its mills. It wasn't a cultural center, like Bialystok. Sarah Bernhardt never acted here in a play. Therefore, don't be surprised if not many in the audience understood what was going on. They didn't know a lot about the great author, Shakespeare. They scarcely had heard of *Macbeth*. What impressed them was how lifelike the storm was, and the thick rolls of cottony fog. They also wanted to know how the owl's eyes lit up, with electrical wires or what? There were many disputes about the witches. Did such creatures really exist? Some people took one side and some another. Finally a Jew said that in his opinion the three harpies were something the kneeling soldier had dreamed. In dreams it's not only possible for women to wear beards, but the worst things you fear, as well as the joys that you long for, often come true.

All of a sudden a Gypsy, or it could have been a Negro woman, came from the wings. She walked up and down in front of the curtain, reading a letter. Her hair was woven into a rope-thick braid, which hung to her waist. Her tight dress had broad shoulders and buttons all down the front. Lipstick, wet-looking, was on her lips. *Bang-bang, thump-thump*, those were the sounds that kept coming from behind the shut curtain. As for the letter, it was about meeting the witches, and told what we already know.

Her reading was interrupted by a little boy, squinting as if he had a headache, who ran onto the lip of the stage. He had round shoulders, like most of our city-born Jews. His mouth opened up, but he didn't say a word.

"What is your tidings?" demanded the woman with the lip-stick.

But the boy from the Hatters' Asylum just stood on his heels. He was wearing hip boots, like a fisherman.

"What is your tidings? Your tidings?"

A pity, the poor fellow was stumped. His eyes screwed tightly shut. The crowd wanted to help him, but no one knew the right words. In the awful silence, even the back-stage noises ceased. In the front row Trumpelman, in an irritated way, slapped his knee. It was as if it were the boy's face he'd struck. For he opened his eyes and spoke at once.

The king comes here tonight!

And the messenger whirled about and ran off in the direction he'd come from.

All eyes, however, were on the woman in front of the purple curtain. What she did then created a sensation in the House of Culture. There had never been anything like it in the whole history of our town. She undid her four top but-

252

tons and pulled her green gown away from her chest. What a tremendous shock! This wasn't, after all, an anonymous actress, a stranger. It was our own Gutta Blit, all grown up. And you could practically see her bosom!

Come, you spirits
That tend on mortal thoughts, unsex me here,
And fill me from the crown to the toe, topfull
Of direst cruelty!

The woman's face was twisted, terrible, as she said those words. The lights, once again, were fading out. Still she stood there, holding her dress that way.

Come to my woman's breasts,
And take my milk for gall!

The stage front went dark. The Jews in the crowd gave a shudder.

Presto! The lights blazed on again. The double drapes of the curtain parted, and the spectators saw something more amazing still. For what had been, only minutes before, a heath or a forest, with a single gnarled and blasted tree, was now—one, two, three!—the great hall of an ancient castle! Real torches were fixed on the massive chunks of the wall, and battle flags hung from the ceiling. On the left, there was a big wooden door; on the right, a staircase, a high one, with a normal-sized door at the top. Without thinking, people applauded. Everything was so well done. There was even moss on the old hand-cut stones.

Mister Smolenskin played the part from *Aida* where the elephants and catapults arrive. The wooden door swung open and a half dozen Hatters' orphans, in Scottish kilts and hats with feathers, stepped into the vaulted room. They were carrying dressed duck on platters, and realistic beef. How good the meat looked! How tasty! Through the door next

253

came a row of archery experts, with their big bows strapped over their shoulders. In the middle of this crowd of lads and lassies stood Nathan Hobnover. He had the same bare knees as the others; the difference was, on the top of his head, glittering, glistening, there sat a round golden crown. The gramophone music stopped. The retainers held still. Then King Duncan, played by Hobnover, pointed across the stage, to the shadowy spot beneath the staircase. His little blond goat's beard waggled when he talked.

See, see, our honored hostess!

Out stepped Lady Macbeth. She had on a sort of nightgown which fit tightly around her neck and swept all the way to the floor. Only her brown head and black braid were showing. "Your servant ever," she said.

"Give me your hand," said the king, and the two actors walked side by side up the long stairway. Something was squeaking: Hobnover's shoes. At the top, the king went through the door; she followed. Then the lights grew so dim that, try as you might, you couldn't see the red beef, you couldn't see the duck.

A bell rang. A pause. It rang again. It was sounding the hour. The eyes of the Jews got used to the lack of light. Mann Lifshits was standing by the foot of the stairs. He was wearing the same armor as before, and the same leather headgear. When the bell rang a third time, he took a step. Then he stretched out his hand. "Is this a dagger which I see before me?" He staggered upward, a step at a time, clutching at the empty air. "I have thee not, and yet I see thee still. Art thou but a dagger of the mind? A false creation?" The knife he meant was right there in his hand. That's what was strange about his behavior. He held the blade out, staring at it, talking to it, as if it belonged to a different person. Raving that way, he went up the rest of the stairs.

At the top he waited, while the bell continued to toll. Twelve times altogether. Midnight.

Hear it not, Duncan, for it is a knell
That summons thee to Heaven, or to Hell.

So saying, Macbeth went into the king's chamber.

Time went by. Maybe after all it would be a peaceful night. But the audience of Baluters was stirring. Something was going to happen, but they didn't know what. Then there was a scream, a real shriek. It alarmed many people. Some of the playgoers wanted to leave. "It's just an owl, an owl," said Popower, Minister of Finance, from his seat at the front. Sure enough, the green eyes of the bird—perched on a beam in the rafters—started to glow. But the next scream was different. It came from behind the upstairs door. All by itself this portal swung open and Nathan Hobnover walked through. He streamed with red paint. His skin, his night-dress, were drenched in the liquid. It was still coming out. Slowly, he began to descend the stairs; the gold crown was still on his head. On the way down the strength of his heart failed him. He clasped his hands to it and opened his mouth. He looked like a tenor singing a song. Then, in a spray, he tumbled all the way down.

What chaos then! Everybody seemed to wake up at once. Macbeth and Lady Macbeth came out of the chamber. They clung in terror together. The servants and archers ran about, rubbing their eyes. Banquo, the second soldier, turned on the lights. "O horror!" he cried. "Horror, horror!" The whole cast was shouting.

Awake! Awake!
Ring the alarum bell. Murder and treason!

But in the audience no one heard these words. If anything,

255

the bedlam there was worse than on the stage. The Jewesses who were not gasping, weeping, were sitting there stunned. Many of the male Baluters were pointing at Macbeth and his mate, as if to say, *There he is! They did it! They're the ones!* Even the members of the Jewish Council were thrown into confusion. "Assassins!" they shouted. "Anarchists!" None paid attention to Popower, the former waiter. He was pulling the sleeves of his colleagues and saying, "But, Verble, but Miss Kleinweiss, it's only a play!"

It's an interesting point the minister raised. The Ghettoites, after all, had been living for years in the most dreadful conditions. Every day they saw things more frightening than witches and fogbanks and hooting owls. Was there a man or woman in the House of Culture who had not lost, one way or another, a person he loved? Could any spectator know for sure that he, himself, would not be deported before the week was out? No! No! Not likely. Here people walked around thin as sticks, with their bones practically showing. In the winter the Baluters froze. They choked from the smell in the summer. You could always hear some mad person shouting, *an English tailor*!, or some other meaningless phrase. It was as if hell had been moved to the surface of the earth. And the worst thing, the horror of horrors, was that the citizens of the Suburb had got used to their lives. Sometimes the newspapers would blow off the corpses: there would be the green face or the blue face or even the healthy-looking pink face of a person you knew. This is what everyone saw, including women, including young boys and girls. No one thought twice about it.

On Assisi Street, however, the Jews were frantic. They pulled on the roots of their hair. Impossible to think they didn't know they were seeing a play. Those were rubber daggers. It was a story from a hundred years ago. No, the Ghettoites knew perfectly well that in a moment Nathan Hobnover would jump up from his pool of bogus blood; yet they wept for him as if he had been an actual king, painfully, mortally, wounded. Has there ever been a better illustration of the wonderful power of art?

By the time things calmed down the stage was nearly deserted. The actors had run off in different directions—the archers in search of the supposed plotters, the retainers carrying Lady Macbeth—who, in all the excitement, had fainted. Mann Lifshits, and poor Hobnover of course, were alone in the castle hall. The former walked down the staircase and put his boot on the latter's chest. The purple walls of the curtain began to close jerkily on them both. Then—it was the last thing the crowd was able to see—the murderer stooped, plucked the bright crown from the head of his victim, and, carefully, using both hands, set it down upon his aviator's helmet. He *was* the king, then, just as the witches predicted.

Ladies and gentlemen, the Manchester of Poland is one thing, America is another. In the New World even schoolchildren know this famous drama by heart. There's no need to dwell on details. Here is what happens next: Macbeth orders some people to kill General Banquo, and, before you know it, it's done. All this took place in front of the curtain, a terrible thing to see. One of the killers ran at the soldier with a sword. It went into his chest, right through his armor, and came out the other side. But Flicker did not fall down. He staggered toward his assassin, who, in terror, let go the weapon. Then a second killer stabbed him in the throat with a dagger. Bright-colored blood came out of the general's mouth. Yet, amazingly, even with the sword blade still running through him, he stood his ground. That's when a third murderer, in a cloak, with a mask on, struck him over the head with a spike-filled club. The brave fellow plunged down. They dragged him away by the legs. All this so that none of Banquo's children could ever be king.

Imagine how our local Jews responded to that scene! The murder of Duncan had been bad enough, but at least it took place behind closed doors. Flicker was killed before their eyes. They had seen the dagger go in to the hilt! But before the uproar had a chance to swell, a line of retainers, Lifshits' now, no longer Hobnover's, marched across the front of the stage. On platters they carried the roast beef and the duck. There was fruit, too: melons and apples and oranges and pears. More: a golden-scaled fish, a pike probably, with its head and its tail attached; round red and round yellow cheeses; and a whole tray of cakes and pastries and—could it be?—crumb-crusted butter tarts. The Baluters were suddenly speechless. One after the other the servants disappeared into the center crack of the curtain. As the last orphan, the one with the sweetmeats, stepped through, these draperies parted, the drama went on.

The scene was just the same, except that a large wooden table, fully set, with chairs all around, had been pulled into the center of the hall. Much of the Hatters' Asylum population were seated around it, drinking goblets of wine. They were meant to be lords and ladies. The queen was at the far end of the table, her white teeth, her white eyes, flashing in her dusky face. What a hubbub! What a jolly feast! The crowd in the House of Culture could actually smell, that's how realistic it was, the smoked fish. After a time Macbeth went to his end of the table. Before sitting down he picked up a silver cup. "Now good digestion wait on appetite," he loudly toasted, "And health on both!"

The company raised their goblets in response; they gulped down the wine. But the king thrust his fingers, wet with grease, into his curly beard. He gasped. He croaked.

Behold! Look! Lo!

If such a thing were possible, his hair, where it was not weighted down with the yellow crown, was rising from his head.

Then two servants, who had been standing in front of Lifshits' seat, now stepped aside. Everyone in the audience saw

258

that someone was sitting in the king's chair. That person was wearing a sheet, with holes cut for the eyes. It was exactly like a child dressed up as a ghost! But the nobles on the stage did not seem to see it. One of them gestured toward the chair.

NOBLE: *Here is a place reserved, sir.*

The guest was practically touching the sheeted figure with his hand, yet not a lord or a lady showed any sign of surprise. The goblin was invisible! Then the spirit rose from the chair and stood on its rubber-soled shoes. What was terrible, awful, unspeakable really, was the sword handle stuck into one side of its body, and the sword blade that came out the other. Ladies and gentlemen: the ghost of Usher Flicker!

"Hee, hee hee!" Someone was laughing. Someone in the crowd, not on the stage. The audience, which had been dumbstruck by the sight of the apparition, now looked around. In her long gloves, in her comfortable chair at the center, Madame Trumpelman was laughing and wiping her eyes. Naturally, the other Jews thought they should be laughing, too. After all, there *was* something comical about the scene onstage. To see a grown man, a man with a beard, trembling, shaking, and popping his eyes! And all the time raving at air!

Hence, horrible shadow!

Thus the more alarming the events in the play, and the more Macbeth shouted, the louder the laughter became. At last the guests fled in confusion, the banquet ended, the two halves of the curtain closed. Madame Trumpelman stood in front of her chair. She lifted her veil. She bubbled with laughter. She gasped and gasped. "Ha! Ha! Don't you see? Trumpelman and Madame Trumpelman! On the stage! Dear Doctor! It's us they are playing! Ha! Ha! Ha! You! And me!"

259

Then old Philosoff, with his string beard, succeeded in standing. "Heavens!" he shouted. "It's true!" Other Judenrat members reached out to pull down the Minister of Charities and Welfare. Trumpelman, the Elder, rose next to his wife. He pushed his spectacles up his nose.

"No, no, no, no, no. It's a coincidence!"

But the purple cloth was already parting on the same scene with which the *Tragedia Makbeta* had begun. Thunder. More thunder. The black, leafless tree. Only this time the fog—or smoke it was, or steam—seemed to be coming from a big metal pot in the center of the stage. Near this kettle hopped the two witches, Tushnet and Shifter, each with a tuft of beard on his chin. They were throwing things into the stew.

> 1st WITCH: *Fillet of a fenny snake,*
> *In the cauldron boil and bake.*
> 2nd WITCH: *Scale of dragon, tooth of wolf,*
> *Witches' mummy, maw and gulf.*

The audience of Ghettoites couldn't help groaning. What an awful feast was this! When only a moment before they had been serving duck! The gardener boy, skipping wildly, holding his hat on, was even worse.

> 3rd WITCH: *Liver of blaspheming Jew,*
> *Gall of goat, and slips of yew!*

Then they all joined hands and, like normal boys, danced around the boiling, bubbling broth.

> TOGETHER: *Double, double, toil and trouble,*
> *Fire burn and cauldron bubble.*

The boy with the tin shook it mightily. The thunder cracked. Lightning flickered. Cellophane strips under the pot writhed like snakes, like bright tongues of flame.

Into this scene came King Macbeth, looking lost. He had his crown on his head and wore his short kilt. But his shoulders, under the weight of his armor, were drooping. He demanded that the hags make predictions. Immediately they told him what to be afraid of, and what not to fear. Good news! Macbeth could never be beaten until the forest of Birnam—an absolute impossibility—marched up Dunsinane Hill.

But the tyrant was not satisfied. "Yet my heart throbs to know one thing," he declared.

> *Tell me, if your art*
> *Can tell so much. Shall Banquo's issue ever*
> *Reign in this kingdom?*

The weird sisters laughed and laughed, as if he'd told a joke. They pointed to the kettle, which just sat there, boiling over. Suddenly a child, a boy, hardly more than a toddler, climbed out of the caldron and began to wander around. A second child, no older than the first, popped up in his place. And then a third one appeared. Mann Lifshits knew how to make his eyes bug from their sockets. He did this now, and staggered backward as well.

> *A fourth! Start, eyes!*
> *What, will the line stretch out to the crack of doom?*
> *Another yet! A seventh!*

Friends, remember that to give birth in the Ghetto was strictly forbidden. No wonder the appearance of so many little ones, each with his folded white napkin, his tiny suspenders, created a sensation. How happy they seemed! How fat their little legs were! They kept coming out of the kettle as if they were woven from the wisps of steam.

"Come, chickee!" the spectators cried. They were cooing and cooing. Even Macbeth seemed affected. He held his arms out to the tots. But they ran by him to where the ghost of

Usher Flicker, on piano wires, was dropping out of the sky. Banquo hovered a moment, then set on each upturned head a paper crown, gold-colored, that tied with elastic under the chin. Thus Macbeth learned the answer to his question. He stared, barren, empty-handed, at the little kings. How they romped! They were having a wonderful party.

"Ha! Ha!"

It wasn't the witches laughing. It wasn't Madame Trumpelman. This time it was the Elder himself. It was frightening to see how his lips came away from his gums. "I'm not upset! Don't look so scared, Jews! Look, I'm smiling. All this is old-hat. The Lipskyites, the left-wingers, mock me the way midgets taunt a giant! They want to put me in a cage! Ha! Ha! So people can laugh! But it takes more than a play to frighten me!"

It was silent throughout the theater. No one knew whether the show was over or not. The Szapiro & Son chandelier started down from the ceiling; Trumpelman looked at it, glared at it, and slowly it rose again.

"Relax! Don't worry! There's only one thing I want to know. A little thing. Who is responsible for this production? Tell me his name! Don't say the children did it! Don't make me laugh! Somebody tricked them into this job. I forgive them. I kiss you, children! I am blowing you kisses! My dears! My darlings! You know I am not a bad man!"

At that moment the owl hooted again. Everyone searched for the bird, for its lit-up eyes. It wasn't there. Not on its perch. Not anywhere. But the hoot-hooting continued, louder than before. It seemed to be coming from far off, perhaps from outside the theater completely. And drawing nearer, too. The audience stirred. People who had pocket watches took them out. From either side of the stage the curtains were coming together. Still no sign of the bright green eyes! What could it mean? Then someone, a person inside the House of Culture, declared, "The train!"

"Not possible!" a different Jew shouted.

"It's only three o'clock in the afternoon!"

Then the whistle blew sharply from the direction of the Radogodsh Station.

"Maybe," said Minister Schpitalnik, "we should go home."

From the benches, from the balcony, from the expensive, upholstered chairs, the whole crowd rose together. They did not know whether to stay or to go. Everyone looked, not at Trumpelman, not at his wife, but over to where Fried Rievesaltes was still sitting down in his comfortable chair.

"Sit, sit," the Police Chief said. "Let's see what happens next." And the crowd, obeying, sank back in their places.

From then on the performance switched back and forth, from one place to another. First we would be in England, where the forces of law and order, led by Myer Krystal, the dead king's son, were preparing to attack the despot. England! Imagine! The next moment we would be back in Macbeth's kingdom, that dark, smoky land. Crowds of orphans dragged over the stage, crying for pieces of bread. Blind people fumbled about, bumping into the props. Worst were the killers, who trotted this way and that way, stabbing whoever they wished. It was a charnel house.

The scene: the hall of the villains' castle. Night. Always night. At the top of the stairs a woman appeared holding a candle. This was Gutta Blit. Her hair was loose and full of electrical charges. Shoeless. Her nightdress undone. Sleepwalking! The beams from the candle glistened on her open eyes. What struck the Jews were the little jerks her head made, just a few centimeters at a time. They heard her sniffing at something. "Here's the smell of the blood still!" she said. Then she began to glide down the flight of stairs.

"Crazy woman!" said Popower, the former waiter.

"Witch!" hissed the oboist, Mordechai Kleen.

The whole front row was whispering. Everyone took little

263

looks at Trumpelman's mate. That woman, pale, with hollows beneath her cheekbones, rose. The Elder rose with her. She gripped his cloak. "Yes," she told him. "It's me. It's what I am. Look at her head. The way it's twisting. It's the weight. The pressure. Like a vise!"

The Queen of Scotland, so dark, so dusky, was by then halfway down the stairs. Indeed, she tossed her head. It was like a horse reacting to flies. "Who would have thought the old man to have had so much blood in him?" she said.

"Poor thing, poor thing!" Madame Trumpelman murmured. "She's suffering!"

Young Miss Blit went the rest of the way down the staircase. In her bare feet, in her dragging gown, she walked to the entranceway. "To bed, to bed, to bed," was what she was saying. But she did not go to bed. She threw back the bolt of the gigantic door. It swung outward. Immediately wind from a machine blew the hair back from her head. *Whoosh!* The candle went out in her hand.

Trumpelman and Madame Trumpelman were leaning against each other. They held each other up. She was stroking the cloth his cape was made of. "Chaim. My Chaim. I see into the future. Yes, like a witch. There will be Jews in this future, honey Chaim. The same kind that are living now. Of us these Jews will say, *They were bad, they did terrible things, but they weren't as bad as the Others.*"

"Look," her husband answered.

Everyone did. The queen, so distracted, was stepping out of the castle, into the sudden blast of the wind. It whistled about her. On this sad scene the two sides of the curtain, like a pair of shutters, drew closed.

Immediately something that looked like a palm tree came tripping across the front of the stage and—it's the only way to describe it—sat down. This was from right to left. Then, from left to right, a thick bush darted out and crouched next to the palm. A pine tree with needles came after, and then two or three little shrubs. Before you knew it there was a line of vegetation across the whole front part of the stage. Their branches were trembling. They shook their green leaves.

The curtains parted. The scene was set in an open place. There were rocks and, here and there, an evergreen tree. The wind was still blowing from some spot offstage. It shook the curls of Macbeth's thick blue-black beard. "Come, put mine armour on," he said. He was already wearing his metal breastplate, and his tight leather helmet was pulled onto his head. He was the soldier of old. But he wanted more protection. "My armour!" he repeated. A Hatters' Asylum orphan ran about, tying on layers of padding and new pieces of mail. Lifshits was swelling. It looked as if, under such a load, he could barely stand. But he drew his sword left-handedly out. Then he laughed. A long, loud laugh that made, inside his armor, a hollow sound.

> *I will not be afraid of death and bane,*
> *Till Birnam Forest come to Dunsinane!*

At that moment one of the evergreens came a step closer. It had feet on the bottom! It moved! So did another one of the firs! One little plant, ragged and windblown, dashed almost to the tyrant's elbow, and then held perfectly still. All the foliage at the edge of the stage began to shake and stir. The twigs were nudging each other.

Someone walked onto the stage. It was the messenger, little blond Citron. This time he spoke fluently.

> *I looked toward Birnam and anon methought*
> *The wood began to move.*

The dictator gaped and raised his blade. "Liar and slave!" he shouted. But already the whole of the forest was closing upon him. New trees ran in from left and right. Not trees!

Children holding branches! With leaves glued on their backs! This was young Krystal's army! The English troops had arrived!

"Hurrah!" cried the Baluters, tremendously excited. "Kill him! Kill the tyrant!"

In an instant the children surrounded the king completely. Snarling, sneering, he waved his sword in the air.

I'll fight till from my bones my flesh be hacked.

No hope for Macbeth. Wherever the Jews looked, even in the aisles of the House of Culture, and along the theater walls, they saw the forces of order. But then the poor devils had to look twice. For those in the aisles were not orphans, but, in their uniforms, with their armbands, grown-up men. They had rubber clubs in their hands. And caps on! Caps! The theater was filled with fifty or sixty or seventy members of the Jewish Police!

And more were still pouring through the Assisi Street door. The train whistle blew. Everyone knew that the train itself was now at the transfer station. But there was not the pandemonium you would expect. The players onstage stood frozen. The audience simply sat. They could not believe this was a roundup. Not in daylight. Not of the Ghetto's most prominent Jews. So it was really rather still in the House of Culture when Trumpelman, upright, with his back to the stage, started to speak.

"I know there are Jews in the Ghetto who hate me and want to kill me. Some of these so-called Jews are in this theater now. Well, here I am! Here's my bare breast! Anyone can shoot me who wants to! From the balcony! The way they shot Abraham Lincoln! Stab me, Communists! Like Caesar! Why should the Elder want to live? You killed his child!"

But no one was watching. Or listening, either. The Elder might just as well be talking to the artificial wind. Anxiously the Jews waved their ration coupons, their identity cards.

266

Then the Minister of Housing, Verble, rose in the midst of the crowd. He twisted one end of his waxy mustache.

"Jews! Jewesses! Look how calm your Judenrat is. We are all sitting, watching the show. We have special information. This is not an ordinary transport. No, no! Just as you are not ordinary Jews! Everyone who goes on this train will be an agricultural worker! This time it's guaranteed! You will be used on the Others' farms!"

"Yes!" a voice—it must have belonged to the daring pamphleteer—rang out from the balcony. "For fertilizer!"

That's all it took, those two words, to set off the panic. People shouting. People screaming. People fainting, too. Some young fellows tried to rush through the door, but the no-neckers drove them back. Hundreds of Baluters were shoving about the place where a Council member was struggling to stand on his chair.

It was Fried Rievesaltes. He threw up his arms, so that his head, with its bulging temples, its wisp of black hair, looked like a ball wedged between them. You could see his revolver strapped in the pit of his arm. His mustache, when he smiled, stretched in sparse strokes across his face. "Friends," he was saying. "Try to be calm." But the crowd yelled louder than ever. They were holding things up to him, not only their coupons, but jewelry, necklaces, brooches of gold. Some people were trying to touch him, or his coat, just his coat hem, as if he were an idol. He was directing some people to go one way, and some in another. "Yellow cards, kindly. Yellow cards, please. Not the ones with the pictures. No, no, they're out of date. The blank yellow cards. Pink cards? Pink cards no longer count. Oh, you Jewish people! You people!"

If anyone had thought to glance at I. C. Trumpelman then, he would have seen that the Elder had grown not merely pale, but completely chalk-colored. The Judenrat President was no child. He knew that this was the moment that marked the transfer of power within the Ghetto. What had he, Trumpelman, to offer his thousands of Jews? Jobs?

Jobs, yes, printed money, and even food. But Rievesaltes, crooking his finger at some cards, turning his thumbs down at all the others—Rievesaltes had become the god of life and death.

The Elder wrapped his cape about his body and thrust out his chin. "I, Trumpelman, came like a robber to rob you of your dearest ones. I, Trumpelman, took you by the hand and led you to death. It's Trumpelman who made you work until your hearts explode. No wonder you turn from him now! Abandon him! What a monster he is! Lock him up in a cage! Ha! Ha! That's your mistake, Jews! A big mistake! We are in the same cage together! There are no bars between you and me! And look! In this same cage with us there is a hungry lion! He wants to devour us all! He's ready to spring! And I? Trumpelman? I am the lion tamer. I stuff his mouth with meat! It's the flesh of my own brothers and sisters! The lion eats and eats! He roars! But he does not spring. Thus, with ten Jews, I save a hundred. With a hundred, I save a thousand. With a thousand, ten thousand more. My hands are bloody. My feet are bloody. My eyes are closed with blood. If your hands are clean, it's because mine are dirty! I have no conscience! That's why your conscience is clear! I am covered in blood completely!"

All at once Chaim started forward. He took long strides up the orchestra aisle. The policemen at the Assisi Street exit made a barrier out of their batons, but the Chairman burst easily through. Behind him, in the House of Culture, the Jews were wailing and clutching each other. They fell on their knees before the Chief of Police. On the stage, machines made a wind that shook the actors' beards and made the pasted leaves toss and tremble. Macbeth threw his warlike shield in front of his body. Above his head he raised his wooden sword.

The Rumkowsky Geyser—naturally the Others had changed the name to something else—still stood in the Walburska quarter. The big houses there, the Mosk mansion, the Jewish estates, had been occupied by the Men of Valor. They took over the Geyser, too, which became their own private spa. It looked just the same, though, with its brick walls holding up the great whitewashed dome. Steam still came from a hole in the top of the structure, and sunshine, in the shape of a moving yellow ball, came in. It was to the front of this municipal bath that the Elder, on his wonderful stallion, came at a gallop.

The Daimler Double Six was parked there already. Trumpelman pulled up beside it and hopped like a young man to the ground. There were guards at the Geyser entrance, Death's-Headers, but once more Chaim, gripping his cane, pushed through. Even at such a distance, deep in the Aryan section, you could hear the whistling at the transfer station. A high sound. A low one. That meant two locomotives, both of them keeping up steam.

Just inside the Geyser there was a big curving hallway where you took off your clothes. Chaim walked through it. With his hat on, and his cloak, with the whole outfit from the gala performance, he entered the chamber of steam. How hot it was! How hard to breathe! Impossible to see through the droplets on his glasses. Then a voice, how well he knew it, echoed about him.

"It is the Jew Trumpelman. Born from the union of two other Jews."

The Lithuanian looked around. Nothing but steam clouds. Plus hot blasts of air. Below him, in a pit, at the center of the rotunda, he could dimly make out the flaming beech logs, the glow of the flat, heated rocks. Water, dripping from wa-

269

ter pipes, snarled and crackled over the stones, like the whites of cooking eggs. "Yes! A hundred percent Hebrew, but he acts like a king!" Something moved above Chaim's head. He took off his blurred spectacles. A left leg, short and thick, was crossed over a right one. The steam parted a second. Wohltat! The native son!

"Chief of the Civilian Authority! I address you as Elder of the Baluty Suburb. An emergency happened! Something must be done!" Trumpelman's hair was already sticking to the back of his neck. He squinted into the mists. He saw the Volksdeutscher, his bright red lips, his dripping breasts. "The Jewish Police have invaded the House of Culture! They are there at this moment! How dare they do it! What nerve! To threaten our citizens' lives! Important, influential Jews!"

"Lives? What lives? Today there will be a big transport. That is true. But the Jews on it will be trained as farmhands. I swear it."

I. C. Trumpelman started shouting. He banged the tip of his cane on the sodden boards. "Don't insult me! I'm not a shit-wagon puller! This is no rabbi with a nose in a book! I know all about it! The forest! The motor fumes in the buses! The mattresses with ladies' hair! You can't fool the Elder of the Jews the way you can a needle threader. He's too smart for you!"

Wohltat leaned forward, plump as a pillow. "What forest? What motor fumes?"

A different voice rolled off the rounded walls. "Why continue the charade? Obviously he knows." Trumpelman could not determine which way to look. The benches in the steambath went around the entire room. They rose, one ring above the other, like the seats in an anatomy theater. The speaker could be anywhere.

"Tell him about the roundup in Warsaw. One-third of the Jews! And Czerniakow swallowed poison. The Elder of Warsaw is dead! Why keep these things a secret? We should an-

270

nounce it to the world! Do you think anyone will object? They'll thank us. They'll applaud. A thousand years from now people will remember us precisely for this, the way they remember Pasteur."

Softly our Elder said, "And Czerniakow's son?"

Wohltat answered. "Escaped! Long ago! An officer in the Red Army now!"

Everything on Trumpelman was by then wilting. The brim of his hat drooped down. His cane felt rubberized. Dizzily he reached out his hand for something to hold to, but nothing was there. "Please, please," he called weakly. "Cancel the roundup. My children! My Jews."

"Ha, ha! Here's an idea!" Now Chaim recognized that laugh, that voice. The Obergruppenführer's. Then he saw, higher up, thin-legged, sharp-nosed, Grundtripp himself. He crossed his arms over his rib cage. "With every corpse we bury a bronze tablet, on which is carved: *In such and such a place, on such and such a date, we alone had the courage to deal with Mister Feinberg or Steinberg or Weinberg,* whatever the name of the Jew."

Trumpelman wrung his hands. "But this was our grand premiere!"

From somewhere, from everywhere, a new voice, high-pitched, excited, began to expound. "No! No tablets! No statues! Not a single sign. It was a mistake to bury them in the first place. Now they will have to be dug up again. So bone crushers can smash up their bones. The whole population must vanish without a trace. As if they had been dropped in the ocean. Or shot in a rocket to space."

The Judenrat President followed Grundtripp's gaze, far up, into the thick of the steam. There was a red-skinned person there. Boiled-looking. With spectacles and a double chin. "Making them disappear, that's easy! The hard part is to perform the task, without reward, without recognition, and still remain good human beings. That takes toughness! Tough-

271

ness! Toughness like Genghis Khan!" The man was beating himself with twigs, like a Finn. Trumpelman knew him. HH! The Schoolmaster! Reichsführer of the SS!

And then the Elder began to beat himself, too. On the head. On his hat. Real, hard blows. "Nincompoop! Nincompoop!" he shouted, again and again. Why a man should attack his own body that way is of course difficult to say. But is it not likely that the Elder, who always thought he was smarter than anyone, had at that instant realized he did not know two plus two? Because any fool could have told him what *four* was: They were going to kill every last Jew in the Balut! *That's* why the Schoolmaster, such a high official, had come. To observe the great day. Blind! Blind! Totally blind! No wonder he knocked his head about. He wouldn't escape like young Czerniakow. He would be murdered with the rest.

Up, down, the steambath started to rock. Mist, bright and white, seemed to be closing around him. He couldn't see anything. But he saw everything. It wasn't just the Baluty Suburb that was being destroyed. And not simply Warsaw either. What about Crakow and Lwow and Pinsk? Every ghetto would be liquidated. If not today, then tomorrow. Budapest, too! And London! And the Jews of New York! Not just Jews! Half Jews! Quarter Jews! Non-Jews with Jewish faces or Jewish husbands or Jewish wives. There was no end to it. It was the mere beginning.

The Lithuanian stood limply, holding his glasses, holding his cane. Would someone tell him why the whole world was spinning? Had he struck his head too hard? He knew that outside, to the west of the city, the sun was going down. But why did it seem to be stuck over the top of the Rumkowsky Geyser? Its light kept pouring in. It made the steam whiter and whiter. Poor Poles! Poor people! That's what he thought. He knew they would be the next to go. And then what? Then who? Slavs! Yellow Mongolians! Negroes in Africa. The earth's population would be turned into Jews!

The High and Mighty, only they would remain.

Then it came to Chaim, with the terrible power of logic, that there could be no exceptions, that even then the killing was not going to stop. The Race of Masters would turn on itself, Blond One on Blond One, until out of millions and millions of human beings just one man would be left alive. Who? Who was he? Trumpelman lifted his head. He peered into the leaping light. Was someone there? Someone else? He blinked against the dazzle, the glare. A movement, a color, caught his eye. Where? There! There, in the highest place, under the dome, a figure was sitting, a person made out of light. Instantly, as if all the steam had been sucked from the roof top, he saw the bare pink body plain. *Big Man! Big Man! It was the Big Man!*

Trumpelman shuddered. It wasn't from fear. Not from awe. Proudly he threw his wet cloak around him. "The dog," he said, his own lips curling. "Uncircumcised!" Then the Elder fell with a thump to the floor.

The Jews are a desert people. Dry. Arid. Always moving around. Not like the Others, a forest folk, deeply rooted, used to mists and dampness and fogs. Thus there was a possibility Trumpelman had only fainted; perhaps he had had too much steam. Indeed, he did awake somewhat later. He opened both eyes. Everything was quiet and shadowy and still. The fire in the fire pit had gone out. There was no one in the upper benches. No one in the benches below. The municipal bath was deserted. Had anyone ever been there?

But when the Elder attempted to rise, he could not. He wanted to lift his head; his head would not move. He saw out the open top of the dome. The sky, not really dark, was covered with powdery light, as if on its surface one professor had just erased all of another's equations.

273

There was more left of that night. It wasn't over. Inside the House of Culture some spectators still remained. Not many. All fast asleep. The Judenrat members and the big rabbis were huddled together, near the orchestra pit. Smolenskin was missing. So was Schotter. Luftgas, up until then an important person, was likewise gone. It turned out that hardly anyone had had a plain yellow card. Maybe two dozen, maybe a half dozen more. The Vocational School students, the wonderful skaters, had been taken away. But the orphans from the Asylum were dozing on the stage. Some of them still had fir branches glued to their clothes. Madame Trumpelman's chair was empty. There was a hat on it, however, as if someone had wanted to save the place.

Let's leave the Jews there, quietly sleeping. Do not ask about dreams.

A little more time went by. Then Philosoff stretched, yawned, and sat upright. Some noise had disturbed him. Clumsily he collected both of his canes. He walked slowly, in quarter steps, to the Assisi Street door. He stopped there, his head cocked, listening to whatever it was that had waked him. The entrance was already open a crack. The minister peeked outside.

"Hello! Verble! Wolf-Kitzes! Minister Baggelman! Hello! Hello!" Philosoff, his beard like ten twisting fingers, called to his colleagues. His voice broke from excitement.

The ministers turned and groaned. Schpitalnik hugged his knees. Popower pulled his collar tight. But the others looked at their pocket watches. Hours and hours to go!

"Wake up! Wake up! Tell me if I'm dreaming!"

The old waiter was pointing into the street where, pale and ghostly, with its pink lips, its milky tail, a stallion stood. Repeatedly it stamped its hoof, and rolled its swollen eye.

The Council members stared at the riderless horse. "The Elder," one of their number whispered, "is dead."

Then they all turned and looked up, to a spot well above the stage. There the lifelike head of Macbeth, its beard black and curly, was stuck on the end of a pike. Its mouth was twisted. Its eyes were blank and white. Though this was a sight to strike one with terror, the Judenrat did not quake. The rabbis and the orphans, who were also gazing up at the usurper, were unafraid. Slowly, unaccountably, all those in the House of Culture began to smile. It was as if a voice had spoken to them: *Take heart, Jews! See the dead butcher! After the night comes the dawn!*

Chapter Nine

The Pulley

I

Alas! When the dawn came to the Baluty Suburb, the Jews wished it were once again night. At daybreak Franz Xavier Wohltat, the coffee roaster, informed the Jewish Council that all children ten years and under, with the exception of the Hatters' orphans, had to report to the Radogodsh Station. Also every Jew not strong enough to hold a regular job. Otherwise the whole Ghetto would be destroyed.

You can imagine the sorrow and anguish this order—soon it was on lampposts, on the building walls—caused. People ran into the streets and rushed up and down. Where were the little ones, whose necks were like wooden pencils, to go? What would happen to the broken-down Jews? Now we know the answers to these questions. At the time, though, there were hundreds of fantastical theories. One was that the boys and girls would grow up in the Conqueror's homeland, and become Lords and Masters themselves. Another was that they were going to be trained to fight in submarines. Because of the small spaces in U-boats, you see. One thing was certain, no more comfortable passenger wagons. Boxcars only, the kind used for cows and steers. Plus this: a whole week went by before one of these cars, leaving full, came back empty. Now the Baluters were going to some spot far away.

Ladies and gentlemen, we won't dwell on those terrible days—which in fact stretched for weeks, for months, for the whole life of the Balut. After the children, after the sick people, came the turn of anyone aged more than sixty-five. Then sixty-two. Then sixty. The policemen, the porters, took whoever could not fully blow up a paper bag. By the end of the year there were only healthy, hardworking Jews left in the Ghetto. Everyone wondered: would these be deported as well? It seemed there was nothing that anyone, in our shrinking population, could do.

Then one day—we are now in springtime, 1943—a Jewish policeman, Pergament by name, was found lying dead on Rybna Street. He was smiling, even though there was a hole just in front of his ear. The very next morning a second body was found, in the muddy Marysin section. This turned out to be Urinstein, Minister of Vital Statistics. Neither the top of his head, nor his top hat, was there. Poor man! Urinstein! So far from his home! The stars of both men had been removed; a note was pinned on their chests instead: *Better to be a Jew than one of* Them!

Better to be a Jew than one of them? The statement amazed the Baluters, not because of what it said—you could argue both sides of that question, like in a debate—but because it suggested they had a choice. *I am a dog, a dog,* Leibel Shifter had said. But everyone knew he had been mad. No, no cure for Judaism. It was a sentence for life.

The next day, when they buried the two shooting victims, was a holiday, the first since the wedding in the Virgin Mary Church. Factories closed. Shops boarded up. And they let out the few who were left in the schools. The official ceremony was in the Baluter Square. There was a band and a bandstand. Hundreds of policemen, with black crepe on their hats, milled around. Also present, also in black, was a big

277

crowd of Judenrat workers—clerks, typists, printers, along with their families. Of course the porters. Naturally the fire brigade. But many plain citizens gathered there, too: café owners, spinning-mill foremen, skilled workers of various kinds. It was a crowd that stood for law and order. They wanted to protest anarchy. NO MORE RECKLESSNESS! That was the banner they raised in the air. The band played. A special honor guard, half ministers, half policemen, carried the coffins through the square.

Then, in the air, there was a strange sound, like a cork coming out of a bottle. One, two, three—all the Jews disappeared. One minute there they were, a crowd of thousands, with big metal tubas, and the next minute there was nothing at all. This was all the more astonishing because no one knew for sure whether the popping sound had indeed been a shot. That became clear only when Rievesaltes' big white stallion, the one that had once belonged to the Elder, dropped onto its knees, the way a camel does to let its rider dismount. Then the beast collapsed completely, and Rievesaltes ran off on his uneven legs.

From that day onward the Jewish Council no longer counted within the Balut. Of course it still ran the soup kitchens and deloused the houses and delivered the mail. But no one paid attention to its rules. When a new tax was announced, with severe penalties for nonpayment, hardly a "Trumpkie," much less hard zlotys, came in. What happened was the no-neckers went around and collected the money first. The police force, in fact, was the real government of the Suburb. Rievesaltes' word was the law. He was the one who set the new curfew hour, made the new spinning-mill quotas, decided whether or not there would be a coupon for coffee in that week's ration book. If you didn't like it, if you had a complaint, your name might show up on the resettlement list.

But for all his power, the Security Minister was just as frightened as the rest of the Judenrat. So were all rich Jews, and the café owners, and the owners of casinos. It was the

Communists, the sharpshooters, who made them tremble. Not a single policeman dared to walk the streets alone. Thus the Lipskyites were like a third government within the Ghetto. The other two did everything they could to bring it down. The Judenrat offered, for the capture of the underground leader, a fifty-thousand-zloty reward. Time after time the police force would sweep through a section of the Suburb, certain they had at last trapped their prize. No luck. No Lipsky. Once they came upon poor Mister Kemp, in the act of slipping leaflets under a door. They poured water on his head. They hit him with rubber rods. But the ex-finisher, a veteran of the Five Day Strike, refused to talk. Where was the little lawyer? The agitator? It was as if he were made from puffs of wind.

Ladies, gentlemen, you know somebody else was missing, too. Trumpelman, Trumpelman! Why talk about the Judenrat, the Lipskyites, the power of Rievesaltes? Had not the *fourth government*, the Conquerors themselves, once declared: "Every Jew and Jewess must obey the Elder's commands"? But the fact was the citizens of the Balut had not seen the Elder for almost a year. Two, then three months went by after the roundup at the House of Culture, and Trumpelman remained in his mansion. Mourning for the deported Ghetto Queen, that was the official explanation. But gradually the word got out, perhaps from the Guardsmen, perhaps from the Jewish Council, that at the Geyser the Elder had suffered a stroke.

This caused no great alarm. First, the Lithuanian's life was not in danger. He could speak, lift his arm, and sit normally in a chair. Also, he did not abandon his official tasks. The Chancellory was shifted from Dworska Street to Tsarskoye Selo. To the estate were summoned all sorts of people—foremen, ministers, Jews with petitions. And from the mansion messengers ran to every part of the Ghetto, carrying orders for this man or that man, holding the text for the latest wall poster decree.

Still, no matter how vigorously Chaim worked to retain his power—and the light in his room burned, as always, through every night—it inevitably slipped away. He would call Wohltat, but Wohltat would not respond. The leaders of the chimney sweeps, his allies till then, found some pretext not to appear. In June the workers at the print shop returned his announcements, claiming that the next run of posters was already filled. It developed that Rievesaltes had occupied the printing house. To secure it from Lipskyites. Not long after that the Police Chief took over the Office of Posts and Telegraphs, too. Trumpelman picked up the phone to fire the Minister, Miss Megalif, but the instrument was dead. Not even buzzing. Worse by far was the way the Ghettoites themselves, with their thousand worries, began to forget the former leader. When they thought of him at all, it was not as a striding, striking figure, taller than anyone, with hair like a lion's mane. He was a sick man, an old man, aged seventy-four: older than any Jew in the world.

We come to 4 August, 1943. Many interesting things were happening in the world on that date. The Americans had practically captured the island of Sicily, and Ben Moses, the boss of the boot, *Il Duce*, was now locked in jail. Hamburg harbor was being bombed. Yes! It was flaming! Lots of *fine fellows* killed. Best of all, the Russian summer offensive just then broke through. The Red Army was in Stich, in Pilatov-ka. Now Orel was about to fall. More! The partisan forces were ranging far ahead of those lines. Getting closer! Burning the oil in Boryslaw! Hope! What a thing it is! Like a worm! Cut it and cut it and cut it! Still it won't die!

But in the other war, the one against the Jews, Horowitz was winning as usual. On that very day the Ghetto of Sonowiec-Bendzyn was liquidated. All of its citizens just disappeared. That left only Minsk. And Vilna. And the Balut.

And in the Balut, just before dawn on August 4, a fearful thing happened. Hasensprung defected. Not only defected, but took all the bullets from the Elite Guardsmen's guns.

280

Now they were defenseless. The whole summer palace could be overrun. At least that is what Rievesaltes said when, later that morning, he brought his men up to the entrance of Tsarskoye Selo. It was for the Elder's protection that he ordered the grounds surrounded. No one could come in or go out. Even the Judenrat was turned away. Imagine how Trumpelman—all his life afraid of being put like a beast in a cage—felt then. A prisoner on his own estate!

Still August 4. Two or so in the afternoon. The light bulb over Trumpelman's head flickered, flickered, and went out. Occupation by the no-neckers of the weak-current station. A few minutes after that, or perhaps it was at that very moment, the Elder suffered a second, far more serious stroke. One-half his body was frozen. The eye on the left did not blink.

Was this the end of I. C. Trumpelman? It seemed surely so. Every day he was sinking and sinking. Now the Jews talked about him. They talked of nothing else. When a Baluter met a Baluter, he didn't ask, "How are you?" or "What color's your work card?" Instead, he said, "What news about Chaim?" Even people who detested the Elder, who blamed him for everything, could not hide their emotion, sorrow it was, when they heard that day by day, then week by week, the last of his strength was ebbing away.

The Balut held its breath. But the rest of the world went on in the usual fashion. One after the other the remaining ghettos were being destroyed. Bialystok's turn came almost right away. Bialystok! Such a cultured and lively town. Then, early in September, Minsk and Lida were made free of Jews. Suddenly the Balut was the last ghetto in Poland. Perhaps that is the reason the Ghettoites, who had nearly forgotten their Elder, now worried so much about his fate. His life and the life of the Suburb were so mixed together in people's minds that they thought as long as the old man survived, the Ghetto would, too. It was as if he had some magical power.

No wonder, then, that on September 22, when the rumor

281

spread that the Elder was actually dying, a shudder went through the streets of the Balut. All that day hundreds and hundreds of people walked from the center of the Suburb to stand beneath the walls of Tsarskoye Selo. They huddled there, thousands altogether, silent, not moving; and they did not go home when it got to be night.

The moon came up, half dissolved, like a pill. Dark clouds blew by. Inside the mansion the current was out. But shadows from candles flip-flopped on the walls. The sickroom itself smelled from their hot yellow wax. Trumpelman lay on his back, in bed. In a low voice, not like his own voice, but still lisping a little, he was telling the orphans a story.

"My dear children, a long time has passed since I last spoke to you of the journey of the *Morgenstern*. So much has happened. It is as if we had all lived ninety years. Never mind! Do not think sad thoughts. It is true, I am ill and at the end of my days. But is it not wonderful that just when my strength has fled, when everything is growing dim, that the adventures of my youth should return with such force to me?"

The Elder was not wearing eyeglasses over his round, bluish eyes. His nose pointed up like a fin. He could not perform the old trick of talking around a lit cigarette. He could hardly speak at all.

"Do you remember how, after my shipwreck, I succeeded in curing the wild Indians, each and every one? Alas! With the winter and its frozen streams, its leafless forests, a new sickness came. It made the men and women and children of the village swell up, in the way that you have seen our citizens do. The time came swiftly when there were more of our number dead than remained alive. Starvation! Starvation, my dears!"

Chaim paused for a moment, trying to breathe. The walls, because of the candles, went on fluttering, flapping. No one interrupted the words of the dying man.

"Never in my life have I felt as helpless as I did then. The

282

Indians fell before me, weeping, in their frenzy scratching their scalps and their skin. I was the legend among men, the white god who had come from the sea. Yet all my magic, my healing art, had dropped from me, just as, during the unaccustomed heat of the previous summer, my very skin had cracked and fallen aside. Bitterly then did I curse the fate that had caused me, a Lithuanian, a Jew, to board the Baltic steamer. Bitterly!

"One night three braves, their faces and upper arms completely chalk-covered, came to the hollow where I slept. Their torch flames woke me. These three then told me that they understood I had lost my luck—*luck* is what, in their own language, they called it—but that if I would follow them they would show me how to regain it. Willingly, I rose and fell in behind them.

"After some time the path that we followed began to incline more steeply upward. It was a mountain we climbed. We continued in darkness, never pausing, until at some agreed-upon signal my companions planted their torches and set about stripping the branches from two saplings that stood nearby. When they had done this they bent the top part of both trees toward one another and bound each to each. Then, with many tears, groaning in sorrow, they bade me to stand beneath the wooden arch. This I did. Each brave then leaped backward, as if the space beneath the bent trees were filled with fire, and from some distance they stared at me, still sighing, their white faces long, sad, and grieving. I could not help thinking they were like three mourners who look lovingly at one who is about to be shut up within a bier. Suddenly they fell upon me with knives, stabbing me, and with great skill passed their leather thongs beneath the muscles of my shoulders and over the bowed trunks of the trees. By means of this harness they drew me upward until my feet no longer touched the ground. Then they seized their flaming torches and vanished without a word down the mountainside."

What a wonderful, thrilling story! The orphans must have

been spellbound, hanging there, not by leather straps, but upon the fragile thread of the Elder's words. All of their lives had been spent inside the Asylum, inside of Poland, and suddenly here they were—half Indians, with painted faces, with arrows and bows. And when the Director of the Asylum continued—sighing now, his voice dropping lower than ever—it became more exciting still.

"Pain? Yes, my dears, pain of an indescribable kind. I was forced to curse every ounce, each cell, the very hairs of my body, all of which conspired to draw me down, downward, when the only relief from my suffering would be somehow to float or fly. I do not know how long I remained thus suspended. I fainted and woke and fainted again. It seemed to me then that nights and days were going by, although I could not have sustained myself in such a condition for more than hours. At last I woke painlessly, thinking that surely I had died. Around me, instead of the gloom, there was only white light. Was this heaven? Was I, so giddy and lightheaded, in the realm of angels? Of clouds? Alas! Not heaven! It was only the bitter dawn. And there, in the snow, not an arrow shot from me, was a yellow-skinned lion, with brown and yellow eyes.

"For some little while we stared at each other. Snow dust, I saw, was on his name. Then he started purposefully toward me. I attempted to scream, to kick at the jowls, at the trembling throat, but like a man in a dream no sound came from me and my legs hung limply down. Suddenly the beast reared upward and—was this not a dream as well?—stood before me upon his hind legs. He roared. He boxed the air. It was the Lion of Judah!

"Then the tan beast dropped his paws upon my wretched shoulders. It was no dream. No! No! I knew then the events of my life had taken place in a trance, and that this was my waking moment. 'My people!' I cried, not knowing whether I meant the Jews I had left behind me—those in the homeland, those who had drowned—or the tribe that since then I had joined. 'I shall never abandon you!'

"The next instant I was on the ground! The lion had gnawed the rope through! I could not move for stiffness, but the beast, gently, although using its jaws, lifted me upon its smooth back. I reached into the mane; I clung there, while the animal carried me swiftly up the mountain. Higher and higher we went, so high that the air became thin, too thin to breathe; and yet, though I was gasping, and the creature itself desperately panted, we went higher still."

The Elder sighed once, deeply, and stopped speaking. He did not move. Was this the end? The end of that lifetime? No. Faintly, having to struggle, he resumed. "How white everything was. Blinding! I let my eyes drop closed, but beneath my eyelids it was just the same. Like looking through eggshells. That whiteness, children! The sun! The clouds! The snow!"

A stop. A start again: in no more than a whisper.

"At last we broke through to the peak of the mountain. The lion and I sat side by side. A vast land stretched out below us, and beyond the land a great panorama, the whole great curve of the earth, green-colored and blue and brown. I saw the various seas, with ships on the waters, sailing ships and steamships, and the continents crossed by the shadows of clouds. And in all this I spied out a single island, saw it as plainly as if I had been a bird flying above it, its green hills and white beaches, the cocoa-bearing plants, the red pepper berries on all of its trees. It was a sight that perplexed me. Why was I shown a vision? What was this place? It is only now, a half century later, and here, in our Ghetto, that the answer to those questions at last becomes clear. Children! My own children! Can you guess it? Ha-ha!"

The Elder broke off abruptly. His laugh, dry, rattling, was awful to hear. But he was alive, panting, opening his mouth again.

"We shall go to that island together."

Then his last breath, a rush of air:

"Madagascar!"

On the floor, against the walls of the room. with their

hands curled like little paws, the orphans of the Asylum were sleeping. There was Citron. There Gutta Blit. Left-handed Mann Lifshits, too. Their bare ankles were mixed up, as if they had been thrown together in a pile. Little Gumbiner— age, not yet three, and motherless now like the others—Little Gumbiner was dreaming something. A frown followed a smile across his face, like a fox chasing a hare. About the mountain, the torches, the lion, and all the other adventures, neither he nor the others had heard a word.

Some moments went quietly by. Then one child untangled himself from the rest and stood up. Instead of a nightgown he had on a big, shapeless coat. His feet were inside of shoes. This young man looked around, into the room's every corner. He squinted, as if even the candlelight bothered his eyes. What he saw was that Elite Guardsman Bass was asleep in a chair, by the foot of the Elder's bed. His colleague, Szpilfogel, was also sleeping, outside the half-open door. That door the lad pulled noiselessly shut. Then, cautiously, carefully, as if Trumpelman were alive and might hear him, he moved to where the old man lay, his lips in a line, his toes pointing up.

Centuries before, in another geological age, the age of reptiles, of fishes, people used to perish on account of diseases. What a world that was! To die in a bed! In modern times that happened to only one in a hundred thousand. Lucky Trumpelman! To have it happen to him. The boy leaned over the Director of the Hatters' Asylum. The man's hair leaped away from his scalp and spread over the linen. A regular fountain of hair. How long his arms were! As long, almost, as his body. And his hand, bigger than a man's head when he balled it up, when he shook it in the air, now lay with knuckles down, fingers open, like an animal left on its back. The American spectacles were lying on the wooden table. It was the sight of these that for some reason made the boy quake.

Impossible to think of a thing more foolish, more pointless,

286

than the tears that at that moment showed up in the young person's eyes. Tears! What next? Sobbing? Tearing his clothes? There is no end to how stupid we are—in other words, to how much we are capable of forgetting. *Fool! Idiot! Coward!* The boy called himself all these names. Nonetheless, his eyes filled right to the brim. He could not help himself. Ladies and gentlemen, where do such things as tears come from? What good are they? And don't they ever dry up?

"Liar!" the boy said, in a half whisper. "Liar! Oh, liar!" He was speaking to the corpse. "You never crossed the ocean in a steamship! You never went to America! Those stories came out of books!" Elite Guardsman Bass stirred a little and made a popping sound with his lips. The youngster hardly noticed. His tears were splashing about—onto the horsehair coat, onto the Elder's stubbly face. Then he cried aloud, "You swore we would live! You swore it! You promised to take us to Madagascar! Now look what has happened! You lied!"

It was not Bass who awoke, not any of the children. It was I. C. Trumpelman. "Where is this? Is this Warsaw?" The Elder was blinking, blinking. Then the lids of his eyes swung right up.

The child was horrified. Even his death was a trick! "Are you alive?"

In the face of the sick man teeth appeared. An attempt to smile. "What's your opinion?"

A joke! Joking! The boy pulled himself to attention. "It is my duty to inform you of the decision of the Edmund Trilling Brigade. The brigade has decided—I have come to inform you—" Up swelled Lipiczany's heart. It was like a gag in his mouth.

Trumpelman spoke instead. "Are you one of my orphans? Step closer. I need my eyeglasses."

Nisel could not stand erect. His head kept drooping. He was shaking, too. Then the Asylum Director, with his right hand, touched the edge of the old winter coat. "Is it young Einhorn?"

"Trumpelman! Elder of the Jews! Because of your crimes against the Jewish people, the Edmund Trilling Brigade has sentenced you to death."

The Elder's blue eyes clouded over, like water mixed into an absinthe drink. "But you shot my stallion already! My noble stallion! Braver than a hundred Ghetto Jews!"

The large hand made its fist. The boy had to thrust his own hands deep into his pockets to disguise their trembling. Here was the Elder as Nisel knew him to be. The trembling was from joy that the old man was still the same. But what he said was: "The sentence must be carried out at once."

Trumpelman lifted his arm, as long, as thin, as a chimney sweep's broom, and stretched it toward the little table where the spectacles lay. He seized them. They flopped open, dangling. It took him a moment, with his one arm, to put them on. "Who are you? I know you. Wait!"

The boy did not stir. It was as if he were standing on the edge of something.

"Lipiczany!"

The knees of the boy gave way. He dropped, like dropping over a cliff edge, to Trumpelman's side. "Chaim!" he said. Their faces almost touched. The top teeth of the Elder came out again. A second smile.

"Lipiczany, my own son! I did not think you could still be alive."

The man turned his head. His chin, his wiry cheek, brushed Nisel's. Everyone, in his sleep, kept calmly breathing.

"Chaim?"

"Yes?"

"You knew."

"Knew?"

"About the forest. About the yellow bus."

"Poor Jews! Poor people!"

"But you still told them to go!"

288

There were tears on the Elder's cheeks. His own? Or Nisel's. "Is it true you have come to kill me?"

Lipiczany, to answer, reached inside his coat and took out a gun.

The Elder, seeing it, shut his eyes. "I can't even use the telephone. Rievesaltes has occupied the telephone exchange."

The gun was a large one, with a wooden handle. Like a pirate's pistol. The boy lifted the heavy weapon. He looked along the barrel. Where to aim it? At the heart? He leaned over the old man's body, touching his ear to the fallen chest. Here it was! Beating and beating!

The Judenrat Chairman spoke to Lipiczany. "Why do I feel that we are living though this moment a second time? Where was the first time? When?"

Instantly Nisel remembered. Trumpelman had been the one standing, weeping. The child was the one on the bed. He saw that room again, the turned-on light bulb, the face of the Director, the Director's shining hair. He had thought he was seeing an angel, a knight.

The moment came back to Trumpelman, too. "It was in the old Asylum. On Krzyzanowsky. I listened to your heart. I was your doctor, and I brought you back to life."

"It isn't true! Zam did it! It was Doctor Zam who gave me the shot!"

"Yes, Zam! With imported suits! Now he's a Communist, ha-ha!"

The boy gripped the gun with both hands. "You're no doctor! You were never a doctor! What lying! It's shameful! We know the truth about you!"

"Not a doctor! Before I was half your age I had cured hundreds of people. Hundreds! I'm not talking about Indians! About America! Not those fairy tales. I'm talking about a little town, my own town. The kind with a puddle in it. This puddle froze in the winter, it shrank in the summer, but it never once went away. This is the truth about me! This town! This puddle! The Jews walked around it all their lives!"

"I won't listen!" cried Nisel. "Stop talking!"

"When I was an infant, before I could talk, the Jews came to me with their boils, their sores. I sat high in a chair. It was like a throne. With cushions! With satin! Why was this? Why such an honor? Because I had blue eyes. *Blue eyes*! That meant I was a wonder-worker! *Should we do this?* the people would ask. *Should we do that?* I did not understand a word they were saying. I just heard their voices and shook my head or nodded, ha-ha, ha-ha, like a clever horse!"

Lipiczany could not help staring at the Elder. The man's eyes were round still, like a child's, and blue-colored. They made you think that what he said was true.

"It worked! People got better. Jews came from other towns. Even from Vilna. *Take this medicine, but don't take that one*, I said. Or, *Buy this potion, fill up a teaspoon with it, and pour the teaspoon onto the ground*. One person I told to swim in water. Another to walk without clothes in the cold. Why I said these things I do not know. It was as if someone else and not I were speaking. One day I looked down from my seat and I saw a whole crowd of people kneeling before me. Thousands, it seemed. My head started to spin! I was like a drunkard! The crowd rose up. *Rabbi! Tell us! Why do we suffer?* That is what they were crying. *Rabbi! Prince!*

"From that day I ceased being a healer. I devoted myself to study. Day and night I was reading. I did not eat. I did not sleep. I never spoke to another soul. Years passed this way. The puddle grew and shrank and grew and shrank, as if it were breathing. The whole world, these thousands of people, were waiting for me to solve their riddle: What is a Jew? Why does he suffer? No scholar knew more than I!"

The boy gazed at Trumpelman, his mouth hanging loosely. He looked as if he were mesmerized. "Did you? Did you solve it? The answer!"

Trumpelman turned his head away. "No! No more study! I cured people by twisting their necks!"

"You know! Tell me! Do they beat us because we're bad?"

"This is what a Jew is." The Elder gripped the horsehair coat. He clung to it. "A Jew is a shit like everyone else."

Enough talk! A cock was already crowing. The orphans started to stretch, to stir. Shoot! Shoot! Why the endless delay? The rooster, way off in the Walburska section, crowed once again. With both hands, Nisel raised the pistol. He pressed the end of it against the Elder's chest. Yes! He was squeezing the trigger! But the blunderbuss did not go off. Not cocked. He pulled back the hammer. But the trigger still did not budge. Perhaps it was rusty, or else the boy did not pull hard enough.

For a moment Nisel simply stood there. His head, on its little neck, drooped.

"I can't," he said.

And why not? Why not seize Bass' pistol? Why not stab the Elder with something sharp? Hurry! Choke him! Choke him with your bare hands!

Too late. Trumpelman started speaking. "Do you call that a gun? It's an antique! Older than I am. How will you attack the warriors with such toys?"

"The Red Army will send us rifles. Until then we must fight with whatever we can."

"Open the drawer. The table drawer," said the Elder. "See what is there."

Nisel, as if following orders, jumped to do it. There was a pistol inside, the kind that shot bullet after bullet. A revolver. The boy snatched it up. He ripped open the chamber for shells.

The Elder—his glasses had slipped sideways on his bony face—gave a tiny wave. "It's loaded," he said.

This gun was not heavy. Lipiczany aimed it with only one hand. "Why did you show me this? Are you giving it to the

291

resistance movement? But the brigade is determined to wipe out the whole Judenrat!"

"If only I had done it before! If I had listened to Lipsky! I know how I have made our people suffer. I hear their voices. Putermilch! Schneour! Mister Szapiro! Blum! Mister Mosk! It's a roar like an underground train!"

Was it getting light outside? Nisel squinted. His face was pinched and lined. He heard Trumpelman speaking, on and on: "Lipsky knew! He is the real hero! I am a traitor! A worm! Tell him to come and kill me!"

"Commander Lipsky does not leave headquarters. I will carry out the sentence alone. I will!"

"No, no. He must come! I have more weapons! Not just guns! I have exploding bombs! Think of it: Jews with guns! Warrior Jews! Armed partisans!"

Lipiczany did not lower his arm. But the lips of his monkey mouth were sucked in. It's obvious he was thinking. What if there were such guns and explosives? Then the Trilling Brigade would be an army!

"I know you do not trust Trumpelman! You want to kill him, to shoot a bullet into his heart. But then who will become Chairman of the Jewish Council? Rievesaltes! The archenemy will get the guns! Don't let it happen! Nisel, my shadow! Run to Lipsky! Tell him to come! I'll give him pistols and bombs. Then he can kill me, if I am not dead already! Smuggle the weapons out in my coffin! Ha! Ha! Like you once did the cow!"

Friends! If only someone would invent a time machine so that we could fly back over the years. Then we could suddenly appear before Nisel and say, *Don't listen! It's a trick! He's cunning! Cunning!* And then, if he paid no attention, if he refused to carry out his orders, we could kill the old fox ourselves. Look! The boy is wavering! His arm, the arm with the gun, is going down! We have to remember he was a child, in spite of everything that he'd lived through. He still had to live through more.

"Hurry! Don't let Rievesaltes take over the Ghetto! Bring Lipsky! The guns will be here at midnight! Run! My son! My child!"

Nisel made up his mind. He moved to the door, threw it open, and jumped over Szpilfogel's outstretched legs. The Guardsman who had grown a small mustache in the Horo-witz manner, woke up in time to see the boy start down the mansion stairs. Then he saw something else, something that made him swallow and gulp. The Elder was sitting up! His feet hung over the edge of the bed. He was moving his arms!

"After him! Follow him! Find out where he goes!"

The Guardsman did not wait for the specter to speak again. In a bound, capless, he took out after the boy in the reddish-brown coat.

The Judenrat President remained propped on the bed. His teeth came out in what once was a dazzling smile. He was watching the children wake up one after the other, using their wrists to rub their eyes. The cock crowed a final time, loudly, loftily, like the one in the fable who thought that his cry made the sun rise.

II

That day, at midday, Verble, Minister of Housing, walked into the Optima Café and got into line. He still looked the same: a mustache with wax, and ruddy cheeks. More like an Englishman than a Jew. In his hands, in his pockets, were hundreds and hundreds of zlotys. His suit was wrinkled, like a brow. The person in front of him was also a Judenrat member, Schpitalnik, of Culture and Entertainment. A stranger, with his hat down, and a mustache that barely covered his lip, stood behind. The line stretched right through the café, so that the waiters had to twist and duck among the close-set tables. There policemen sat, sipping drinks, smoking

293

cigarettes, laughing at popular jokes. For instance, *A fat Pole and a thin Warrior fall off the Zgierska Boulevard Bridge together. Question: Which one hits the ground first? Answer: Who cares?* In short, the Optima Café was the headquarters of the Jewish police.

The line moved slowly forward to where, on a couch, with his feet up like a pasha, Fried Rievesaltes attended to tasks. At last Schpitalnik arrived. He looked at the Police Chief, whose head, because of the way the light struck his temples, seemed to shine. Like a halo, almost.

"Mister Minister!" Rievesaltes exclaimed. "What are you doing here? You have not been arrested!"

Schpitalnik just giggled and opened his tin of snuff. Verble, from over his shoulder, responded.

"Yes! Arrested! The same as I! We're both supposed to report! To the Radogodsh Station! Here is the order, which you signed yourself!" The Minister of Housing thrust the document toward Rievesaltes. The latter did not blink or budge. "This is a pity. A tragedy. Even Judenrat members!"

"It's no pity! It's a joke! You arrest us in the morning and free us in the afternoon. For cash! What a racket!"

"And what does the Housing Department now charge for a mattress? Is it not sixty zlotys? That's for a mattress filled with rags. But what if a Jew should want something soft? He has to pay exactly one hundred. And where does such stuffing come from? You bribe the feather cleaners. You smuggle from the Christian church. Stealing the property of the Occupying Power is a capital offense. You could be shot!" The whole room fell silent. No more jokes. Impossible not to hear what the Security Minister said. "I shall not, however, mention this matter when I discuss your case with my friend, the Obergruppenführer. The price of this negotiation is twenty-five thousand zlotys—ten thousand in advance, fifteen later."

Everyone gasped, even the waiters. It was a ransom for a king. "Swindle!" poor Verble cried.

Rievesaltes now swung his feet off the sofa, onto the floor. "If by any chance we should not have success," he said, "never mind about later."

Schpitalnik, meanwhile, had been going through his coat pockets, his pants pockets, turning everything out. He stood there, with little inverted bags all over his body. "Ha! Ha! I've only sixteen Trumpkies!"

Verble snorted. "Trumpkies are not worth a thing!"

"Ha! Ha! Completely worthless. But I don't want to be transported. I could play on the piano. I could learn to sing. *Tum-tum-de-tum!*"

Fried Rievesaltes cut in. "Time always passes. Jews, shadows grow. Look at the size of the line. For another five thousand, five thousand on top of the rest, I'll argue for you both with my friend. Come, Minister Verble! Just fifteen thousand! Not a word about the feathers! Come! I'll get down before Grundtripp on my knees!"

Now it was the Housing Minister's turn to pick through his pockets. He found, he handed over, the staggering sum. This was the equivalent of one hundred and fifty mattresses, the soft kind: enough for one hundred and fifty Jews to dream, on those feathers, they were flying away.

The next man stepped forward and removed his hat. Simultaneously somebody screamed, "Watch out! A Guardsman!"

Rievesaltes reached into his armpit. A dozen policemen, in theory unarmed, did the same. The stranger held up empty hands.

"Yes, I know him! Szpilfogel!" The speaker was the former orphan Nellie Brilliantstein. How greatly in the last years she had changed. Heavy set, a rumbly voice, a steady smoker. And her eyes, which had been wide, were now deep, narrow, and green. She went to Trumpelman's guard. "Tell us! Has it happened? Or is the old man still alive?"

Rievesaltes swayed just a little. "Now who is the Elder? Him? Or me?"

295

The Elite Guardsman did not answer this question directly. Instead he lowered his arms, as well as his voice, and said to the head of the Jewish police, "My message is for your ears, nobody else's." Then to Rievesaltes he whispered a thing so astonishing, yet so delightful, that the Minister's mouth at first dropped open, then spread in a beaming smile.

We know precisely what the Police Chief found out from Szpilfogel. This: that at midnight, at Tsarskoye Selo, the terrorist Lipsky could be caught in the act of smuggling contraband guns. Unfortunately what Rievesaltes did not discover was that at that very moment, Bass, also a Guardsman, was revealing to Obergruppenführer Grundtripp that the Security Minister, up to then such a trustworthy Jew, might be observed just after midnight at Tsarskoye Selo, plotting with the traitor Lipsky.

Is the old man still alive? What a question! Who else could have thought up such an ingenious plot? Here was a miraculous recovery. First he is in his bed, his deathbed, with not enough breath to make a mark on a mirror, and then he's smarter than Machiavelli!

Now who is the Elder? Are there any doubts? Trumpelman still! Even the Others, the High and Mighty, were nothing more than puppets in the puppetmaster's hands.

III

Midnight then. A light rain. Just enough to make you wipe your eyeglass lenses. Chilly, too. Smoke came from the chimney at Tsarskoye Selo, lingering at the top. Inside the mansion, Trumpelman, the Elder, was sitting on a chair. His hands were tied in back of the frame. On the floor in front of him, a man with a nose and a mustache and glasses was examining a crate of guns. That is when Fried Rievesaltes, with a pistol in his hand, stepped through the unbolted door.

Rievesaltes: "You can take off the rubber nose. For I know it is you, Attorney Lipsky."

Lipsky was armed as well. "Hands up, traitor."

"Not true," Rievesaltes remarked. "Everyone knows that I save hundreds of doomed Jews each day. I don't shoot them, the way you do."

"We execute only those who have grown rich and powerful on the sufferings of their own people. The ones who enjoy their jobs."

"The money I make is spent inside the Ghetto. Isn't there a reward for your capture, Lipsky? Fifty thousand zlotys from the Judenrat? Thus we take from the rich and give to the poor. Hands up, Mister Smuggler, please."

But neither man raised his hands. Each pointed his weapon at the other.

"It's a stalemate," said the old man in the chair. Then he began to issue sharp commands. "Rievesaltes, back up ten paces. You too, Lipsky—in the other direction. Back, back, near the door. Don't point your guns, idiots! Not until the Chairman gives the command. He will say, *Get ready!* He will tell you, *Aim!* Don't shoot until you hear the word *Fire!*" Thus the Elder arranged the duel.

Rievesaltes looked at Lipsky. "Are you willing?" he asked.

"Willing," said Lipsky.

Force of habit, that is the explanation for why the two gunmen obeyed the Elder. Or else they recognized there was nothing else to do.

"One condition," the Bolshevik called. He was standing with his back to the door, across the room from the Chief of Police.

"And that is?"

"Whoever survives executes Trumpelman."

"Agreed."

Trumpelman's lips pulled up, off his teeth and gums. Then he shouted, quite loudly, "Get ready!"

Lipsky raised his gun arm. He had not removed his

money-lender's disguise. His hat rode on the tuft of his hair. "Rievesaltes! For your crimes against the Jewish people, the Edmund Trilling Brigade sentences you to death!"

The condemned man raised his arm as well. "What is death? Who knows the answer to that, Lipsky? Not you and not I. It's possible we'll find out together."

"It can't," said Lipsky, "be worse than life."

"Aim!" cried Trumpelman.

The Chief of Police released the catch on his gun. "They say that *up there* even the poorest Jew can make a good living."

Lipsky turned his profile, with a hand on his hip. "Better than in the Aryan section."

At that instant the door next to the lawyer flew open and Grundtripp, the Totenkopfer, burst into the room. "Don't move, Jews!" he commanded. "Not even a finger!" It was then that Isaiah C. Trumpelman bellowed, "Fire!"

A bullet came out of each duelist's gun. Lipsky's went wild, into the floorboards. But Rievesaltes' sailed into the chest of the Obergruppenführer, and stopped.

"You are under arrest!" cried the Other, without realizing he had been shot. Then because his heart was not beating, he dropped straight down.

Fried Rievesaltes let go of his weapon. He undid the button of his collar. "I'm dead!" he exclaimed. "Dead! Not living!"

Now Trumpelman started to shout. "Help! Help! It's a rebellion! Communists!"

A detachment of Death's-Headers rushed through the doorframe. F. X. Wohltat was right behind them. His face was different from usual. Red, not white. As if he were choking. "I almost went first," he said.

A horrible scene followed then. All the Death's-Headers rushed over to Rievesaltes and began to beat him, to kick him with their shoes. Suddenly there was a crash and a tinkle and rainwater came into the room. Lipsky, with an armful of guns, had jumped through the window. The Others ran to the spot and began to shoot into the dark. Missed! Missed again! The underground leader was gone.

"Stop! Stop shooting!" It was Trumpelman, still tied to the chair. "The Police Chief is a Judenrat prisoner. And so is the Bolshevik, Lipsky. He won't escape from the Elder. The Judenrat will punish them both."

"Both! Both! We'll kill you all! We'll smash the Ghetto to pieces! What if I'd gone first through the door!" It was the Volksdeutscher. His voice rose and rose, practically shrieking. "Twenty-four hours! Just twenty-four hours! If the partisan is not captured by then, we shall attack with tanks, with artillery guns, with planes. No one will be left alive. There will be nothing but corpses!"

Those last words made everyone think of Grundtripp. Blood kept coming from his body, as if it were still being pumped. His mouth was wide open. So were his eyes. The look he had was of shock, of surprise. Who can blame him? It was difficult to believe that such an important man, with the rank equivalent to a Lieutenant-General in the British Army, could be killed by a single bullet shot by a Jew.

IV

The dawn of that day, drizzly, dim, leaking in a hundred places, was the last one our Baluters would ever see. Such, at any rate, was a widely held opinion—an opinion that had been formed as soon as our Jews awoke and read the poster in fresh, black, wet-looking ink. Lipsky, provocateur Lipsky, had to be handed over by midnight. Otherwise the Suburb would be destroyed. Signed: the Judenrat Chairman. As if that weren't enough, the Ghettoites next discovered there was no place to work. The mills were locked. The shops—twine makers, brush makers, crystal sorters, and such—did

299

not open. That meant one thing: the threat on the posters would be carried out. But who was to capture this Lipsky? The Jewish police had disappeared. Rievesaltes was now a prisoner in his own jail. Worst, most awful, Grundtripp, the Blond One, was dead! Shot, some said, by a Jew! Hopeless, then, to beg for mercy. What to do? There was nothing to do. That is why the Jews simply went into the streets and stood there, in their coats, in their caps, by the hour, like wheat.

Then, because the Ghetto was so quiet, many people heard, first a pounding noise and then the sound of someone cutting wood. Everyone began to walk toward the Baluter Ring, where the sounds came from. Other Jews were already there, filling up the streets that lined the square, pressing right to the edge of what had once been—with its birds and squirrels and blue-and-white benches—an attractive park. Nothing but tree stumps there now. And among these stumps, on the burned patches of grass, a man was hammering and a man was sawing, while the Judenrat Chairman, in his new wheelchair, rolled up and down.

It was Brauwatt with the hammer, a real carpenter, with nails in his mouth. What was he building? Too soon to tell. The one man kept sawing planks; Brauwatt joined them together. After a time you could see there was a platform, a kind of stage. On top of this two vertical supports went up, like two big capital A's. Then two teams of sweepers climbed up these structures and lowered a stout crossbar between them, nearly four meters above the ground.

"Look!" came a voice from the crowd. "It's a scaffold!"

Of course! Why hadn't they seen it before? The Baluters began to laugh and shout. "Yes! Yes!" they cried. "We'll hang the traitor!" How every man's spirit soared! It was as if rays of sunshine had broken through the thick, spongy clouds.

What came through the clouds in actual fact was an airplane. It dived straight for the thousands of Jews. For a moment it seemed that the pilot meant to crash into the wooden

300

scaffold. He got closer and closer. One of his rubber wheels was spinning. The wings shook and dipped. Then, thundering, it swooped up and away, making a wind that knocked off dozens of caps. The Jews understood: this meant that they would be bombed. A cry went up from the crowd. *Lipsky! Lipsky! We want Lipsky!* It was an understandable reaction. Against the lives of so many thousands, the fate of one man weighed no more than the wing of a fly.

The manhunt went on all afternoon. Bands of Jews ran through the streets, shouting, *Hand him over! Give him up!* Search parties broke down apartment doors. They swept through attics, through cellars, and poked the hollow walls. Everywhere they found people hiding, in wardrobes and bunkers and inside chimney flues. But no matter how frantically, how carefully, they searched, they were unable to find a single member of the Edmund Trilling Brigade. The rain, needles of it, came thicker, faster. Down some whirlpool went the light of the day. That meant the Baluty Suburb, the last ghetto in Poland, had only four or five hours to live.

Suddenly, at the intersection of Jakuba and Franciskanska, in the factory district, there was a disturbance. *There he is! Stop him! Kill the traitor!* Down the length of Jakuba a little man came dashing. His cheeks were puffed up. He had a wing collar on. Behind him, with sticks, ran the mob. With each step they were gaining. And from every side street came more Jews. A roar went up. The poor man was trapped. He stopped. You could see his black mustache, his white collar. Then somebody grabbed him by the knees and another person took hold of his shoulder. He disappeared.

"He came out of a manhole! I saw him!"

"Like a rat!"

"We should have looked there from the start! Ha! Ha! An underground leader!"

In a moment a man came with a gasoline lantern. The Jews stepped back. Lipsky, with his arms broken, lay on the

301

ground. The trouble was, it wasn't Lipsky the lawyer. The yellow light flashed and sizzled. It was the tailor Lipsky. Originally from Kamenets-Podolsk.

Where was the Bolshevik, then? The answer, of course, is that he was at the brigade headquarters, the same little room, the one with the slanted roof, the paper over the windows, that James Faulhaber had once been led to—upstairs and downstairs, blindfolded, on hands and knees. It was so cleverly disguised that no one—not the Ghettoites, not even the Warriors—would ever find it. Faulhaber, the American, was in that room now. He was wearing the wool suit in which he had arrived at the Ghetto gate, nearly two years before. In all that time his hair had not once been cut. With those locks, with the loose strands of wool, he looked more like a poet than anything else. "It's unbearable!" he moaned. His hands were over his ears. "Won't they ever stop?"

No one in the room—and there were a dozen Jews, all crowded together—responded. So the awful cries—*Give him up! Hand him over!*—continued to drift up from the streets, sometimes near, sometimes far off, but never, not for a moment, ceasing. Finally Chaffer, his hands over his ears, burst out in wordless musical notes.

"La! La! La!" Old Pipe, surprisingly loud, joined in too.

"Quiet! Silence!" Hersh Einhorn hissed at the two elderly men. "Do you want to give our position away?"

"Maybe that *is* what they want! There are some people here who would like to meet the demands." That was the Widow Trilling, after whose husband the brigade had been named.

"No, no, no, no—" said the buttonholer. "Not in the least. Not at all."

The room fell silent again. Some fighters sat—on sandbags, on a corner of a table, on the floor; the rest, in small ovals, were pacing. A Jew asked the time. "Twenty-one minutes past ten," another Jew told him. The voices in the street went on and on.

Thus it was almost eleven, the proverbial eleventh hour, before the next person spoke. It was Zam, the Warsaw physician, and what he said chilled them all. "Jews! Partisans! Kill me if you want! But here is my opinion. Our leader Lipsky should turn himself in!"

"Of course," cried the widow. "It's a non-worker speaking. A fancy dresser."

"A doctor's job is to save lives, not to waste them," replied Miss Bibelnieks, Zam's assistant.

Kleiderman, one of the Mosk mill workers, said, "No one will be saved if Lipsky surrenders. The ultimatum is just a pretext to attack the Ghetto. If it doesn't happen tonight, it will tomorrow. If not tomorrow, the next day. Our turn has come. We have to fight."

"Yes! Fight! Fight!" a half dozen voices, heedless of everything, cried.

"Fight? Fight who?" Zam demanded. "Listen! Do you hear them? Our enemies will be the Jews in the street."

"Pardon, pardon—" The big presser was trying to get people's attention. "Between today and tomorrow, there's a big difference. I mean, what if we put off the showdown for two more months? Then the Soviet Army will be here to join the fight. Just two months!"

Nachman Kipnis stood. From all appearances he had, in the last year, or two years, simply stopped growing. But the lenses in his glasses were thicker, like milk-bottle glass. "Comrades! Whether it's two months, or four months, or even six months, our orders are to keep the Ghetto alive! The Red Army needs us. We have to start the revolt from within!"

The presser was red in the face. He was blushing from shame. "This Lipsky! I love this Lipsky! Before I met him I was just a presser, a pants worker. He taught me to struggle. From him I learned the purpose of life. Now friends, dears,

I am like Atlas. The world is a ball in my hands!" The big man in three strides crossed the room. He leaned over the Brigade Commander. "Lipsky! Our hero! Forgive me! You have to go!"

The lawyer, looking like himself, in a plain, open, faded shirt, was sorting through a box of bullets. He was so feverish, so busy—choosing shells that fit the revolvers, putting them in—that he had not heard anything of the debate. But he saw the presser standing near. "A minute. A minute. Let's say every other shot is a hit. So we shoot one hundred Others! A hundred! It's enough! They'll turn. They'll run."

Old Pipe in his pullover—it had a diamond design—came over. "Mister Lipsky. We have decided. You have to surrender to the Judenrat."

"It's not true! Don't listen! There's been no decision!" Sitting on a sandbag, holding his knees, Nisel Lipiczany continued. "There is a chance the Warriors are bluffing. Has anyone thought of that?"

Lipsky let the cartridges slide through his fingers. "What is this? I should surrender? Surrender? It is the eve of the battle. It's when the Ghetto needs its leaders most."

"It seems," said Faulhaber, "we should take a vote."

Hersh Einhorn: "This isn't America, Faulhaber. We don't vote on this and that."

Kleiderman: "We are a military force, in wartime. Anyone who doesn't follow orders is shot."

"And Lipsky is our Commander. He gives the orders here."

"Yes, that's so, Madame Trilling," young Kipnis said. "But don't forget, our brigade, like the whole resistance movement, is only a single unit of the Red Army. Lipsky is our Commander, but above Lipsky, above all the generals and admirals, there is only one leader: the Man of Steel!" The boy wheeled. He pointed to the portrait, pasted to the wall, of the man with the mustache, the smoking pipe.

A sigh went up from the fighters. In the street someone

screamed. Glass was breaking there. People were begging, as the deadline drew nearer, for a miracle to save them.

The cannibal woman—remember, she had not eaten her son—broke the silence. "Vote," she said.

Everyone looked at Lipsky. He was squatting and, like a bird on a branch, turning his head. "No resistance group in history has handed over its own leader. Don't be the first ones."

Faulhaber took over. His suit was shredding in places. He brushed the hair from his eyes. "Everybody who thinks we should not turn Lipsky in, put up his hand."

Nisel's hand was first in the air. Then Einhorn's, and Kleiderman's, and of course the one that belonged to the widow Trilling. Four altogether. Then the cannibal woman raised her arm, too. A total of five. A pause.

Faulhaber: "What about you, Lipsky? Not voting?"

Across his chest the lawyer folded his arms. Not voting.

"Wait!"

The Jews looked over to where the last surviving Bloomgarden, Ignacy, stood with his hands in his pockets. He put one of those hands in the air. Six, then.

Said Faulhaber, "All opposed?"

The following raised their hands: Pipe, Chaffer, Kipnis, Faulhaber himself, the presser, Miss Bibelnieks, Zam. In other words, seven.

Imagine the astonishment of all the fighters when Lipsky burst into tears. The drops poured out of his eyes like water from pipes. Of course everyone looked at his or her shoes. But they had to hear what their Commander was saying.

"I'm not crying for myself. I don't care about having to die. Poof! One more Jew! I'm crying for Trilling and Szypper and Professor Zygmunt because they gave up their lives. For what? So that we could behave exactly like their great foe, the Judenrat! *Hand one over, we'll save many!* For that we sentenced the ministers to death. It's the hopelessness, the hopelessness, brothers and sisters! I can't stop the tears!

There is something in history that makes all men act the same!"

Zam's eyes were a little wet, too. "What's the alternative? The alternative is to act like the Blond Ones. Go into the street and battle the Jews!"

Faulhaber was gripping his hair, handfuls of it. "The choices!"

"To tell the truth," said the finisher, Pipe. "To tell the truth, for the first time I feel sympathy for the Jews on the Judenrat."

The cannibal woman then lifted her dress off her body. Underneath she had panties, probably made out of cotton, but nothing on top of her small, pointing breasts. Naked like that, she went to Lipsky. "Quick," she said, "Put it on."

The Commander's wet head disappeared into the dress, a blue one, with white, daisyish flowers. When it came out again, his eyes were dry and narrow, his teeth made a grinding sound. "Stand back!" he ordered his fellow fighters.

"It's all right," said the presser. "No one will stop you."

"No one," said Kipnis and Zam together.

The widow of Edmund Trilling had been all her life an Orthodox woman. That explains how she was able to take her hair off and push it down on the head of Lipsky. "Run, run," she said.

With a gun in his hand, wordlessly, he did so. Out the secret exit, down flights of stairs. Behind him, in the room, the cannibal woman placed her hands on her neck. Her elbows, dropping, modestly covered her breasts. Next to her stood the Widow Trilling. Her head, like a bulb that was planted, sprouted the tiniest hairs.

"What's the time?" asked a Jew.

No reply.

At street level, Lipsky opened a door a crack and slipped outside. He glanced in both directions, as if looking for traffic, and walked quickly to the far side of the road. There,

306

in the shadows, Szpilfogel nudged the Elder. "That's the door," he whispered. "That's where I followed the orphan boy."

Trumpelman, in his wheelchair, peered at the approaching woman. Lipsky was a short man; the dress he wore came below his knees, almost to his ankles. But it did not cover his pants cuffs, or his shoes. The Guardsmen raised their rifles, the sweepers lifted their clubs. "Alive," said the Elder, and released them.

The lawyer saw the ambush just in time. He whirled, he ran, but he tripped on his blue-and-white hem. The clubs fell on his body. The butt of a rifle knocked off his wig. Far off, in the Aryan section, the chimes of the steeple struck the first notes of twelve.

V

Rain, rain. It wouldn't stop. The long, low clouds passed so near it seemed you could touch them. The top floors of the buildings on the Baluter Ring had all disappeared. Sometimes the bulging bottom of a cloud would roll over the ground, splitting, spilling; or just a crooked finger of mist would descend, suddenly, as if it meant to lift a Jew by the collar. And how wet these Jews were! The water streamed off the brims of their hats like Spanish tassels. Their skin was wrinkled, like after a bath. They did not mind. They hardly noticed. Six deep, numbering thousands, they stared into the center of the park, where the damp wood of the scaffold showed through a cloud that bubbled and frothed like the head of a beer.

Rievesaltes was on the platform and so was Lipsky. They both stood on square boxes and both, from their beatings, were bruised and blue. There were nooses around their necks already. The odd thing was that these knots were made

307

out of either end of a single rope, a rope that went up and through a wheel, a pulley, attached to the scaffold beam. Verble was on the platform, too. He was the new head of the Jewish police. By himself, without a speech, without anything, he kicked the box out from underneath each doomed man.

Naturally, Rievesaltes went down and Lipsky, a slight man, ascended. Verble pushed the boxes beneath both men again. Then he gave a command. Four policemen—one was the old hand, Pravenishkis—jumped onto the platform. They began to drop stones, cobblestones, into the seat of the lawyer's pants. Again Verble removed the boxes. Rievesaltes sank, but more slowly. Lipsky still rose. The test was repeated. Now Lipsky, with stones in his pockets, stones in his crotch, actually dropped—while Rievesaltes, whose vest had only a single pearl button, climbed into the air. A final test. A perfect balance. Both men weighed exactly the same.

The policemen dropped down from the platform and arranged themselves on either side of the Elder's wheeled chair. Vigorously Trumpelman raised his arms.

"Jews, listen! Lwow! Sosnowiec-Bendzyn! Bialystok! Minsk and Lida! All these ghettos have been liquidated! They no longer exist. And now, fresh news! Weep, Jews! Vilna, a center of learning, of light—yesterday Vilna disappeared! Any idiot can see, if we had not caught these traitors, yesterday would have been the end for us, too. But here they are! Look at them! The big shots!" Here the Elder waved over his shoulder toward Lipsky, toward Rievesaltes, each standing on his own special box.

"Where are their armies now? The police force is stringing its own minister up! Ha! Ha! And what about the anarchists? Those snot-noses with popguns? Why don't they rescue their leader? It's because they don't dare! Those pipsqueaks know the Elder has got back his strength! He's not the one who's going to die! What about that, Mister Rievesaltes? What, Mister Lipsky? Let's hear your last words!"

But neither the minister nor the lawyer, even though each was conscious, even though the rope was not yet tight, said a word. By stillness, by silence, they showed their disdain. But when Verble pulled out the boxes again, this time in earnest, they could not help squirming and jiggling on the ends of the line.

What happened was this: during their struggles, one of Rievesaltes' shoes struck the platform planks, and up he rose. This caused the rope to go slack, and the former Police Chief snatched a breath or two. Lipsky, down on the platform, made the identical discovery. If you kicked yourself upward, you could slacken the noose, you could breathe. The result was, both men rose and fell, rose and fell, kicking and gasping and popping their eyes. It lasted for hours.

The Jews in the crowd did not wait that long. They sloshed through the puddles. They turned from the scene. Even the policemen decided to go someplace indoors. After a time there was no one in the Baluter Ring. The park was deserted. It was then that Trumpelman, in spite of his stroke, in spite of his age, rose from his special chair. For a moment he stood there, leaning on his cane. Then, astonishingly, he threw down even that weak support.

Bing! Bing! It was Krystal. It was Lifshits. Is it possible, then, that somewhere on earth a photo exists to prove that the events of this scene are true? Not likely. For a cloud, a big one, churning and foaming, had come down like a whirlwind and hid the Elder, along with his two bitter enemies, from view.

Chapter Ten

Fighters

I

Some scientists say the whole universe is expanding, we're flying away from each other, and one day in the future every sun will go out, every planet will be cold. Ladies and gentlemen, think of it! No life anywhere! Just space! Nobody! Nothing! However, there's another school of thought. These astronomers maintain we won't expand forever; instead we'll collapse, we'll all come together in a kind of a ball—and then, after the explosion, everything, all of history, will start over again. Over again! It's terrible, it's unforgivable, but at that you just want to laugh.

How the Baluty Suburb came to an end. That's our topic now. Let's start with the big presser, the one from the underground movement. One, two, three! And he turns on his electric torch. It was just a weak yellow beam, going up barely three or four meters. But from this simple action much can be learned. First, a Jew was alive. Next, the Ghetto existed, since he was standing in the Marysin section, in the fields behind the summer palace. And why turn a light on in the daytime? Thus, we know it was a warm, dark night in the autumn, the fall. 1943? Alas, 1944. In other words, since Rievesaltes was hanged, together with Lipsky, a whole year had gone by. Tens of thousands of lifetimes. Hundreds and hundreds of trains. What had happened to the Red Army? At the time of the executions, the resistance had been in direct contact with the advancing people's forces. The brave soldiers and sailors had been only months away. The two sides were supposed to have linked arms together. To share the victory!

"Comrades! Comrades!" the poor presser groaned, gazing at the sky. With a stiff arm he held the light upward. Insects poured out of it, over his chin, his broken nose. "Comrades! Where are you?"

"*Shhh!*" a voice hissed from nearby. Hersh Einhorn's. "Listen!"

Somebody else, James Faulhaber, declared, "They're here!"

There was a buzz, a humming sound, like a beetle. It came closer. It was practically over their heads.

Suddenly everything became brighter than daytime. The clouds lit up, like shades for enormous lamps. At the same time there was a thumping, a crashing, a roar. The Men of Valor had let loose an antiaircraft barrage. Illuminated bullets went into the air. The ground was shaking. In the midsts of these blasts, the presser did not budge. Minute after minute his signal light steadily shone. Then the cannons stopped shooting. The members of the Edmund Trilling Brigade strained to hear. Nothing. No sound at all.

"Woe!" cried Faulhaber.

Two or three shouted together: "They've shot him down!"

A last shell, a low one, exploded. The whole Jewish graveyard, with its hills, its ditches, and even a tombstone, showed up in the light.

Hersh Einhorn pointed upward, into the sizzling sparks. "Wait! What's that?"

The brigade members peered overhead. The glow in the clouds lasted for another half second. But in that time they all saw something. It looked as if a circular patch on the sky had come loose, or as if someone had cut a section out of the dark bowl above them and with a finger pushed it down. Then the inky object was gone.

Everybody exclaimed at once.

"Where is it?"

"Gone! Disappeared!"

"Where's the light? Shine it here! Here!"

The big presser aimed his torch in every direction. He spun around. Nothing to be seen.

"Silence, Comrades!" commanded young Einhorn. "Hold the light up. Be still."

No person moved. Or breathed even. A moment went by. Then, into the fuzzy beam, two boots dipped down. After that, two legs appeared; and then, ever so slowly, the body of a man. The revolutionaries stood rooted, gaping. It was as if they were at the bottom of an ocean, watching a deep-sea diver descend. The light from the torch struck a chest, a head, and above the head something dark, black, cloudy: this umbrella collapsed and the night diver rolled into a ball on the ground.

The Ghettoites ran to where the parachutist had landed. They formed a circle around him. Up the daredevil sprang, and with vigor saluted. "Code name: Taradash. Red Army Commando. Regiment of the Fourth Guards."

Awkwardness. Silence. Everyone stared at the jumper, who remained blinking and smiling in the light of the presser's lamp. What a strange-looking fellow this was! Wisps of beard, like an adolescent's, were stuck on his cheeks and his chin. His nose was a long one and his eyes, like those of a dissipated person, were dark underneath and on the lids. Smiling, he kept on smiling, while behind him, attached to his narrow shoulders, the black silk canopy billowed and swelled. There was a red star on the front of his crashproof helmet.

At last one of the underground fighters, Pipe, born in Odessa, said shyly, "Taradash. Clever. From *taradaj*, a talky woman."

"No," the commando replied. "From *Torah Dat*. Torah law."

"Ah! Ah!" went the presser. "A Jew!"

At that, the discipline within the little band gave way completely. The fighters began to totter, to weave. Some sat on the ground. Nisel Lipiczany clutched at the stranger. "I am kissing you," he said. "Kissing you!"

The leader of the resistance recovered first. He came to attention in front of the Soviet airman. "Commander Einhorn here. The Edmund Trilling Brigade."

Nachman Kipnis, who could barely see anything, only outlines, cried for all to hear: "Friends! It's an historic moment! Stand up! The progressive forces have joined!"

The buttonholer Chaffer, however, lay down completely. He began to throw dirt over his knees.

Then the Commando, in perfect Polish, started to speak. "Comrades! Brothers! Now you know you have not been forgotten!"

Yet another person, the cannibal woman, sank down on her haunches. And the brigaders who remained on their feet were swaying, as if they too might fall.

Taradash continued. "Comrades, the day of your liberation is at hand. In forty-eight hours you will see the brightness of its dawn. I must, therefore, speak briefly. Together we have much to decide." For an instant he paused, blinking in the torchlight. Like a mantle, his parachute spread out behind. "The partisan forces, the Fourth Guards, and the Second Division of the Red Army have now combined. All are racing westward, racing to you, Comrades, and in two days' time the advance units will arrive at the bank of the Dolna. Naturally we expect the Beast, in his last frenzy, to blow up the bridges. To prevent this we have a plan, Operation Ural Mountains, in which your brigade has been assigned a crucial role.

"By surprise, from behind, in darkness, you will break out

313

of the Ghetto and seize one of these vital spans. It is understood that you will be unable to hold this position for any length of time. Therefore, before your assault on the bridge, two inflatable boats, under my command, will have already set out from the eastern shore. Within two minutes after you open the engagement, these boats, each with twenty fighters, will join you in the battle. You should know this: the landing party will be made up entirely of Jews, Jews who have escaped from Poland and who have fought so bravely with the partisans and the People's Fourth Guards. This is an honor we have been given! The instant the bridge has been secured—in no more than a quarter of an hour—the Red Army will stream forward in force to liberate the Ghetto and the town. Thus we shall destroy the enemy together, arm in arm. Revenge, Brothers! Revenge!"

"Forward! We are with you!" A single voice let out that cry. That of Nachman Kipnis. The rest were still.

With his bruised, shadowy eyes, the parachutist looked around. "What is it, Comrades? Do you object to the plan?"

A fighter replied: "Too late."

"We can't do it," another added.

It was odd how, in the light from the electric torch, Taradash only widened his smile. "But we are fighting in a war. You are soldiers."

"On your feet! It's an order! You're deserters!" Hersh Einhorn screamed at the squatting brigaders. He shook them. But no one rose. Chaffer was still pouring dirt over his body, like a child at the shore.

"We know you are short of supplies. We shall drop you guns, bullets, antitank weapons. The Red Army is counting on your support."

"No, no, you don't understand—" It was Doctor Zam. He took the presser's arm and guided the light onto the Bloomgarden orphan, who was sitting off to one side. "Look. See."

Ignacy immediately shielded his eyes. You could see both bones inside the arm he flung up. He swallowed. The bulge

314

moved down his neck. Zam forced the light onto Faulhaber. The American sat cross-legged, his head in his hands. He looked like a beggar in India, or a holy man there. Miss Bibelnieks next, leaning on Faulhaber's shoulder. She breathed through her mouth. Her teeth were long, yellow, like a horse's. On to little Kipnis. Only the mole beneath his eye had kept growing. It was dark, furry. With one hand he raised the other, in order to make a fist. Next the scalp of the cannibal woman, which showed through her hair. On Nisel's chest you could see where the drum of his heart was beating. Quite a show! Just skeletons! In America you say, like something the cat dragged in!

"Enough!" said the brave airman. "Turn off the light."

The presser obeyed—and at once dropped down next to the others. It was as if it had been the energy of the light, with the bugs and gnats flying in it, that had held him upright.

Quiet, quiet. Then someone said, "He who does not work does not eat." A quotation from the Ghetto King. The plain truth was that the brigade members were starving. Indeed, only weeks before the widow of Trilling had in that way died.

"We will drop food from the air, rations—" the commando began. Then he, like the others, grew still. Another moment went by. A cricket, under a rock, started cricketing. Dew came down. Of course it was pitch-black again.

Mister Pipe, of the Mosk Works, in a low voice spoke first. "Tell me, Comrade. Is it true that in the new Russia the workers own the means of production? I wanted to ask."

Before the airman could answer, Hersh Einhorn cut in. "The government, land, and machinery are controlled by the working class. It is a dream that has come true. Like in Plato's *Republic*."

Young Bloomgarden: "No bosses? No exploiters? No one orders you around?"

"That's so," said Kipnis. "All the goods are held in com-

315

mon. No one has too much. Everyone has enough. That's why, under socialism, the instinct for domination, the urge to seek power over others, and all the brutality of life just disappear."

The cannibal woman: "I have heard that in the Soviet Union there is no discrimination against women. Can this be? Are there woman doctors? Do women steer ships and pilot planes? Perhaps there are women policemen, who stop streams of traffic with their hands."

"There is so much we are eager to ask you, dear friend," Einhorn said. "So much we want to know. What about the success of the second five-year plan? Were the quotas all filled? And the wonderful blast furnace at Magnitogorsk? Has it been completed on schedule? It is time to pour the molten iron! To hammer it into molds! A new society will be forged!"

"In the Soviet Union there are over seven hundred universities and colleges!" said Kipnis, whose voice rose several notes. "Here is another fact. Did you know the Soviet Union comprises one-sixth of the land area of the earth?"

"Perhaps one day we shall visit your cities," Faulhaber said. "They say that the domes of churches are covered in gold, that in summer the sun shines on them through the night."

The presser: "In the underground railway the stations are made out of marble. I saw a picture. Ha, ha! Marble!"

"And there are flowers and trees in the center of highways!"

"This is better than Palestine!"

"Better than Madagascar!"

It was Lipiczany who realized that throughout this conversation Taradash had not said a word. "Comrade!" shouted the boy. "Where are you?"

The voice of the airman came back—not from nearby, but from well up the hill leading to Tsarskoye Selo. "Farewell, brothers! I must return to our lines."

316

"Not that way!"

"Watch out!"

"You're going to the Elder's palace!"

The commando had moved still farther off. "I know my way. The Elite Guard will take your place at the bridge."

Not a single member of the Edmund Trilling Brigade heard those words correctly. They gasped, then, when the parachutist went on: "In case you were not willing, or not able, we have included the Elder in our contingency plan."

Einhorn: "Trumpelman will never agree. The Elite Guard is for his own protection."

The voice came out of the darkness: "But he has agreed. He was the one who first contacted us."

Chaffer sat up, like a dead man reborn. "It's a trick!"

"The Elite Guard are fifth columnists!"

Taradash, halfway to the mansion, paused. "Listen to me. The Blond Ones are determined to defend the city. It's from here they want to mount their counteroffensive. Operation Ural Mountains isn't just a matter of the liberation of the Ghetto, but of the whole course of the war. It must be carried out."

Zam, the medical doctor, spoke next—slowly, calmly, not in the least excited. "You are making a big mistake. The Chairman of the Judenrat is a collaborator. He was the one who murdered our leader, Lipsky. He stood shoulder to shoulder with the Others when they shot Edmund Trilling, the Bundist, for whom our brigade is named. His wife took part in the execution of the painter, Klapholtz. From the beginning he urged the citizens of the Balut to join transports, and he went on doing this after he knew what happened in the forests and camps. His Judenrat makes the selections, conducts the roundups, and helps load the trains. He starved the Jews. He worked them like slaves until they dropped at their benches. He enforced the regulations that deny them the right even to be born. All this continues. It goes on. Do not

317

say he has done this out of necessity, in sorrow, knowing that the Others would be worse. He sought his position. He smacked his lips."

"He is," said the cannibal woman, "a devil."

But the commando merely shrugged this indictment off. "What you say may be true. Yes, it is true. But so is something else. Of all the ghettos of Europe, only Trumpelman's yet survives. How could this be accomplished except through the measures you describe? Whether or not he enjoyed his task is beside the point. I am from Warsaw. A Jew like you. I know what happened to the Elder there. He felt anguish. He felt torture. He couldn't collaborate any longer. Suicide. An honorable act. And the next day the Others rounded up all the children."

Hersh Einhorn, in the blackness, stood stiff. "Comrade, I must inform you that the Judenrat President, Trumpelman, has been sentenced to death by the underground movement. I warn you: the Red Army must not associate with such a man."

"Of course you feel this way," Taradash answered. "From your point of view, with all that you've lived through, it's proper to have passed this sentence. The Red Army will not interfere if, after Operation Ural Mountains has been completed, and after the liberation, you still wish to carry it out. In my opinion, however, it would be a mistake to do so. In the eyes of history, it is you who will appear violent, vengeful, not your Elder. You must attempt to put aside your sufferings and see the wider perspective. Trumpelman has always known precisely what he was doing. He was in a race with time. And he won."

Just then, from the midst of the resistance fighters, there came a hissing, sputtering sound. For an instant everyone feared that a pin had come loose from one of the homemade grenades. But there was no explosion. It was Nisel laughing. "Yes! Yes! I see! I see!" he cried. "He's going to be a hero!"

The next thing you knew, Nachman Kipnis began to yip

318

more or less like a dog. "Ha! Ha! Ha! A statesman! That's the wider perspective!"

"A freedom fighter! That's what they'll write in the books. Ha! Ha! The history books!" This was Bloomgarden. He began to roll on the ground, squeezing his sides.

Then Einhorn, the last of the children, began to giggle, to grunt. "They'll teach about him in school!"

The outburst, it was hysteria really, did not stop there. Within minutes the grown people were laughing, too. Not just laughing, but roaring, screeching, striking their thin chests, their bony kneecaps, with real force. Chaffer was the most animated of all. He shook and rolled. The dirt on top of his body flew in every direction. "Do you know what?" he finally managed to gasp. "Hee! Hee! The Russians on one side. The Americans—Ha! Ha!—on the other!" He broke off, whooping, howling. What he said next made the entire brigade, like the silk parachute, collapse limply onto the ground. "They're going to say that Horowitz lost the war!"

What could the buttonholer mean by such a remark? He meant this: the war that Horowitz had already won wasn't going to be mentioned. The Big Man would be robbed of his victory over the Jews! And in just that way, Trumpelman, the criminal, would become their savior. What the Ghettoites—the children first, and then the older people—had glimpsed, what became clear to them, was the nature of history. A farce. A misunderstanding. A kind of joke.

Finally, one after the other, the underground leaders came to their senses. Wordlessly, they got to their feet. They stood at attention. The Red Army commando had not left for the mansion. There he stood.

Lipiczany spoke. "Not Operation Ural Mountains."

Taradash, only an ink blot, a shape, said nothing.

"Szypper."

"Szypper?"

One dozen voices: "Operation Szypper!"

Which is how the daring plan got its new name.

319

When the sun rose that morning, the Others blew up one of the Dolna River bridges. Krystal and Lifshits saw this, from the top of the Mosk Works chimney, near Jakuba Street. There was a flash, a geyser, a bang; planks, like tiny splinters, spurted into the air. Then the two halves of the bridge writhed on the water, like a cut worm. That left two bridges remaining—the so-called Tower Bridge, which, because it was high above the water and had a turret at either end, reminded people of the famous structure in London, and the King Ladislaus Bridge, three lanes wide. Across both of these, throughout the day, Warriors came streaming, their faces as dark as Moors'. Behind them, stretching into the sky, turning it brown, was a great column of dust. It threw a shadow over the town. Those in the Balut, seeing this, became excited. Here was the wrath of the Red Army! How they marched! Pulverizing the earth!

On the next day the cloud was even thicker. The sun behind it was red and glowing, like the heating element of a stove. At two in the afternoon one end of the Tower Bridge crumpled, the other end rose; then the whole thing fell into the river. The King Ladislaus Bridge still stood, however; even when the first people's soldiers, and then the first people's tanks, appeared on the horizon, it did not explode. From the chimney top Krystal and Lifshits could see that the Others meant to defend it. Guns were brought up to the approaches, and a squad of Death's-Headers took positions along the nearby embankment.

Such forces could not halt the advancing soldiers. The reason the Red Army stopped, then fanned out along the far bank of the Dolna, was that at the first sign of a crossing the bridge would surely be destroyed. That the Warriors had not already done this could only mean that they hoped to save the bridge to mount their counterattack. Thus the two armies stared at each other across the river. Then the sun went down and the Edmund Trilling Brigade prepared an attack of its own.

Since the war started not a single Man of Valor had been killed by a citizen of the Balut. Rievesaltes shot Grundtripp, but that had been bad luck, sheer chance. The bullet had been meant for a Jew. So it was an occasion when Kleiderman plunged his knife into the chest of a sentry, and gave it a twist. Down dropped the Blond One; the finisher stood there, looking stunned. The rest of the brigade slipped through the rip in the fence and gathered in Zgierska, the Aryan boulevard. They could hear the footsteps of the next guard down the block. The presser, with his forearm, knocked him cold. Hersh Einhorn then sliced his throat. Kleiderman still had not moved. Miss Bibelnieks went to him.

"Why didn't somebody tell us?" he said. She understood him. He meant, *that this could be done.*

Einhorn tapped his wristwatch crystal. Like their food, their cannon, all of their bullets—this had been parachuted into the graveyard by air. It read, by a match, ten minutes past ten. The two rubberized boats would set off from the eastern shore at exactly eleven thirty. The crossing would take eighteen minutes. The brigade had to begin their attack at precisely a quarter to twelve. Three minutes later the boats would land and the artillery barrage would begin. There could be no slipup. At midnight, when the watch was changed, the dead sentries would be discovered. But by then the whole combined might of the progressivist forces would be rolling over the open bridge; the Warriors, instead of dealing with an escape from the Ghetto, would have other things to do. Operation Szypper in a nutshell.

Lipiczany led the way down the pitch-black boulevard, following the same tram lines he had ridden over in December, 1941. The brigade, dodging from wall to wall, crouching, came after. The problem was, how to reach the near side of

321

the bridge without firing a shot? The streets were patrolled. Poles ran by, caught by the curfew. More than once the fighters had to scatter into doorways, while a troop of Death's-Headers marched past. All at once Hersh Einhorn dropped down; he was on his hands and knees. "Quick! Do what I'm doing." The boy was smearing mud from the un-paved roadway onto his hands and wrists, his face, his throat, his neck. Nachman Kipnis did the same thing. He even rubbed it into his hair. It took the others a few minutes to finish. Then they stood up and, like Negroes, flashed their teeth and rolled their eyes. When they moved off, again in single file, not even an owl, with its wonderful eyesight, could see them.

By the time they reached Alexsandrowska it was nearly eleven o'clock. The boulevard was too wide to dash over, even singly. And a group of soldiers stood on the opposite side: you could tell by their cigarettes.

"Go back," whispered Doctor Zam.

"No time," said Einhorn.

"I'm thinking," said Chaffer. "But I can't think of a thing."

Then Pipe stepped off the sidewalk and threw up a hand. Like a normal person, he said, "Taxi!"

The others shrank back, aghast. "He's gone mad!" said Kipnis.

"Ha! Ha!" laughed the presser. "Two sausages, please. On a soft roll! Might as well ask for that!"

"Get him!" Hersh Einhorn commanded.

But before anyone could move, Pipe—it was so dark you could not see his pullover's diamond design—took another step into the thoroughfare and said, "Taxi!" once again.

And lo, with its headlamps dimmed, and a band of green and white squares along its side, a taxi rolled up to the curb. This was a Packard, an American car, with room for the entire brigade. Faulhaber opened the back door and crept inside. Bloomgarden climbed into the front. The driver was a Pole, with an open shirt and a cap. "What's this?" he said,

322

looking at his passengers' blackened faces. "A Purim party?" Then, with a gun butt, Einhorn cracked the back of his head.

Now, more than three decades later, we can stop and ask, *was this right or wong?* At the time, however, no one gave it a thought. The antitank gun went into the trunk, along with the radio. The fighters slunk down on the seats and piled over each other on the carpeted floor. Bloomgarden took the wheel and at once drove off, in the direction of the Central Square. Yes! All right! It was murder, then! And thievery, too! The driver was in the rain gutter, so that anyone seeing him would think it was a drunken Pole.

The Central Square was dark, empty. The Packard swung into it, off Alcxsandrowska, and circled counterclockwise. Then it began to lose speed on the far side of the monument to Rumkowsky. It went slower and slower and finally, in front of the Hotel Europa, came to a stop. "What is it?" Faulhaber asked. "What's happened?" No explanation. Everyone was peering through the right-hand windows. Lipiczany and Einhorn stuck their heads completely out. Even Nachman Kipnis, in his frosted glasses, was trying to see.

"Butter-crumb tarts," Bloomgarden said.

"With the tops crisp and burnt."

Inside the auto it was perfectly still. Across the square, however, came a dull, soft, clanking sound. It kept repeating. The brigaders swung around. At first, in the blacked-out square, there was nothing to see. Then, from behind the invisible bulk of the Donati Station, a series of twinkling lights appeared.

"A train!" said the cannibal woman.

And the others, seeing the sparks fly up from beneath the iron wheels, like from whetstones, also murmured, "A train."

"To the river!" said Commander Einhorn.

Faulhaber leaned forward, as if toward a real taxi driver. *"Don't spare the horses,"* he said, in English. He wanted to lighten the mood.

* * *

At sixteen minutes after eleven the strike force of Operation Szypper drew near the Dolna River. This was a neighborhood of apartment houses, shabby ones mostly, in which—according to reports from the Mosk chimney top—Poles continued to live. The taxi moved down a street that ran parallel to, and a block from, the river. There seemed no way to get to the waterfront proper. Each side street they passed was blocked with coils of wire. Behind the wire there were undoubtedly troopers with guns. Einhorn signaled with his hand.

"Stop there. At that house."

The big car pulled up before a wide three-story building, with an iron fence in the front. The gate in the fence was secured by a metal chain. The presser cut through this with his shears. Keeping low, the resistance fighters moved from the taxi to the courtyard. The presser went back for the equipment in the trunk. From there he heard—it was too dark to see—a Death's-Header patrol. Einhorn heard them, too. He ran up the steps of the building and threw himself against the large wooden doors. Locked. Bolted. Kleiderman gave it a try. The entrance held.

"Whoops!" It was the presser. He scooped up Lipiczany and hoisted him onto his shoulders. "Jump!" he cried.

At once the boy sprang for the window ledge. Then he squirmed through the open window. In the nick of time he unbolted the door from the inside. The brigaders rushed into the building and crouched by the street windows, holding their guns. The patrol reached the taxi. The trunk was open and so were the curbside doors. The courtesy light was burning inside. One of the Totenkopfers slammed down the trunk. Another closed the front and rear doors. The light went out. The patrol marched briskly off.

A match. The Soviet watch. Eleven twenty-one. Einhorn led the way across the marble floor. They could not stop their boots, in this large, open hallway, from making an echo.

They went from room to room—bumping into furniture, into chairs—toward the back of the building. The Commander raised his hand: rear windows. On their hands and knees now, the Jews approached them. Even before they got there they heard what sounded like an audience coughing, whispering to each other. They peeked through. A hundred Warriors were gathered just beneath them. Here and there, plainly enough, came the gleam from a barrel of a gun. The coughing, the murmur—that was the rush and splash of the river, only thirty meters away.

The Jews deployed through the building in the following manner. On the ground floor, with the bazooka: the presser, Ignacy Bloomgarden, and Mister Pipe. Nachman Kipnis went to the second floor, to operate the transmitter-receiver. With him went Kleiderman, Chaffer, and the cannibal woman. Up top: Einhorn, Lipiczany, Faulhaber. Zam, because he was the doctor, and Miss Bibelnieks, his assistant, were free to roam where they were needed. In addition, it was their job to watch the front courtyard, so that the Others did not take the strike force by surprise. For the moment, everyone waited at one window or another. There was dust, from the dust cloud, on the windowsills. It was still falling.

Hersh Einhorn checked his watch. "Eleven twenty-nine," he said. His voice, which had not been raised, carried all the way down to the first floor, where Pipe was slapping himself, like a person who wants to keep warm. "Comrades," Einhorn said one minute later, "the operation has now begun."

Across the river, approximately three hundred meters upstream, two portable rafts were slipping into the water. The Jews inside the boats started to row. The other Jews, the ones inside the building, leaned forward and back, forward and back, again and again. Do not think that at such a moment of danger the materialists had started to pray. Certainly not! Instinctively they felt themselves to be in the boats also, also pulling the oars.

325

Commander Einhorn: "Eleven thirty-two."

The members of the Edmund Trilling Brigade stared and stared out the windows. They strained to hear. Little waves were slapping against the shore. On all three floors there was the click of the bullets going into the guns.

"Ha! Ha!" laughed the presser. "Nervous!"

"Eleven thirty-seven." Seven minutes in the boats! Seven minutes on the water! Not quite halfway.

"At this moment, in New York City, it is not night. It is afternoon. A sunny afternoon!" This was, of course, James Faulhaber.

No one spoke after that. Not even to ask for the time. Nothing to do but look out the windows. How dark the night was, how dark the town. Houses, factories, streets, all the thousands of people—did they even exist? Impossible to tell the black earth from the black sky. That darkness! Like a mouth! Eating you up!

Then the dawn, as promised, arrived. The eastern half of the sky flared up, as if someone had set it on fire. Overhead there was a flapping sound, like pigeons, and then, behind, somewhere in the city, a series of explosions.

"Lightning!" screamed Chaffer, on the second floor. "Thunder!"

"No! It's not! It's the artillery barrage!"

And so, eight minutes early, it was.

"Comrade Kipnis." Hersh Einhorn was surprisingly calm. "You may break radio silence. There has been a mistake. Tell them to stop their fire."

But before the boy could respond, there was a second round.

Downstairs, Pipe cried, "Ah! Look there!"

The Jews gazed out the windows. Hung between the bright sky and the dark water, like an immense, shining harp, was the King Ladislaus Bridge.

"Hello, Comrades! Hello, Comrades!" That was Kipnis,

326

shouting into the radio. Then he reported to his friends. "They're playing music!"

Another salvo. This time the two little boats were illuminated, for all to see. The Jews in them were paddling madly. You could see their faces. Their mouths made many black O's.

"This is the Edmund Trilling Brigade. Cease fire! Cease fire at once!" Kipnis tore his earphones off. "They heard me!" he said. It was true. The distant batteries had fallen still. The night was coal-black again.

Outside, between the house and the river, the Others were jumping up from where they had taken cover. They ran to their tanks. They manned their artillery gun. But they didn't shoot bullets. They shot up, one after the other, three blazing flares. This brought once more into view, with the white froth around them, the twin bobbing boats. Was it possible the Warriors still hadn't seen them? Why didn't they shoot?

It was Kleiderman who realized that the Others were not looking at the water, but at the bridge above it. The Warriors pointed. They laughed. The finisher looked, too. "There's somebody there!" he exclaimed.

One floor higher, a fighter sighed. Lipiczany said, "Chaim."

No doubt about it: the black cape, the white hair, the spectacles winking, blinking—it was the Elder. He banged his cane. He started to speak. "Don't shoot! No shooting, soldiers! The war must end without bloodshed. We have to be friends!"

The flares drifted downward, swaying beneath their tiny tufted umbrellas. The Blond Ones stood there, transfixed. Trumpelman lifted his arms. "The Elder of the Jews has a peace plan. He is a neutral figure! The only one in the world both sides can trust!"

Carefully, slowly now, the rubber boats made for the shadow of the bridge, which lay like a slick on the water. The

327

Jews inside the building held their breath. They saw Taradash, the commando, in one of the bows. He was stroking the little vines of his beard.

"This is the peace plan! We'll hold an international conference! The Great Ones will come! All the big fellows! And the Pope! The whole idea came to me in a dream!"

Nisel laid the muzzle of his automatic rifle on the windowsill. He pressed his cheek along the stock of the gun. "Now," he said.

"Don't!" Einhorn slapped the weapon aside. "He knows about the operation. This isn't madness. It's a deliberate diversion."

"So they won't see the boats," Faulhaber added.

Zam: "The brave man!"

One of the flares, sizzling, fell into the water. The first raft ducked under the bridge, almost directly beneath the feet of the Elder. "Peace! Peace, gentlemen! Men will love each other! They will dance! And sing!"

The second flare, even before it struck the water, went out. The third one slipped sideways, like a leaf falling, giving out light. But both boats were safely under the bridge. Above them the Elder had actually started a dance, a jig. He sang a Yiddish song. *"Bai nakht verft der alter fisher, hoopla! Zem netz ber de glanzende fish."*

Suddenly his whole body stopped, as if something had frozen him there. He scowled. The light passed off his hair, off his spectacle lenses. Then he pointed his cane, as if it were a gun, through the slats of the bridge. It was the commando, the daring airman, he aimed at. "That one! I know him! His father was the Warsaw Elder! He wants to take over! To kill me! It's Czerniakow! The son!"

The tragedy that followed took only a minute, only as long as it takes to lace up your shoes. One of the boats turned about and began desperately rowing toward the far-off eastern shore. In the other, Taradash—or perhaps it really was the young Czerniakow—placed a foot on the side of his craft and raised his arm toward Trumpelman. His pistol went off at the same time the Warriors fired their guns. Many bullets hit him, in many places, and he fell into the river and sank right down. The boat itself lost its air. It lay on the water like the pad of a lily. But the Men of Valor did not stop their fire. Off swam Jews in every direction. Some were able to take only one or two strokes, or three or four; and some swam meter after meter. Whether soon or late, each one vanished beneath the surface of the water. It was as if a big fish were gobbling them down.

Nor did the other raft escape. The two tanks onshore swung their powerful guns about. The first volley traveled too far and struck out of sight. But the very next shot landed right on the target. A big tree of water, with a white trunk, with white branches, sprang out of the Dolna. The rubber boat, with all twenty Jews, vaporized.

Then the shooting stopped. You could just get a glimpse of the river, which was smooth, not boiling; and you could see, drooping over the edge of the bridge, the black cape of the Elder. Then the last flare flickered out. It is true that the brigade members were weeping. But not because I. C. Trumpelman had at last, as they say, departed this earth.

Hersh Einhorn, the adolescent, temporarily lost his nerve. He asked, "Now what do we do?"

As if in reply, the cannibal woman leaned from the second floor window and began to fire her rapid-shooting gun. Over her shoulder Kleiderman hurled out a grenade. It exploded, the way it was supposed to. Then the top and bottom floors joined in. The Jews were shooting from every window. They were throwing their bombs.

To the Blond Ones, it must have seemed like a whole army attacking. In their surprise, their panic, dozens of Warriors ran pell-mell toward the embankment, and over into the river. Other soldiers either retreated to the brickwork under the bridge, or took cover behind the two gray-green tanks.

One of these started its engine and immediately rumbled

329

off down the promenade. The other held its ground. It aimed its gun point-blank at the ground-floor windows; out of those windows, with a roar, the presser fired first. *Poof!* Like a flaming dessert, the machine ignited. Blue fire came from the turret, the peepholes, the barrel of the gun. Then it detonated inside, and the blue flames turned into orange ones, which steadily burned.

Then Einhorn gave the command: "Ground floor out! Second floor out! Top floor, maintain covering fire!"

Right away six Jews rushed from the rear exit of the house, shooting automatic guns. Simultaneously, the Warriors beneath the bridge scattered left and right, along the embankment. Some of them threw their weapons down.

And that was that. The Edmund Trilling Brigade controlled the approach to the bridge. The Blond Ones had not fired a shot.

"Ha! Ha!" laughed the presser. "We've done it!"

"*Shhh!*" said Chaffer. He was listening.

"Come in, Comrades. Come in, Comrades. Comrades, come in." It was Nachman Kipnis, up on the second floor, talking on the radio. "Bridge secure. Repeat: bridge secure." The boy's voice droned on and on, while in the yard below him, and at the edge of the river, the wounded Warriors gasped and groaned. The flaming tank hissed terribly and lit the scene. At last the Jews heard what they were waiting for:

"They answered! They heard me! Now they will come!"

"Three cheers for Comrade Kipnis!"

Wearing his earphones, the lad appeared at the window. Like a boxer he clenched his hands.

Faulhaber, Einhorn, Lipiczany—the whole top floor raced down the stairway and out of doors. "To the bridge!" cried Faulhaber.

"To the bridge!"

The brigade ran to where the abandoned artillery piece still pointed down the length of the arching span. Miss Bibelnieks reached inside her blouse and removed a small bou-

330

quet: horsetails, buttercups, daisies. "Only paper," blushing, she said.

"Brigade, attention!" Einhorn commanded.

Everyone stood rigidly, in parade formation. Then, as if they had communicated secretly to one another through the ether, each man, each woman, each child burst into "The Marseillaise." How lustily they sang it! Loud enough to hear clear across the swift Dolna! And when they had finished the first verse—about the hateful tyrants, about the peace which lay bleeding—they repeated the chorus, *Victory or Death!* and began to sing the second. Only not so many brigaders knew the words. They had to drop out. They had to hum. Silence soon. Miss Bibelnieks held out her damp, drooping horsetails. There was no one on the King Ladislaus Bridge.

Faulhaber turned toward the wireless operator. "What did they say, exactly?"

Kipnis dug the toe of his boot into the ground. "Something in Russian," he answered. Then added, "But I know they'll come!"

From far off there came the sound of explosions. Then gunfire. A faint glow appeared in the sky. All this occurred not in the east, where the Soviet forces were poised, but behind the brigaders, to the west. Zam, the lookout, appeared in the windowframe.

"The Balut," he announced, "is on fire!"

In the dying flames from the tank, the underground fighters looked at each other. The pitch on their faces had almost worn through.

Then Kleiderman shouted, "The train!"

"It's a roundup!"

Mister Pipe then said something awful. "Is it possible that we have been tricked?"

"Tricked?" asked Bloomgarden. "By who?"

Pipe pulled his head into his shoulders. It was a shrug. "Without us, the Ghetto is defenseless."

"True!" cried the cannibal woman. "We have to return!"

331

Einhorn tried to sound cheery. "Don't worry! The Red Army is coming! Our orders are to keep the bridge open. That way we'll help the Balut, too!"

A shot rang out much nearer by. Chaffer sat down. He sighed.

Zam screamed from the building, at the same time firing his Soviet gun. "Counterattack!"

The Jews looked down at the buttonholer. There was a round hole in his throat. Through this he sighed.

More shots from the embankment. The presser, by the field gun, clutched at his shoulder. "Shot me, ha-ha!" Then, moving slowly, smoking, snorting, the second tank returned.

In the original plans for Operation Szypper, the Edmund Trilling Brigade had been expected to hold out for a quarter of an hour. And that was to be with the assistance of a landing party and a constant barrage. Yet not only had the fighters secured the King Ladislaus Bridge upon their first assault, but they now beat back the sudden counterattack. This is how it was done.

First, the brigade members snatched up as many arms as they could from the Blond Ones and made their way back to the three-story building. From this fortress, shooting out the top-floor windows, they were able to drive the foot soldiers back. The pity is the tank rolled up and fired a shell into the house. It exploded on the ground floor, killing Miss Bibelnieks and Chaffer, her patient. A second shell burst in the identical spot. Luckily, you can't kill the same people twice.

Lipiczany and the presser, who had remained at the embankment, at last managed to turn their artillery cannon. The shot they sent off exploded to the side of the tank, but with enough force to snap one of its treads. The dreadful machine spun in a circle. Then the top sprang open and the Warriors within jumped out. Kleiderman, turning a toothpick end over end in his mouth, shot each one: either in the heart or the head. Thus, by themselves, with no commandos and no supporting fire, the brave Jews kept control of the vital bridge. Remember them! *Children of their Nation,* in the words of "The Marseillaise."

But where were the Russian forces? Where? Even with binoculars, Hersh Einhorn could not see the slightest movement on the eastern bank. In the Suburb, however, the shooting continued. Lights blazed as if there were no need for a blackout at all. At times the brigaders imagined that, across half the city, they could hear people scream.

"Don't they know there is a roundup in the Ghetto? Why don't they cross?" Kleiderman, in his anguish, beat a fist on a wall.

Kipnis touched him on the shoulder. "This war is only part of the world revolution. What appears to be a struggle between nation and nation is in reality a battle between classes." They boy looked up. He raised his finger. "To advance merely for the sake of the Ghetto would be reckless adventurism!"

"But there are still fifteen thousand people in the Balut!"

Zam came forward. "There has to be an explanation. The bridge might be mined. That's why they have not yet come."

Kleiderman wrenched away. He backed from his fellow fighters. "Fools!" he told them. "Fools!" Then he leaned well out the window and began to shout. "I know! I understand! I know what you're doing!"

A sniper, lying quietly by the river, shot his rifle in the direction of that voice. Kleiderman doubled up, like a person in a fit of laughter, and pitched out the window. There was a crack from his bones when he hit the ground.

Immediately a second sniper opened fire.

"Yes! Ha! Ha! Hit me in the thigh!"

The presser, though wounded, managed to set off the cannon again. The big gun ripped a crater in the stone-covered embankment. "Ha! Ha! It's the last shell!" There was a lull in the shooting. Then you could hear men running across the gravel behind the house.

"They're charging!"

"Fire!" ordered Einhorn.

This time the Blond Ones did not retreat. Instead, they flung themselves down where they were. There was nothing for the Jews to aim at, except the occasional flash from an enemy gun.

"No more bullets!" Mister Pipe called.

The cannibal woman said she had ten shots left.

The fighters all moved to the second floor. They gathered around the old wireless set. Purplish lights ran up the length of the tubes. Between the transformers, electricity leaped and cracked, making a smell like toast. Kipnis put on the earphones. Endlessly he repeated the single word: *Comrades.*

The Jews leaned forward, their faces sweating like plums. Nothing. Silence. No reply.

Doctor Zam straightened up. He handed his bullets to Pipe. "I will contact our allies in person," he said. "I must show them the bridge is not mined."

"But how—" asked Einhorn.

Zam was already down the shattered stairs. He shouted over his shoulder, "The taxi!"

Sure enough, a moment later the interior light went on in the Packard, and the doctor, who had once driven a sports car, slid behind the wheel. The engine started. The bulb on the roof, indicating the car was for hire, began to wink. The vehicle roared off. At the first intersection the Packard made a right turn and disappeared. Immediately four shots rang out, one atop the other. Not shots, it developed. The taxi had plunged through the barricade; the barbs on the wire coils had punctured the tires. Yawing one way, veering another, the auto lurched down the embankment and onto the three-lane bridge. Recklessly, with abandon, the underground fighters crowded into the window. Nobody fired. Nobody attempted to halt the careening cab.

On went Zam. The loose rubber slapped against the surface of the roadway. The rims of the wheels began to shoot out a stream of sparks. He was a quarter of the way across.

Now a third. Spinning, skidding, the auto reached the half-way point. The Jews were holding their breath. Their hearts were pounding. But no mine exploded. Thus their comrades would know: the bridge was safe to cross! Far off the blinking bulb—*taxi! taxi!*—slid from one side of the roadway to the other, across all three lanes. *Toot! Toot!* Yes! Joyfully, triumphantly, Doctor Zam was sounding the Packard's two-note horn. When the taxi was only a hundred meters from the eastern embankment, the Red Army responded. With a flash of light. With the zoom of a rocket. The auto stopped dead, turned over, and burned.

Inside the building the Jews were clutching their heads.

"They have killed him! Killed him!"

"This cannot be! How could this be?"

Faulhaber was sobbing. "What does it mean? It's a tragedy!"

"Comrades," said Einhorn, wet-eyed like the others, "there is room for doubt here. Perhaps they did not know who it was. Perhaps they thought it was the counterattack."

At the radio, Kipnis was agitated. "Quiet! Quiet! A signal! The Red Army is going to speak."

Instantly the room was silent. Pipe, from Odessa, grasped the earphones from the boy. He put them on.

Skolka eeshaw zheevee? The old man repeated what he had heard aloud. "This means, *How many of you are still alive?*"

Eight, they might have replied. *Or maybe seven. Possibly six.* But the brigade members, speechless, stunned, did not answer the question. No matter: the bombs which flew through the window, which rolled here and there among them, soon made any such figure invalid.

What happened was that the exploding grenades created a tremendous hole in the floor of the second story, and that half the resistance fighters fell through. Namely: Pipe, the cannibal woman, and—with his pug nose, his Tatar eyes—Hersh Einhorn. If they had survived the blast, if they had lived through the fall, then they were killed by the Blond

335

Ones, who rushed into the ground floor and shot many more bullets than needed into their bodies.

The remainder—Bloomgarden, Kipnis, Faulhaber—were also blown from the room, into a smoky hallway. As best they could they crawled up the staircase to the top floor. They had no weapons. Kipnis' spectacles were gone. And Faulhaber discovered that much of his blood was pouring from a wound in his side. At any moment, they thought, the Others would swarm up the stairs and shoot them, too. The stairs, however, collapsed, along with the rest of the second story. It took the Warriors ninety minutes to dig each other out, after which they simply withdrew. The building, though trembling, was still.

An hour went by. Then another. The sound, of distant shooting kept coming in the front windows. There had never been a roundup that lasted so long. Two sounds came in at the rear: the splash of the little river waves and something—no one knew what—squeaking and squeaking. Then the sky began to glow, just faintly, like the light in a vacuum tube.

Dawn. The three Jews looked out the window. Across the river, all along the bank, were the tents of the Red Army. Here and there smoke rose. Here and there a tiny figure walked around. It was like a painting of a sleeping, peaceful village. Nachman Kipnis stared intently, even though, without his glasses, he could see little more than a tan-colored foam. "The Jewish question," he said.

Neither of his comrades—pale Faulhaber; the boy, Ignacy—replied. Kipnis continued:

"After the last Ghettoite is dead, then they will come."

It got lighter out. Sunbeams came in the windows. Thus the fighters discovered that the three-story building was in fact some kind of schoolhouse. The room was full of desks with built-in chairs. Blue inkwells were screwed into the tops. Books were tucked inside them. On the wall in front there was a blackboard, with a ledge for erasers and chalk. It was bright enough to see the last lesson.

Kopérnik, Mikołaj 1473–1543
De revolutionibus orbium coelestium

A breeze sprang up. The sky turned blue. Kipnis was reading a book—that is, he wet his finger, he turned the pages. Faulhaber? Faulhaber's lifeless head was on a desk top, for all the world like a drowsy pupil. Bloomgarden went to the window. The schoolyard below was in shambles. You could see in the gravel where the Warriors had dragged their countrymen away. Of all the playground equipment—the overturned slides, the climbing bars twisted and bent—only a single swing remained standing. Lipiczany was in it, going back and forth. It made a squeaking sound.

"Look!" cried Bloomgarden, and he began to beat two erasers together.

"You look!" answered Nisel, pumping himself into the air.

A big cloud rose from the window. It was as if Bloomgarden, with the chalk dust around him, were a Red Army of his own.

Nisel swung even higher, so that his hair flew back and his toes pointed at the center of the sky. "Hurrah!"

Bloomgarden pounded and pounded. "Hurrah!" he shouted, too.

III

The transport had been scheduled to leave at dawn, but there it was, still in the Radogodsh Station, well after nightfall. Every time the Others thought the roundup was finished, out came a fresh bunch of Jews. So new cars—not just boxcars, but tenders, flatcars, even first-class passenger coaches—had been hitched to those that were already full. By noontime the Jewish police, busy for twelve hours straight, were relieved by Death's-Headers. Then Verble and his men were driven into stockcars of their own.

No one could be left behind. Ghettoites who were dead—in other words, the ones who had resisted, or who had attempted to hide—were stuffed beside the ones still alive. Ladies and gentlemen, enough. Enough. Let's just say they caught everybody. Even Lifshits and Krystal, high up in their chimney roost, were shot to the ground. Look: the Baluty Suburb is empty. The windows are open, the lights are ablaze. Pots and pans are scattered over the roads. Engineer, blow the whistle! Ring the bell! Time to get under way!

But still the train stood, as if the thousands and thousands of people inside it were too heavy a load. At last a limousine came down Krawiecka Street and stopped near the terminal shed. It was the Daimler Double Six. Up and down the track the Others came to attention. F. X. Wohltat came out the rear door. It looked as if someone had blown him up to more than his normal size. The buttons on his shirt had popped open. His jacket had split its seams. Even his face, his wrists, his neck, like a frog's, were swollen. At once he went round the back of the car and opened the other door. Out stepped—how many lives had he? More than a cat!—I. C. Trumpelman. His cape was gone, and so was his hat and his cane. The old spectacles still hung on his nose.

Through cracks in the boards of the stockcars, through peepholes, the Jews saw the Elder. They recognized his mane of hair. A cry went up. A tremendous wailing.

"South!"

"We're going south!"

Wohltat, sweating, excited, pulled his revolver out. He beat the butt on the side of a cattle car. But the lament passed from wagon to wagon. "Save us!"

The Elder walked forward, briskly, without assistance, to the first sealed car. The guards, the Totenkopfers, saluted. "Messiah! Messiah!" cried the trapped Ghettoites. But they quickly fell silent when the Others slid back the door. Wohltat leaned into the unlit hole.

"You see, there is everything. A big coffee urn. Lots of black coffee. And pails for a latrine."

The men and women shrank back inside. Trumpelman glanced in, then turned to the next car. This time the Volksdeutscher actually hopped inside. There were too many Jews there to see the kettle. Wohltat pushed them backward. He beat them down. "The coffee," he said. "There, the latrine."

And so went the inspection. The Daimler followed along, shining its spotlight into each opened car. Trumpelman did not say a word, not even when people called him or when he saw someone—an Elite Guardsman, a big rabbi, black-haired Nellie Brilliantstein—he knew. All he did was peek inside, for an instant, then turn his back to wait for the man in charge.

This took more and more time. Wohltat liked to wade into the wagons, so that people tripped before him. He walked on them. He crushed them against the walls. "Coffee!" he screamed. "Latrine pails!" Then he would stagger from the car, like a drunken person. By the time they reached the wagon that held the Jewish Council his clothes were stained and torn. For some reason he ran into the crowd of ex-musicians, ex-waiters. He charged them with his head down like a bull. The Judenrat members shrieked in terror. Nomberg, of Religious Affairs, thrust his hands outside.

"Help us! There are ladies in the car! People's wives!"

But Wohltat, the wild man, would not leave the wagon. He plunged deeper inside, trampling on the men and women.

Trumpelman continued the inspection alone. It was obvious he did not care about the sanitation arrangements, or whether the Baluters would have enough coffee to drink. He did not break stride as he moved past the opened doors. But then, in front of a deep, open coal car, he came to a stop. With both hands he gripped the sides of his spectacle frames. He was trembling. Stretching his neck, he peered.

Up came the limousine, playing its light on the side of this tender—an old one, battered, with steep, slanting walls. Only the faces of the oldest children—Rose Atlas, Gutta Blit, Usher Flicker—showed over the rim. And the gardener boy, the pinhead: he was there, too. Then someone inside the coal car began to pound on its walls. It made a booming, hollow sound. "Chaim! Chaim!" Citron's voice. "Chaim!"

In four strides Trumpelman was next to the dark tender. He leaped to the ladder that hung down its side. From there he could look in. All the children from the Hatters' Asylum were standing at the bottom. Their faces were black from coal dust. The same dust matted their hair.

"I'm a fast runner!" It was little Gumbiner, now aged almost four. He raced across the bottom of the car and up the slanted wall toward the Elder. But partway up his legs—fat ones, inside short pants—stopped churning, and he sprawled onto the metal floor.

Then Citron tried, holding his arms out, and so did Leibel Shifter. They fell back, too.

Hobnover shouted, "It's too high!" He began to cry.

"What will they do to us?" Tushnet said.

At that instant the whistle blew, a long, screeching blast. Another whistle came from the far end of the train.

Trumpelman remained on the rim of the coal car. He hung there, uncertain, half in, half out.

Then Wohltat came running along the railway bed, his elbows working like the rods of the train. He stopped beneath the tender. He was bloody. His chest was heaving. He clasped his fat hands together and looked straight down.

"Oh, sir!" said Rose Atlas. She was staring at him over the edge of the car. "What has happened to you?"

The Volksdeutscher heard her. His lower lip went farther and farther out, like a pouting child's. Then he stamped. He kicked the ground and uttered a pitiful wail.

"I could do whatever I wanted!"

340

Both whistles sounded again, from either end of the transport. The cars began to rattle, to shake. Trumpelman swung his legs over the rim of the tender and dropped within.

It would be pleasant to say that for the whole of that dreadful journey, while the children clasped his neck, his knees, the Elder entertained them with more of his adventure tales. But it only started that way. Somehow, from somewhere, Trumpelman produced a cigarette. He lit the end of it with a match. Then, like in the old days, in the old singsong voice, he started speaking.

"Dear children, do not be afraid. Take heart! You know how many dangers I have safely passed. How many times I have been on the brink of death. The same fate that protected me as a youth in America will preserve me throughout my last days. Again and again my enemies, continually plotting, have attempted to complete with their bullets, their bombs, what weakness and age have already begun. I do not speak of this to gain your pity, but to give you courage in your own moment of danger. Look up, my doves! For I would not have been saved from death except to fulfill a great destiny. Nothing, no one can kill me until we complete our journey together. And now we have started! We are moving! To Madagascar!"

It was true. The train, after starting, shuddering, stopping, now slowly, by centimeters, began to roll. The orphans moaned and clutched the Elder more tightly. He embraced them.

"Our wonderful adventure begins! Southward we go—to Budapest, to Constantinople, through deserts of Arabia, across the Red Sea! Think of it, my dears! We shall ride high on the backs of camels! We shall sail down African rivers in canoes. Look! A crocodile floats on the water! Yellow leopards are sleeping on the branches of trees! There, on the shore, black men with masks are howling, howling. Do not be

341

frightened. Don't tremble! The children of the Hatters' Asylum are under the Elder's protection. You share his immunity!"

In a corner of the coal car, a shadowy place, two children attempted to speak. Their voices cracked and creaked, as if they had been in the desert already.

"Camels!" said one.

"A crocodile!" said the other.

They laughed together, making an awful sound. Who could this be? Ignacy Bloomgarden, Nachman Kipnis, of the Edmund Trilling Brigade. They had been captured that morning, not long after dawn. Someone else was there, too—someone Trumpelman stared at, with his lips pulled away from his teeth.

Lipiczany stared back, mud-covered, not blinking once. His voice, when he spoke, was dull, flat, toneless. "There is no Madagascar. The train stops at Oswiecim. That's where they burn. They burn!"

"No! No!" the old man shouted. He rose, so that Citron and Shifter and the other children dropped from him. "Soon we shall be at our homeland!"

Lipiczany: "Oswiecim is the homeland of the Jews."

Trumpelman stood there, his strong teeth grinding against each other. Then a shudder, like a visible wave, passed over his body. "Outlaws!" he roared. "Lipskyites!" Turning away from the children, he hauled himself to the rim of the creeping car.

The orphans flung themselves at the Elder's legs. They did not want him to go. Nisel, still on his back, only stared. You could not tell, looking at him, whether or not he was breathing.

"Look! The lights!" cried the Elder, swinging outside, to the ladder, and from the ladder to the ground. Rose Atlas, Blit, Flicker, rushed to the tender wall. From there they could see him, moving along Krawiecka Street, into the Suburb. The smaller children could only hear him shout.

"You think the Judenrat is a gold mine! That we're rich! But we have to pay for electrical current! Off! Turn them off! It's brighter than daylight!"

The Elder was going into the houses on Lutomierska. He switched off all the lights. Then he veered into the Marysinska Corner, and the lights began to blink out there, too. "Big spenders! Showoffs! You'll ruin us all!" The sound of his voice faded away. It was not possible to see him. But wherever he went it got darker. Drenowska Street. Jakuba Street. Soon it began to get dark near the Baluter Ring. Trumpelman was turning off every switch in the Ghetto. He pulled every cord. Of course there were thousands and thousands of light bulbs still burning. Who knows? Perhaps he put out every one.

Chapter Eleven

Urania

I

On an unusually warm day for October the *Urania*, a steamship, backed out of the harbor at Liverpool. The passengers lined up for deck chairs, wearing shorts, or trousers without any shirts. Children ran about, shouting. Young men and young women played on guitars. The war, on all fronts, was over.

At the end of the third day this weather changed. The ship rolled from side to side. All night long came the sound of glassware sliding and breaking. Then, halfway across the ocean, the sky cleared and the sun came out again. But it was not the same as before. A cold wind, a cold sea spray, kept people indoors. The rest of the trip was like winter.

Two passengers, boys, remained on deck no matter the weather. They sat in the same spot, toward the back, near the rail. After the storm they covered themselves with a blanket, a brown one, and huddled together with the material to their chins. You already know them: Nachman Kipnis, Lipiczany.

What a sight! Kipnis, totally blind, was wearing a large pair of smoked glasses. He looked, under his woolly blanket, like a little nocturnal animal, a tree shrew, a lemur, with enormous black eyes. Now Lipiczany. His head, with the hair cropped, was pale and somehow transparent. It was like your own hand when you hold it over a light: there were the blue veins, the green veins, the shadows from bones. The doctors said it was because of his swollen heart. At the railing, Kipnis spoke to Nisel:

"A boat is coming."

Lipiczany squinted. He could see the whole gray globe falling away on every side. The *Urania* was alone on the ocean.

"No," he replied.

"Wait."

Lipiczany stared. In a quarter of an hour, on the horizon, he saw a line of smoke. A moment later the dark shape of a ship appeared.

"Do you see it?" asked Kipnis. It was amazing, really. He knew it was there because of the pressure of the waves.

"Yes," said Nisel.

The boys clutched each other. They clung together. The boat got nearer. Then it passed them, going in the other direction, and the smoke from its smokestack spread out behind it like a cloak.

II

Ladies and gentlemen, a natural question. How did these Ghettoites, on board a train for Oswiecim, end up on an ocean liner? There is no miracle here—only confusion, only luck. When the transport arrived at the camp, the death house was already full—with Slovaks, mostly, and Jews from Terezin. There was no selection on the platform: all our citizens, even children, got safely in.

Then, in November, when the killing machine was once again vacant, the order of choice was by barracks, not by age or sex or the state of one's health. What point in saving strong people, if the front was drawing near? But almost as soon as this process started, it stopped. Someone—they say it was HH, the Schoolmaster—gave a command to blow the baths and the chimneys and the whole business up. Two months later, when the ground was frozen, all the prisoners were marched away.

Thus, of the Baluters on the last transport, a third underwent the special treatment, another third—from illness, exhaustion, from starving—died in the camp, and the rest perished in this spot or that spot, along the snowy road. As for Lipiczany and Kipnis, they were too weak to join the marchers. They could not even get out of their bunk. They simply lay there—for months it seemed, for years, though in fact the Red Army entered the camp in a matter of days.

There are perhaps two hundred Baluters who lived through the three months at Oswiecim and the many years that have passed between now and then. Let's say we wrote them, in America or South America or wherever, to ask a different question: *What happened to I. C. Trumpelman?* It's surprising how many Jews would answer—surprising, too, how many would say that the Elder died there, in the killing camp.

In one version of this story, there was an additional transport—for the Jews who had managed to hide in the Suburb—and the Elder was on it. Another version has it that Chaim drove up in a special command car, just for himself. Many Baluters believe he had a letter, from Wohltat or some other high official, that supposedly guaranteed him all sorts of favors inside the camp. However, as soon as the letter was opened, Trumpelman was led to a wall, where he was shot. But other Jews say that, to amuse the Kapos and guards, the Elder was allowed to carry on as if he were still in the Ghetto, strutting about, giving orders, with his black boots and his cane. There are people who swear they saw him on a hilltop, shouting, *hup-hup-hup!*, as our Baluters paraded by: then he got onto the end of the line and marched into the death house. Here is a different tale. Chaim tries to make himself as inconspicuous as possible, he crouches down, he wears a disguise. But he is recognized by a crowd of Baluters—some say by Judenrat members—who beat him to death on the spot. Rumors! Gossip! Guesses! The Jews from Oswiecim can't bear to think he died someplace else.

In the springtime, well after the liberation of the camp, a new rumor sprang up. It seems a handful of Jews *had* managed to hide in the Ghetto, and more had saved themselves on the Aryan side. Now these folk were saying that the Elder had not left the Balut, that, in fact, he was still living inside. It was because of this story, mainly, that the two underground fighters, Nachman and Nisel, decided to return to the town where they had been born.

But when they arrived there, Trumpelman could not be found. At Tsarskoye Selo, Red Army men blocked the mansion door. And only Poles were living on Krzyzanowsky, in the original Hatters' Asylum. There was a report that Trumpelman took baths at the Rumkowsky Geyser; but the fire was out there, and boards had been placed over the top of the dome. Next, the boys stood opposite Dworska Number 20, studying each person who went in and came out. They had heard that the Elder was working for the undercover police, the Bolshevik ones, who had taken over the old House of Lords. A dead end, that clue, the same as the others.

What the hunters did find—everywhere—were pictures of the Elder: on thousands and thousands of paper "Trumpkies" and—with his head surrounded by cotton bobbins and clouds—on the Ghetto stamps. Souvenirs. The Poles even found some of Krystal's photos: Chaim on his stallion, making a speech; Chaim in the doorway of the brothel on Assisi Street; getting married, he in a dark tuxedo, she, Madame Trumpelman, covered by a veil. But of Chaim himself, the man in the flesh, there wasn't a trace.

A month went by. It was June. It was July. At last a Jew

347

told them that he had seen the Elder, not once, but many times, with his own eyes. Where? At the Astoria Café, at the front table, drinking a clear-colored drink. There the orphans, so frightful-looking, blind, bald-headed, arrived. The café had been completely redone. No Putermilch. No Baggelman. No musicians of any kind. The boys sat down and from one glass of wine got tipsy, got dizzy. They giggled. They crossed their legs. It got later and later and nobody came. The top of the room started spinning. Their chairs, like in a séance, rose into the air. Drunkards! Fools! They didn't notice that the front table was no longer empty. Never mind, never mind. For while the person who sat there was tall, almost two meters, and with a whole head of silver hair, he was not old Trumpelman.

A short while after this the city announced it was going to dedicate a monument to the Ghetto dead. People began to arrive from near and far. Among them was a Mister Impik, from the Hatters Young Men's Benevolent Association, who took a room at the Hotel Europa. With red hair, with red-colored freckles, he was a healthy fellow, the size of two of our Jews. It was he who offered the orphans the steamship tickets. However, they politely said no. For a whole week he struck his chest, with his lips he made the sound of horses, of an army, so that they would change their minds. But the boys said they wanted to search for the Elder. Then came the day of the dedication.

The man and the two boys went to the ceremony together. A platform had been erected in the Baluter Square. Thousands were there. It was sunny. It was balmy. The memorial itself was made out of marble and stone, huge block on huge block, with near-naked figures crouching inside. The mayor stood to make a speech. This was the same hairless man, the bullethead, who had held that job during the reign of the Others. It seemed he got along with the new Occupying Power as well. Indeed, he was slapping the Soviet general, the Liberator, on the back. The two of them shared a loud laugh.

Kipnis, behind the dark balls of his lenses, gasped. "I heard them!" he said.

Then the mayor started to speak. A real oration! About the rights of man, about the dignity of men and women. A silver tongue! He said that suffering makes people noble. He said that in the end goodness would prevail.

But Kipnis was whispering in Impik's ear. "It's a bet! They made a bet with each other!"

Then he turned to Nisel. "He's going to make the whole speech without once saying *Jew!*"

The next morning, at sunrise, the orphans showed up at the Hotel Europa. As they walked down the hallway, toward Impik's room, they passed a half-open door. Kipnis stopped. He wanted to know what was there. Lipiczany looked. It was a small room, on the corner, with a washstand and a circular window. A pair of black boots stood at the foot of an unmade bed. This sight, a perfectly ordinary one, filled the orphans with terror. Who had been sleeping in the rumpled bed? The boots—so large, so black, so shiny: whose were they? Kipnis gripped Nisel's hand. Lipiczany threw his arms around Kipnis. Each one was thinking the very same thought. What if this were the room of the Elder? What then? Would they denounce him? Call the police? They could not strangle him alone! Trembling and shaking, holding each other, they squeezed through the door of the American's room. They told him yes, they wanted to go.

It's time to end now. To end. No comments. No questions. You know how these children happened to sail from Liverpool. As for Trumpelman, every now and then you hear some fantastic story that he has turned up in one place or

349

another. Still breathing. Still alive. Impossible! Not true! His age would be more than one hundred! Ladies and gentlemen, we do not have to think of him any more.

III

The ship, the *Urania*, had been scheduled to dock in the morning, but because of all the rough weather it did not reach the harbor until late in the afternoon. The sun, aquiver, was going down on the left, over the land. The passengers crowded against the rails on the starboard side. At first Lipiczany thought that the city looked like a plaything, like piled-up blocks you could knock down with your hand. But as they drew nearer, and turned up the river, it loomed larger, more frightening, and it was the boat that seemed like a toy.

Kipnis, from cold, from excitement, was shivering beneath the blanket. "What do you see? Do you see the towers? Are they shining? Is it true that they reach the sky?"

Lipiczany stared at the city. It was like some awful machine. The cold red light of the sun beat at the windows of buildings. From the doorways, and on the streets, people were walking, stumbling, pressing against each other. Above them the smoke and steam from thousands of chimneys spread like a lid on the air.

"Tell me! The New World! The city! What is it like? Here is the palace of the common man!"

Nisel rested his head against Kipnis' shoulder. "Yes, like a palace," he said to his friend.